PRAISE FO

The Siren of S

"What I love about Mimi Matthews is that in the crowded field of historical romance she always finds new and interesting slants for her plots and characters. That, along with her wonderful writing and meticulous research, makes every book she puts out a rare treat to enjoy and savor. Highly recommended!"

—*New York Times* bestselling author Kate Pearce

"Unflinching, tender, and moving, the delicately crafted *The Siren of Sussex* might just be my favorite work from Mimi Matthews; it certainly is one of my favorite historical romance reads this year."

—Evie Dunmore, *USA Today* bestselling author of *Portrait of a Scotsman*

"Lush, seductive, original—*The Siren of Sussex* drew me in from the first page, and wove its magic. A fresh, vibrant, brilliant Victorian romance, making it an unforgettable read."

—*New York Times* bestselling author Jane Porter

"A moving love story and a vivid recreation of Victorian life, *The Siren of Sussex* by Mimi Matthews is a treat of a book for the historical romance lover."   —Award-winning author Anna Campbell

"Impeccably researched, brimming with passion and chemistry, and a loving tribute to Victorian fashion and horsemanship, *The Siren of Sussex* is a page-turning, powerful, and endearing love story about two people rising above the pressures of society to follow their hearts. A five-star fantastic read!"   —*USA Today* bestselling author Syrie James

"A tender and swoonworthy interracial, cross-class romance in Victorian London . . . Readers will delight in this paean to women's fashion and horseback riding."   —*Publishers Weekly* (starred review)

"Matthews brings the Victorian era to vivid life with meticulously researched details and an impossible romance made believable and memorable."   —*Booklist* (starred review)

"Romance aficionados who love fashion and animals will delight in this tender romance and will be excited to see Evelyn's friends in future installments."   —*Library Journal* (starred review)

"Readers should expect emotional heft and fascinating historical detail . . . Matthews explores cultural identity conflicts, exoticism, and the difficult position of a merchant catering to the whims of a privileged class, all within a tender, empowering love story."
                                    —*Shelf Awareness* (starred review)

"An exquisite historical romance that is so captivating I had to force myself not to gallop through it at a breakneck speed, wanting to savor the author's obvious care and delicate attention to detail . . . A must read for lovers of historical fiction."
                                    —Meg Tilly, author of *The Runaway Heiress*

"Marvelously crafted, Evelyn and Ahmad's world is ripe with nuanced social perceptions and characters that winnow heart deep. At times passionately intelligent and achingly vulnerable, *The Siren of Sussex* is destined to dazzle readers of Evie Dunmore and Harper St. George."
                                    —Rachel McMillan, author of
                                    The London Restoration and *The Mozart Code*

"Readers have learned to expect absorbing dramas from Mimi Matthews, and her latest—in which a strong and intelligent woman finds a way to save her family's fortunes while following her own heart—is no exception. Any reader who has ever loved horses, high fashion, and brooding protagonists will fall hard for *The Siren of Sussex*. I savored it to the final page."   —Stephanie Barron, author of *That Churchill Woman*

Also by Mimi Matthews

BELLES OF LONDON NOVELS

The Siren of Sussex

The Belle of Belgrave Square

MIMI MATTHEWS

BERKLEY ROMANCE
New York

BERKLEY ROMANCE
Published by Berkley
An imprint of Penguin Random House LLC
penguinrandomhouse.com

BERKLEY and the BERKLEY & B colophon
are registered trademarks of Penguin Random House LLC.

Library of Congress Cataloging-in-Publication Data

Names: Matthews, Mimi, author.
Title: The Belle of Belgrave Square / Mimi Matthews.
Description: First Edition. | Berkley Romance, 2022. |
Series: Belles of London; 2
Identifiers: LCCN 2022001074 (print) | LCCN 2022001075 (ebook) |
ISBN 9780593337158 (trade paperback) | ISBN 9780593337172 (ebook)
Subjects: LCGFT: Novels. Classification: LCC PS3613.A8493 B45 2022 (print) |
LCC PS3613.A8493 (ebook) | DDC 813/.6—dc23
LC record available at https://lccn.loc.gov/2022001074
LC ebook record available at https://lccn.loc.gov/2022001075

First Edition: October 2022

Printed in the United States of America
2nd Printing

Book design by Daniel Brount

For my father, Eugene.
Kind, steadfast, honorable; a true hero.

Such is the effect of the excitement of novel reading upon the nervous system, that the only way to obtain momentary ease, is to plunge into another as soon as one is finished.

—*Confessions and Experience of a Novel Reader*, 1855

One

Julia Wychwood was alone in Rotten Row, and that was exactly the way she liked it.

Well, not quite alone.

There was her groom, Luke Six. And there were some humbly clad men and women tarrying along the viewing rail. But otherwise . . .

Yes. Alone.

It was often the case at this time of morning—those early moments after break of dawn, when the air was misty cool and the rising sun was shining brightly to burn away the fog. Some ladies and gentlemen chose to ride at this time of day, but not many. Certainly not as many as during the fashionable hour. Then, all of society was out in force.

Which was precisely why Julia preferred riding in the morning. There were fewer stares and whispers. Less judgment.

With a squeeze of her leg, she urged Cossack into a canter. It was the big ebony gelding's best gait—a steady, even stride, with a sway to it like a rocking chair. She relaxed into it. When cantering, Cossack required nothing more of her than that she maintain a light contact on the double reins. He did the rest, which left her ample time to daydream.

Or to fret.

She wasn't only alone in Rotten Row. She was alone in London.

Her three best friends were all out of town, with two of them not set to return until Sunday. That left four days for her to get through on her own. Four excruciating days, and on every one of them, an equally excruciating society event.

Julia considered taking to her bed. She'd done it before to get out of attending a ball or a dinner. But she'd never done it for more than two days at a time. Even then, her parents insisted on summoning Dr. Cordingley—an odious man who always came with his lancet and bleeding bowl in hand.

She shuddered to think of it.

No. Faking an illness wouldn't work this time. Maybe for one day, but not for all of them.

Somehow, she was going to have to get through it.

Cossack tossed his head at something in the distance.

Julia's gloved hands tightened reflexively on the reins. She squinted down the length of the Row at the rider coming toward them. "Easy," she murmured to Cossack. "It's just another horse."

An enormous horse. Bigger and blacker than Cossack himself.

But it wasn't the horse that made Julia tense in her sidesaddle. It was the gentleman astride him: a stern-faced, battle-scarred ex-military man.

Captain Blunt, the Hero of the Crimea.

Her mouth went dry as he approached. She was half-tempted to bolt. But there was no escaping him. She brought Cossack down to a trot and then to a walk.

She'd met the captain once before. It had been at Lady Arundell's spring ball. Viscount Ridgeway, a mutual acquaintance of theirs, had introduced him to Julia as a worthy partner. In other circumstances, the interaction might have been the veriest commonplace—a few polite words exchanged and a turn about the polished wood dance floor.

Instead, Julia had gawped at Captain Blunt like a stricken nitwit. Her breath had stopped and her pulse had roared in her ears. Afraid she might faint, she'd fled the ballroom before the introduction had been completed, leaving Captain Blunt standing there, his granite-hewn features frozen in a mask of displeasure.

It had been one of the most mortifying experiences of Julia's life.

And that was saying something.

For a lady prone to panicking in company, mortifications were a daily occurrence. At the advanced age of two-and-twenty, she'd nearly grown accustomed to them. But even for her, the incident at Lady Arundell's ball had marked a new low.

No doubt Captain Blunt thought her actions had had something to do with his appearance.

He was powerfully made. Tall, strong, and impossibly broad shouldered. Already a physically intimidating gentleman, he was made even more so by the scar on his face. The deep, gruesome slash bisected his right eyebrow and ran all the way down to his mouth, notching into the flesh of his lip. It gave the impression of a permanent sneer.

Rather ironic that he was hailed as a hero. In looks, there seemed nothing heroic about him. Indeed, he appeared in every way a villain.

"Miss Wychwood." He removed his beaver hat, inclining his head in a bow. His hair was a lustrous raven black. Cut short to his collar, it was complemented by a pair of similarly short sideburns edging the harsh lines of his jaw. "Good morning."

She scarcely dared look him in the face. "Good morning."

He didn't reply. Not immediately. He was studying her. She could feel the weight of his stare. It set off a storm of butterflies in her stomach.

Ride on, she wanted to say. *Please, ride on.*

He didn't ride on. He seemed intent on making her squirm.

She suspected she knew why. She'd never apologized to him for her behavior at the ball. There'd been no opportunity.

Perhaps he wanted her to suffer for embarrassing him?

If that was the case, Julia was resigned to take her medicine. Heaven knew she deserved it.

She forced herself to meet his gaze. The butterflies in her stomach threatened to revolt. Goodness. His eyes were the color of hoarfrost—a gray so cold and stark it sent an icy shiver tracing down the curve of her spine. Every feminine instinct within her rose up in warning. *Run,* it said. *Flee.*

But this wasn't Lady Arundell's ballroom.

This was Hyde Park. Here in the open air, mounted on Cossack, she wasn't the same person she was at a ball or a dinner dance. For one thing, she wasn't alone. She had a partner—and an imposing one, at that. Cossack lent her his strength and his stature. Made her feel nearly as formidable as he was. It's why she was more confident on horseback.

At least, she'd always been so before.

"How do you do?" she asked.

"Very well." His voice was deep and commanding, with a growl at the edge of it. A soldier's voice. The kind that, when necessary, could be heard across a battlefield. "And yourself?"

"I'm enjoying our spell of fine weather," she said. "It's excellent for riding."

He flicked a glance over her habit. Made of faded black wool, it did nothing to emphasize the contours of her figure. Rather the opposite. It obscured her shape, much as the net veil on her short-brimmed riding hat obscured her face. His black brows notched into a frown.

She suppressed a flicker of self-consciousness. Her clothing wasn't meant to attract attention. It was meant to render her invisible. But it hadn't—not to him.

The way he looked at her . . . Hades might have regarded Persephone thus before dragging her down to hell to be his unwilling bride.

And everyone knew Captain Blunt was looking for a wife.

If one believed the prevailing rumors, it was the sole reason he'd come to town. He was on the hunt for a vulnerable heiress he could spirit back to his isolated Yorkshire estate. An estate that was said to be haunted.

"You ride often at this time of day?" he asked.

"Whenever I can," she said. "Cossack is glad for the exercise."

"You handle him well."

Some of the tightness in her chest eased at the compliment. "It's not difficult." She stroked Cossack's neck. "He may look imposing, but he's a lamb underneath. The biggest creatures often are, in my experience."

Captain Blunt's own mount stamped his gigantic hooves as if in objection to her statement.

She gave the great beast an interested look. He was built like a medieval warhorse, with a broad chest, heavy fetlocks, and a thickly waving mane and tail. "What do you call him?"

"Quintus."

"And is he—"

"A brute through and through," Captain Blunt said. "Sometimes, Miss Wychwood, what you see is precisely what you get."

Julia wondered if that was true in the captain's own case. Could he really be as menacing as he appeared? She didn't know to a certainty. All she knew was that, according to society gossip, he was positively dangerous—especially to marriageable young ladies.

It didn't excuse how she'd behaved toward him at the ball.

She moistened her lips. "I believe I owe you an apology."

He looked steadily back at her.

"When Lord Ridgeway was introducing you to me at Lady Arundell's ball . . ." She faltered. "Perhaps you don't remember—"

"I remember," he said gruffly.

Heat rose in her cheeks. "Yes, well . . . I'm sorry to have run off like that. I'm afraid I'm not at my best when meeting strangers."

"Do you often run off during introductions?"

"Not generally, no. Not unless I fear I'm going to swoon." Her mouth ticked up at one corner in a rueful smile. "You wouldn't have appreciated having to catch me."

Something flickered behind his icy gaze. An emotion impossible to read. "You don't know me very well, ma'am."

Were it any other gentleman, Julia might have suspected him of flirting with her. But not Captain Blunt. His scarred countenance was as coldly serious as his tone.

Her smile faded. "No, indeed." She tightened her fingers on the reins. "But I apologize all the same." She dipped her head to him as she urged Cossack on in the opposite direction. "Good day, Captain Blunt."

He didn't return her farewell. He didn't say anything. He only sat there atop his horse, watching her ride away.

Julia felt the burning impression of his stare at her back. And this time, she didn't will herself to be brave. She did what she'd wanted to do since she'd first laid eyes on him.

She pressed her heel into Cossack's side and she fled.

Jasper was tempted to ride after her, no matter that she'd just dismissed him.

But no.

He held Quintus to a standstill as Miss Wychwood rode away. She kept to a walk for several strides before kicking her horse into a lofty, ground-covering canter. Her seat was impeccable, her gloved hands light on her reins. She had a reputation for being a good rider. And she must be one to handle a horse so obviously too big for her.

Good God. She couldn't be more than five feet and three inches in height. A petite lady, with a gentle way about her. Had she no one to choose her a more suitable mount?

Jasper suspected not.

Her parents were well-known invalids, prone to all manner of fancies. Their elegant town house in Belgrave Square played host to an endless stream of doctors, chemists, and an ever-changing roster of servants.

Even Miss Wychwood's groom was of a recent vintage—a different fellow from the one who had accompanied her three days ago. He cantered a length behind her, the pair of them disappearing into the distance.

Jasper's frown deepened.

He'd learned many things about Miss Wychwood in the past several weeks, enough to know that marrying her and whisking her away to Yorkshire was going to be anything but simple.

Damn Viscount Ridgeway for suggesting it.

Exiting the park, Jasper returned to Ridgeway's house in Half Moon Street. It was a fashionable address, if not an ostentatious one, tucked between the house of a rich old widow on one side and that of a well-to-do solicitor on the other. After settling Quintus in the stable with his groom, Jasper made his way up the front steps to the door.

Ridgeway's grizzled butler, Skipforth, admitted him into the black-and-white-tiled hall. "His lordship has requested your presence in his chamber," he said as he took Jasper's hat and gloves. "He's breakfasting there."

Of course he was.

Ridgeway rarely emerged from his room before ten, and then only on sufferance.

Jasper felt a flare of irritation. Not for the first time, he regretted accepting Ridgeway's invitation to stay.

"Shall I take you to him, sir?" Skipforth asked.

"No need." Jasper bounded up the curving staircase to the third floor. He rapped once on Ridgeway's door before entering.

The heavy draperies were drawn back from the windows. Sunlight streamed through the glass, revealing an expansive bedchamber decorated in shades of rich crimson and gold. On the far side of it, opposite his unmade four-poster bed and the silver tea tray containing the remains of his breakfast, sat Nathan Grainger, Viscount Ridgeway.

He was sprawled in a wooden chair in front of his inlaid mahogany dressing table, eyes closed as his valet trimmed his side-whiskers.

"That you, Blunt?" He squinted open one eye. "Back so soon?"

"As you see. Skipforth said you had need of me?"

"So I do. And excellent timing, too. Fennel's just finished shearing me." Ridgeway dismissed his valet with a wave of his hand.

Fennel, a weedy man with a shifty expression, promptly withdrew into the dressing room, shutting the door behind him with a click.

"I require your opinion on a horse I've been eyeing at Tattersalls," Ridgeway said. "Unless you have other plans today?"

"Nothing that can't be changed. When are you leaving?"

"Presently." Ridgeway sat forward in his chair, examining his freshly trimmed side-whiskers in the glass. "What do you think?"

Jasper could detect no difference from the way Ridgeway usually looked. "I suppose they're shorter."

"I despaired of them growing too full. A man wants to appear dignified, but after all, one doesn't wish to look like the prime minister."

"No chance of that." Jasper crossed the floor to take a seat in a velvet-upholstered wing chair near the fire.

Ridgeway kept only enough servants to support a bachelor establishment. His house was, nevertheless, comfortable and well tended—a definite improvement from the hotel Jasper had been staying at when he'd first arrived in town.

Not that he'd had much choice in lodgings.

He had no family in London to impose upon. No real friends on whom he could inflict his company.

Even his connection with Ridgeway was tenuous at best.

They'd met six years ago in Constantinople—both men at their lowest ebb. Ridgeway had come to Scutari Hospital to collect the body of his younger brother, killed in the skirmish that had taken the lives of the rest of Jasper's men.

Jasper had been at Scutari, too; not on an errand, but as a gravely injured patient—the sole survivor of the skirmish, rendered all but unrecognizable by the severe wound on his face.

Ridgeway had spoken to him, attempting to rally his spirits. A futile task. Jasper had been in no mood to speak to anyone. But later, upon his release from hospital, when Ridgeway had written to him, Jasper had grudgingly replied.

An occasional correspondence had followed.

It wasn't a friendship. Not anywhere near it. Jasper hadn't any friends. And unless he was mistaken, neither had Ridgeway. They were merely two men brought together by circumstance. Cordial acquaintances—and sometimes, not even that.

Indeed, since coming to stay with him, Jasper had found Ridgeway's cold-bloodedness increasingly repellent.

"Why so glum?" Ridgeway cast him a glance. "No luck with Miss Wychwood?"

"Luck has nothing to do with it."

"You did see her?"

"I did," Jasper said. Despite the fact that she clearly didn't want to be seen.

Given the drab, ill-fitting clothing that shrouded her figure and the riding veils that concealed her face, one might think she had reason to hide. That her face and body were something to be ashamed of.

It wasn't true.

Julia Wychwood was beautiful.

He'd realized that from the first moment he'd set eyes on her.

In another time—another life—he might have been in grave danger of losing his heart.

Ridgeway continued admiring his reflection. "What's the problem, then?"

"The problem," Jasper said, "is that this business is becoming quite a bit more mercenary than I'd intended."

"Courtship *is* mercenary. And marriage is positively cutthroat. If you don't have the stones for it you may as well resign yourself to a permanent state of bachelorhood." Ridgeway smoothed his hand over his side-whiskers. "Which isn't so bad, now I think on it. So long as you can afford it."

"Which I can't," Jasper reminded him.

Ridgeway shrugged. "There you are."

"Yes," Jasper said. "Here I am. And there you are, being absolutely useless, per usual."

"I say. That's unfair. Didn't I introduce you to her?" Ridgeway met Jasper's eyes in the glass. "She's an heiress. A sickly heiress, too. Take my advice and marry the chit. She won't overburden you for long."

Jasper's jaw tightened on a surge of anger. Mercenary he may be, but he hadn't yet sunk to marrying an invalid and praying for her early demise. "You're very sure of yourself."

Ridgeway shrugged. "She took to her bed last month for several days. I hear that the doctor was called in to bleed her. She's already a pasty thing. How much more blood do you suppose she has left to offer?"

"She's stronger than she looks."

"You can't know that. You've only seen her a handful of times."

"I've seen enough. I've seen her ride. She's not yet at death's door." Jasper paused, adding, "And she's not pasty."

"No? What would you call her complexion? It's not marble or alabaster. Not like her friend, Lady Anne." Ridgeway again looked at Jasper in the glass. "By the by, if you take my advice, you'll make the most of that lady's absence from town. You might have noticed, whenever she's here, she guards her little protégé like a hydrophobic mastiff."

"Lady Anne has left London?" That *was* news. "For how long?"

Another shrug. "A few days. She and her mother have hared off to Birmingham to look in on that child medium everyone's talking about. The one who claims to have contacted Prince Albert."

Jasper's lips compressed. He'd heard of the boy. When one was out in fashionable society, it was impossible not to. Jasper put no stock in such tales. No more than he put in spiritualism as a whole. It was all so much nonsense. Ghosts and spirits and proclamations from beyond the veil.

As if he hadn't enough of that to deal with in Yorkshire.

"I wonder that Miss Wychwood didn't accompany them," he said.

"The Wychwoods don't involve themselves in such things. They've enough trouble on this side of the grave, what with their rapidly failing health." Ridgeway stood abruptly. "Speaking of which, Fennel tells me that Miss Wychwood will be attending Lady Clifford's musicale this evening. Good thing you didn't refuse the invitation."

Jasper sighed. A musicale meant a crowded room filled with the cream of London society. It meant him sitting shoulder to shoulder with eligible young misses and their overbearing mamas.

"Having second thoughts?" Ridgeway asked.

Yes. And third ones, too.

But Jasper wasn't going to confide all of his doubts in Ridgeway. The man already knew too much. "There must be someone else who will suit."

"What?" Ridgeway gave him a narrow glance. "Another heiress, do you mean?"

"Yes," Jasper said. "Exactly that. Someone who . . ."

Someone who didn't nearly faint at the sight of him. Who wasn't afraid to look him in the face.

From anyone else, he could have tolerated well-bred disgust. It was a frequent enough reaction to his appearance. But he couldn't accept it from *her*.

"Blast it," he muttered under his breath. "This shouldn't be so complicated."

"It isn't." Ridgeway reached for his coat and tugged it on. "You require an heiress with no family or connections—no one to ask questions about you or to come snooping to Yorkshire. The only heiress who fits the bill is Julia Wychwood. If not her, then you may as well let the bailiffs take your estate."

Jasper ran a hand through his hair in frustration. The bailiffs. Bloody hell. It wasn't going to come to that, was it? Not after everything he'd already risked to forge a new life for himself.

Ridgeway laughed. "The look on your face. One would think you were too high-minded to follow through with it."

An image of Miss Wychwood materialized in Jasper's mind, her sapphire blue eyes shining vividly from behind her black net riding veil.

I believe I owe you an apology.

She'd taken him completely off of his guard. Had puzzled and disarmed him.

Was she really who she appeared to be? A sickly wallflower heiress, ripe for the plucking?

He was beginning to have his doubts. "I might be."

"Bah," Ridgeway scoffed. "That's not the man my brother wrote to me about during the war. The cruel, ruthless, bloodthirsty Captain Blunt who had all of his men shivering in their boots. Surely, you remember him?"

"Only too well," Jasper said grimly.

"Do you? Because it sometimes seems to me that you're not that man at all."

Jasper's gaze jerked to Ridgeway's face. There seemed to be no ulterior meaning in his words. No hint of a threat. "I may well have been ruthless," he replied, "but never with women. And never outside times of war."

"My dear fellow, this *is* a war," Ridgeway said. "It's the London season."

Two

❖

Julia sat immobile on the silk damask–cushioned bench in front of her carved walnut dressing table as her lady's maid, Mary, put the final touches on her evening coiffure. It was a pretty enough style—a cascade of tightly pinned rolls at the back, secured with dozens of hairpins and several spritzes of liquid bandoline.

Julia hardly noticed it.

She turned the page of the small blue clothbound volume of *Lady Audley's Secret* on her lap, her attention fully engaged by author Mrs. Braddon's lavish prose. Never mind that she'd read the story countless times before.

"Miss Lucy Graham was blessed with that magic power of fascination, by which a woman can charm with a word or intoxicate with a smile," Julia read aloud. It was one of her favorite lines in the entire book. "Can you imagine, Mary?"

"She was a murderess, she was." Mary placed a spray of spring roses into Julia's hair. "Nothing to admire about that."

"Yes, but . . ." Julia met her maid's eyes in the gilt-framed trifold looking glass that stood atop the dressing table. "Can you imagine what it must be like to be so attractive? So fascinating to everyone you meet?"

"Trouble is what it would be, miss, and no two ways about it. A woman has enough to contend with without having magic powers of fascination." Mary smoothed a stray hair back from Julia's temple. "And I don't see what you've got to worry over. There's no one who sees you who wouldn't admit to your beauty."

"Even beautiful women can be thought unattractive. If there's something in their character people take a dislike to—an unbecoming shyness or awkwardness—it doesn't matter how fine their appearance. But to be like Lady Audley . . ."

"You read too many of them sensation novels. It ain't real life, you know."

Julia's mouth quirked. She wasn't offended by the impertinent observation. Unlike the other servants in the house, Mary had the privilege of tenure. A plain woman in her middle forties, she'd been hired as a lady's maid three years ago when Julia embarked on her first season. Since then, Mary had seen her at her best—and at her worst. She knew all Julia's little foibles.

"Gentlemen don't like girls what read books," Mary continued, sinking the final bit of greenery into Julia's coiffure. "And you want to find yourself a husband this season, don't you?"

"Yes, but—"

"I'd be surprised if one of them society gents don't propose, now you've come into your bloom." Mary stepped back with an encouraging smile. "Just look at yourself."

Julia gave her reflection a dutiful glance. Her black hair was drawn back from her face, lending focus to the contours of her cheeks and jaw, and to her wide mouth and similarly wide-set gaze. Her eyes were very blue in the candlelight, and her skin seemed translucently pale. Luminous, one might even call it.

And there was so much of it exposed.

The low neckline of her mazarine shot silk evening dress left little to the imagination, baring her throat, shoulders, and the rounded swell of her bosom.

Mama wouldn't approve of it.

But Mama wasn't here. She was still recuperating in Bath. And Papa may as well have been with her for all he emerged from his rooms.

"Well?" Mary prompted.

"It's lovely." Julia rose from her seat. Her flounced silk skirts rustled over her crinoline. "I shall need a shawl."

While Mary darted off to find one, Julia collected her gloves and her silk-fringed reticule. Opening the drawstring closure, she dropped her novel inside. A society musicale was no place for reading. But it never hurt to be prepared.

Jasper descended the stairs after Ridgeway, both of them dressed in evening black accented by light-colored silk waistcoats and cravats. The gasolier in the hall was turned up, casting a diffuse ring of light over the checkered tiles.

Skipforth emerged from the shadows. "A letter for you, Captain Blunt."

Ridgeway gave his butler a look of irritation. "The post? At this time of night?"

"A boy just brought it round from the Cavendish Hotel." Skipforth handed the missive to Jasper as he stepped down into the hall. "It appears to have been misdirected."

Jasper examined the letter. The address on the envelope had been penned in a child's unartful scrawl. It was at once recognizable.

Charlie.

Jasper had told him to write if there was any difficulty. And with Charlie, there was *always* difficulty.

"One of your by-blows, I presume," Ridgeway said.

Jasper stiffened. The description was insulting, both to his own honor and to that of the children. But it wasn't inaccurate, not so far as society was concerned. They believed the worst of him.

Which was exactly how it had to be.

"It looks like it," he replied.

Ridgeway's expression of irritation grew more pronounced by the second. "Must we delay?"

"Not at all. I'll read it in the carriage."

Ridgeway nodded his approval. "Good man. Lady Clifford despises latecomers to her musical soirees. Claims it disrupts the performers."

Jasper collected his hat and gloves before following Ridgeway out the door. The viscount's carriage awaited them in the gaslit street—a black lacquered coach with the family coat of arms emblazoned in gold on the door. A liveried footman set down the steps.

Ridgeway climbed in without assistance.

Jasper followed, taking the seat across from his host. He settled himself in the corner beneath the light of the carriage lamp. As the horses sprang into motion, he opened the seal on Charlie's letter and began to read.

Dear Sir,

The roof is leaking again. This time it leaked in the nursery right down on Daisy's head. Mr. Beecham says I am not to burden you and that you have more important things on your mind than the likes of us. But even you would not wish Daisy to catch her death from neglect. Please send fifty pounds for repairs.

P.S. Alfred says to remind you that the roof in the workhouse did not leak.

Sincerely,
Charles X.

A muscle ticked in Jasper's cheek as he refolded the letter and slipped it into the interior pocket of his evening jacket. He didn't know which part was more offensive. Was it the implication he was neglectful? Or was it the suggestion that conditions in the workhouse had been superior to that at Goldfinch Hall?

No, he realized. It was neither.

The most offensive was Charlie's signature. *Charles X.* As if he were still the same bastard-born boy Jasper had taken from the workhouse. A lice-ridden mite who hadn't known his letters and who had barely been able to scratch out his mark, a single X taught to him by his similarly illiterate mother.

Charlie had been six at the time, and Alfred five.

Jasper had been little more than a lad himself then. Only five and twenty, with scant experience in handling domestic affairs. But he'd done his utmost in the circumstances. He'd sent the boys to school in the nearby village of Hardholme. Had made sure they learned to read and write.

It had done little to elevate him in the boys' estimation.

Six years later, Alfred was, at best, indifferent to him. But Charlie still blamed Jasper for all the ills he, his mother, and his siblings had suffered.

No doubt Dolly had filled his young ears with all sorts of grim tales about the heartless Captain Blunt. A wicked, unfeeling monster who had left his mistress and three illegitimate children to starve and die while he went off to war.

And Dolly *had* died.

By the time Jasper had returned from the Crimea, the consumption had all but devoured her. She'd mustered the strength to travel to Goldfinch Hall, baby Daisy on her hip, demanding Jasper retrieve Charlie and Alfred from the workhouse before she died.

Demanding. Threatening.

Jasper had been tempted to give up the game then and there. To leave Yorkshire forever and start again somewhere new.

He hadn't, of course.

But he wasn't going to think of any of that now. Not on the same evening he was meant to be wooing a bride. Whether Miss Wychwood or someone else, he still didn't know. Nothing about this bloody endeavor was turning out the way he'd planned.

"Dare I ask?" Ridgeway inquired blandly.

Jasper glanced up at him, frowning.

"Your by-blows. I can't imagine what one of them has written to you."

"Nothing to concern yourself with," Jasper said. The carriage rolled through the busy street, the cab rocking as the coachman turned the horses onto Grosvenor Square. "Just a reminder of why I'm here."

"An unpleasant reminder, by the look of it." Ridgeway sighed. "It serves you right for sending them to school. A nightmare if you ask me, receiving disagreeable letters from one's bastards."

"I don't recall asking."

The carriage came to a halt in front of Lady Clifford's residence. A footman opened the door of the coach for them. There was no line of carriages waiting in the street, and no crowd of guests milling about the stone steps leading up to the door. Flickering light emanated from the windows of the town house, accompanied by the soft tinkling of piano keys and the plucking of harp strings.

Ridgeway scowled. "We're late."

Jasper climbed out after him. A butler welcomed them at the front door and, after relieving them of their hats and coats, escorted them upstairs to the drawing room.

The connecting doors had been opened between rooms as if for a ball, making an enormous space for the more than one hundred ladies and gentlemen in attendance. Dozens of chairs and upholstered benches were arranged in long rows, set back from a dais on which two silk-clad young ladies played a sentimental duet on the piano and harp.

On catching sight of them, an attractive blond woman in the fourth row beckoned to Ridgeway with her painted fan.

"There's Lady Eastlake," he said. "If you'll excuse me?"

Jasper nodded. He preferred to be on his own. And he was never more so than in a crowd. There were no ladies awaiting his company. None who knew him in London save by reputation. But his own popularity didn't concern him. His name garnered him invitations enough for his purposes. As for the rest of it . . .

He could manage well enough for himself.

Entering the room, he kept to the back wall. Papered in pale green watered silk, it was adorned with evenly spaced gas wall sconces. Some gentlemen stood in the gaps. Some young ladies, too. Wallflowers, by the look of them. They dropped their eyes as Jasper moved past them, whispering to one another as soon as they thought him out of earshot.

"That awful scar!" one of them breathed.

"Have you ever seen anything so horrible?" her comrade breathed back in a dramatic undertone.

"And that's not the worst of it. I heard . . ."

Jasper kept walking until the whispers faded away. He knew full well what he looked like. And he knew even better what people said about him. About how ruthless the notorious Captain Blunt had been in the Crimea.

God knew it was true enough.

Had Miss Wychwood heard such rumors? She was certain to have heard something.

He hadn't seen her yet. He wasn't confident she would be here. During the last month, she'd been expected at several events he'd attended, only to beg off at the last moment because of illness or indisposition.

His gaze drifted over the crowd. There were benefits to being tall. When standing, he could easily see over the rows of seated ladies and gentlemen. If Miss Wychwood was here, she wouldn't be sandwiched in the middle of the audience. And she wouldn't be exposed in the front row. She didn't like crowds. And she didn't like drawing attention to herself.

No. If she was here, she'd be nearest the exit. That much better to make her escape.

And that's exactly where he found her.

She was seated in a chair in the third row from the front. On her left were the open doors of the drawing room, flanked by two liveried footmen, and on her right was the newly widowed Earl of Gresham. A heavily bewhiskered gentleman well past his fiftieth year, the earl had the look of a stout country squire. He was leaning over her, whispering something in her ear.

Her head turned as she listened, revealing her beautiful face in profile—the lustrous ebony hair, a dark arching brow, and the strong line of her straight nose and elegantly sculpted cheek and jaw.

Jasper's pulse quickened the instant he laid eyes on her.

She wore a dark blue dress that exposed her pale throat and softly rounded shoulders. Some elaborate silk confection with fringe and ribbon bows. It shimmered in the gaslight, the color of the sea at midnight. The same shade as her eyes.

It was wholly unsuitable.

Much like Miss Wychwood herself.

The more he knew of her, the less he could envision her living at Goldfinch Hall. Even less could he imagine her acting the part of mother to Charlie, Alfred, and Daisy.

As if any lady of quality would ever consent to such a thing.

He would have to find another wealthy woman to marry. Someone who was less gently bred. Less sheltered and refined.

Less beautiful.

He was running out of time. He hadn't needed Charlie's letter to remind him. Jasper knew full well what was at stake. The burden of his obligations was ever present.

Marriage was the only solution.

All he needed was a likely candidate. Someone he could woo and wed with all speed. A distasteful business, but a necessary one.

Ridgeway was sure to know of another lady who might suit. Until then . . .

The music stopped and the crowd burst into a swell of restrained applause.

Jasper's thoughts were wrenched back to the present. He tore his gaze from Miss Wychwood.

Hell and damnation.

Had he been staring? Staring and scowling like some miserable cur fretting over a bone? He grimaced at the thought, even as he joined in the brief round of applause for the two young ladies on the dais.

They curtsied and withdrew, smiles and blushes on full display. Lady Clifford took their place. Known for her keen interest in the arts, she was always hosting some sort of musicale or dramatic evening. Like many events of the season, they largely served as thinly veiled showcases for young ladies on the marriage mart.

"A fine effort by Miss Lydiard and Miss Bingham," Lady Clifford said. "For our next performance, Miss Rumple will grace us with an air on the harp. Miss Rumple?"

An angelic young lady dressed all in white ascended to the dais. She curtsied to the audience before seating herself at the harp.

Her anemic performance was followed by that of one eligible young miss after the other, all expensively coiffed and clad. They sang and played in solos and duets, songs performed in German and Italian, in soprano and contralto.

Jasper remained standing against the back wall of the drawing room, arms folded across his chest. Among all the young ladies, he saw none to stir his interest. They were pretty enough, to be sure, and doubtless they all boasted respectable dowries. That should have been his foremost concern. His *only* concern.

And it was.

He required money to replace the roof at Goldfinch. Money to repair the years of rot and neglect. If he could manage to set the whole of the estate back on the right track, in five years' time, it might be self-sufficient. All it required was an influx of capital.

As for the rest of the business, wedding and bedding some suitable heiress—a lady with no friends or relatives to interfere—he'd simply have to steel himself and get on with it. He didn't have to like the girl, let alone be attracted to her. Many men married for mercenary reasons. It was the way of the world among the upper classes.

The prospect, nevertheless, left him chilled to the heart.

As the voice of the current performer rose to match its thundering accompaniment, he couldn't help but glance, once again, in Miss Wychwood's direction.

Lord Gresham was still there, his lecherous attention now focused on the lady to his right. The seat to his left was empty.

Julia Wychwood was gone.

Three

❦

*J*ulia huddled in the corner of the empty receiving room on the second floor, her novel open on her lap. A gas wall sconce above her illuminated the words on the page. Reading them, her pulse began to slow and her muscles gradually relaxed. Her surroundings faded—the shrill soprano of a performer, and the noise of the accompanying piano—as she sank into the now familiar story of Lady Audley.

No sedative could have worked with such efficiency.

In a novel she was safe. Her throat didn't close up and her palms didn't grow damp. She could experience things in a way that didn't overwhelm her.

Obviously, it wasn't ideal.

She shouldn't be hiding in an empty room during Lady Clifford's musicale. Still, Julia doubted whether anyone would notice her absence. Not her inattentive chaperone, society matron Mrs. Major, who had departed to join her fashionable friends shortly after their arrival. Not even Lord Gresham—though he *had* spent the better part of the first three performances talking into Julia's bosom.

Men always talked *at* a female rather than *to* her.

As a rule, Julia didn't mind it. When surrounded on all sides by strangers, she often found it difficult to formulate a word. An overbearing man could be a blessing in such circumstances. But Lord

Gresham was overbearing with a purpose. Recently widowed, the elderly earl was seeking a new young wife to bear his heirs.

Such an arrangement might suit someone else, but it didn't suit her. When she married—*if* she married—it wouldn't be to some man who was old enough to be her father. Only look at what had happened to Lady Audley.

"That must be quite a book to hold your attention in all this din."

Julia's head jerked up. Her heart lurched.

Captain Blunt stood, silhouetted, at the entrance to the anteroom, his broad shoulders nearly spanning the doorframe. His scarred face was shadowed in the gaslight, making him appear even more sinister than he usually did—something she hadn't thought possible.

He wasn't old enough to be her father. Indeed, he couldn't be much above thirty.

"What is it?" he asked.

Julia hastily closed her book. She cleared her throat. "It's, um, *Lady Audley's Secret.*"

"Ah. I see." He advanced into the room. Slowly. Deliberately. As if he was approaching a wild horse that might shy away from him.

Julia rather felt like one.

Her heartbeat quickened as he drew closer. She instinctively shrank back against the silk-papered wall behind her, wishing she could disappear.

No such luck.

She was well and truly caught. And it was her own fault. She was the one who had chosen to hide in this particular corner. There would be no escaping him now.

He came to a halt in front of her. "Don't be afraid."

Don't be afraid? He could say that when he was looming over her like a great beast in a fairy tale?

"I won't spoil it," he said.

Comprehension came like a lightning strike.

Julia inwardly groaned.

He wasn't talking about *himself.* He was talking about the *book.*

She felt more than a little foolish. "You couldn't spoil it. I've read it six times before."

"Six times?" His black brows lifted. "Any particular reason?"

"Some stories are better the more you read them. You notice things you didn't the first time. And not only that." She hesitated. "Books you've already read are like old friends. It's comforting to revisit them."

He nodded once, as if in unspoken understanding. "And this is why you slipped away from the drawing room? To revisit an old friend?"

"No. That is . . . yes." She couldn't keep the stammer from her voice. Neither could she formulate a creditable excuse. The truth tumbled out unchecked. "I was feeling lonely out there."

He gave the empty room a dubious look. "As opposed to in here?"

"Here I'm alone, but I'm not lonely. There's a difference."

Here, there were no fashionable crowds to exclude her from their midst. No one to provoke her anxiety. To make her feel unwanted or unworthy. There was only herself.

And now him.

"You must like the story tremendously," he said.

"Oh, I love the story. It's one of my absolute favorites." Her gloved fingers fidgeted on the book's cover. "Did you like it?"

"I did. Very much so."

She stared up at him, speechless.

His mouth tipped at one corner. It was a semblance of a smile. A brief one at that. It vanished as soon as it materialized, his mouth reverting to its characteristic scar-snaggled sneer. "You look surprised."

"I am rather. Most gentlemen wouldn't deign to read a novel. And if they did, they'd never admit to liking it."

He shrugged. "Novels provide an inexpensive escape from the realities of life. One would be a fool to discount them." He cast a glance at the empty place beside her. "May I?"

Julia's mouth went dry. "Er . . . yes. If you wish." She moved her flounced skirts out of the way, making room for him on the silk-cushioned bench.

He sank down next to her. The bench creaked in protest beneath his weight.

He was close. *Too* close.

His leg brushed hers. She felt it through the barrier of her petticoats and crinoline, as surely as if their knees had touched without anything between them. Her already racing pulse skipped a beat.

She'd never been this near to him before. Never yet had the opportunity to fully appreciate his size and strength. The peculiar power of his presence. It was commanding. Almost menacing. And why not? He was a soldier. A dangerous soldier, if rumors were to be believed.

If she knew what was good for her, she'd stand up and walk straight back to the drawing room. Instead, she remained where she was, a hair's breadth away from one of the most ruthless men in recent military history.

He may have been known as the Hero of the Crimea, but the moniker was rarely spoken with honorable connotation. Captain Blunt had been notorious during the war.

She wasn't privy to the particulars of his conduct. At the time, she'd been too young to read the papers. And now, among the ladies with whom she associated, there was only the vaguest of murmurings. All Julia knew for certain was that his notoriety had increased since returning to England.

If what her best friend, Lady Anne, said was true, the captain's haunted estate in Yorkshire was presently playing host to his brood of illegitimate children. A scandalous fact. What sort of gentleman flaunted his sins in public? The answer was evident: a man who was no gentleman at all.

If he wanted to compromise Julia, he could, and easily.

She contemplated running away, but glancing up at the captain, she found him gazing down at her with single-minded attention.

"Miss Wychwood . . ."

"Yes?" Her voice was a breathless whisper.

"I wonder . . . What is it that appeals to you about that novel?"

Julia blinked up at him. "You want to know about *Lady Audley's Secret*?"

"I do."

She owned to a flicker of disappointment. What had she thought he was going to say? Something scandalous?

Something thrilling?

Stupid of her. One might think she wanted to be thrilled by him.

"What is it in the story that captures your interest?" he asked. "That makes you read it over and over again?"

That was simple enough. "It's the way she transforms herself. I've always found the idea fascinating."

Captain Blunt gave her an inscrutable look.

"Reinvention," she explained. "Changing oneself into someone else."

His gray eyes were glacial. "To what purpose?"

She feared she'd said something wrong, but she couldn't for the life of her imagine what. "Why . . . to be happier."

"How so?"

"By being another person," she said. "Obviously."

"You'd still be the same person underneath it all."

"Yes, but circumstances would be different. You could start fresh in a new place. Somewhere you would be welcomed and admired. Where you'd feel as if you belonged."

Captain Blunt appeared skeptical.

"It's true," Julia insisted. "For ladies, anyway. Everything with us is based on outward appearances. On rumors and innuendo. Once a lady develops a bad reputation, she may as well retire from London society completely. The only option is to reinvent herself somewhere else. In India or America or some spa town or other. Many ladies have done so."

He studied her in the gaslight. "You don't have a bad reputation."

"I wasn't talking about myself." Her silk reticule hung from her wrist. She drew it open, dropping her book back inside. "And anyway," she muttered, "I have a reputation for being strange. It's much the same."

"Strange? How?"

"Different. Odd. I don't fit in." She pulled closed the drawstring mouth of her reticule. "That must be abundantly clear."

"Not to me it isn't."

"Perhaps you haven't noticed it yet."

His voice deepened to a husky growl. "I've noticed everything about you."

Her eyes widened in vague alarm. "Have you? Goodness. I don't know why you should. I'm singularly uninteresting."

"Is that a fact? And yet you interest me very much." He searched her face. "I wonder why you haven't married."

The statement, made so casually, was as insolent as it was unexpected.

Julia drew back from him, her words emerging in an outraged squeak. "I *beg* your pardon?"

"Forgive my impertinence," he said. "It's only that I can't fathom how it is you remain unattached."

She was indignant to her marrow. "You're mocking me, sir."

"I don't mock. I speak plainly. You're free to do the same."

Her gaze was riveted to his. She'd never spoken plainly to a gentleman in her life. Not a stranger, anyway. Given the choice, she rarely spoke at all.

But what would it hurt?

He appeared interested. And she had nothing to be ashamed of.

She exhaled an unsteady breath. "If you must know, my circumstances are complicated. My parents are in poor health. And my own health is often indifferent."

"You're ill?"

"Not ill. I suppose you might say I'm . . . fragile."

He regarded her steadily. "You didn't look fragile on that horse of yours this morning."

"That's different. Cossack makes me stronger. Without him, I'm generally viewed as inadequate. Except in one respect." Her pulse throbbed in her ears. A voice in her head warned her to hold her tongue. She didn't heed it. "I have a sizable dowry."

Captain Blunt said nothing in reply. He merely looked at her, still holding her gaze, even as the tension crackled palpably between them.

She pressed on against all better judgment. "Perchance you've heard of it?"

"I have," he admitted.

Naturally, he had. Why else would he be paying her any attention? She'd known that from the moment he'd first requested an introduction to her at Lady Arundell's ball. Even so, his confession left Julia deflated.

So much for thrills and danger.

The infamous Captain Blunt was, when it came down to it, nothing more than a garden-variety fortune hunter.

"I expect you've heard a thing or two about me as well," he said.

She couldn't deny it. "I have."

The silence grew between them. It was too painful to endure.

She rose abruptly from the bench. Captain Blunt was immediately on his feet. She took a step back in a futile attempt to put space between them.

He closed the distance. "Miss Wychwood."

"Captain Blunt," she uttered at the same time.

He paused, allowing her to proceed.

She made herself continue, despite the anxiety tightening her chest and the scorching blush burning its way up her throat and into her face. "I hope you won't trouble yourself to pursue me. We'd never suit."

His gray eyes flickered. "You think not?"

"I-I do. That is, we wouldn't." She stumbled a little over her words.

"I have a substantial dowry, it's true, but no amount of money lasts forever. And after you've run through it, you'd be stuck with me."

His expression hardened. "An observation that flatters neither of us."

"You asked for plain speaking."

"So I did." He offered her a rigid bow. "Miss Wychwood."

"Captain." She inclined her head to him and, catching up her heavy skirts in her hands, swiftly took her leave. As she exited the room, she sensed him staring after her just as he had that morning in Hyde Park.

She hastened her step, once again reminded of myths and fairy stories. Of dark, brooding villains abducting young maidens who were guilty of doing nothing more than minding their own business.

And Captain Blunt *was* a villain. Everyone said so.

She would do well to remember it.

Four

❖❖❖

Sunlight shone through the tall morning room windows, warming Julia's bent head and shoulders as she sat at her mother's dainty Boulle-inlaid writing desk. She dipped her sharpened quill pen into the open inkpot, tapping away the excess before marking a heavy X through yesterday's date in her diary.

Only three more days until her friends returned to London.

Three more days of society events to get through alone.

She set down her pen. She'd gone riding this morning, half expecting to run into Captain Blunt again. But he seemed to have heeded her request. There had been no sign of him in Rotten Row. None that she could see.

And she'd looked for him.

Looked and looked. As if she was disappointed by his absence.

Which wasn't the case at all.

She was glad to be free of his interest. She wasn't some feather-headed heroine in a novel to be lured in by his imposing height and his magnificently broad shoulders. By his raven-black hair, with its faint threads of silver at the temples, and by his piercing eyes as cold and gray as the Thames in winter.

Goodness. If not for his scarred face and his black reputation, he might almost have been handsome.

Almost.

But this wasn't a novel. No adventure awaited her in the arms of a villain, only ruin, misery, and disgrace. If she was to find a husband this season, it must be among decent men. Men who weren't blood-thirsty former soldiers, and who didn't live in haunted Yorkshire estates with their brood of illegitimate children.

Strange, that. She couldn't imagine Captain Blunt keeping a mistress. There was nothing of tenderness about him. Nothing terribly romantic. Although . . .

He *had* admitted to reading *Lady Audley's Secret.*

She wondered what Anne would have to say about it.

Lady Anne Deveril, only daughter of the late Earl of Arundell, had been Julia's best friend for as long as she could remember. They were opposites in every way—Anne was bold, confident, and opinionated where Julia was shy, uncertain, and often tongue-tied in company. Yet together they fit, each of them providing what the other lacked.

In many ways, Anne acted as Julia's protector. It was a role that was almost mother-like, guarding Julia from impertinent men, and saving her from her own self-indulgences. Only recently, when Julia had been tucked in her bed with chocolates and a novel, pleading illness to avoid her social obligations, it had been Anne who had persuaded her to get up and face the London season.

Until two days ago, they'd been navigating it together, along with their bosom friends, Stella Hobhouse and Evelyn Maltravers. The four of them were excellent horsewomen, more comfortable in their side-saddles than in a ballroom. Their rides in the park were the highlights of Julia's days. As for the evenings, even dances were more fun with her friends in attendance.

Would that they were here now!

They'd all left London on the same day. Evelyn had accompanied Anne and Lady Arundell to Birmingham to see the child medium. And Stella had abruptly departed town with her clergyman brother, made his unwilling companion to an ecumenical conference in Exeter.

Both Stella and Anne would be returning on Sunday. Evelyn would come a few weeks later, after a brief visit home to her village in Sussex.

Julia missed them dreadfully. In their absence, she didn't know quite what to do with herself. As always, in such circumstances, the security of her bedchamber beckoned. The warmth of her bed and the temporary escape of a novel.

Rising from her chair, she rang the bell for the maid.

Moments later, a hard-faced young woman in a starched apron entered. Jane Seven, she was called—the seventh maid employed in her position. They were all of them called Jane, just as all the first footmen were called Jenkins, the second footmen were called George, and all the grooms were called Luke. Julia's parents insisted it was easier that way. Though, it never seemed entirely right to Julia's mind.

"You rang, miss?" Jane Seven inquired.

"Have the carriage readied," Julia said. "And summon Mary. I have some shopping to do this morning."

"Yes, miss." Jane Seven wobbled a curtsy before turning to leave.

"Why are these curtains opened?" The thin, querulous voice of Julia's father, Sir Eustace, preceded him into the room. He entered, still in his slippers, wearing a shawl-collared silk and velvet banyan over his loose shirt and trousers. A thick scarf was tucked in at the neck as protection against imagined drafts. "Draw them at once, Jane."

Jane Seven hurried to the bank of windows on the opposite wall. Reaching up, she pulled the heavy curtains shut, moving from window to window, until the bright sun was once again blocked from the morning room.

Julia frowned. "It was I who ordered them opened, Papa."

Her father gave her a long-suffering look. "You'll be the death of me, child. And yourself, too, if you're not careful. Up at dawn again? Riding that horse of yours?"

"I'm perfectly well," she said. "And you? You must be feeling a little better to have emerged from your rooms."

"Still poorly, as anyone can see." He dropped into an overstuffed armchair with a weary sigh. "I must go over the quarterly accounts with Hicks, though the strain of it will probably put an end to me. You must summon Dr. Cordingley as a precaution."

Julia went to her father. She sank down on the tufted ottoman at his feet, the full skirts of her day dress pooling around her in a spill of Clarence-blue cashmere. "Can't Hicks manage without your assistance?"

"The man who doesn't mind his own accounts deserves to have his servants rob him. And they will, mark my words." He broke off to utter a hoarse bark at the maid as she exited the room. "Fetch me a tonic, girl! And bring a blanket, and a fresh pot of tea. And send in one of the footmen to lay a fire."

"Yes, sir. At once, sir." Jane Seven scurried out the door.

Papa rested his head against the cushioned back of the chair. His gray hair was thinning across his scalp, his whiskered face pale from lack of sunlight. If left to their own devices, he and Mama would spend all their days in darkness, nursing their various indispositions.

"Should you be up at all?" Julia wondered.

"How could I help it with all this noise? Have I not told you to tread quietly on the stairs? If you must insist on rising early to ride—" His eyes narrowed. "Mind you, I object to the activity. You know I'm sensitive to the smell of horses. The headaches I suffer on every occasion I travel in the carriage. And now, my own daughter stinking of the stables. One day I shall instruct Hicks to sell that horse of yours."

It was an old threat. An idle one, too. She bristled at it nonetheless.

"Really, Papa. You know very well that Cossack belongs to me. I bought him with the money I inherited from Aunt Elinore. You haven't the authority to sell him."

"Oh, haven't I? Try me and see, my girl. Your aunt may have left you a sizable portion, but I'm still master here—though I may be on my deathbed."

"You're not on your deathbed. And you wouldn't rob me of my one joy in life. It's bad enough you prevent me from having a dog or a cat to ease my loneliness. But to threaten me with losing Cossack—"

"Loneliness?" he wheezed. "Bah. What's that compared to my health and the health of your poor dear mama? You can't comprehend what we suffer."

She didn't wish to argue with him. Certainly not *this* ancient argument, one that had first arisen when she was in leading strings. From childhood, she'd loved animals. The fact that her parents had forbidden them was a source of lingering bitterness to her.

"If you attended to your duty, you'd have no time to be lonely," Papa went on. "Your mother and I require looking after. What else is a daughter for?" At that, he fell into a coughing fit, the violent hacking muffling the long-standing lament with which he closed most of his complaints: "Would that I'd had a son!"

His words didn't hurt her. She'd heard them too many times before. In the Wychwood house, her parents' invalidism reigned supreme. Everyone existed in service to it, her most of all.

She took her father's hand. "You don't mean that. If you did, you wouldn't force me to have another season."

"Force!" He jerked his hand away. "Since when is a young lady forced to wear pretty gowns and attend balls?"

"You know I don't like to."

"What you like has little to do with it. You must marry. Your husband will help to look after us. He'll see to Hicks in future, and to accompanying your poor mother to Bath when her illness commands it."

Julia had heard this, too, with increasing frequency. According to her parents, her future husband would be yet another caretaker for them. Julia's own happiness—or lack of it—mattered not at all. "I don't think I shall ever marry," she confessed.

"Nonsense. You'll do your duty, and willingly."

"I *have* been doing my duty."

"Not according to Mrs. Major. She sent a report round this morning, says you wandered off during last night's musicale."

"A report?" Julia was incredulous. "You make it sound as though I'm a probationer."

His wiry brows lowered. "With your proclivities, you may as well be. Why else would your mother impose on Mrs. Major to chaperone you? She's meant to prevent this kind of behavior. And so I've reminded her."

Julia expected he had. Her father was a great one for dashing off complaining notes from his sickbed. When he was in residence, the second footman was forever on the trot.

"Setting a dour old matron to guard me isn't going to make me any more attractive to suitors," she said.

"I'll hear no arguments on the subject."

"But Papa—"

"Enough, child." Beads of perspiration gathered on her father's brow. He withdrew a linen handkerchief from his pocket to blot his face. "Away with you, now. You'll tire me out before I've done my work."

Her shoulders slumped. There was, indeed, no point in arguing with him. He and Mama always won. Naturally, they did. It was they who held all the power.

"Yes, Papa." She rose from the ottoman, smoothing her skirts. "I'm going shopping for a new book. I'll return directly."

"Mind you do," he said. "I may have need of you."

Bloxham's Books was a small shop at the end of an alleyway off of Charing Cross Road. Julia was a frequent visitor to the premises. In the last month alone, she'd been there three times on the hunt for new novels to read.

Mr. Bloxham served as both bookseller and publisher. He did a steady business in lesser-known sensation novels, adventure stories, and romances. Books written by people like J. Marshland or Mrs. Trent-Watkinson. Authors most of the general public had never heard of before.

"They write them fast and we print them fast," the shop clerk confided as Julia explored the shelves. "Not much in the way of literary value, but they pass the time."

Mary trailed behind them, looking as dour as a crow in her black stuff dress and bonnet. As lady's maid, she was obliged to accompany her mistress on errands, but she made no secret of her opinions about novels. She seemed to think they were the main reason Julia hadn't yet been successful on the marriage mart.

Julia knew better. It wasn't novel reading that caused her crippling anxiety. Quite the reverse. Along with riding Cossack, it was one of the only things to grant her respite from it.

She removed a small book from a cramped middle shelf on the wall. *The Nobleman's Secret Child*. "Who says they don't have literary value?"

"Why, the best people in the book business, miss." The clerk drew closer. He was a keen young man in an ill-fitting suit who smelled strongly of cheap pomade. "The reviewers at *Blackwood's Magazine* and them at the *Weekly Heliosphere*. You won't often see our titles included in their pages, but on occasion one of them gets a mention, and never to the good. Only look at Marshland's latest. 'Tripe,' the reviewer called it. 'Excessively earnest tripe.'"

"That's not very nice."

"No indeed, miss. Not for Mr. Bloxham, it isn't. He's left with one hundred copies of the book, and since the write-up in the *Heliosphere*, we can't sell them for pittance."

Julia returned *The Nobleman's Secret Child* to the shelf. She walked further down the narrow aisle, her wide skirts brushing the shelves on either side. "It can't be that bad."

"Have you read Marshland's novels?"

"Not recently, no, but I used to devour them as a girl. I still count *The Fire Opal* as one of my favorites of all time."

"Ah, *The Fire Opal*." The clerk waxed nostalgic over the popular sensation romance. "It's Marshland's bestseller to this day."

"She doesn't publish much anymore, does she?"

"Not regular like, no."

"And when she does, her stories aren't at all like they used to be."

"Marshland's style has changed and no mistake," the clerk acknowledged. "For the worse, some say."

"I can't believe that. Her writing is generally a cut above the others."

"Aye, so it is." The clerk followed after her, with Mary not far behind him. "But a bad review puts people off. Don't matter the quality of the story. If word gets out that a book's rotten, we can't move it."

"I'm sorry to hear it." Julia examined first one book and then another. She didn't know what she was in the mood for. A romance, certainly, but not one featuring brutish husbands, self-sacrificing damsels, or even secret babies. She wanted something a bit more hopeful, with a heroine she could believe in and a hero worthy of the name.

Replacing yet another book onto the shelf, she returned to the front of the shop. A round wooden table was arrayed there, holding multiple copies of the same novel—a slim volume bound in dark green cloth.

It was Mrs. Marshland's new book.

Julia picked up a copy, examining the title stamped in gold on the spine. *The Garden of Valor*. "What is it about?"

"A knight come home from the wars," the clerk said.

"It's medieval?"

"Indeed, full up with swords and jousts and unrequited love."

"Unrequited? But I thought it was a romance. Romances are supposed to have happy endings."

"So it does, eventually. Too happy for the *Heliosphere*. The reviewer didn't like the romantic elements. Compared them to treacle."

She frowned as she flipped through the pages. *Tripe. Treacle.* "The reviewer must have been a man. Only a man would describe a romance in such a way."

The clerk nodded. "He is, miss. He goes by the name of Bilgewater."

Her mouth quirked. "Gracious. Is that a nom de plume?"

"Expect so. He wouldn't want any angry authors coming after him. Not after some of the things he's written about their books. Marshland isn't his first victim."

"Poor Mrs. Marshland. I'm sure she doesn't deserve such censure." Julia tucked a copy of *The Garden of Valor* under her arm. Impulsively, she selected three more.

Mary approached, curious. "Four of the same book, miss?"

"One for me, and one for Lady Anne, Miss Hobhouse, and Miss Maltravers." Julia crossed the short distance to the wood counter near the shop's front window. She set the books down on it in an untidy stack. "It will be my gift to them when they return to London."

It wasn't completely altruistic. Julia was in the mood for a bit of treacle. If she could support a lady novelist while she was at it, so much the better. Besides, she liked to discuss books with her friends, and how could she discuss *The Garden of Valor* if Anne, Stella, and Evelyn hadn't read it?

The clerk beamed. "Excellent, excellent." He darted behind the counter to tally her charges.

As Julia fumbled in her reticule for the coin to pay for her purchases, the shop bell rang, signaling the arrival of another customer. She cast a distracted look at the door.

And then she froze.

Captain Blunt did the same. He stood inside the entrance, his black hat in his hand. His usually unreadable expression betrayed a faint flicker of surprise.

If not for that flicker, Julia might have suspected that he'd followed her here. That he hadn't respected her wishes at all. That he was continuing to pursue her despite the objections she'd voiced to his suit.

But no. The sight of her had set him back on his heels.

He recovered quickly. "Miss Wychwood."

"Captain Blunt." She stared at him for a long moment, her heart thumping with an odd mixture of anxiety and excitement.

The clerk gave a discreet cough. "That will be one pound six, miss."

"What?" She turned back to him, flustered. "Oh yes. I beg your pardon." She pushed a one pound coin and six shillings across the counter to him.

"Shall I wrap them, miss?" he asked.

"Please."

Captain Blunt approached the counter. His gaze dropped to her stack of books. A strange stillness came over him.

"Yes, I know," she said. "They're for me and my friends. We've enjoyed Mrs. Marshland's work before."

"Have you." His voice was peculiarly flat.

She sensed judgment in his words. "You sound as though you don't approve of her."

"On the contrary." He leaned against the counter. He was wearing a black three-piece suit, impeccably tailored, but plain to the point of austerity. A faded gold pocket watch chain glinted at the front of his single-breasted waistcoat. "Marshland's prose can be very affecting."

"Then you've read her? And liked her?"

"I wouldn't go that far," he said. "But I'd be interested to know your thoughts on the novel once you've read it."

"Of course. I daresay I shall finish it before this evening."

His mouth curved. What might have been a smile in another man appeared more like a snarl because of his scar. "So quickly?"

She managed a sheepish smile in return. "I've never been successful at postponing my pleasures."

"I trust it *will* be a pleasure."

"I have reason to hope. The plot points the critics complained about are the elements I like best." She paused, explaining, "The romance."

Her words were met with silence.

Awkward silence.

She felt a rush of self-consciousness. Some gentlemen didn't approve of romances. But Captain Blunt wasn't one of them, surely. After speaking with him at last night's musicale, she'd been left with the impression he had some interest in the genre.

Looking at him now, it was hard to believe it. He appeared so fierce and formidable. A gentleman impervious to finer feeling. A man with ice in his veins.

It must be nice not to feel things. Not to stammer and blush in the presence of the opposite sex. She couldn't imagine Captain Blunt blushing over anything. He seemed invulnerable.

She wished she could say the same about herself.

Mere proximity to him was enough to set her stomach fluttering. To make her insides quiver and quake.

She had felt just the same when he'd approached her at Lady Arundell's ball. At the time, she'd mistaken the sensation for fear.

But it wasn't fear. She realized that now, much to her chagrin. It was something else. Something worse.

It was attraction.

Despite all she knew of him—despite the warnings of her friends, and of her own mind and conscience—her body was disposed to *like* the man.

More than like.

She wondered if he felt it, too; this low thrum of physical awareness. It was impossible to tell. His scarred face was wiped clean of expression.

"You must be shopping for a new book yourself," she observed for lack of anything better to say. The stupidity of the remark struck her the instant she uttered it. "But of course you are. Why else would you be here?"

"Why indeed?"

The clerk eyed them with thinly concealed interest as he finished wrapping her books in brown paper.

Mary eyed them, too, her broad face etched with disapproval. No doubt Julia would get an earful when they returned to the carriage

"Any book in particular?" she asked.

Captain Blunt hesitated a fraction of a second before answering. "A new adventure story for my eldest boy."

Understanding came over her. Embarrassment swiftly followed. He was talking about his child. His *illegitimate* child. One of the many he housed at his estate.

Julia supposed she should be offended. A gentleman wouldn't speak of such things in the presence of a lady.

But she wasn't offended.

Her foremost feeling was one of curiosity. "Your son enjoys adventure novels?"

"He does."

She waited for him to elaborate. When he didn't, her curiosity outweighed her discretion. "How old is he?"

For the first time since she'd met him, Captain Blunt seemed uncomfortable. "He's, er, twelve."

"Your purchases, miss." The clerk pushed Julia's wrapped books across the counter to her. "Will there be anything else today?"

"Thank you, no. That will be all." She collected her package, conscious of Captain Blunt's regard. She gave him a look of apology. "Forgive my curiosity."

"Forgive my indelicacy," he replied.

Something about the gravity of his manner warmed her to her soul.

She knew she was reading too much into it. That she was allowing this strange attraction for him to overpower her reason. He wasn't kind. He wasn't handsome.

He certainly wasn't a hero.

Anne would never forgive her for entertaining such thoughts. She'd say that, faced with the canvas of the captain's complete lack of emotion, Julia was painting him with the broad brush of her own sentimentality. That she was imagining him into someone he was not.

But Anne wasn't here. And really, what harm was a secret attraction? So long as Julia never spoke of it. Never acted on it.

"You're forgiven." Hugging her books to her bosom, she moved to leave. "Good day, sir."

He bowed to her. "Good day, Miss Wychwood."

Julia exited the shop with her maid, keenly aware that Captain Blunt was still at the counter, looking after her. It was only as the shop door swung shut behind her that she heard him address the clerk.

"Get me Bloxham," he commanded gruffly. "At once."

Five

Jasper folded the bank draft for fifty pounds in with his letter to Mr. Beecham before sealing the envelope. He was writing out the direction when a rap sounded at the door.

"Come," he said.

Ridgeway strolled in, already dressed for their evening engagement. "Attending to your correspondence?"

"Estate matters."

"At this hour? How dreary."

"Indeed." Jasper sat back in his chair. He was still in his shirt-sleeves, his black evening coat draped over a chair near the bed.

It hadn't been easy getting the money for the roof repairs. He didn't dare send it directly to Charlie. The boy was too sullen and secretive for his own good. God only knew what he'd do with the money. There was as much chance he'd use it to spirit his two siblings away as there was that he'd pay someone to patch the hall's roof.

From the moment Jasper had appeared at the grim workhouse in York where Dolly had surrendered her two sons, Charlie had viewed him with suspicion.

The condition of Goldfinch Hall had done nothing to alter his opinion.

Jasper supposed the estate had its charm. It was a large, sprawling property, with a certain fading grandeur to it. The kind of place that appealed to one's gothic sensibilities. But such dubious attractions were no replacement for a roof that didn't leak and floorboards that weren't rotting beneath one's feet. A few months ago, Beecham had nearly fallen to his death.

The ancient retainer was the only full-time servant Jasper employed. A remnant from the past. He'd been caretaker of Goldfinch Hall for over a decade, remaining there long after the death of Erasmus Blunt, the reclusive great-uncle who had left the estate to Jasper in his will.

Would that old Erasmus had left some money for its maintenance.

In hospital after the fall of Sebastopol, Jasper had imagined Goldfinch Hall as a refuge. A place where he could find peace and quiet, far away from the miseries of war. Instead, it had proved to be an albatross around his neck.

If not for the children, he'd have walked away from it without a backward glance.

That was out of the question now. And not only because he was bound by his promise to Dolly, but because he was bound by the bonds of affection.

Charlie and Alfred could be difficult, it was true. He'd come into their lives too late. They still hadn't forgiven him for abandoning them. But Daisy was different. She'd been less than a year old when he'd returned from the Crimea. Nearly seven now, she couldn't remember her mother. Jasper was the only parent she'd ever known.

It should have made things easier between them.

It didn't.

Daisy was an odd child. Painfully shy at times, but with a streak of feral independence. Not for her the sewing room or the sampler. She preferred climbing trees, swimming in the lake, and napping in the hayloft of the barn.

He'd had no luck in persuading her to behave with more decorum. What she needed was the civilizing influence of a female. A lady who would take her in hand.

Bastard boys had a hard enough road ahead of them, but for a girl, the taint of illegitimacy would color her entire life. The least Jasper could do was to assure she had the wherewithal to live that life with dignity—good manners, a decent education, and a ready supply of money.

A wealthy wife would go a long way toward providing those things. A wife who wasn't Miss Julia Wychwood.

Which reminded him. "I need to see a solicitor while I'm in town."

Ridgeway's brows lifted with interest. "I thought you had a man in York."

"Piggott is my late uncle's solicitor, not mine." Jasper had only met the fellow on one occasion. Mr. Piggott had administered Erasmus Blunt's will. He was an aged attorney, prone to discussing the private affairs of his other clients. "I need someone of my own. Someone who can exercise a bit of discretion."

"I see."

Jasper sincerely hoped not.

"Any particular area of expertise?" Ridgeway asked.

"Criminal," Jasper said.

Ridgeway's face was impassive, betraying no sign of surprise. "You might try my neighbor, Mr. Finchley. I can't promise he's taking on new cases or even that he dabbles in criminal matters any longer. But he was once rather renowned. He counted the most powerful gentlemen in the city among his clients."

"He sounds expensive."

"I daresay he's worth it, as much for his skill as for his silence. The man's a veritable vault of secrets, though you wouldn't know it by looking at him."

"He has offices in town?"

"In Fleet Street." Ridgeway paused. "It's nothing serious, I trust?"

"Not serious. Tedious." Yet another obstacle to Jasper marrying and returning to Yorkshire. One more of conscience than of actual impediment. His mind would be easier if it could be settled. "As tedious as all the rest of this business."

"I have news that might cheer you," Ridgeway said. "Miss Throckmorton will be at Lady Holland's dinner this evening."

Jasper gave him a blank look.

"Daphne Throckmorton," Ridgeway prompted. "The Northumberland toffee heiress?"

Jasper rubbed the side of his face. He had a vague memory of Ridgeway mentioning the girl in passing. "She owns a manufactory, doesn't she?"

"Absolutely not." Ridgeway appeared insulted by the suggestion. "I wouldn't have suggested her if she was in trade."

"She's a toffee heiress."

"Naturally, her *people* were in trade—nothing to be done about that, I fear. But according to my sources, on her father's death, the toffee business went to a distant cousin. Miss Throckmorton herself was left with only a monetary inheritance. Forty thousand pounds, to be precise."

Forty thousand pounds.

It was ten thousand less than Miss Wychwood was worth. Still, it was no paltry sum.

Jasper stood to retrieve his coat. "Your sources being the fellows at your club."

Ridgeway didn't deny it. "There are already wagers in the betting book over which penniless younger son will swallow his scruples and marry the girl. The odds are in Aldershott's favor. He hasn't a bean to his name. But my money's on you, Blunt. You can easily win Miss Throckmorton and her fortune if you put a little effort into it. Ladies love a war hero." He cast a narrow glance at Jasper's letter to Beecham. "Though I wouldn't mention your by-blows to her just yet. Cits tend to take a provincial view of such matters."

"No doubt," Jasper said dryly. As if he was likely to mention the children to a lady—any lady. It simply wasn't done. And yet . . .

Only a few hours ago, in Bloxham's Books of all places, he'd spoken of Charlie to Miss Wychwood. And she was as well-bred a young lady as they came. Daughter to a baronet, for God's sake. He'd expected her expression to shutter against him. For her tone to take on the sharp bite of disapproval.

Neither had happened.

Quite the reverse.

Jasper recalled her reaction with perfect clarity. The vision of her face—her blue eyes widening and her lips half parting in surprise—was emblazoned on his brain. *"Your son enjoys adventure novels?"* she'd asked.

Not *your by-blow* or *your bastard* or any of the other unflattering epithets used to describe children born on the wrong side of the blanket. But *your son*.

Jasper couldn't remember when anyone had ever described Charlie thus.

"Forty thousand pounds," Ridgeway said. "You did hear me, didn't you?"

Jasper shrugged on his coat. "I heard you."

"You asked for an alternative to Miss Wychwood and I've found you one. A tad less polished perhaps—"

"Am I likely to care about that?" Jasper asked crossly.

"No need to bite my head off," Ridgeway said. "All gentlemen care. A wife should be an ornament to one's masculine pride. But any fellow can make allowances, given the right inducement."

Jasper felt a flash of irritation. But he couldn't argue with Ridgeway's logic. Money was required for the estate. For Charlie, Alfred, and Daisy. It's why Jasper had come here. Not for sentiment or self-gratification. Certainly not for romance.

It didn't matter that Miss Wychwood was sweet and beautiful. That her eyes lit up like polished sapphires when she discussed her favorite novels—novels written by J. Marshland of all people.

If there was ever a sign that Jasper should give up on the very idea of her, that had surely been it.

And she wanted him to give up. She'd told him point-blank not to pursue her. To continue to do so would make him no better than a rogue.

Besides, a man didn't have to be smitten by a young lady in order to court her. Marriage was a business transaction. All that was wanted was a necessary incentive.

And Miss Throckmorton's forty thousand pounds was nothing if not incentive.

Julia plucked at the set of pearl-sized buttons on the wrist of one of her evening gloves. She was seated on a jade velvet settee in Lady Holland's spacious drawing room next to two other young ladies—Miss Throckmorton and Miss Bingham. Side by side, the full skirts of their respective dinner dresses billowed against each other in a rainbow of amethyst silk, Eugenie-blue grosgrain, and apple-green poplin.

Miss Throckmorton and Miss Bingham were angled toward each other, engaged in animated conversation. They were both younger than Julia. Not more than nineteen, if she was to guess, and possessed of all the enthusiasm of being in their first season.

Julia knew them only a little. A consequence of having been guests at so many of the same parties. But they weren't her friends. She had nothing in common with either girl. For one thing, they were neither of them the least bit ill at ease. Not even Miss Throckmorton, an heiress to a fortune her late father had accumulated in trade. One might think she'd be self-conscious of the fact. Instead, she was brimming with confidence, poised in both her speech and her manner.

"I was finished in Paris," she said in answer to a question from Miss Bingham. "Papa spared no expense."

"Paris!" Miss Bingham sighed. "I haven't been in ages. But my gown was made in Paris." She fluffed her ruffled skirts. "Mama ordered it specially."

Julia smoothed her hands over the skirts of her own gown—a dark amethyst silk trimmed with bands of plaited black ribbon. It wasn't especially flattering to either her complexion or her figure. For that she'd need to employ a new dressmaker. Someone like her friend Evelyn's beau, Mr. Malik. His designs were stunning to behold. A marvel of cut, fabric, and color, they fit a lady like a custom-made kid glove, making her the envy of all who saw her.

Not the best choice for someone who preferred to be invisible.

Julia wished she could be so now. But there was no opportunity to shrink into the shadows—or to slip away to a private anteroom. Her chaperone, Mrs. Major, had arranged herself near the exit doors, preventing her charge's escape. Per Papa's orders, she was keeping an eagle eye on Julia tonight.

It was all quite depressing.

"Have you, Miss Wychwood?" Miss Throckmorton asked.

Julia turned to her. "I beg your pardon?"

"We were speaking of Paris," Miss Bingham said. "Miss Throckmorton asked if you'd been there recently?"

"I have not," Julia said. "I've never been out of London."

"Never?" Miss Throckmorton was aghast. She was a tall, dignified young woman, with seal-brown hair drawn back in a tight cluster of ringlets. A strand of lustrous pearls hung from her neck. "How can that be?"

Julia explained, "My parents don't like me to stray far from home. They rarely leave town themselves, except to take the waters in Bath."

"You don't go with them?" Miss Throckmorton asked.

"Oh, they don't go together," Julia said. "One always remains behind, and me along with them."

"Miss Wychwood's parents are both ill," Miss Bingham said. "And Miss Wychwood, too, on occasion."

"A pity," Miss Throckmorton murmured. "You're not unwell now, I hope?"

"You do look a little green," Miss Bingham said.

Julia expected she did. She had no desire to be in a crowded drawing room. The setting provoked the worst of her anxiety. All the people huddled in groups, whispering and chattering, and exchanging dry witticisms.

How did they come up with them? All those droll remarks and witty rejoinders. Did they memorize them in advance?

Julia couldn't imagine how it would work. Not for her, anyway. When confronted by a clever stranger, most times she couldn't remember her own name, let alone some amusing scrap of rehearsed dialogue.

"Miss Wychwood?" Miss Throckmorton prompted, a trace of irritation in her voice. "Are you all right?"

"I'm very well. Only . . ." Julia flashed a glance about the room. Mrs. Major was still by the exit, as immovable as a sentry. But there was no one near the curtained French doors that led onto the terrace. "This room is a trifle close. If you'll excuse me. I might just step outside."

She moved to rise, but was forestalled by the arrival of a gentleman. It was Viscount Ridgeway.

He was a familiar figure in London society. A handsome golden-haired gentleman, with a calculating air about him. The sort of man who enjoyed making sport of bluestockings and wallflowers. Ladies like Julia who were awkward and tongue tangled in company.

Indeed, it was he who had first presented Captain Blunt to her.

Stomach tensing, she sank back into her seat.

"Ladies." Lord Ridgeway sketched them an elegant bow. "Please don't get up. I haven't come to interrupt your conversation."

Miss Bingham blushed and batted her lashes. "Why *have* you come, my lord?"

"To impose on Miss Throckmorton." He addressed her as if Julia and Miss Bingham had ceased to exist. "You look charmingly this evening, ma'am."

"I thank you," Miss Throckmorton replied.

"May I introduce you to an acquaintance of mine?" Lord Ridgeway gestured to someone in the crowd. "Lady Holland has informed me he's to be your partner at dinner."

"Oh?" Miss Throckmorton followed Lord Ridgeway's gaze.

So did Julia.

It was Captain Blunt. He came toward them, looking as solemn and soldierly as he had at Bloxham's.

Her heart performed a disconcerting little somersault.

But like Lord Ridgeway, Captain Blunt wasn't looking at her. He was looking at Miss Throckmorton.

As Lord Ridgeway introduced the pair of them, Julia could do nothing but sit woodenly on the drawing room settee, her hands clasped in her lap.

The scene before her was unsettlingly familiar.

Just so had Lord Ridgeway introduced Captain Blunt to her at Lady Arundell's ball. In response, Julia had fled.

Miss Throckmorton, by contrast, was perfectly composed. "It's an honor to make your acquaintance," she said. "I've heard of your exploits, of course. The Hero of the Crimea, isn't that what they call you?"

"An overstatement," Captain Blunt said. "I'm no hero." As he spoke, his icy gray eyes met Julia's. It was the barest glance. A mere heartbeat of connection—of acknowledgment—before he turned his attention back on Miss Throckmorton.

Julia's chest constricted almost painfully.

No. He wasn't a hero. He was just a man. One that, only yesterday evening, she'd asked to stop pursuing her.

And he had done so. Obviously.

It wasn't a rejection. He was respecting her wishes. An honorable action, really. It made no sense that it would hurt.

She schooled her features, even as she again cast about her for some means of escape. Her gaze lit on the Earl of Gresham. Newly arrived, he stood at the entrance to the drawing room, speaking to Mrs. Major.

Mrs. Major replied, motioning toward Julia with a toothy smile.

Julia's palms dampened beneath her gloves. She had no affection for Lord Gresham. Not only was he too old for her, he was rather insensitive, too. The kind of blustering gentleman who always talked over a lady or insisted she do this thing or that.

He made a direct line for her from across the drawing room, wasting no time in presenting himself.

"Miss Wychwood," he said, bowing. "Ridgeway. Captain Blunt. Ladies."

"Gresham," Ridgeway said.

Captain Blunt gave Lord Gresham a stiff nod. He didn't seem pleased to see the earl.

Julia wondered if they knew each other.

"You will excuse me, gentlemen." Lord Gresham offered his hand to Julia. "Miss Wychwood's estimable chaperone has granted me the honor of escorting her into dinner."

"An honor indeed," Ridgeway said.

Captain Blunt said nothing. But he wasn't looking at Miss Throckmorton any longer. He was frowning at Julia.

She took Lord Gresham's hand, permitting him to draw her to her feet. Escape was escape, even if it came in the form of a long-winded, condescending old man who stared overlong at one's bosom.

"Take care you avoid the drafts," Lord Gresham said, guiding her away. "There's a chill in the air this evening. Your father mentioned it particularly."

She gave him an alert glance. "You've spoken to my father?"

"I called on him this afternoon in Belgrave Square. The poor fellow. He's a martyr to his health."

"He is. Though he seemed to be a little stronger today."

"I'd have said he was worse. I've asked my personal physician to look in on him. The least I can do, all things considered."

Before Julia could ask what he meant, a footman in scarlet livery appeared at the drawing room door to announce that dinner was served.

Lady Holland rose from her chair. She was a curvaceous dark-haired widow of thirty-odd years, newly out of mourning. The golden thread of her elegantly embroidered dinner dress glistened in the gas-light. "Ladies and gentlemen, if you would follow me."

She led the way into a high-ceilinged, silk-papered dining room. On one side was a cavernous marble fireplace. On the other, a line of liveried footmen stood at the ready in front of a grand mahogany side-board. The long dining table was adorned with clusters of roses and greenery, and ablaze with candlelight. Dancing flames sparkled in the crystal goblets and reflected in the polished-silver serving dishes.

The guests entered in order of precedence. Lord Gresham and Julia were among the first. She glanced back at the line of couples behind them. Near its end, Miss Throckmorton was on Captain Blunt's arm, looking remarkably at home there.

Julia felt a peculiar twinge in her midsection. What kind of twinge, she wasn't certain. It couldn't be jealousy, could it?

But no.

She wasn't some dog in the manger, to covet a gentleman she'd already rejected.

At least, she didn't think she was.

"Lady Holland was careful to seat us near the fire." Lord Gresham maneuvered Julia to her chair, pulling it out for her. "There'll be no drafts to trouble you here."

"Thank you, my lord." She sat down, carefully arranging her full skirts. The seat on her right belonged to Lord Gresham. And on her left . . .

The thick cream-colored place card bore the name of Captain Blunt.

She scarcely had time to register it before he was there, a great gruff presence, appearing as if she'd conjured him. He filled up the space beside her, broad and tall and heart-clenchingly dangerous.

Her already trembling insides vibrated like a tuning fork.

She chanced a shy look up at him through her lashes.

He returned it, unsmiling. "Miss Wychwood," he said. "It seems this seat belongs to me."

Six

<hr />

$\mathcal{J}$ulia wasn't a proponent of tight lacing. On leaving the house that evening, she'd been cinched only snugly enough to fit into her dinner dress. Nevertheless, after an endless succession of rich cuisine forced on her by Lord Gresham, she could feel the rigid bones of her corset digging into her flesh.

"We've opened up my house in Grosvenor Square for year-round occupancy," his lordship said from his seat beside her. "I mean to host a dinner myself next month. Perhaps you'll see fit to act as my hostess."

Julia swallowed a morsel of roast beef. It stuck in her throat. She hastily washed it down with a sip of wine from her crystal goblet. "Your hostess?" She endeavored not to choke. "I don't think *that* would be very appropriate."

"There's nothing more appropriate, my girl, under the circumstances."

It was the second time the earl had alluded to these mysterious circumstances. Given his recent visit to Belgrave Square, Julia suspected the worst.

"And what circumstances are those? If you mean—" She broke off as Lord Gresham motioned the footman to bring her more roast. "Please, my lord. I couldn't eat another bite."

"Nonsense. You require feeding up. We must have you healthy, Miss Wychwood."

Julia quailed at the sheer amount of food already on her plate. She had a large enough appetite, to be sure, but she'd never been comfortable gorging herself in public. Much like everything else she enjoyed, overindulging was better done in the privacy of her bedchamber. There, tucked in bed with a novel, she'd often laid waste to an entire box of chocolates.

But Lady Holland's packed dining room, with its flickering candlelight, clinking crystal, and hum of fashionable conversation, was a far cry from Julia's curtained four-poster in Belgrave Square. How could she enjoy anything with so many people around?

She grudgingly speared a piece of potato on the tines of her fork, only half listening to Lord Gresham's descriptions of the renovations to his London residence.

If this was what the future held for her, she didn't know if she could face it. Year after year, wed to some aging nobleman, the entirety of her life lived under his constant scrutiny.

And not only his.

All of London society would be watching and judging. It was the very essence of town life. Julia knew that better than anyone. She'd been born here and had spent every day of the last two-and-twenty years a veritable prisoner in her parents' house. Marriage was to be her one means of escape, and even that was merely exchanging one prison for another.

"What do you say to that, Gresham?" The elderly lady seated on his lordship's right commanded his attention.

Julia exhaled, glad for the reprieve, however brief. Lowering her uneaten forkful of potato back to her plate, she dared another look at Captain Blunt.

Throughout dinner, she'd heard the intermittent murmur of his deep voice in low conversation with Miss Throckmorton.

But he wasn't talking to Miss Throckmorton now. Like Lord

Gresham, the young toffee heiress was occupied with the person on her opposite side, leaving Captain Blunt temporarily at his leisure.

His frost-gray eyes met Julia's. "Miss Wychwood."

Her heartbeat quickened. "Captain Blunt."

For a taut moment, neither said another word.

Julia was the first to break the silence. It was either that or risk him turning his attention back to Miss Throckmorton. "This is a merry party, isn't it?"

"It is." He continued to regard her with the same quietly appraising look.

She was certain he must think her very strange.

Though why he should come to that conclusion tonight of all nights, she couldn't fathom.

So far, she'd behaved with near perfect decorum. She'd sat in the drawing room with the other young ladies, she'd engaged in conversation at table, and she hadn't once let her anxiety get the better of her.

Not yet.

Indeed, despite the clamminess of her hands and the trembling of her stomach, her unruly nerves were under creditable control.

Why then did he look at her so? His gaze searching hers, cold and emotionless, sending a shiver of awareness through her vitals?

"Do you, er, have many such parties where you come from?" she asked lamely.

"Dinner parties? No, ma'am."

"None?"

"We live an isolated life in Yorkshire."

"*We*," she echoed before she could think better of it. Her voice sunk to a whisper. "Do you mean you and your . . . your children?"

A frown notched his heavy black brows.

At Bloxham's he'd referred to the subject as indelicate. And it was. Julia *knew* it was.

She was on the verge of apologizing when he startled her with an answer.

"Yes." His words emerged in a gruff undertone. "There are four of us altogether. Five if you count the estate's caretaker, Mr. Beecham."

Julia considered this information for a moment. Society gossip would have one believe that Captain Blunt had an entire houseful of illegitimate children. A half dozen or more. Instead, there were only three of them. *Three*.

She supposed even one illegitimate child was a shocking number. A gentleman, after all, shouldn't have any. Still . . .

Three was a great deal more palatable than seven or eight.

"Are they all boys, your children?" she asked.

Captain Blunt raised his crystal goblet to his lips. "Not all. I have two boys, Charlie and Alfred. But my youngest is a girl, Daisy. She'll be seven this August."

Julia's mouth curved in an involuntary smile.

It was hard to picture the fearsome Captain Blunt as father to a six-year-old girl. She wondered how much interaction he had with the child. Most well-to-do fathers had precious little until their children were older and better behaved.

"I expect you have a nurse to look after her," she said.

Captain Blunt downed the remainder of his wine in one swallow. "Nothing of the kind. As I said, there are five of us in the house. No one else."

"No servants?"

At first, he didn't seem disposed to answer. He returned his goblet to the table, his long fingers lingering on the stem.

"It must be a large house," Julia said.

His shoulders stiffened, as if he was bracing himself to administer a piece of unpleasant news. His scarred mouth set in a grim line. "It is a large house, and formerly a great one. But live-in servants are difficult to come by, and my estate lies on the moors, many miles from the nearest village. In poor weather, one can go weeks at a time without seeing another soul."

She lifted her own goblet, taking a drink. "It sounds divine."

Her response provoked an odd flicker in his gray gaze. "You think so?"

"Oh yes. A secluded estate in rural Yorkshire, far away from meddling neighbors and disapproving villagers? I can imagine nothing better." She paused. "I don't suppose it has a moat?"

His lips twitched. "It does not."

"And is it, by any chance, overgrown with wild roses?"

"Ah. There you have me. It is indeed overgrown, but it's no castle in a French fairy tale, Miss Wychwood."

And I'm no Beast, he might have said.

Julia's cheeks warmed. She set down her goblet, chastened. "Forgive me. My imagination often runs away with me."

"An imagination is nothing to apologize for."

She flashed him a rueful grimace. "You wouldn't say so if you knew half of what I was thinking at any given moment."

"I should give a great deal to know what you're thinking," he said gravely.

The warmth in her face spread to her midsection. Her corset felt at once even tighter than it had before. It made her a trifle breathless. "If you truly want to know . . ."

"I would be honored."

"Very well. I'm thinking about how marvelous it must be to live an isolated life in the country. To wake up in the morning, knowing the day doesn't hold another ball or dinner or musicale."

The faint hue of amusement faded from his expression. "You sound as though you really mean that."

"I do. Most sincerely. Which is rather ironic, since I'm destined to live the rest of my life here in town."

Captain Blunt appeared as though he had more to say on the subject, but before he could utter another word, their conversation was interrupted by Miss Throckmorton.

"Isn't that right, Captain?" she asked loudly. "It's always the way when traveling by steamer ship."

He gave Julia a long, frowning look, before reluctantly turning to answer Miss Throckmorton.

Julia was left alone with only the food on her plate to occupy her. Food that was growing colder by the second. She pushed her remaining roast beef around disconsolately with her fork.

Lord Gresham snapped his fingers at a footman. "More gravy for Miss Wychwood."

"Oh no. I couldn't—"

"Tut-tut, Miss Wychwood. You must finish your meal." The earl's cheeks were ruddy from too much burgundy. "You'll need your strength to accompany me on the piano after dinner. Lady Holland has asked me to sing."

Julia's already flagging spirits sank still further.

It was difficult enough to be here as a guest, seated at the table or in the drawing room, obliged to say *yes* and *no*, and *please* and *thank you*, and to keep this infernal smile pasted on her face. But to stand in front of the assembled company? To perform on the piano while everyone watched and judged?

She took another sip of wine to fortify herself.

This was going to be a catastrophe.

Jasper sat at the edge of Lady Holland's drawing room. His attention was fixed, along with the rest of the guests, on Lord Gresham and Miss Wychwood. The latter was seated in front of the Hollands' square rosewood piano, her delicately tapered fingers stumbling through the accompaniment to the earl's boisterous tenor.

She was visibly uncomfortable. A pale pink flush suffused her throat as Lord Gresham loomed over her, turning the pages of her music and intermittently correcting the errors in her playing.

He was an overbearing man. A bully, though he hid it behind a facade of paternal condescension. Jasper had seen enough of them in his lifetime to recognize the breed on sight. And Gresham had the potential to be one of the worst.

His true character manifested in the way he ignored Miss Wychwood at dinner, heaping her plate despite her objections, and in the way he subjected her to embarrassment in front of the crowd, insisting she play a song with which she was clearly unfamiliar.

Jasper's temper rose with every fumbled chord.

Couldn't the man see that Miss Wychwood was shy and anxious in company? That she disliked being made a spectacle?

Jasper hadn't known her above a month when he'd realized it for himself.

"Poor Miss Wychwood," Miss Throckmorton murmured from her seat beside him. "Shall I rescue her?"

Jasper gave Miss Throckmorton a rare look of gratitude. "An excellent idea."

Miss Throckmorton rose and walked to the piano, her skirt floating about her legs. She was a lovely young lady in her way. Poised and polished, and entirely self-assured. She leaned down to Miss Wychwood's ear.

What she said was too soft to hear, but whatever it was, it prompted an expression of relief in Miss Wychwood's face. Without further ado, the two young ladies switched places.

Gresham's song faltered. He cast a hard look at Miss Wychwood as she stood from the bench in front of the piano.

"Pray go on," Miss Throckmorton said to him, sitting down. She picked up right where Miss Wychwood had left off, continuing the song with a resounding swell of expertly played chords.

Gresham resumed singing, but there was no mistaking the cloud of displeasure that marred his brow. Miss Wychwood had disobeyed him. Not an auspicious start to their relationship.

And it *was* to be a relationship. Jasper recognized that much.

Gresham needed a young wife to bear him an heir, and for better or worse, he'd set his eyes on Miss Wychwood.

Why wouldn't he?

Miss Throckmorton, Miss Bingham, and all the rest of the season's young ladies may be polished to a shine, but Julia Wychwood was as beautiful and unspoiled as a wild rose.

No doubt Gresham thought he could tame her. Mold her into a proper countess.

Is that what she wanted? To be the wife of a wealthy titled lord?

After their conversation at dinner, Jasper had cause to doubt it. And now, watching Miss Wychwood edge her way through the crowded drawing room in search of a seat, he doubted it even more. She appeared a hair's breadth away from losing her composure.

Damn Gresham.

Jasper stood, intercepting her as she passed his chair. "Miss Wychwood," he said in a voice for her ears alone. "You look as though you require a breath of fresh air."

Her hands were shaking. "I do, rather."

"Will you permit me to escort you onto the terrace?"

"Yes, I—"

"Shh!" Mrs. Major swiveled in her seat to glare at them. She waved her lacquered fan, motioning for Miss Wychwood to either sit down or remove herself.

Miss Wychwood mutely took Jasper's proffered arm.

He led her to the row of glass-paned French doors at the back of the drawing room. Swathed in heavy red velvet draperies, they opened onto a torchlit balcony. It ran the entire length of the house, looking down over the formal gardens below.

The evening air was cool and sweet, redolent with the fragrance of Lady Holland's prize roses and . . .

Tobacco?

Jasper shot an irritated look to the right. Two gentlemen were huddled in the shadows, talking and smoking cigars.

Miss Wychwood didn't seem to notice them. The moment she and Jasper stepped through the French doors, she released his arm and walked straight to the furthermost edge of the balcony. Setting her hands on the rail, she exhaled a shuddering breath.

Her face was illuminated in the torchlight—brow drawn and lips trembling. For one alarmed instant, Jasper feared she might cry.

He came to stand at her side. "Miss Wychwood—"

"I want to go home," she said in a colorless voice.

"Of course. I'll fetch your chaperone." He moved to return to the house.

"No!" She caught at his sleeve. "No, please. Mrs. Major won't permit me to leave early. Not even if I—" She broke off, shaking her head. Her hand fell from his arm, resuming its place on the rail. "It doesn't matter."

A swell of frustration tightened his chest. He didn't know how to help her. How to put her at her ease. After the ordeal she'd been through at dinner and then in the drawing room, she needed more than fresh air. She needed to feel safe.

"Surely, she'll allow it," he said. "If I tell her you're unwell—"

"I'm not unwell. I'm being silly."

He made a scoffing noise.

"I am," she insisted. "Ask anyone."

"I don't need to," he said. "I can judge for myself."

The renewed sounds of rousing piano music, and a doubly rousing tenor, drifted out from the drawing room. Some idiot must have demanded an encore from Gresham and Miss Throckmorton.

Miss Wychwood's fingers curled tight around the rail.

Jasper was possessed by the urge to gather her up in his arms. To protect her from all this. To hold her until her breath was steady and her trembling had ceased.

A ludicrous impulse.

He couldn't embrace her. Not here. Not anywhere.

He could do nothing but offer the support of his proximity. Standing there, shoulder to shoulder, his arm close enough to brush hers.

She smelled of lavender water and herbal soap. A fresh, clean scent. It clung to her as softly as a whisper, as intoxicatingly feminine as all the rest of her—the gentle curve of her pale shoulders, the twinkling jewels that studded her silken hairnet, and her overflounced gown, with its ruffles and ribbons and ridiculously full skirts.

Skirts that were even now bunched against the side of his leg.

A peculiar warmth pooled within him. It was all mixed up with this bloody sense of powerlessness, leaving him cross, and restless, and damnably hot under his cravat.

"Miss Wychwood . . ." His every instinct demanded action.

She gave him a wary look in the torchlight. No longer sapphire blue, next to the rich amethyst of her silk gown, her eyes had taken on a violet hue.

A bewitching sight. It provoked a thrum of longing in Jasper's veins.

"Yes?" she asked.

He cleared his throat. "Did you, ah, finish your book?"

"Mrs. Marshland's novel?" She brightened. "Yes, I did, actually."

Some of the tension in his muscles eased.

This was how he could help her. Not by holding her. Not by carrying her off to safety somewhere. But by talking to her. By engaging her on the subject she loved most.

"What did you think of it?" he asked.

She replied without hesitation. "I enjoyed it immensely."

"You disagree with Marshland's critics, then."

"I suppose I must. Though I don't know anything more about what the critics said than what the clerk at Bloxham's told me. Something about the story being tripe or treacle?"

Jasper grimaced. "That about sums it up."

She turned to face him. "You read Mr. Bilgewater's column in the *Weekly Heliosphere*?"

"Sometimes."

"And follow his recommendations?"

"The critics and I rarely agree when it comes to popular novels." He regarded her in the light of the torch. "I'm more interested in what *you* think."

Her eyes were wide and guileless, but her expression wasn't without intelligence. Indeed, there was a kind of earnest passion in her gaze. The look of a true devotee of romance. "I told you," she said. "I enjoyed it. Which should be evident enough, given how fast I finished reading it."

"What did you enjoy about it?"

"So many things." She warmed to the subject, more animated than he'd seen her all evening. "Mrs. Marshland's work isn't as thrilling as it once was, but her prose is beautiful. She writes with such a depth of emotion. As if she's felt it all herself—the love and the yearning. Even the romantic disappointments. One can feel it right along with her."

A surge of secret pride made him stand a little taller, a litter straighter, even as he leaned into her, craving more of her favorable opinions. He warned himself to tread carefully. Romance was a dangerous subject to discuss with a lady.

And not only romance.

"You assume J. Marshland is a woman."

"Naturally," she said. "No man could write about romance in such a way."

"And yet . . . I've heard that Marshland is, in fact, a man."

She drew back, skeptical. "Who says so?"

"I read it somewhere," he said vaguely.

"Where?"

"I can't recall. But it's true nonetheless."

Her soft mouth tugged into a frown. "Well . . . I don't suppose it matters overmuch. A good writer is a good writer, no matter their sex."

"Even when it comes to love?" he asked.

"If he's experienced it himself, he may well write about it."

He set his hand next to hers on the railing. Their little fingers nearly touched. "And if he hasn't experienced it yet?"

"But he must have done to write about it so eloquently. If he *is* a man, I expect he's suffered some terrible tragedy in love. How else could he explain what Sir Richard feels when Lady Elaine refuses his offer and marries another?"

"Anyone might feel the same who's had something valuable slip out of their grasp."

"Not *something*," she pointed out with the apple-tart sternness of a schoolmistress. "A *lady*. The lady he's loved the whole of his life."

Jasper had to make an effort not to smile. For all she was shy and romantic-minded, Miss Wychwood had starch in her. "You didn't find his constancy difficult to believe?"

"No. He was a knight, adhering to a code of chivalry. And anyway, it *is* just a novel."

"A fantasy, then."

"Unfortunately. Real men don't go to such lengths for love. I daresay some never experience the emotion at all."

His mouth hitched at one corner. "You're well acquainted with gentlemen's hearts?"

"Not personally, but I know plenty of ladies who are." She paused, confessing, "When one isn't comfortable talking in company, one learns to be a prodigiously good listener. I've heard the most dispiriting things as a consequence."

Jasper could well believe it. If there was one thing he knew about ladies, it was that they talked freely among one another, often with a level of candor that would put most gentlemen to the blush. "I wouldn't believe everything you hear."

"Oh, I don't. But I believe enough to know that real gentlemen are nothing like the heroes in novels. For one thing, they wouldn't pursue a lady for as long as Sir Richard did, and with so little hope of having their feelings reciprocated."

"No indeed," he said quietly. "A real gentleman would respect a lady's wishes and cease his pursuit."

Understanding registered on Miss Wychwood's face. A blush followed with it. But she didn't look away from him. She held his gaze, her bosom rising and falling on a tremulous breath.

"He would leave her alone," Jasper murmured. "Unless she'd changed her mind about him."

Silence stretched between them. There was no muffled conversation from the other people on the balcony. No music drifting from the interior of the house. Only a thick band of tension, pulled so tight it felt as though it might snap at any moment and obliterate them both.

Jasper's heart thudded hard. "*Have* you changed your mind?"

Miss Wychwood's flustered gaze dropped to their hands, side by side on the railing. "I don't know you well enough to say." Her soft, halting words were husky as velvet. "I . . . I'd like to know you."

Triumph surged through him. It wasn't a full-throated endorsement of his intentions toward her, but by God, it was a start. "Then you shall," he vowed.

The sound of the French doors opening prevented him from saying anything more. He removed his hand from the rail, turning around to come face-to-face with Miss Wychwood's redoubtable chaperone.

"Miss Wychwood," Mrs. Major said in ominous tones. "What are you doing out here? And without your wrap! You'll catch your death."

"I needed some air," Miss Wychwood replied. "Captain Blunt kindly offered to escort me."

"Captain Blunt." Mrs. Major's attention lingered on his scar. Her lip curled in unconscious revulsion. "You've done quite enough, sir. I shall take charge of her now."

"I trust you won't neglect her, ma'am," Jasper said.

Mrs. Major bristled at the reproof. "Indeed. Come, Miss Wychwood. Lord Gresham has been asking after you."

Miss Wychwood caught Jasper's gaze as she moved to rejoin her chaperone. "Thank you," she said under her breath.

He inclined his head. "Enjoy your ride in the morning, Miss Wychwood."

She glanced back at him, eyes round.

Mrs. Major nudged her through the French doors. "Inside," she said. "And promptly. His lordship is waiting."

Seven

——❦——

The Wychwoods' carriage rolled down the streets of Mayfair, the team of matched bays heading home to Belgrave Square at an easy pace. It was only a short distance from Lady Holland's residence, but long enough for Mrs. Major to fit in a stern lecture.

"Captain Blunt is *not* the sort of gentleman with whom you should be associating," she pronounced from her seat across from Julia. "I would have thought that was evident."

Julia was in no mood to placate her chaperone. From the moment Mrs. Major had discovered her on the balcony with Captain Blunt, she'd pushed and pulled her around like the veriest rag doll, paying no heed to Julia's own wishes, and showing not one speck of compassion for her anxiety. "Why should it be?"

"*Why?* Have you no eyes in your head, girl?"

Julia wrapped her wispy scrap of a silk shawl tighter around her shoulders. "You're referencing his scar, I suppose."

"Among other things," Mrs. Major replied.

The carriage rumbled over an uneven patch of road, jostling them both in their seats.

"It isn't right to judge a person by their appearance," Julia said.

Mrs. Major's already thin lips disappeared from view completely. "Not only his appearance. His character."

"What about his character?"

"He lacks the qualities inherent in a gentleman. His conduct in the Crimea—" Mrs. Major stopped short of describing it. "One can excuse many things during war, but the cruelty—the cold-bloodedness. A gentleman would not have behaved so."

Cruelty?

Julia frowned at the word. It was impossible to reconcile the ugliness of it with the man who, only this evening, had shown her such tender concern. "I've heard he had a reputation for being rather hard, but—"

Mrs. Major uttered a derisive snort. "You don't know the half of it, my girl."

"I'd like to."

"Doubtless. But it's not my place to say."

"I don't see why not. I already know about his illegitimate children. What else can—"

"Miss Wychwood!" Mrs. Major's tone held an unmistakable warning. "This is not to be borne. If you cannot cease prattling on about subjects that you plainly do not understand, then you will be silent."

Julia's mouth clamped shut. She wanted to argue. To raise her voice, even. But Mrs. Major wasn't her enemy. She was here at the request of Mama and Papa, doing their bidding, keeping Julia in line as strictly as if she were an army captain herself. Marching her straight into the arms of the Earl of Gresham.

And it wasn't only Mrs. Major.

Back in her bedchamber at Belgrave Square, clad in a thick cotton nightgown that covered her from her neck to her toes, Julia sat in front of her dressing table as Mary briskly brushed her hair.

"Captain Blunt?" Mary's nose scrunched in thought. "Not him with the country house full of by-blows?"

"Not a houseful," Julia said. "There are only three of them. Two boys and a little girl."

"*Only three*, she says." Mary clucked her tongue. "You listen to me, miss. You forget Captain Blunt and marry that earl of yours. You'll be a grand lady. A countess. Isn't that worth a minute or two of discomfort each night?"

Julia caught Mary's eyes in the trifold looking glass. "What discomfort?"

Mary gathered the bulk of Julia's hair in her hand and brushed the ends of it. "That's for your mama to tell you. But I'll say this, it's a small price to pay for your own coach, fine gowns, and a grand house in town. *The Countess of Gresham.* I like how that sounds. To think, I could be your maid. Me, lady's maid to a countess!"

"He hasn't even asked me yet," Julia said. "And there's more to life than coaches and gowns."

"Easy to say when you've never gone without them."

Julia privately acknowledged the truth of it. Her world was exceedingly small, all of it reduced to one suffocating section of fashionable London. A cage, indeed, but a gilded one. "I must sound very ungrateful to you."

"You sound young is how you sound," Mary said. "You take my advice. You marry his lordship. A fine life you'll have, presiding over balls and dinner parties, and having all the papers write about what you're wearing."

"It sounds dreadful. I've never wanted— Ouch!"

Mary raked the silver-plated brush through a thorny tangle in Julia's hair. "Beg pardon, miss, but what you want isn't the point. The earl's an old man. He'll leave you a widow soon enough. You can retire to the country then, and read all the novels you like."

Julia gave her outspoken maid an injured look. "Really, Mary. I would think it a sad thing if my happiness must depend on anyone dying."

"Most ladies' happiness does." Setting aside the hairbrush, Mary proceeded to twist Julia's long hair into its nighttime plait. "There's no woman better off than a widow. That's what me mum always says."

Julia stood, reaching back to take charge of her plait. She drew it over her shoulder, swiftly finishing it and securing the ends with a scrap of purple satin ribbon. "I daresay she's right, but what of all the peril that exists in the years between marriage and widowhood?"

Holding the candle aloft in her left hand, Mary pulled the quilted coverlet on the bed back with her right. She waited as Julia climbed in. "Aye. True enough. But it's our lot as women, ain't it? If I were you, I'd thank my lucky stars the earl had taken a fancy to me. He's better than most men. Richer, too."

Julia settled back against her down pillows. The four-poster's heavy draperies were already drawn on three sides, making her bed feel as warm and safe as the den of a woodland animal. "But what about love?" she asked. "What about romance?"

"With who? Not that Captain Blunt fellow?"

Julia's pulse gave a rebellious flutter.

If she closed her eyes, she could still feel the warmth of him standing next to her on the terrace. The size and strength of him. It had been a little like being next to Cossack. That bone-deep sense of safety and security garnered from being aligned with a larger, more powerful animal.

But Captain Blunt was no animal. He was a man.

A big, virile man who—unless she had mistaken him—was going to meet her for a ride in the park in the morning.

"I don't know," she said quietly.

Mary tucked her in. "You're overtired, you are. Worrying your head about romance, when you've a perfectly good gentleman paying court to you." She drew the bed-curtain, engulfing Julia in darkness. "Sleep, now. I won't have you looking tired at the ball tomorrow."

The ball.

Julia had been trying not to think of it.

It would be her third evening engagement without her friends. Another night of dressing up and making a spectacle of herself, alone and exposed, with no one to stand at her side.

But Captain Blunt would be at the ball, wouldn't he?

She nestled deeper into her bed, comforted by the thought of him. By the very real possibility that he would be there for her. Not a hero, it was true, but not quite a villain, either. Something in between, perhaps.

Someone who made her feel a little less lonely.

Jasper reined Quintus in the moment he caught sight of Miss Wychwood riding down Rotten Row.

She was wearing the same black riding habit and veiled hat as on the last occasion they'd met in Hyde Park. An unbecoming shroud of fabric, but—to her—a necessary one. He comprehended that now. She didn't want to be seen.

For her, invisibility meant safety. It was why she preferred solitude to the excitement of the crowd. Why she disappeared into empty rooms rather than staying where there was music, singing, and dancing.

Being alone wasn't the same as being lonely, she'd said.

Damned if he hadn't understood exactly what she meant. Even so . . .

Good God.

He'd never met a young lady so ill-suited for town life.

After all, what was the London season if not a stage on which eligible young ladies were kept on endless display? Paraded here and there for the benefit of every interested individual? It wasn't a system set up for sensitive females. Delicate creatures like Miss Wychwood, with anxious minds and romantic hearts.

How in the world was she to thrive in such a charged environment? How was she to breathe?

Surely, it would be a mercy to marry her and take her back to Yorkshire with him.

Or so he'd been telling himself ever since they'd parted last night.

Goldfinch Hall was no palatial estate, but there, at least, she could have a little freedom. And if the price of that freedom was somewhat steep . . .

Well.

Such was the fate of beautiful young maidens who put themselves in the path of villains.

"Captain Blunt," she said, bringing her black gelding to a halt.

The sun was shining brilliantly in a cloudless azure sky. It was a perfect morning for riding. As a consequence, they weren't the only two in the Row. Several ladies and gentlemen were about, making the privacy Jasper had envisioned when he'd suggested this meeting impossible.

But beggars couldn't be choosers.

He was resolved to take what he could get. "Miss Wychwood. Good morning." He sketched a bow. "How are you?"

"Very well."

"No ill effects after last night?"

She ducked her head, giving a breathless laugh. "No, no. Not unless you count embarrassment."

He rode up to her. Her gelding was impossibly large, but next to Quintus, he may as well have been a palfrey. "What have you to be embarrassed about?"

"Behaving like such a ninny. You would think I'd never played the piano in front of anyone before."

"I thought nothing of the kind."

She nudged her gelding into a walk, her gloved hands steady on the reins. "What *did* you think?"

Jasper fell in step beside her on Quintus. Miss Wychwood's groom followed after them at a distance. "That you needed someone to come to your aid. I hoped I wouldn't be too objectionable a candidate."

"You weren't," she said. "You were perfect. I'm so very grateful. I wanted to tell you—"

"You needn't." Gratitude was the last thing he wanted from her. "It was a privilege."

"I can still be grateful for it." She gave him a shy glance through the fine net of her veil. "You've come to my aid so often these past days."

A stab of guilt pricked at his conscience. It was in his interest that she think well of him. Even so, he wouldn't permit her to make him out to be something he was not. "Perhaps it's because I have ulterior motives where you're concerned."

Her voice took on a serious note. "My dowry, you mean."

"Among other things."

"I'm glad we can speak plainly about it," she said.

He inclined his head. No doubt it would be wiser to woo her with honeyed words and empty promises, but he'd never excelled in that regard. Besides, there were enough secrets between them already—secrets he was destined to take to his grave. In this, at least, he could be honest with her.

And he *wanted* to be honest with her.

It was a dangerous urge. He hadn't felt the like of it in years. This dratted desire to reveal himself to another person. To have them know him for who he truly was.

"What do you require it for?" she asked.

"For my estate. Goldfinch Hall."

She smiled. "Is that what it's called?"

"It's named after the goldfinches that gather there every winter. There are hundreds of them, with red crowns and bright yellow wings—a colorful display. It's quite striking to see them." He looked at her. "Are you fond of birds?"

"I love all animals," she said. "All."

He wasn't surprised. "You have pets?"

She resumed staring straight ahead as they rode. "Only Cossack. My parents won't allow any others. They can't abide them."

Jasper waited for her to elaborate, but she said nothing more. He had the sense she was refraining from voicing some private grievance. A criticism of her famously eccentric mother and father, perhaps.

He wondered about her life with them. She, an only child. A daughter, shackled to their invalidism—be it real or imagined—there in that imposing white-stuccoed house in Belgrave Square. It can't have been a happy life for her as a little girl.

It couldn't be a very happy life for her now.

"I've had to learn more than I'd like about birds during my time at the Hall," he offered by way of conversation. "Did you know that a flock of goldfinches is called a charm?"

She flicked him an uncertain glance. "Is that true?"

"I swear it."

"A charm." Her lush mouth curved with pleasure. "Oh, but I like that."

"Better than a murder of crows."

"Much better," she agreed. "Though I haven't anything against crows. They're very intelligent birds, you know. I once read a novel where the heroine had a talking crow as a pet. When she died, it was he who revealed the identity of the villain who had poisoned her. He even testified in court."

"An unlikely occurrence."

"Novels needn't be realistic to be entertaining. Some of the most thrilling I've read are filled with outlandish twists and turns. Secret babies, lost heirs, falsified deaths, and hidden identities."

Not quite so outlandish, Jasper thought grimly. Not if one had seen the things he'd seen. Done the things he'd done. Indeed, elements of his past made popular fiction seem rather tame in comparison.

But a young lady of Miss Wychwood's breeding wouldn't know about that. To her, it was the stuff of entertainment.

"Like *Lady Audley's Secret*," he said.

"Exactly like that." She gave a gentle tug on her gelding's reins, preventing him from nipping at Quintus's neck. "The way you describe Goldfinch Hall makes it sound like something from a novel. I know you said it wasn't a castle in a French fairy tale, but—"

"It isn't. There's nothing romantic about the state of it. When I returned from the Crimea, I found it in an appalling condition." He grimaced to recall it. "My uncle—God rest his soul—was a recluse, not entirely in his right mind. He'd let the fields run fallow and allowed the house to crumble down around his ears. It's a miracle it still stands."

"I'm sorry to hear it," she said. "You must have been disappointed to find it so."

"Disappointed. Yes."

An understatement.

He'd been shocked. Gutted. And the condition of the estate had been only the first of many unpleasant surprises to greet him on his arrival in Yorkshire.

But there was no point in repining.

He'd made his decision and he was bound to stay the course. Not just for a week or a year, but for all time. The children's future depended on it.

"Has it always been in your family?" she asked.

"Not always. My uncle's grandfather bought it at the end of the last century. It had been standing vacant before he took residence. The house has a history of neglect."

"You mean to repair it?"

"I do. And not out of any misplaced sense of vanity. I don't require a grand estate. Were it up to me, I'd have abandoned the place long ago. It's for the children I do it. It's their birthright."

A soft breeze ruffled her black net veil, briefly shaping it to the contours of her face. "Some might argue that children born outside of wedlock have no birthright."

His jaw hardened reflexively. "Is that what you believe?"

She seemed to consider the question. "I don't know. I've never given any serious thought to the matter. But I know what people are like, and how unforgiving they can be about anything that doesn't fit their ideas of propriety."

"So do I," Jasper said. "It doesn't diminish my responsibility to the children. The house is theirs, and the land along with it. I won't permit it to fall to ruin. Not if I can contrive a way to save it."

"What about your own children?" she asked.

A jolt of apprehension made him stiffen in his saddle. "They *are* my children."

"Yes, I know that. What I mean is . . . What about the children you'll have with whomever it is you marry?"

Jasper thought he detected a flush of color in her cheeks. It was difficult to tell through that dratted veil of hers.

If she *was* blushing, he couldn't blame her. He felt a little warm under the collar himself now he understood her meaning.

It was something he'd never considered. An unforgivable oversight on his part. Of course she must want children of her own. Children with *him*.

And why shouldn't he oblige her?

There was little else he was capable of giving her. The house was derelict. Charlie, Alfred, and Daisy were half-wild.

And worse.

Miss Wychwood would have to contend with having Jasper as her husband. His great scarred, hulking self in her house—and in her bed.

His muscles clenched low in his belly.

It had been a long time since he'd been with a woman. No opportunities existed in Yorkshire. And on those rare occasions when the chance had presented itself elsewhere, he'd felt no great impulse to exert himself.

He was a dashed sight too romantic-minded, that was the problem.

Perhaps that was what he and Miss Wychwood had in common.

"I suppose," he said carefully, "a certain amount of my wife's dowry must be set aside for any children arising from our union."

Her brows knit. "But not the estate?"

It was a valid question. Jasper cursed himself for not having prepared for it. What had he expected? That his future wife wouldn't want their children to inherit the one thing of value he possessed? That she'd quietly accept him leaving the whole of it to his bastards?

"It's rather complicated," he said.

"Undoubtedly." She fell quiet, the clip-clop of their horses' hooves on the hard-packed earth the only sound. "Does the children's mother live with them at the Hall?"

Jasper failed to suppress a flinch. Her question was as startling in its frankness as a sharp slap across the face. To be sure, he'd have preferred the slap.

She hastened to apologize. "Forgive me. I'd assumed your children all shared the same mother."

If her first question was a slap, the conclusion she drew from his response to it was as brutal as a punch in the jaw.

Good God. She must take him for a whoremonger.

"They do," he said tightly. "I'm not completely lost to decency."

It was a ridiculous distinction. He knew it as soon as he made it. After all, what was the difference between one mistress and three of them? A whoremonger was a whoremonger. The rest was only arithmetic.

"And no," he added. "She does *not* live with us. She hasn't been a part of our lives for a long while. My youngest scarcely remembers her."

Miss Wychwood went quiet again.

Her silence set Jasper's teeth on edge. He hated that they must discuss this. Hated that any gently bred young lady—Miss Wychwood in particular—should be obliged to give voice to anything so coarse and unsavory.

He nevertheless continued, though the words stuck in his throat. "Allow me to say that I would never ask a lady to join me in living at the Hall if I thought the situation there would degrade her."

"I didn't think you would," Miss Wychwood said. Her words were softened by the trace of a smile.

"You don't find the presence of my three children too scandalous to be borne?"

"It *is* scandalous," she acknowledged. "But I suspect many ladies would be willing to bear the scandal if it meant marrying well and being mistress of their own property."

For an instant, he took leave to hope.

"Are you one of those ladies?" he asked.

"Does it matter? If it's money you require, I daresay any heiress would do. If not me, then someone else. Miss Throckmorton, perhaps."

He couldn't dispute the fact. Money was his primary concern. It was what had brought him to London in the first place.

But it wasn't what had brought him here this morning.

On rising from his bed, he hadn't thought of riches, or even of Goldfinch Hall. He'd thought only of seeing Julia Wychwood again.

"Miss Throckmorton is an impressive young lady," he said.

"She is," Miss Wychwood replied without a hint of malice. "It was good of her to come to my aid last night."

"As I say, an impressive young lady. However . . ." He cast her a weighted glance. "She wasn't my first choice."

"I know that." She straightened her habit skirt—a restless movement not entirely in keeping with her quiet hands and seat. "What I don't understand is why."

Honeyed words might have been difficult, but the truth came easily enough. Jasper didn't hesitate to utter it. "You're beautiful."

She returned both hands to the reins. Her horse tossed his head, sending the curb chain of his Pelham bit clinking. "I'm flattered you think so. But beauty doesn't last."

"Your kind will."

She gave him a doubtful look.

He gazed steadily back at her, as solemn as he'd ever been. "I believe, ma'am, that you have a beautiful soul. That you *are* a beautiful soul. I don't expect that will alter with age."

She stared at him for an instant, seemingly speechless. Her mouth trembled. "What a lovely sentiment."

He shrugged. "It's the truth."

"I don't know what to say."

"Don't say anything," he returned. "Or better yet . . . tell me something of your own feelings."

Her expression became wary. "What about them?"

"You said you wished to know me better. I assume that's why you're here. You must have known I'd be here, too. That I intended to speak with you away from your chaperone."

"I always ride at this time of morning. But . . . Yes. I understood what you meant when we parted last night. I may be silly on occasion, but I'm not a fool."

"No indeed." He frowned. "Yet still you came."

She gave him a bemused glance. "You sound as though you're trying to warn me off."

"I should," he said. "I still might."

"Your very changeable, sir."

"I suffer from pangs of conscience. An unfortunate condition. I'm endeavoring to overcome it."

She laughed.

The sound provoked a lump of yearning in his chest. He realized, to his disquiet, how much he wanted to be the one to make her laugh.

"Unfortunate, to be sure," she said. "Given your purpose for being in town."

Naturally, it was. A fortune hunter was meant to be conscienceless. Ruthless. A role that anyone would have said suited Captain Jasper Blunt to a certainty. And yet . . .

He hadn't been ruthless with Julia Wychwood, not by a long chalk.

When she'd asked him to stop pursuing her, he'd done so. And then, last night, when he might easily have compromised her on Lady Holland's balcony, he'd chosen instead to talk to her about romance novels.

J. Marshland's novels, for God's sake.

"My purpose hasn't changed," he informed her.

"I'm aware," she said. "But you've been nothing but kind to me. It's one of the reasons I wanted to see you this morning. I never got a chance to properly thank you for rescuing me last night."

"That wasn't a rescue. That was naught but a minor service." Jasper's eyes held hers, his voice dark with promise. "When I rescue you, Miss Wychwood, you'll know it."

Eight

————✦————

$\mathcal{J}$ulia's breath caught at his words. She supposed she should be afraid. Any sensible lady would be. Captain Blunt had all but outlined his plan to marry an heiress and use her dowry to repair his fortunes. He was making no effort at deception. Quite the opposite.

Thus far, they'd talked of his finances, his illegitimate children, and even the children he might sire with his future wife. A wife who, only a few short days ago, he'd imagined would be her.

An unseemly conversation.

Anne would be horrified. But Anne didn't subsist on a steady diet of romances and sensation novels.

To Julia, there was nothing very evil about Captain Blunt's plans. He wasn't, for example, anything like Sir Percival Glyde, one of the characters in Mr. Collins's novel *The Woman in White*. Sir Percival had been charming on the surface. But underneath, he'd been a thorough villain; marrying a vulnerable heiress only to steal her fortune, falsify her death, and have her committed to an asylum under an assumed name.

Not so Captain Blunt.

He'd been honest and straightforward with Julia from the beginning. She admired him for it, even if she didn't wholly understand him.

"I hope I won't need rescuing at Lord and Lady Claverings' ball tonight," she said. "Will you be there?"

"I will."

She smiled, relieved. "I confess, I'm not looking forward to it. It helps to know I shall have a friend in attendance."

Captain Blunt's battle-scarred face was void of emotion.

She realized, belatedly, what she'd said. She'd called him a friend.

Were they friends? One wouldn't think so. Not judging by the way he was looking at her now. But she was learning that his countenance wasn't a reliable indicator of his feelings. For that she need only look at his actions. At his words.

He'd assisted her last night when she needed him. Had stood by her side, talking to her about novels until she'd regained her composure.

And that wasn't all.

Only moments ago, he'd told her that she had a beautiful soul. That she *was* a beautiful soul.

Julia glowed with warmth to recall it.

Had any gentleman ever said anything half so wonderful? Not that she'd ever heard. Not that she'd ever read, either. It was surely the most romantic sentiment ever uttered.

And it had been uttered to *her.*

A lady could live off such a compliment for a lifetime.

"You needn't feel in any way obliged to me," she added. "I shall do very well on my own."

"You'll be in company with your chaperone?" he asked.

Their two horses walked abreast, as companionably as if they were stablemates. Only Cossack's occasional attempts at nipping Quintus revealed the newness of their acquaintance.

Julia tightened her hands on her reins. "I will. My parents have enlisted Mrs. Major for all my engagements this season."

"She's a formidable protector."

"Yes, she is. Though my father has had to remind her of her duties once or twice."

"She forgets?"

"On occasion. She prefers the company of her friends at parties. It's why she's so eager to hand me off to Lord Gresham."

Captain Blunt gave her a look that was hard to read. "Lord Gresham has taken a particular interest in you."

"I suppose." Julia could think of nothing else to say on the subject. There had been no opportunity yet to speak to her father. Until she did, she had only her suspicions to inform her. She hoped she was wrong, that Papa hadn't come to some agreement with the earl.

The mere idea of it was enough to dispel the glow of warmth within her.

Up ahead, a thin gentleman trotted toward them on a rangy gray hunter. It was Lord Milburn. He gave them an interested look as he passed.

A scalding flare of self-consciousness took Julia unaware.

Good gracious.

How long had she and the captain been riding together, immersed in private conversation? And how many people had observed them?

Owing to the fine weather, the park was growing busier. Gentlemen were out alone and in pairs, and ladies were riding in company with their grooms. Glancing back, Julia caught the eye of her own groom, Luke Six. His face was set in a frown of disapproval.

Her spirits sank. No doubt he would report her meeting with Captain Blunt to Papa.

"I had better head back," she said.

Captain Blunt followed her gaze, taking in both the increasing presence of riders and the look on her groom's face in one comprehensive glance. "Of course. I won't detain you."

She turned Cossack around. "Good day to you."

He bowed to her—the same stiff, militaristic inclination of his head with which he'd greeted her. "Good day, Miss Wychwood."

She pressed her heel into Cossack's side, anxious to put as much distance between herself and Captain Blunt as possible. Until she did, she'd continue being the recipient of knowing whispers and curious stares.

Thank goodness for her veil. No one could truly see her face through it. Not when she was moving at a quick clip. But she couldn't be seen to be running away. She was careful to keep Cossack to a walk.

She'd gone no more than a few lengths when another rider fell in beside her. An exceedingly fashionable, and all-too-familiar, blond lady mounted on a graceful little mare.

It was Viscountess Heatherton.

Julia's pulse surged on a rush of anxiety.

Lady Heatherton was one of the most prominent figures in London society, famous as much for her beauty as for her vicious and vindictive nature.

Julia hadn't seen her since a recent ball at Cremorne Gardens. There, on one of the gardens' dark walks, Lady Heatherton had instigated an altercation with Evelyn and her beau, Mr. Malik. Julia had been present, along with Anne and Stella. Only the intervention of Anne's mother, Lady Arundell, had prevented the incident from erupting into a full-blown scene.

Since then, Julia and her three friends had steered clear of the viscountess. Not out of fear. They weren't intimidated by her. But as Anne said, there was no need to provoke her ladyship into another senseless attack, the result of which could only serve to harm their own reputations.

Julia kept that firmly in mind. She had no wish to provoke anyone. In truth, she felt a little sorry for Lady Heatherton. Everyone knew her marriage to the much older Lord Heatherton was an unhappy one.

"Miss Wychwood," her ladyship said. "You're without your friends today, I see."

"I am, my lady. They're out of town at present."

"And Miss Maltravers with them?" Lady Heatherton's face spread into a self-satisfied smile. "Well, well. I thought she had more mettle."

Julia's gloved fingers curled tighter on her reins.

The viscountess had taken a particular dislike to Evelyn, owing to Evelyn's involvement with Mr. Malik. Julia didn't know the full story. It was something about Mr. Malik having once been Lady Heatherton's dressmaker. A falling-out had set the two of them at odds. A *romantic* falling-out, Julia suspected. As a result, Evelyn had become Lady Heatherton's enemy.

"Miss Maltravers will be back," Julia said. "She's only gone home to Sussex for a fortnight."

"Oh?" The smile froze on Lady Heatherton's lips.

"Miss Hobhouse and Lady Anne will be returning soon as well. I expect them by Sunday evening."

"You're quite alone until then, are you? Or, not quite alone." Lady Heatherton's eyes glittered with renewed malice. "Was that Captain Blunt I saw you with?"

Julia didn't know why the viscountess should ask when she clearly already knew the answer. "It was."

"Fascinating." Lady Heatherton's blond hair glimmered in the sunlight. It was caught up beneath a silvery-gray felt hat, trimmed in black and white ostrich feathers. The stylish chapeau complemented her formfitting riding habit, a costume made to showcase her narrow waist. Her ladyship was a well-known proponent of tight lacing.

Next to her, Julia felt a veritable dowd.

"Brave of you, too," Lady Heatherton added. "To be alone with him that way."

"We weren't alone," Julia said. "No more than anyone else riding in the park."

"I should be nervous myself," her ladyship went on, "given the man's history."

Julia gave her a sharp look. "What do you mean? What history?"

"You don't know?" Lady Heatherton affected an expression of surprise. "A shame. If you did, you wouldn't risk his company. Not without your chaperone."

"I'm sorry . . ." Julia's brows knit into a puzzled frown. "Are you acquainted with Captain Blunt?"

"One needn't be acquainted with a man to form an opinion of his character. One need only keep their ears open." Lady Heatherton gave her little mare a tap with the crop, urging her into a faster stride.

Julia easily caught up with her on Cossack. "You've heard something?"

"It's not my place to say," her ladyship replied airily. "I daresay you'll catch wind of it eventually."

Julia's temper flared at Lady Heatherton's casual tone. How *dare* she malign Captain Blunt in such an offhand fashion? Spreading reckless innuendo about town in an effort to blacken his name—and why? Simply because she was bored and wished to amuse herself?

"I abhor gossip," Julia said. "It's bad enough to listen to it, but to repeat it—"

"I've done nothing of the sort." Lady Heatherton's gimlet eyes flashed sparks. "And it isn't gossip. My husband was in the Foreign Office during the war. He read the dispatches from the front. What I know, I learned from him."

"What did you learn?"

"That your Captain Blunt was a ruthless soldier, feared as much by the British as by the enemy."

Julia huffed. "That's no secret." Captain Blunt's reputation had been alluded to often enough in her presence. "If that's all you've heard—"

"There's more," Lady Heatherton said.

Julia steeled herself. "Go on."

Lady Heatherton dropped her voice as they rode past a gentleman on a prancing bay. "According to Heatherton, Captain Blunt gave no quarter to the enemy. He was known to execute captives in cold blood rather than imprison them."

An icy chill seeped into Julia's veins. "Even if that's true . . . It was wartime. And if they were indeed the enemy—"

"It wasn't only his adversaries who aroused his cruelty. His conduct toward his own men was just as pitiless. He marched them until they collapsed, and flogged those who were insubordinate to within an inch of their lives, making them subsist on half rations, starving at his pleasure. And the way he dealt with deserters! There were executions. Brandings. Horrors you can't imagine."

Julia stared at the viscountess, stunned.

"He nearly killed one of his lieutenants once," her ladyship continued with ill-concealed relish. "The bookish son of a country vicar, I understand. He'd taken bread to a dying prisoner against Blunt's express orders. Blunt repaid the man's kindness by flogging him almost to death."

Julia shook her head, unwilling to believe it. "That can't be true."

"It is. Heatherton says by the time Sebastopol fell, the captain had developed a taste for brutality. How else do you suppose he managed to survive?"

Julia could make no reply. Her heart was beating like a smith's hammer.

"Is that news to you as well?" Lady Heatherton laughed—a sharp, unfriendly sound. "You really know nothing about him, do you? Silly girl. Why do you imagine he's called the Hero of the Crimea? He survived an ambush, during which he single-handedly killed an entire patrol of Russian soldiers. It was for that he earned his name. Never mind that he lost the lives of the rest of his men in the bargain."

"It can't be true," Julia said again, as much to herself as to Lady Heatherton. "If it were, he wouldn't have been welcomed into society the way he's been. No one respectable would ever have issued him an invitation."

"Why shouldn't they? Everything he did was done with the goal of defeating our enemy." Viscountess Heatherton's lips curled into a smile. "And now he's set his sights on you. A sweet little morsel of a bluestocking heiress. Do you know, Miss Wychwood, I rather pity you."

Nine

—✦—

*L*ater that morning, after a brief stop at Doctors' Commons, Jasper bounded up the steps of the Wychwood town house in Belgrave Square. It had been less than a week since he and Miss Wychwood had embarked on their tentative friendship. Just a few short days of talking to each other. Confiding in each other.

She hadn't exactly approved of his suit. She'd only said she'd like to know him better. It wasn't much in the way of encouragement.

But time was of the essence.

Charlie, Alfred, and Daisy awaited him in Yorkshire. Every day that passed was another spent away from them. Away from his duties on the estate. It was that which had compelled him to go to Doctors' Commons to obtain a special license. A presumptuous act, but a necessary one given the time constraint.

Miss Wychwood was certain to understand.

Jasper hadn't the luxury of prolonging things. The sooner he spoke to her father the better.

Though, by the looks of it, it may not be the most auspicious time to do so.

The windows of the enormous white house were covered in black fabric, and the knocker had been removed from the front door. It gave every appearance of being a home where someone had recently died.

How ill *was* Miss Wychwood's father?

Jasper had been inclined to think of Sir Eustace and Lady Wych-wood as a pair of eccentrics. Two bored, wealthy aristocrats who had made a life's work out of their imagined ailments. But perhaps they truly were afflicted with some malady or other?

He rapped at the oaken door. It was opened a moment later by a balding footman in canary-yellow livery.

Jasper handed the man his card. "Tell Sir Eustace that I would have a word with him."

The footman gave Jasper's dour, black-clad figure an uncertain look, as if he didn't know quite how to place him. "This is in regard to—?"

"His daughter," Jasper said brusquely.

A knowing gleam shone in the footman's eyes. He admitted Jasper into the hall, relieved him of his hat and gloves, and directed him to a shadowy salon where he could wait while the footman inquired if Sir Eustace was at home.

Of course he was at home. Where else would he be? It was only Lady Wychwood who was away at the moment. In Bath, or so Jasper understood, taking the waters.

He couldn't blame her for decamping.

The house wasn't a welcoming place. Though luxuriously appointed, it had the air of a sickroom to it—dark and overwarm. Vaguely suffo-cating. It was the sort of environment designed to make a healthy person feel ill at ease.

It made Jasper exceedingly uncomfortable, as much for its present oppressiveness as for the unhappy recollections it inspired from his past. He *hated* sickrooms. Hated the smell and the cloying heat. The knowl-edge that a person one cared about—that one loved—might slip away at any moment. Gone forever. Never to see again. Never to talk to.

No wonder Miss Wychwood was unhappy here. She was a bright shining spark of a girl, full of romantic daydreams. She didn't belong in this . . . this *mausoleum.*

As Jasper waited in front of the carved marble fireplace, he gave an absent tug to his waistcoat, straightening an imagined wrinkle. There were none. His black three-piece suit was immaculate, his boots buffed to a high gloss, and his jaw freshly shaven.

Never in the whole of his two and thirty years had he performed an errand of this nature. Once resolved to it, he'd embarked on the business with extraordinary care.

By God if he wasn't a bit nervous.

He could almost believe it was real. That he was some infatuated boy approaching a young lady's father for permission to court her.

But he wasn't a boy any longer. And he wasn't infatuated.

He *wasn't*.

This was about Miss Wychwood's fortune. And if he liked her a little, too . . . Well. That was all the better for their future together.

His visit here was merely a formality. Jasper prayed it would go quickly. He still had that solicitor to call on in Fleet Street. And afterward, there was this evening's ball to prepare for. He was conscious of the passing seconds, each of them marked by the ticking of an ornate ormolu clock on the mantelpiece.

The footman returned momentarily. "Sir Eustace will see you in his study. This way, if you please."

Jasper followed him down the hall. Sir Eustace's study was at the back of the residence. Heavy draperies were drawn shut over the windows, and a fire blazed in the grate, making the room as uncomfortably warm as the rest of the house. Far worse, it reeked of animal lard and herbs. A chest plaster, Jasper suspected, or some other manner of medicinal.

Sir Eustace looked as though he needed it. Seated behind a mahogany desk, he was as pale as a waxwork effigy. He wore a quilted banyan, with a cap on his head, a muffler tucked at his throat, and a rug draped over his shoulders. "Captain Blunt," he said weakly.

Jasper bowed. "Sir Eustace."

"Come in and have a seat." Sir Eustace waved away the footman. "That will be all, Jenkins."

The footman departed, shutting the door behind him.

Jasper sat down in a leather-upholstered chair, facing Sir Eustace across the desk. He saw no resemblance to Miss Wychwood in the man's face. No similarity in shape, coloring, or expression. Perhaps she took after her mother?

Or perhaps not.

An oil portrait on the study wall depicted an expensively dressed woman with dark hair and drooping, aristocratic features. Lady Wychwood, Jasper presumed. She looked no more like Miss Wychwood than the baronet.

Which begged the question: Where did Julia Wychwood get her beauty? Her sweetness? It wasn't from her parents. For all she resembled them, she might have been a changeling left on their doorstep. A fey child, merely biding time among mortals until the fateful day she was retrieved by her people.

She didn't belong here.

Jasper felt the truth of it even more than he had when he'd first entered the house.

Sir Eustace regarded him narrowly, a shrewd expression in his eyes. "Jenkins tells me you've come about my daughter."

"I have," Jasper said.

It had been his plan from the beginning. A mercenary plan. To woo her and win her. To claim her fortune for his own. Ridgeway had insisted it could be done without any trouble. Miss Wychwood was a wallflower. A self-proclaimed oddity with two failed seasons behind her. Surely, Sir Eustace would jump at the chance to see her married off.

But something wasn't right.

It was that look in the baronet's eyes. That shrewd, measuring look, completely at odds with his frail demeanor.

Jasper was at once on his guard.

"Your visit is ill-timed," Sir Eustace said. "I've been too long from my bed today. My constitution can't abide it. The prospect of death is a constant companion to me."

"You have my sympathies," Jasper said.

"Sympathy is poor medicine. But I don't complain. I've long accepted that it's my lot in life, never knowing which day will be my last." Sir Eustace emitted a long-suffering sigh. "The doctor's been summoned. He'll be here shortly."

"I'll endeavor to be brief." Jasper paused. "Unless . . . If you'd rather I return some other time—"

"There's no point in delaying. I'm rarely better off than you see me now. And I confess, I've been expecting you. There have been reports." Sir Eustace withdrew a handkerchief from his pocket. "You've been spending time with my daughter."

"I've had that privilege, yes. We're invited to many of the same functions."

"And that's all? Come, sir. I may be confined to my bed the majority of the day, but news still reaches me from various quarters; my daughter's chaperone and others. It seems you've singled my daughter out for your attentions."

Jasper was unaccustomed to being challenged. Given his reputation, most men wouldn't dare. But there was no mistaking the querulous thread in the older man's voice.

He knew about Jasper's pursuit of Miss Wychwood and was plainly unhappy about it.

Jasper couldn't altogether blame him. Any father who loved his daughter was bound to be protective of her. "Miss Wychwood is a charming young lady. I've come to admire her very much."

"Charming?" Sir Eustace chuckled. "She's an heiress. I've made no secret of it. And you . . . You're an ex-soldier in straitened circumstances."

"A fact of which *I've* made no secret," Jasper said.

"I'll give you that, Captain. There are others who would attempt to hide their poverty. But you've been aboveboard, haven't you. Is it honesty, I wonder, or some variety of stratagem? A tactic meant to disarm an enemy?"

"Your daughter is not my enemy."

"But you don't deny it? A soldier of your character. A man accustomed to winning—to getting what he wants, no matter the cost."

A whisper of warning prickled at the back of Jasper's consciousness. The same damnable feeling he used to get when the tide of a battle was turning against him. It was an unmistakable signal he wasn't going to prevail, no matter how fierce his efforts.

"I'm afraid you've been listening to idle gossip."

"One hears things," Sir Eustace admitted. He blew his nose into his handkerchief. "You have an estate in Yorkshire, I understand."

"I do," Jasper said. "Goldfinch Hall."

"That's your only property?"

"It's a substantial one."

"In Yorkshire," Sir Eustace repeated.

"As I said."

"And that's what you propose? To marry my daughter and to take her and her fortune away with you to the other side of the country?" Sir Eustace gave another watery chuckle. "I'm precipitate. You haven't yet offered for her hand. But that's why you're here, I gather. To ask my permission to court her. Well, you can't have it."

And there it was.

Given Sir Eustace's manner, Jasper wasn't entirely surprised by the rejection. He nevertheless stiffened at the callous way in which the baronet had delivered it. "May I ask why I'm to be refused?"

Sir Eustace tucked away his handkerchief. "You aren't suitable for my daughter."

"If this has anything to do with my natural children—"

"I haven't an issue with your bastards. A man must sow his wild oats. Though you'd be advised to put them somewhere else before you wed. No female wishes to share a home with a whore's leavings."

Jasper's voice turned cold. "What is your objection, then?" he asked. "Is it to do with my war record?"

Aside from the children, it was the only truly objectionable thing about him. His evil history. A blackened past no amount of goodness and decency could ever hope to erase. He was destined to spend the rest of his life atoning for it.

The irony didn't escape him.

"I don't object to your conduct in the Crimea," Sir Eustace said. "Had I been an officer—and I would have been one of exceedingly high rank if my health had permitted it—I'd have ruled my men with an iron fist. It's the only way one can turn common rabble into soldiers, is it not? Floggings and other punishments. Wellington himself once said that a man is no soldier until he's received fifty lashes."

Jasper was vaguely aware that his right hand had clenched into a fist. He willed it to relax, opening his fingers one by one to lay flat on his thigh. Nothing could be gained by losing his temper. Certainly not with Miss Wychwood's father. Like most gentlemen, safe at home during the war, the baronet had no idea what he was talking about.

"No, no," Sir Eustace went on, wheezing. "It isn't your military history that makes you ineligible. It's your choice of residence. As if I would ever permit my daughter to remove to Yorkshire! Her place is in London. She's needed here by her mother and myself. We're too ill to spare her. Any gentleman she weds must reside in town."

Realization sunk in slowly. Jasper was loath to accept it. "And that's your only requirement?"

Sir Eustace didn't appear to see anything odd in this. "It is, sir."

"I would think, given your daughter's lack of offers, you might be more willing to entertain my suit. After two failed seasons—"

"You're mistaken. My daughter has had several offers these past years. All by gentlemen who would take her away from here. Naturally, I refused them out of hand. Just as I must refuse you." Sir Eustace stood. "I've already given my permission to Lord Gresham. He's refurbishing his house in Grosvenor Square and has pledged to reside in town all the year round. It will suit Lady Wychwood and I to a nicety."

Jasper slowly rose to his feet. He felt a peculiar numbness at his core. It was directly at odds with his burgeoning sense of outrage.

Miss Wychwood hadn't been a failure on the marriage mart. She might have been married anytime these past two seasons.

Bloody hell.

Did she know her father had been refusing all offers? Did she even suspect? And all because he wanted to keep her here, within a stone's throw of Belgrave Square.

And for what? To be a sickroom attendant for the remainder of her life? First to her parents, then to some aged husband?

Jasper fought to control his temper. "What about Miss Wychwood? You say that her marrying Gresham will suit you and your wife, but how will it suit *her*?"

"She's our daughter. She will do her duty."

"She's of age."

"Indeed. But if she marries without my permission, she inherits nothing from me. Not a pound. Not a farthing." Sir Eustace tugged the tasseled bellpull to summon the footman. "I daresay a pauper bride isn't as attractive to you."

Jasper stood silent, his emotions roiling dangerously beneath the surface. There was nothing he could say. Nothing he could do. The facts were incontrovertible. He needed Miss Wychwood's fortune. It was necessary for the children. For the survival of their estate. It was the whole reason he'd come to London. The impetus for everything he'd done thus far.

It made no difference if his affections had been engaged in the process. His own feelings didn't matter. *He* didn't matter. All that mattered was the money.

A smug smile shone in Sir Eustace's eyes. "I thought not."

Ten

—✕—

I t was nearing one o'clock when Julia returned to Belgrave Square. She hadn't meant to linger so long at Bloxham's. And now she had but a few minutes to tidy herself before her receiving hours.

Not that anyone ever called. Not so long as Anne, Stella, and Evelyn were out of town. But today might be the day someone did. Someone in particular.

The prospect of it boosted Julia's spirits for a fraction of a second only to send them plummeting again as she recalled the terrible revelations Viscountess Heatherton had imparted about Captain Blunt.

Julia had been agonizing over the information all morning. It was why she'd gone shopping, hoping to forget her anxieties, if only for a while, in the purchase of a new novel—or five.

But even as she'd browsed the shelves of Bloxham's for the second time in as many days, the knowledge of Captain Blunt's extraordinary cruelty during the war had been there, nagging at her like a sore tooth. She couldn't leave it alone. Couldn't stop wondering what sort of man would do such things.

The answer came easily enough: a monster.

And not the beastly kind from a fairy tale. But the dishonorable kind who committed unspeakable crimes. A man who was cruel and heartless and incapable of mercy.

If what Viscountess Heatherton said was true.

And there was the rub.

Lady Heatherton had claimed the intelligence had come from her husband, but Julia knew how rumors could grow out of all proportion. She had only to consider how exaggerated reports had been about the number of the captain's illegitimate children.

What if the rumors of his cruelty were no different? Nothing more than ugly stories built around a smidgeon of truth?

She wondered what that smidgeon would turn out to be in the tales of Captain Blunt's conduct. Would it be something justifiable? Something she could understand? That she could forgive?

There was only one way to find out. She would have to ask him herself.

The mere idea of it was enough to make her stomach perform a nauseating flip-flop.

Entering her bedroom, she dropped her newly purchased stack of novels onto the bed. There were five altogether. Nearly one third of J. Marshland's entire catalog.

"I still don't see why you had to get so many of them," Mary grumbled as she assisted Julia out of her velvet-trimmed carriage gown. The street had been dusty and dirty, soiling the hem. It would have to be sponged and pressed.

"Because," Julia explained, stepping out of her heavy skirts, "Captain Blunt is familiar with Marshland's works. The more I read of them, the more we'll have to talk about."

That had been the idea anyway.

Though once she learned the truth about his actions in the Crimea, heaven only knew whether she'd want to speak to him ever again.

"You've read Mrs. Marshland before," Mary said.

"Yes, but not all her novels." Julia's brow creased. "Or his." She went to the basin and washed her hands and face, drying them on a flannel towel. "Captain Blunt insists Marshland is a man."

Mary snorted. "Does he, now?" She retrieved a fresh afternoon dress from the wardrobe; a soft, striped wool grenadine with an *Imperatrice* collar of white piqué. She helped Julia into the skirts before tugging the loosely cuffed sleeves of the bodice over her arms. "Seems to me he's playing with you, miss. Everyone knows gentlemen don't read novels. Not great big Crimean soldiers, anyway."

"He may well be," Julia allowed. "Even so, he *has* read Marshland's novels—and other novels, too. He couldn't talk about them the way he does if he hadn't read them."

"Huh." Mary fastened the small metal hooks that closed the front of Julia's bodice. "He don't seem the type."

"No, indeed. He looks too fierce, doesn't he? And perhaps he is."

Julia was far from certain of him anymore. The only thing she knew was that he'd been kind to her. That he'd left her alone when she'd asked. And that he'd come to her aid when she needed him. He hadn't taken liberties or attempted to insinuate himself. He'd been gentle with her. Almost protective.

Of course, it could all be a trick. An elaborate trap laid by a master, meant to ensnare both her *and* her fortune.

She didn't want to believe it.

A rap sounded at the bedroom door. Mary answered it, opening the door only an inch. "What d'you want?"

The voice of the first footman, Jenkins Four, emerged through the crack. "A message for Miss Wychwood."

"If it's a gentleman caller, you tell him she'll be down in five minutes," Mary replied tartly. "It won't hurt him none to wait."

"Not a caller," Jenkins Four said. "It's Sir Eustace. He asks her to come to him directly."

"What is it, Jenkins?" Julia walked to the door, finishing the topmost two hooks on her bodice as she went. "My father hasn't taken a turn for the worse?"

"I couldn't say, miss, but the doctor's just been." Jenkins Four stepped back as Julia exited her room. He hurried alongside her down the thickly carpeted hall. "And Sir Eustace has sent a telegraph to her ladyship."

A jolt of alarm hastened Julia's step. "He telegraphed my mother?"

"Yes, miss. He sent the message off with George over an hour ago."

Her father's bedchamber was in the opposite wing. By the time Julia reached it, she was out of breath. She knocked softly before entering. "Papa?"

The room was dark and overwarm, the air heavy with the pungent fragrance of liniment and mustard plaster.

She found her father not in bed, but seated in front of a blazing fire, his pallid face illuminated by the flames. He was swaddled in blankets from his chin to his slippers. A glass of yellowish liquid sat, half-full, on the little round wooden table beside him. Julia recognized it as one of his tonics. A patent medicine that contained a greater portion of opiates than it did of any healthful ingredients.

"Back at last," he said thinly. "I trust you enjoyed your shopping."

She felt a twinge of guilt. No doubt he meant her to. "What's this I hear about Dr. Cordingley stopping in?"

"Not Cordingley. Dr. Hurt."

"Dr. *Hurt*?" Julia had never heard of the man before. "That's not a very promising name for a physician."

"Don't be ridiculous. He's Gresham's man. An excellent fellow. The earl recommended him to me himself."

"How obliging of him." Julia pressed a hand to her father's waxen brow.

He jerked away from her. "No fussing. I've already been seen to. Hurt says I'm to keep to my room for the remainder of the week. He'll be back this evening to look in on me."

"What seems to be the trouble?" She perched on the edge of the chair opposite him. The upholstery was heated from the fire, warming her all the way through her petticoats and crinoline. "Is it your heart, Papa?"

"Would that it would stop beating and put an end to my suffering," he grumbled.

She instinctively leaned toward him. "You mustn't say that."

He shrank from her, his expression petulant. "Don't pretend concern. If you cared one jot for my health, you'd have been here with me and not gallivanting around the city for your own pleasure."

"I only went to Charing Cross. You hadn't any need of me. And I didn't think—"

"*You didn't think*," he repeated. "There's a surprise."

Julia possessed herself in patience. It wasn't easy. She didn't like to be scolded unfairly. Her every instinct urged her to defend herself. But she wasn't going to argue with him. Not when he was in this condition. "Did you truly send a telegraph to Mama?"

His wiry brows snapped together. "The servants have been gossiping, have they? Which of them spoke to you? I won't tolerate back-fence prattle. Not in my house."

Julia knew that well enough. Her father had dismissed many a maid and footman on the flimsiest suspicion of telling tales. Prolonged illness had made him prone to paranoia. "The servants weren't gossiping, Papa."

"No? What else did they say to you? Lies, I'll wager."

"Pray don't distress yourself. They only said the doctor had come, and that you'd sent George off to the telegraph office."

Mollified, he relaxed back in his chair. "I had no choice, did I? I've the state of things with Gresham to consider. You'll need someone to keep you out of the clutches of fortune hunters until he comes to the point. I'm not well enough to do it myself. Would that I'd had a son!"

A sense of foreboding crept over her. The same ominous feeling she'd had when Lord Gresham had mentioned she might, someday soon, play hostess to one of his dinner parties. "What has Lord Gresham to do with it? I know he's visited you, but—"

"Just as any gentleman should, given his interest in you." Her father's hand emerged, white and frail, from the cocoon of his blankets to retrieve his glass of tonic. "He's a fine man, Gresham."

"He's an *old* man," Julia retorted before she could curb her tongue.

Annoyance flashed in her father's eyes. "Too right. A young girl requires a seasoned husband to take her in hand."

Husband.

Her breath stopped. "Are you saying . . . Has the earl asked to marry me?"

"Not as yet, but he intends to." Her father drank the remainder of his tonic, swallowing it down in great noisy gulps. "Until such time, I've given him permission to pay court to you. He'll be here this evening to escort you to the ball."

She shook her head. "No, Papa."

"*No*, you say?" A flush of anger darkened his face. "You forget yourself, my girl."

"Not without reason." She folded her hands in her lap, trying hard to ignore the panicked skittering of her pulse. "I don't like him. Not in that way. We don't suit at all."

"What do you know of it?"

"I know myself," she said. "And I know enough about him to make me uneasy."

She knew Lord Gresham was arrogant and overbearing and that his wife had perished in childbed.

There had been talk of the late countess's plight. Rumors that Gresham had kept the woman in a perpetual state of pregnancy, desperate for her to produce his heir, even if she might die in the attempt.

And she had.

It was why Gresham was in London looking for a new wife. A *young* wife.

"Rubbish," her father said. "These matters are a man's business. It's for me to decide who suits you. I say Gresham will do nicely. He has a house in Grosvenor Square. An easy distance from here."

Julia continued to shake her head in protest. She was being backed into another cage. An even smaller one than she resided in now. Once married, there would be no escape from it, not until Lord Gresham died.

Or she did.

"You don't understand," she insisted. "I could never bring myself to—"

"If you've any maidenish apprehensions, your poor dear mama will quell them. I've commanded her to leave Bath this very day."

Her mother was coming home?

The prospect did nothing to alleviate Julia's fears.

Her mother could be as tyrannical in her infirmity as her father. They both of them believed that children should obey absolutely. That the entire purpose of a daughter was to be of service to her parents. But unlike Papa, who dismissed Julia the moment she became quarrelsome, Mama didn't flinch from enforcing her orders with a hard pinch or a slap.

"She'll be home by morning," he said. "And then you may speak with her on the subject."

"What about tonight?" Julia asked. "I don't wish to attend the ball with Lord Gresham. I'd rather go with Mrs. Major. Either that or not at all."

"Enough."

"Indeed, I'd much prefer staying home."

"*Enough.* I'm too poorly to listen to your screeching. My heart aches and my head's a misery. If you knew what I suffer you wouldn't plague me so. Go on now, and leave me in peace."

Julia rose, her legs unsteady beneath her. "My heart is aching, too, Papa," she said quietly. "If you force me to marry Lord Gresham, I fear it will break."

"Bah. You and your romantic claptrap." He returned his hand to the shelter of his blanket cocoon. "Away with you before you send me to an early grave."

Eleven

During the London season, there were many hostesses who measured the success of a ball by the number of fashionable bodies they were able to pack, sardine-like, into the confines of their home. To Julia's vast discomfort, Lady Clavering was one of them.

There were easily more than four hundred people inside the Claverings' lavish gaslit ballroom, with its gilded cove ceiling painted to resemble a cloud-covered cerulean sky. Couples swirled in harmony around the polished wood floor; gentlemen in understated eveningwear and ladies in extravagant gowns, their tinsel-festooned skirts floating out over enormous crinolines.

Music from the orchestra swelled from the dais, and the air was redolent with the scents of perfume and pomade. Those who weren't dancing lined the walls, both sitting and standing. Wallflowers and matrons alike, staring, whispering, and wafting their fans.

Julia had never felt more stifled. As she moved around the floor in Lord Gresham's arms, doing her best approximation of a polka, she found it rather difficult to breathe.

The earl was having no easier a time of it. He guided her ineptly through the crush of dancers, treading on the skirts of first one lady's ball gown and then another.

"Beg pardon," he grunted. Perspiration dotted his brow. "Dashed close, isn't it?"

"It *is* crowded," Julia said. "We needn't finish."

"Nonsense." He trotted her around the room with renewed vigor. "I'm as fit as a man half my age."

Julia gritted her teeth. It was their second dance of the evening. One more and they may as well announce their engagement to the world. The earl certainly seemed keen enough.

Already well in his cups when he'd arrived to collect her, he'd sat beside her in the carriage, clutching at her hand and talking at her décolletage the entire journey from Belgrave Square.

Seated across from them, Mrs. Major had only smiled complacently, so satisfied in her success at helping to engineer a great match that she'd willfully ignored both the earl's behavior and his inebriated condition.

A condition that had only grown worse as the evening progressed.

Parched by the heat of the ballroom, Lord Gresham had been making free with the unending supply of punch provided by footmen who circulated the floor offering cups on silver trays.

He wasn't drunk. Not yet. But his cheeks were ruddy and he was gripping Julia with a clumsy strength. She couldn't get loose of him. The more she wiggled, the tighter he grasped.

A grim foreshadowing of what their life together would be like.

Julia hadn't accepted it yet, but she recognized the signs. The walls were closing in on her. Or perhaps they already had and she was only now beginning to realize the full extent of her captivity.

She saw no means of escape. Not even Captain Blunt provided her any hope. For one thing, there was his past to contend with. And for another, he wasn't even here. At least, he didn't appear be.

Which didn't mean he hadn't come.

The sheer density of the crowd made it impossible to locate anyone. At any given moment, people were flowing from one room to the next, clogging the halls before spilling out into the drawing room or card-room, or onto the terrace.

Julia wished she had as much freedom. If she did, she'd run straight out into the garden. Into the darkness and the fresh evening air. She wouldn't stop running until she was alone. Until Lord Gresham and Mrs. Major and all the rest of them were too far away to catch her.

"Miss Wychwood?" Lord Gresham inquired loudly.

She blinked, bringing the earl's face back into focus. "I'm sorry. What did you say?"

"I said you must save me the waltz."

Julia recoiled at the prospect.

Mercifully, the music came to a close before she was obliged to reply. His lordship released her, bowing. It was a short reprieve. Only a fraction of a second of freedom before he took her arm again to guide her from the floor.

"It's the supper dance," he said. "We can dine together afterward."

"Oh no. I can't think of dancing again, or of dining. Not until I've had a breath of air." She tugged her arm in a fruitless attempt to extri-cate herself. "If you would please excuse me."

"Not a bit of it." He tightened his grip. "If you must step out into the garden, I'll accompany you—and happily so." He propelled her toward the terrace doors. "I've a word or two to say to you in private."

Jasper escorted Miss Throckmorton to a seat at the edge of the ball-room. The polka had enlivened her features. She looked flushed and pretty. Entirely unobjectionable. Any gentleman would be honored to partner her for a dance. To fetch her refreshments or to take her into supper.

He reminded himself of that fact for what felt like the hundredth time.

"How serious you look," Miss Throckmorton remarked as she sat. "Are you not fond of dancing?"

"Fond enough to accept Lady Clavering's invitation," he said.

What choice had he?

His visit with Sir Eustace had dealt him a devastating blow. Indeed, on leaving Belgrave Square, Jasper had felt as though he'd come face-to-face with another patrol of enemy soldiers. Only this time, he hadn't prevailed. This time, the enemy had given him a thorough and merciless kicking.

He'd emerged onto the street, scarcely registering the sound of a footman calling after him as he strode off in the direction of Half Moon Street. His emotions in turmoil, he was halfway to Piccadilly before he'd realized that he'd forgotten his gloves.

It had been the least of his problems.

Returning to Ridgeway's house, Jasper had shut himself up in his room, as brooding and sullen as any rejected lover, until—through sheer force of will—he'd once again resigned himself to his task.

He'd come to London to find an heiress. It wasn't for his own inclination. It was for the children. For the estate. He had no choice in the matter.

If Julia Wychwood was beyond his reach, then Miss Throckmorton and her fortune would have to do.

That hadn't stopped him from searching the crowd for Miss Wychwood this evening.

He'd caught a glimpse of her during the polka. She was dancing with the Earl of Gresham, her expression shuttered, as if she'd withdrawn somewhere inside herself. A secret place filled with books and horses and endless expanses of verdant green countryside. Somewhere far away from the overwhelming crush of London.

It isn't your concern.

And it wasn't. He couldn't involve himself. Setting his shoulders, he refocused on the lady before him.

"But you're not enjoying yourself," Miss Throckmorton said. "That's plain to see."

"I rarely wear my feelings on my sleeve, ma'am," he replied.

"Indeed. It's part of your charm. Still . . . One wonders why you came." She opened her painted fan, wafting it in front of her face with a thoughtful air. "Surely, it wasn't on my account."

He couldn't answer her. Not truthfully. Instead, he forced a smile, certain it must look more like a rictus of pain. "May I bring you a cup of punch?"

Miss Throckmorton's own smile dimmed. "Thank you, yes. I am rather parched."

He took his leave of her. A footman with a tray of punch glasses hovered near the doors to the terrace. Making his way toward him, Jasper couldn't help but cast about the crowd once more in search of Miss Wychwood.

As always, his height was an asset. He found her almost at once.

Wearing a steel-blue gown cut low off her creamy shoulders, she was exiting through the terrace doors on Lord Gresham's arm. She glanced back into the ballroom, her expression faintly desperate. Gresham didn't falter. He tugged her out along with him, seemingly against her will.

Every nerve in Jasper's body sounded a warning.

Good God. What was Gresham up to?

He moved to follow after them, all thoughts of Miss Throckmorton and her cup of punch forgotten.

A tall gentleman in flawlessly cut eveningwear stepped in front of him, barring his way. "Blunt. I thought that was you."

Jasper gave the man a distracted look. It was Felix Hartford. A wealthy denizen of fashionable society, he was the grandson of the Earl of March and one of Jasper's few acquaintances in town.

Though *acquaintance* might be a stretch.

Jasper was even less familiar with him than he was with Ridgeway. "Hartford. I didn't know you were here."

"I don't wonder. It's impossible to find anyone in this crush."

"Quite." Jasper looked past him to the terrace doors. "Excuse me. I have something I must attend to."

Hartford followed his gaze. "An assignation?" He grinned. "Consider me surprised."

Jasper glowered at the man. "It's not an assignation, damn you. If you must know, Gresham's taken Miss Wychwood outside. She didn't appear too keen on the idea."

Hartford's brows notched in a disapproving line.

He was known to take a particular interest in Lady Anne. To what extent, Jasper didn't know. The whole of their relationship seemed to consist of long looks and pointed barbs. As if the two of them were engaged in some private battle.

One could almost believe they were enemies, except for the fact that, given the opportunity, Hartford never failed to render Lady Anne a service.

And Miss Wychwood was Lady Anne's bosom friend.

"Oh, she didn't, did she?" Hartford moved past Jasper. "Well, Blunt? What are you waiting for?"

The Claverings' tiered garden was landscaped for sin. Strategically placed torches illuminated the curving paths, but left plenty of nooks and crannies in shadow, perfect for midnight trysts. Muffled laughter and the sound of rustling fabric punctuated the splash of water flowing from a grand marble fountain nestled in a private clearing surrounded by statuary and manicured box hedges.

Lord Gresham guided Julia to one of the curved marble benches at the base of the fountain. He urged her to sit.

Julia stood her ground. She'd had enough of being pushed and pulled about. "My lord, I would you would stop pressing me."

"Now's not the time for missishness, girl. Have a seat so I might speak with you. Come. I'll sit beside you—"

She struggled to free herself. "Pray, let me go. I mean it, sir."

"Miss Wychwood, you compel me to be blunt." He grasped both of her arms. "I require a wife. An heir. And your father has assured me you're the one to fill the role."

"I'm not, I promise you."

"I'll be the judge of that." His intoxicated breath was sickly warm on her face. "You must know I find you ravishing beyond description. I may not be as young as I once was, but rest assured, I shall have no trouble rousing myself to—"

"Lord Gresham, *really*." Julia pushed against him, horrified by the sentiments he was expressing. They weren't a surprise. But to hear them—and to know how close she was to being obliged to submit to his desires—made her stomach roil in protest. "You go too far."

The earl was past the point of heeding her. "My dear"—he strained to kiss her—"you drive me to be forceful."

"Likewise." She brought her foot down hard on his instep. The little heel of her silk slipper landed with a satisfying crunch.

"Argh!" Lord Gresham released her. Groaning plaintively, he hopped about the clearing on one foot. "Damn and blast it!"

"You have only yourself to blame, sir," she said primly. Backing away from him, she glanced around the darkened clearing for her best route of escape. "I told you to let me go."

"Miss Wychwood!" Captain Blunt emerged through the shrubbery. His black-and-white evening clothes, so understated and civilized, stood in stark contrast to the dangerous glint in his ice-gray eyes. "Are you all right?"

Her already racing pulse kicked into a gallop. "Captain Blunt. What are *you* doing here?"

Felix Hartford appeared in the captain's wake.

Julia took another step back.

She'd known Mr. Hartford for most of her life, but theirs wasn't anything resembling a friendship. He'd always been more interested in Anne than in her—an interest that manifested itself in razor-sharp jests that never failed to rile Anne's temper.

Seeing him now, Julia wasn't entirely confident he was there to assist her. Not until he moved to intercept Lord Gresham.

"What's the meaning of this, sir?" Lord Gresham blustered.

"I could ask the same." Mr. Hartford grasped the earl by his coat. "Dragging off a defenseless young lady? And in your appalling condition?"

Lord Gresham shrugged free of him. "You have a damned nerve, Hartford. There's nothing wrong with my condition."

"You smell like a distillery."

His lordship turned the color of a ripe tomato. "I may have lost my head a little owing to drink, but—"

Captain Blunt advanced on the earl, something savage in his expression. In that moment, Julia could easily imagine him as Hades, God of the Underworld.

Or as a merciless soldier, cruel and pitiless to his core.

A shiver went through her.

Captain Blunt saw it. His face darkened like a thundercloud. "If you've hurt her—"

"*I?* Hurt *her?*" Lord Gresham was indignant. "It's you who's frightening her, Blunt, not I. Miss Wychwood and I have an arrangement. The girl's father—"

"Her father be damned," Captain Blunt said. "You have no right—"

"On the contrary. I have every right." Lord Gresham gave Julia an aggrieved look. "Tell him, Miss Wychwood."

Julia met Captain Blunt's eyes. "It was a misunderstanding," she said. "That's all. I'd rather not have a scene."

"Quite right." Mr. Hartford took Lord Gresham's arm. "I'll see you into a carriage. You can make your apologies to Lady Clavering tomorrow."

The earl dragged his feet. "What about Miss Wychwood?"

Mr. Hartford looked to Julia. "Shall I fetch your chaperone?"

"Oh no." She retreated until she felt the bench press against the back of her skirts. "Please don't summon Mrs. Major. It will only inflame the situation. I'll be quite all right here. I only require a moment to compose myself."

"I'll stay with her," Captain Blunt said.

Julia's gaze lurched to his. Her heart skipped a beat.

Mr. Hartford nodded once. "Very well, but don't linger. People will talk." With that, he marched Lord Gresham from the clearing, leaving Julia and Captain Blunt alone in the moonlight.

Entirely alone.

Nothing but the crackling torchlight and the tinkle of the fountain to break the silence between them.

Julia sank down on the marble bench. She breathed deeply of the cool night air, willing her wild pulse to return to something like normal.

Captain Blunt remained where he was, standing at the edge of the clearing. A great menacing beast glowering at her as surely as he had at Lord Gresham.

But no.

There was something else in his gaze now. Something equally unsettling.

"You didn't answer me," he said.

She pressed a hand to her corseted midriff. "I beg your pardon?"

"Are you all right?" he asked again.

"I . . . Yes, but . . . I can't catch my breath."

He came closer. "Is there anything I can do?"

"No. I'm fine," she said. "Just . . . give me a minute."

He paced the grass in front of her as she marshaled her senses. His large frame was wrought with tension.

She studied him covertly, feeling that same unsettling pull of attraction she'd felt on every other occasion they'd met. Strange, that. He wasn't a classically handsome man. His countenance was too saturnine. His features too harshly hewn. Indeed, there was no softness or gentleness in his face at all.

Nowhere except, perhaps, in the shape of his mouth.

His lips curved with a vague sensuality. The faintest suggestion of tenderness, marred forever by the trajectory of his scar.

Once, she'd been afraid of him. But now . . .

Now, she wondered what it would be like to kiss him.

A scandalous notion. She blamed Lord Gresham for putting it into her head. If he hadn't attempted to kiss her, she wouldn't be thinking about kisses at all.

"I'm grateful you and Mr. Hartford arrived when you did," she said when she'd regained some of her composure.

Captain Blunt flashed her a dark glance. Apparently, it had been the wrong thing to say. "Would that I had arrived sooner."

"I'm glad you arrived at all," she said frankly.

He scowled. "Why the devil did you go with him?"

"I could hardly refuse. Not when he was gripping me so tightly and tugging me along with him. He's bigger than me, in case you hadn't noticed. And he *is* an earl."

"Are you certain he didn't hurt you?"

"No. He only scared me a little. I'm fine now."

"Until your next encounter with him." Captain Blunt's jaw tightened. "Will there be another?"

Julia shuddered at the thought. She had no desire to see Lord Gresham ever again. But given the circumstances, her own desires counted for very little. Not when they stood against the adamantine will of her parents.

Good gracious. Mama would be coming home in the morning. And then, who knew what would happen?

Julia had hopes that Anne's return the following day would alleviate some of her anxiety. But even Anne—her dearest friend in all the world—had stated in no uncertain terms that Julia's best chance of escaping Belgrave Square was to marry. The fact was, despite all her ardent opinions, Anne was, in many ways, as much a prisoner of her family as Julia was of her own.

A dispiriting truth.

"I don't know," she said.

"You should refuse to see him again," Captain Blunt advised.

"You imagine I have a choice?"

"*Everyone* has a choice."

"Spoken like a man," Julia said under her breath. She arranged the voluminous skirts of her ball gown with restless hands. "If you knew anything about ladies of my rank, you'd know our own preferences don't matter. Not when it comes to marriage."

Captain Blunt didn't reply. He only paced and muttered to himself. "I knew he would try something like this. From the moment I saw him with you—"

She raised her brows. "You saw us together tonight?"

"Tonight. And at Lady Clifford's musicale. And then again at Lady Holland's dinner. I knew he was the type of man who—"

"I wasn't aware—"

"Of course not," he said harshly. "Your opinions of him must be guided by your father. And if your father approves—"

Julia gave Captain Blunt an alert look. "What do you know of *that*?"

"I know you deserve better." He paused, adding, "And I know Gresham deserves a good thrashing."

She smiled in spite of herself. "He can be in no doubt of your opinion of him. I've never seen you look so fierce as you did when you stepped into the clearing."

He gave a humorless laugh. "Consider yourself fortunate."

"I didn't know you *could* look that way. As though you would tear a man limb from limb."

"I was a soldier, Miss Wychwood. One not known for his pleasant disposition."

Her expression sobered. "Yes. So I've heard." Her hands dropped to her sides, fingers curling around the edge of the marble bench. "Indeed, only this morning, as I was leaving the park, someone told me the most alarming stories about your time in the Crimea."

He stopped pacing and turned to face her. His gaze held hers, but he said nothing. Admitted to nothing.

A frisson of uneasiness made Julia hesitate. She considered dropping the matter altogether. After all, what difference did it make? The two of them weren't going to end up together. But she wanted to know. She *had* to know.

"I wonder how many of those stories are true," she said.

Captain Blunt appeared strangely unmoved. "All of them, very likely."

She stared at him. "But . . . you don't even know what this person said, or how terrible it might have been."

"I don't need to know. If the actions described to you were brutal, cruel, and entirely lacking in humanity, I probably committed them at one time or another." His scarred mouth twisted in a sardonic smile. "I told you, Miss Wychwood. I wasn't a very nice man."

Twelve

The fine hairs lifted on the back of Julia's neck. She hadn't anticipated Captain Blunt admitting to the behavior Lady Heatherton had accused him of.

Perhaps he didn't fully understand the crux of the accusations?

"You can't have done those things," she said.

His black brows lifted a fraction. "Did you not hear me, Miss Wychwood? I deny nothing."

"But you don't know the—"

"What did this person tell you? That I was a monster? I freely own to it." A faint thread of bitterness colored the captain's voice. "Surely, you don't require the particulars."

Julia frowned. She didn't know what response she'd anticipated from him, but it wasn't this scathing admission of guilt. It was too frank. Too brazen.

Something about it wasn't right.

It was that hint of bitterness. That, and something else. An odd glint of iron-forged resolve in his eyes, as if he were a man who was willingly—almost determinedly—confessing to a crime he hadn't committed.

"Ah. I see that you do," he said. "Where to start? Shall I begin with the way I executed prisoners who were trying to escape? Or with the manner in which I dealt with cowardice and insubordination in the ranks?"

He came to stand in front of her. His posture was vaguely combative.

She drew back from him, her fingers gripping tight to the bench.

"There were floggings. Brandings. Other punishments—as creative as they were cruel. Naturally, I insisted on carrying the sentences out myself." He came closer still, his legs brushing the swell of her skirts. "The deserters I sometimes shot, depending on my mood. And for minor infractions—"

"You don't have to tell me," she managed at last. "I don't want to know."

"Don't you? Forgive me. It seemed you were curious."

"No. That is, I am, but only because . . . Because I can't believe—" Julia struggled to give voice to the worst of it. The accusation that he'd been not only excessively harsh in his punishments but unjust, too. Unchristian. "Is it true you beat a soldier nearly to death for giving bread to a dying prisoner?"

Captain Blunt went as still as one of the statues in the Claverings' garden. A strange expression passed over his face. "Who told you that?"

Julia saw no reason to prevaricate. "Viscountess Heatherton. She claims her husband read dispatches during the war."

"Did he, by God." Captain Blunt loomed over her. "What else did her ladyship say about this ill-fated Good Samaritan? Did she tell you his name?"

Julia's heart thudded heavily. "No. Nothing like that. She only said he was the bookish son of a country vicar."

"Bookish." Captain Blunt huffed. "Yes, I suppose he was."

"*Was?*" Her voice dropped to an apprehensive whisper. "You didn't kill him, did you?"

"No, I didn't kill him. But he's dead all the same. Pity. You'd have liked him."

"Why do you say so?"

"He was a dreamer. He loved novels—reading them and writing them." Captain Blunt's expression turned pensive. "He was a brave lad, too. Noble, you might say. All the same, he wasn't made for soldiering."

"How did he die?"

"In the same skirmish that killed the rest of my men. He took a sharpshooter's bullet to the face."

Julia was hard-pressed not to flinch.

Captain Blunt grimaced. "Forgive me. I shouldn't have said that."

"Poor man. It sounds dreadful."

"It was. All of it. Would that I could forget."

She couldn't be certain, but she thought she detected a note of remorse in the captain's words. "Are you sorry?"

"That he's dead?"

"For that, or . . . for any of it?"

He sank down beside her on the bench, as close to her as he'd been in the anteroom during Lady Clifford's musicale. "Every day, every hour, I'm sorrier than I can express."

Julia exhaled the breath she'd been holding. "You regret your conduct? I suppose that's a start."

"My regret is nothing new, Miss Wychwood. I've had years to come to terms with my past. Six long years since I returned to England." His gaze captured hers, solemn and steady in the torchlight. "I want to tell you—and you must believe—that I came back from the Crimea a completely different man. Since that time, I have been doing my utmost to right the wrongs of the past."

She stared up at him, the warmth of compassion stirring in her veins. "The war changed you?"

"Utterly." His face was half-shadowed in the flickering flames, making him look very much the part of a man caught between the forces of light and darkness. "You do believe people can change?"

"I do," she said. "I-I want to."

"Then believe it. I am not now the man that I was then. That person—the soldier you've heard stories about—is dead."

"And in his place?"

"Someone else. Someone who's trying very hard to do the right thing in extremely difficult circumstances."

Julia's compassion for him grew. She was beginning to understand. This was the reason he was committed to raising his illegitimate children. To repairing their home and restoring their birthright. He wasn't some rogue determined to flout society. He was a changed man—a *penitent* man—attempting to make amends.

"Is this why you need a suitable lady at your side?" she asked.

"It is," he said. "Very much so."

The fountain trickled behind them in a melodic splash of water.

And Julia knew—she simply *knew*—that that lady wasn't her. Not because she'd told him so, but because he'd discovered it for himself. It's why he hadn't come to her when she'd arrived in the ballroom. Why he hadn't appeared to claim a dance with her or offered to bring her a cup of punch.

He'd admitted to having seen her. If he had wanted her company, he'd have sought her out. Nothing would have stopped him. But he hadn't. Not until he'd felt honor bound to save her from Lord Gresham.

The realization should have been enough, but a small vulnerable part of herself demanded she verify it absolutely.

"How long have you been here?" she asked. "At the ball, I mean."

"Since half ten."

"I didn't see you. Were you in the cardroom?"

He looked at her, something inexplicable in his eyes. "I was with Miss Throckmorton."

Julia had suspected it already. Indeed, she had nothing to reproach him with. She'd told him they didn't suit. Had asked him to stop pursuing her. Nevertheless . . .

His admission hit her like a blow.

Only last night she'd confessed that she wished to know him better. And he'd promised her she would.

What had changed his mind?

Was it something she'd said during their ride this morning? Some foolish remark or awkward gesture?

Or was it merely that Miss Throckmorton's dowry was greater than her own?

Julia wasn't aware of the exact amount the wealthy toffee heiress was worth, but it must be substantial to tempt Captain Blunt. He'd made no secret that money was his primary concern.

"I thought you might be," she said, forcing a smile. In moments such as these, a lady had little left but her dignity. She was resolved to hold fast to it. "I like her. She's far more suitable for you than I ever was."

"Miss Wychwood." Captain Blunt's voice deepened. "My admiration for you—"

She inwardly winced. "Please don't. You needn't. I'm not sad or disappointed. I'm happy, you see. It's enough for me to have become your friend, and to know you've changed your life for the better. How could I ever be sad knowing that?"

"I hope we *are* friends," he said.

Her smile wavered. She didn't know how much longer she could sustain it. "Yes. We are." She rose from the bench. The urge to escape swelled within her. "Thank you again for coming to my aid."

He stood, frowning at her, as if he had something else he wished to say. Some kind remark, no doubt, meant to soothe her injured pride.

She wanted to flee and save herself the humiliation. But she couldn't run. She was frozen to the spot, waiting for him to speak.

"I'm sorry about Gresham," he said at last. "And I'm sorry you had to see me like that, looking fierce, as you said. I—" He broke off, only to continue gruffly, "I don't want you to be afraid of me."

"I'm not afraid of you. Not anymore." She wasn't. Quite the opposite. "As for how fierce you looked . . . I suppose it was in a worthy cause."

He gazed down at her. "The worthiest."

Heat rose in her cheeks. She was keenly aware of their surroundings. The two of them, standing alone in the clearing, under a moonlit sky. Not even in her dreams could she have conjured a more romantic setting.

"No one's ever defended my honor before," she confessed.

"No? When I arrived, you were doing an excellent job of defending it yourself." He smiled slightly. "It didn't seem fair that I should knock the man down when you'd already injured him."

Her brows notched. "I hope I didn't hurt him too badly. He was only trying to steal a kiss."

"*Only.*" Banked flames smoldered in Captain Blunt's eyes. "You must have objected to the liberty to have responded as you did."

"I didn't object to the liberty. I objected to the man." She explained, a little self-consciously, "A first kiss is important. It's something a girl remembers forever. I'd rather mine not be with Lord Gresham."

Captain Blunt looked at her, silently, steadily. There was an endless pause. And then: "Have you someone else in mind?"

Butterflies fanned their wings in her stomach, fluttering up to her breast, making her heart quiver with romantic expectation.

Unreasonable expectation.

Was he thinking what she was thinking? But he must be to look at her so. He *must* be.

He took a half step toward her. Her silk skirts swirled about his legs. "Do you?" he asked.

"It wouldn't be fair," she said. "Y-you belong to Miss Throckmorton."

He came closer still. His head bent to hers, his voice a rough scrape of sound. "I belong to no one."

She swallowed hard. "Nor do I. Not yet."

"Well then." He brushed his knuckles along the edge of her jaw. The gentle caress sent a tremor of longing through her frame. "Would you like me to be your first?"

She drifted into his touch, swaying toward him almost against her will. Her body's answer was plain enough. *Yes, yes*, it seemed to sing, reaching out to him with every nerve and sinew.

But it was her mind that was in control.

For now, anyway.

She moistened her lips. The unconscious action riveted the entirety of Captain Blunt's formidable attention. "Yes." She admitted it both to him and to herself. "*Yes*. But you needn't feel obliged—"

His mouth captured hers, swallowing what was left of her words.

Julia gave a muffled moan—part pleasure and part surprise.

Oh, heavens.

His lips were as sensual as she'd imagined. They molded to her own, strong and searching, coaxing a response from her.

She yielded to the tantalizing pressure.

It was more than a first kiss. It was an acknowledgment. A physical validation of their unspoken attraction to each other. Something raw and honest and imbued with an undercurrent of soul-quaking passion.

He wasn't particularly suave or seductive about the business. On the contrary, there was a certain masculine ruthlessness to his kiss. It spoke of the soldier he'd been. A man used to taking what he wanted. To prevailing against all odds.

Had he wished to, he could have easily overpowered her.

He didn't.

She was nonetheless overwhelmed by him. A prisoner to sensation; the ridged scar on his lip, the heat of his body, and the curve of his gloved palm cradling her face.

Knees trembling, she lifted her hand to clutch weakly at the lapel of his black evening coat. Her touch seemed to bring him back to his senses.

He broke the kiss, his chest expanding once, twice, as if—like her—he had difficulty getting enough air into his lungs. "There," he rasped, bringing his forehead to rest gently against hers. "Is that a first kiss worthy of remembering?"

Julia inhaled a tremulous breath, taking in the delirious scent of him—bergamot shaving soap, clean linen, and the spice of warm male skin. Her own body was hot all over, her face awash with blushes. *Good Lord.* Captain Blunt had kissed her! Their first kiss.

And their last.

Moisture pricked at the backs of her eyes. It was silly to be so affected. But what lady wouldn't be to have shared such a kiss with such a man?

"I shall remember it for as long as I live," she said.

"So will I, Miss Wychwood," he vowed softly. "So will I."

Thirteen

—✳—

The trouble with an unforgettable kiss was that, within a startlingly short period of time, remembering it wasn't enough. Julia was no sooner back in her bedroom in Belgrave Square than she was consumed by thoughts of repeating the experience.

Her foolish heart couldn't accept that it was never going to happen again.

But it wasn't.

It couldn't.

Henceforward, all Captain Blunt's kisses belonged to Miss Throckmorton.

As Julia sat in front of her dressing table, head bent for Mary to brush her hair, a sickening jealousy sank its claws into her soul.

She was unaccustomed to the sensation.

It wasn't in her nature to be jealous of anyone. Not young ladies who were prettier than she was, or who had experienced more of life. She prided herself on being a good friend. On being genuinely happy for those of her acquaintance more fortunate than she was herself.

But not now. Not at this moment.

"You're quiet tonight," Mary remarked. "And here I thought you'd be chattering my ear off about the ball." She ran another stroke of the brush through Julia's hair. "You're not really ill, are you?"

"I don't know," Julia said. She certainly felt poorly.

It's what she'd told Mrs. Major anyway.

After parting ways with Captain Blunt in the garden, Julia had returned to the house in search of her chaperone. She'd found Mrs. Major at the edge of the ballroom, all atwitter over Lord Gresham's departure.

"*Quite a to-do,*" she'd said. "*The earl over imbibed. He's gone home in a cab.*"

"*I'd like to go home, too,*" Julia had said. "*I'm not feeling at all well.*"

In the Wychwood family, there was no statement more powerful than one intimating ill health. Even Mrs. Major had snapped to attention. The earl had left his carriage at their disposal. She'd wasted no time in bundling Julia into it and seeing her straight back to Belgrave Square.

On arriving, Mrs. Major had accompanied Julia into the hall to leave a note for her father. While writing it, she'd fretted loudly over Lord Gresham's drunkenness, Julia's sickness, and the prospect Sir Eustace would blame Mrs. Major for both.

All the servants had heard her.

"You *are* pale," Mary acknowledged as she set aside the silver-plated brush. "Is there anything I can bring you? A cup of chocolate? Or some warm milk?"

"There's nothing you can do for me," Julia said bleakly. "Not unless . . ."

Once again, she thought of Miss Throckmorton and her boundless fortune.

Was that the reason Captain Blunt had chosen her instead of Julia? Not because of Julia's personal failings but because of her financial ones?

There was only one way to find out.

"Not unless you can discover how much Miss Daphne Throckmorton is worth," she said.

Mary's brows shot up. "That toffee heiress everyone's talking about?"

Julia wasn't surprised Mary had heard of her. As the longest-serving servant in the Wychwood household, Mary prided herself on knowing all the fashionable comings and goings in Mayfair.

"Hmm. I suppose I could find out." She gave her a quizzical look. "Why do you want to know?"

"Because," Julia said, "the information might make me feel better." Or not.

Either way, at least she'd know the truth.

"The state you're in, you don't need information." Mary examined Julia's face in the mirror. "What you need is bed. Or a doctor. You sure you don't want Jenkins to send for one?"

"No. No doctors." Julia didn't wait for her maid to plait her hair, or even to draw back the coverlet on her bed. Rising from her dressing table, she crossed the room and climbed up onto the mattress, slipping beneath the covers to burrow her head in her pillow.

Mary followed after her, her brow creased with uncharacteristic worry. "What's wrong, miss? It's naught to do with the earl, is it? I heard as how he was in his cups."

"He was."

"Did he take liberties?"

Julia made no reply.

Mary tsked and shook her head. "There's some men made foolish by drink. You can't judge 'em too harshly."

"What does it matter?" Julia grumbled. "He could be the drunkest man in Christendom, and if he proposed, I'd still be obliged to marry him."

"You'll be a countess," Mary reminded her.

"I don't want to be a countess."

"What do you want, then? To stay in this room all day? In this bed, reading your romances?" Mary cast a disparaging glance at the teetering stack of J. Marshland novels on Julia's bedside table. "Much more of that and people will say you're an eccentric."

"They already say that."

"You want them to say worse?"

Julia turned over onto her back. "What I want is for a gentleman to love me like a hero in a story. Someone who doesn't care about my dowry or my pedigree or whether or not I can give him an heir. I want a gentleman who'll take me in my underclothes, exactly as I am."

Mary scoffed. "You can't compare your life to one of them novels. Haven't I told you? None of that's real."

"I know it isn't real. If it were, I wouldn't have endured nearly three seasons only to receive an offer from a man like Lord Gresham. And now I must accept him because Papa has said I must."

And because no one else wants me.

Her vision blurred in spite of herself. "I suppose I am sick. Pray leave me alone, Mary."

In the absence of her friends, Julia had so far refrained from claiming illness to avoid her responsibilities. It was an unsustainable excuse. But Mama was arriving in the morning. There would be Lord Gresham's suit to contend with. And then, as if that weren't enough, there was to be a picnic in Richmond Park. Everyone who was anyone would be in attendance. Miss Throckmorton, certainly. And if she was there, Captain Blunt was sure to be present as well.

Julia couldn't face him. Not after that kiss. She couldn't face any of it.

She'd rather stay in bed, safe and secure, huddled within the draperies of her four-poster. If the price of that security was a visit from the odious Dr. Cordingley, then so be it.

Julia was awakened in the morning not by her maid but by her mother. Seated on the edge of the bed, Lady Wychwood was clothed in a black silk carriage dress, as if she'd only just arrived from the railway station. She stared down at Julia with an expression so severe Julia was tempted to close her eyes again and feign sleep.

Once acknowledged as handsome, Mama's face had long since been etched by unhappiness and infirmity. Her features were drawn, her skin sallow, and her eyes prone to watering—a consequence of the camphor oil she used to alleviate the aches in her limbs.

"Awake at last," she said in tones of deep disapproval. "Would that I had had the luxury of sleeping late this morning."

Julia made no effort to sit up. She remained tucked safe in bed, her white cotton nightgown rumpled and her long unplaited hair tangled about her shoulders.

Mama's gaze narrowed. "Nothing to say for yourself? Very well. You can listen."

Julia's stomach sank. Her mother's lectures could be as dismal as her father's.

"My journey's overtaxed me," Mama said. "I must retire to my room before I do myself a permanent injury. But know this: Your father may have tolerated your obstinate carrying on, but I will not. If a gentleman as illustrious as the Earl of Gresham has indicated an interest in you, you will do your duty, or by heaven you'll feel the consequences for it."

A rare flicker of defiance sparked in Julia's breast. "I'd rather take the consequences."

Mama's eyes kindled. "Ungrateful girl! To think of how I suffered to bring you into this world, sacrificing my health, very nearly my life, and all so you could defy me in this fashion. Have you no sense of what you owe me? Of what you owe your poor father? That I should have birthed such a thankless child!"

"Why did you?" Julia asked. "You needn't have married Papa. You had a fortune in your own right."

"I did my duty," Mama snapped back. "I did what my family required of me. And so shall you."

Julia regarded her mother in silence. Mama had been but seventeen when she'd been betrothed to Papa, the coddled only son of a wealthy family, decades older than his young bride, and prone to prolonged bouts of illness.

In the aftermath of Julia's birth, his perpetually frail condition had seemed to rub off on her mother.

Julia could scarcely remember a time when Mama hadn't been the victim of megrims, the vapors, or the ague. Her list of ailments had grown over the years, leading to a great deal of time spent alone in her rooms, or away from home, cloistered in a luxurious hotel in one of the fashionable spa towns.

As Julia had grown older, she'd often wondered if her mother had used the excuse of poor health as a means of securing her privacy and independence. She and Papa had never had another child. They kept separate rooms and maintained largely separate lives. It was the closest thing to Mama being a widow. And Papa couldn't complain, not when his own health was in such a precarious state—though he regularly lamented his lack of a male heir.

Women had so little power in life to control their destinies. Julia had experienced the lack of it firsthand.

She was experiencing it now.

If claiming illness could offer her a fraction of the same freedom it had given her mother, Julia didn't see why she shouldn't take advantage of it.

"I can't do my duty in this condition," she said. "I'm not able to do anything."

Mama's lips thinned. "Maidenish nerves, I don't wonder."

"It isn't that."

"What is it, then? Mrs. Major claims you were indisposed last night, but she failed to report the specifics of your complaint."

"My stomach aches," Julia said. "And I have pains in my chest." That much was true. Her heart felt as though it had been trod on by an elephant. "I need a few days of rest to restore myself."

Mama expression became pensive. "Your eyes *are* swollen. And your nose is red. Dr. Cordingley warned me about danger to the mucous membranes in those with imbalanced humors."

The only danger Julia was in was from excessive weeping. She'd cried last night into her pillow. She felt a little like crying now, truth be told. But she was done with feeling sorry for herself. Done with pining over Captain Blunt.

If she could just be alone with one of her books, the world would right itself eventually.

"Have you a fever?" Mama pressed the back of her hand to Julia's brow. She withdrew it, frowning. "I'm so feverish myself I can hardly tell." She stood. "I'll summon the physician."

Julia's pulse quickened with apprehension. It was one thing to contemplate bloodletting in the abstract. But faced with the imminent possibility of it, her composure began to crack. "I don't need Dr. Cordingley. I only need a few days in bed."

"Nonsense," Mama replied. "You'll feel better after a good bloodletting."

Julia did not, in fact, feel better after a good bloodletting. She felt weak, light-headed, and entirely incapable of defending herself against Dr. Cordingley's backward opinions on women's reading habits.

"Novels are at the root of it, mark my words," he said as he packed away his brass scarificator. The octagonal brass casing of the horrible instrument housed a mechanism of spring-loaded blades used to create cuts in the flesh. It was more efficient than a lancet, allowing for greater blood flow with one strike.

And there had been so much blood this time. By the time the procedure was completed, Julia was scarcely able to lower her bandaged arm from the bleeding bowl back to the bed.

"Reading novels promotes an excess of heat in the body," Dr. Cordingley went on. "Fevers, palpitations, and so forth. It cannot be permitted in the female sex. In young ladies like your daughter, the passions must be repressed rather than stimulated."

Mama sat in a chair near the door, a lace handkerchief pressed over her mouth. She nodded her head in agreement. "As you say, Doctor."

Dr. Cordingley cast a disdainful look at the stack of novels on Julia's bedside table. "You'd do well to dispose of these, and any others in her possession."

"I shall," Mama said.

"No." Julia managed a faint objection. "You can't. They're mine."

"Your parents will do what's necessary, Miss Wychwood," Dr. Cordingley replied sternly.

"They're *mine*," Julia repeated. "*I* bought them."

"Never mind who bought them," Mama retorted. "If the doctor says you mustn't read them anymore, you won't read them, and there's an end to it."

Dr. Cordingley was complacent. "It's as I've told you, Lady Wychwood. Novel reading pollutes the body and corrupts the mind. Do you wonder your daughter finds herself in such a sad condition?"

"Will your treatment be enough to cure her, Doctor?" Mama asked.

"To start." Dr. Cordingley snapped shut his leather medical bag. "I recommend a second course of venesection to rebalance her humors."

Mama didn't appear alarmed by the suggestion. She had a zealot's faith in the medical profession. "Administered when?"

"An hour from now."

Julia struggled to draw breath to object. Her room was sweltering hot. Mary had been placed in charge of keeping the fire stoked. She stood near the hearth, her face gone white. She knew as well as Mama that Julia had never yet undergone two consecutive rounds of bloodletting.

"Mama," Julia said weakly.

"Be quiet, child," Mama chided. "Doctor? May I offer you some refreshment?"

"You are very good, my lady."

Mama rose from her chair. "You'll understand why I can't join you.

My own health has deteriorated to such a degree, I fear I haven't the strength."

"You traveled straight from Bath?" Dr. Cordingley crossed the room to her side, giving her his full attention. "I wouldn't have advised it."

"I but obeyed my husband's command," Mama said. "To my own detriment." She opened the door to leave without sparing a look in Julia's direction.

"You're a dutiful wife, my lady, and a caring mother. Will you permit me to examine you? I may have something I can prescribe for your relief." The doctor glanced back at Mary. "Attend to your mistress, girl. I'll return in an hour for her next treatment."

The door shut behind them both.

Julia felt the heavy air stir as Mary came to stand beside her.

"Oh, miss." Mary's usually no-nonsense voice quavered with uncertainty. "If you're pretending, I swear I'll—"

"Mary . . ." Julia looked at her maid. "Don't let them."

Mary all but threw up her hands. "What can I do? He's a doctor. He must know what he's about." She fussed with the coverlet. "He's right about those novels. I've told you so dozens of times, haven't I?"

Julia couldn't manage a reply. She was too tired. Too weary of it all.

The last time Dr. Cordingley had bled her, it had been taxing, but she'd got through it with aplomb. Within a few hours, she'd been tucked up in bed reading a delicious novel that featured a missing will, an honorable highwayman, and a courageous damsel on the run. Compared to the pleasure of the characters' romance, her own loss of blood hadn't mattered at all.

But she hadn't reckoned for Dr. Cordingley.

She hadn't known that, with subsequent bleedings, the amount of precious fluid taken would increase beyond all tolerable proportion.

What if she should succumb to the treatment? What if she should die?

In her bleary-headed state, she didn't know how many of her fears were real and how many were a product of her excess imagination.

Perhaps she *had* read too many novels.

"Miss?" Mary said. "Didn't you hear me?"

Julia opened her eyes, uncertain when she'd closed them. She felt as if she was waking from a fever dream. "What is it?"

"I said I found out about that toffee heiress for you. You asked how much she was worth. The answer's forty thousand pounds. And I didn't even have to leave the house to discover it."

"How . . . ?"

"You'll never credit it. Remember Florence? The maid Sir Eustace turned off last month? Her who used to be called Jane? She's a parlor maid in Green Street now, at the very house Miss Throckmorton's putting up at. Cook had tea with her not two days ago. It was she who told me."

Of course Julia remembered their former maid. Jane Six, she'd been called. Papa had dismissed her for gossiping. But it wasn't the information Mary had imparted that stuck in Julia's head. It was the fact that the girl's name was Florence. Julia hadn't realized.

The knowledge provoked a swell of regret.

What right had Mama and Papa to steal the servants' names? And why hadn't Julia rebelled at the practice?

She hadn't spoken up. She hadn't taken a stand.

She'd gone along with her parents for the same reason she always went along with their edicts—part filial obedience and part fear. The world wasn't a kind place for young ladies who were shy and vulnerable. Ladies who were often too anxious for company. Julia had always believed she was safest at home.

But she wasn't.

Perhaps she'd never been.

And if she wasn't safe here, where would she be safe? She had nowhere to go. No relations to take her in. Not even her friends could assist her. Not in any substantial way. Anne, Stella, and Evelyn had their own battles to fight.

Julia would have to fight her own battles, too. A daunting prospect.

Though not an impossible one. She had a vague idea where she could begin.

"Forty thousand pounds," she murmured. It was a generous sum for a dowry, but not as sizable as Julia had feared. Her eyes drifted shut, her pulse slowing to a crawl in the oppressive heat of the room. "I wonder if he knows . . ."

Fourteen

The day after the Claverings' ball, Jasper made the hour-long journey to Richmond Park in company with Lord Ridgeway. Lady Desmond was hosting a picnic there, and guests were expected to arrive by noon. Most of fashionable society would be in attendance, Miss Throckmorton among them.

"The weather's clear, thank God," Ridgeway remarked as they disembarked from his carriage. "Last picnic I attended, we had all of thirty minutes to eat before the rain started. A dashed nuisance. And I'd brought my curricle, too." He tapped the closed body of the coach with his silver-topped walking stick. "Lesson learned."

Passing through the gates, the grounds of the park spread out before them. Formerly a royal hunting preserve, it was nearly ten miles in circumference, studded with ancient trees, glistening waterways, and antlered deer grazing peacefully on the grassy slopes.

Jasper settled his hat on his head. He'd worn a black suit, just as he always did. He was in the minority. Most of the gentlemen present had favored sack coats and garish plaid trousers. The ladies, by contrast, were in soft whites and pastels, with flowing skirts and wide bell-shaped sleeves. His gaze slid over them.

She wasn't here.

"Try not to look so disappointed," Ridgeway said under his breath as they trudged onward. "The ladies will take offense."

Jasper cast him a dark glance.

He was in a dangerous mood. Since returning from the ball last night, he'd been unable to think straight. Unable to sleep or even to breathe without the overwhelming weight of his unhappy situation bearing down on him.

It was intolerable.

On rising this morning, he'd saddled Quintus and gone for a bruising ride in Hyde Park. He'd told himself it wasn't because he hoped to see Miss Wychwood. And yet he'd looked for her all along Rotten Row. She hadn't been there.

And now she wasn't here.

A fact that made him want to roar with frustration.

Damn and blast it all to hell.

What had he been thinking last night? As soon as he'd known her dowry was out of reach, he should have let the thought of her go. He'd had years of practice in forgetting. In hardening his heart against all finer feeling.

And then he'd seen her in the moonlight. He'd stood over her, listening to her tell him she'd never been kissed before. All reason had left him.

He hadn't planned to kiss her. And when he had, he hadn't meant to linger over the business with such passionate attention. But the moment his head bent to hers, all his hard-won resolve went straight out the window.

Her lips were so soft and voluptuous, half parting beneath his own with trembling anticipation. Their breath mingled, softly, sweetly, and in that moment . . . God help him, he'd felt something very near to heaven.

But it was over now. Miss Wychwood realized that as well as he did. If she hadn't, she'd have been in Hyde Park this morning.

She'd be here now.

A ridiculous part of him had hoped she would be.

Gazing out over the sun-filtered landscape, he couldn't help wondering how he would proceed if things were different.

If *he* was different.

He'd spent the past six years wondering—to no avail. The life he was living was his own now, for better or worse. The life of an ex-soldier encumbered with a failing estate and three illegitimate children.

The fact was, if given the choice, he wouldn't change it even if he could.

Had he never gone to Yorkshire, Charlie and Alfred would have remained in the workhouse. On Dolly's death, Daisy would have ended up there, too. The life expectancy for orphans in such places didn't bear speaking of. The three of them might have died.

No. Jasper couldn't regret his actions. From the moment he'd set foot in Goldfinch Hall, he'd been bound by the dictates of honor. Like it or not, he recognized his duty.

"I'm only concerned with one lady's opinion," he said.

"Quite. Miss Throckmorton is certain to be here somewhere. Ah. There she is, by the pond with Miss Bingham." Ridgeway set off in their direction. "Best hurry. Aldershott is upon them. He may have finally decided he can stomach the taint of the shop."

"She'd do well to accept him." Jasper walked alongside Ridgeway across the grass. A warm breeze whispered over the banks of the pond, stirring the fragrance of heather and flowering meadowsweet. "He's young, well-bred, and unencumbered. All he lacks is a fortune."

"All *you* lack is a fortune," Ridgeway retorted.

Didn't Jasper know it. At the moment, his lack of funds was at the root of everything that was wrong in his world. If not for want of money, he'd be free to pursue whom he pleased. "It doesn't follow that Miss Throckmorton will be willing to grant me hers. She's shown no particular interest in my attentions."

"No? She looks at you a good deal. Granted, not as much as Miss Wychwood did. But a man can't have everything."

Or anything, Jasper thought bitterly.

Ridgeway shot him a narrow look. "Is this you brooding? I confess, I don't much care for it. You've little enough to recommend you already."

"I'm not brooding," Jasper said sourly. At least, he was trying not to—and failing miserably, he didn't doubt. His mood was too foul, his heart too heavy. He regretted having come. He was in no fit state for this cold-blooded charade.

"Good. Because you have an excellent chance with Miss Throckmorton. She may act as though she has the luxury of choice, but she's as eager to tie the knot as you are. For a cit, a gentleman of your stature would be a prize. All you need do is make yourself moderately agreeable—"

"Yes. So you've said." Jasper was ill-disposed to make himself agreeable to anyone. But he was aware of how forbidding he appeared when he was in a black mood. And he was already forbidding enough. As they approached Miss Throckmorton and the others, he made an effort to school his features.

Miss Throckmorton and Miss Bingham were kneeling on a blanket beneath a tree on the bank, unpacking a picnic hamper. Aldershott had just sat down beside them. He was a fair-haired gentleman, with a thin frame and an angular face.

"Blunt. Ridgeway," he greeted the two men stiffly. "You're not thinking of joining us?"

"Do, please," Miss Throckmorton said. "I brought plenty for everyone."

"Eating already?" Ridgeway asked.

"No, indeed. We're only claiming our spot. Within another half hour, all the best ones will be taken. Lady Desmond's invited half of Mayfair."

"Splendid," Ridgeway said. "I prefer a bit of exercise before luncheon. Come, Miss Bingham. Shall we have a stroll around the pond?"

Miss Bingham giggled. "Oh yes. Let's." She took Ridgeway's hand, allowing him to assist her up. "You don't mind, Miss Throckmorton?"

"Not at all. I daresay we could all use a walk to whet our appetites." Miss Throckmorton stood without assistance. She collected her delicate lace parasol and opened it over her head. "If you wouldn't mind, gentlemen?"

Jasper offered her his arm. She tucked her hand through it as they moved to join Ridgeway and Miss Bingham. Aldershott walked with them on Miss Throckmorton's opposite side.

The pond was one of many in Richmond Park. Fed by a spring, the still surface reflected the lush azaleas and rhododendrons surrounding it, their bright blooms fading as spring drifted inexorably toward summer.

Old oaks provided intermittent shade along the wide path that circled the water. They'd gone halfway around, engaged in sporadic conversation, when Miss Bingham glanced back from her place on Ridgeway's arm to frown at Jasper and Aldershott as they flanked her friend.

"I abhor odd numbers," she said. "Such a pity Miss Wychwood was too ill to come. If she'd been here, we'd have been perfectly matched."

Jasper very nearly froze where he stood. It was only with an effort that he continued walking alongside Miss Throckmorton. Though his emotions roiled, his voice was one of creditable calm. "Miss Wychwood is ill?"

Miss Throckmorton made a soft sound of sympathy. "Terribly ill, apparently. It's dreadful, really. I understood she was frail, but I'd no notion it was so serious."

This time he did stop, coming to an abrupt halt on the path. His heart stopped right along with him. Whatever calmness he'd managed up to now vanished into the ether. "What do you mean? How serious?"

Miss Throckmorton's hand fell from his arm. She turned to face him. Ridgeway and Miss Bingham turned as well, doubling back to join them.

"Miss Bingham and I called on her this morning in Belgrave Square," Miss Throckmorton said. "I'd hoped she might agree to accompany us to the park. But just as I raised my hand to knock on the door, it opened and a man in an old-fashioned frock coat came out."

"Dr. Cordingley," Miss Bingham said with an eloquent shudder.

Ridgeway frowned. "That old vampire?"

"He's never met a patient who didn't need a bleeding," Aldershott remarked unhelpfully. "The older generation swears by him."

Miss Throckmorton tipped her parasol to better shade her face. "Indeed. He told us he'd given Miss Wychwood two consecutive treatments this morning and that she wasn't fit to receive anyone."

Jasper stared at Miss Throckmorton. *Two bleedings?* A sense of icy foreboding settled over him.

"He was very severe, too," Miss Bingham added. "I swear I saw Miss Wychwood's blood on the cuff of his sleeve. It was horrible."

Ridgeway looked at Jasper. And then he sighed. "If you'll excuse us, ladies. Aldershott."

Jasper scarcely heard him make his excuses. He was already stalking off across the park.

Ridgeway trotted to catch up with him. "Damn it, Blunt."

"Don't try to stop me," Jasper said.

"Stop you from what? What do you plan on doing? If she's as ill as they say—"

"She isn't. And if she is, it's because they've made her so. They don't understand—"

"Yes, and I suppose you do. You who have known her all of two months. Even less if you discount the occasions on which she was terrified of the sight of you, fleeing like a frightened rabbit every time you crossed her path."

"It isn't like that anymore. She—" Jasper broke off with a scowl. "Why the devil am I explaining myself to you?"

"Because I'm the only friend you've got." Ridgeway kept pace with him as he strode over the grass, through the gates, and to the line of carriages in the street. "Has it not occurred to you that perhaps her parents know best?"

Jasper flashed him a sardonic glance.

"No. Of course they don't." Ridgeway sighed again. His carriage was but a few yards away. The coachman had already unhooked the horses and was walking them along the grass. "Hitch them back up, Rufus. Captain Blunt's returning to Mayfair."

"It isn't necessary." Jasper wasn't averse to taking a hansom or an omnibus. One means of transportation was as good as the other. So long as he got there as quickly as possible. "I'll find another way back."

"Yes, because that's the definition of heroic, arriving at a lady's home in a hired cab."

Jasper grudgingly waited for Ridgeway's coachman to ready the carriage. "This isn't heroism. This is selfishness. It's for my own peace of mind." It was partially true. He couldn't rest until he knew she'd be all right.

"Whatever it is . . . it's not in your best interest. Nor in the interest of those bastards of yours. You do know that?"

Jasper knew it. By God, how he knew it. "I only want to see her. To assure myself things aren't as bad as Miss Throckmorton said."

"Sir Eustace and Lady Wychwood aren't likely to invite you in."

"I don't expect they will," Jasper acknowledged grimly. "But if history is any indication, the pair of them will be confined to their beds. It's their servants I'll have to deal with. Given the rate of turnover in their ranks, I can't imagine any of them are very loyal. A decent bribe should gain me admittance to any room in the house."

Ridgeway's eyes shone with appreciation. "And to think you once objected to being ruthless where women were concerned."

Jasper thrust his hands into his pockets, pacing as the coachman finished hitching up the horses. Perhaps he *was* being ruthless. If so, it was in a good cause.

He'd seen men die of blood loss in the Crimea. Strong men, laid low from battle wounds or fever, bled by some well-meaning quack who achieved nothing more than draining the last remnants of life from them.

Miss Wychwood was no soldier. She wasn't strong. Not as strong as a man. If Cordingley had administered two courses of bloodletting . . .

Jasper's chest tightened painfully. He'd only just found her. A woman who spoke to his soul. To his secret self. Not to the monstrous man everyone believed him to be, but to the man he truly was. It was one thing to give her up for the children's sake. But for her to be ill, or worse—

The prospect sent a stab of helpless anguish through him. It burned like acid, eating away at his ironclad self-restraint.

He couldn't think of losing her.

"*Have* you a decent bribe?" Ridgeway asked.

"On my person? No. I'll have to—"

"Here." Ridgeway withdrew his purse and extracted a handful of banknotes. He passed them to Jasper. "That sum should be sufficient. Especially when coupled with your menacing presence."

Jasper folded the notes into an inner pocket of his coat, frowning. "I don't know why you insist on bestirring yourself on my account."

"For my brother's sake," Ridgeway said. "Clearly."

Jasper well remembered Ridgeway's brother. Rupert Grainger had been a lanky young fellow with a broad smile and a contagious laugh— characteristics that had faded the longer they'd remained in the Crimea. He'd died in the skirmish at the fall of Sebastopol. An easy death in comparison to the hell he'd been living through as a soldier serving under the merciless Captain Blunt.

"I was no friend to your brother," Jasper said.

Ridgeway looked at him steadily. "His letters said otherwise."

Jasper went still as the significance of Ridgeway's words sank into his brain.

Good God. Was it possible? Had the viscount somehow ascertained the truth?

A month ago, the mere suggestion would have shaken Jasper's world to its foundation. He would have been alarmed or, perhaps, even afraid.

Not today.

In truth, all he felt was a vague sense of relief.

"How long have you known?" he asked.

"I don't know anything," Ridgeway said. "But I suspected almost from the beginning."

"And still you befriended me. Why—"

"I told you. For my brother's sake. And for my own, I suppose. It amuses me to see how you navigate this quagmire you've got yourself into." Ridgeway brushed a speck of dust from his sleeve. "I wonder, has it all been worth it?"

"It might be," Jasper said. "If I can have her."

"Then take her, by all means," Ridgeway replied. "No one's stopping you. Who would dare? You're the infamous bloody Hero of the Crimea."

Fifteen

⧫

The dimly lit interior of the Wychwoods' house in Belgrave Square was as cloyingly overwarm as on Jasper's previous visit. Long shadows fell across the entrance hall, stretching out to darken the curving oak staircase that led to the floors above. It was only two o'clock in the afternoon, but one would never know it. Not with the windows covered and the gaslight turned down.

Again, Jasper had the impression of entering a dwelling where a person had died. The sensation did nothing to allay the sharp thrum of anxiety that had accompanied him all the way back to Mayfair.

He followed the Wychwoods' yellow-liveried footman up the steps. The same footman who had opened the door to him last time—a knowing fellow of passing middle age.

A fellow who was now several pounds richer.

Jasper had anticipated that a bribe would work to his benefit. He hadn't realized just how effective it would be. Two ten-pound notes later and the footman was telling him everything except where the silver was stored.

"Dr. Cordingley's never bled any of the family twice in one visit," he said. "Not since I've been here. And Lady Wychwood and Sir Eustace are too ill to sit vigil. They've both withdrawn to their beds in opposite wings of the house. It's fallen on Miss Wychwood's maid, Mary, to see to things."

"Is her maid with her now?" Jasper asked.

"She is." The footman led him down a carpeted hallway. "She's to summon the doctor back if Miss Wychwood takes a turn for the worse. She won't like it one bit, me bringing you up here."

Jasper didn't give a damn what the maid liked or disliked. Nevertheless, as the footman knocked on the large wood-paneled door of Miss Wychwood's bedchamber, Jasper stood back, silent.

The door opened a crack. "What is it now?"

"A gentleman's come to see Miss Wychwood."

"Does she look like she's receiving?" the maid answered back tartly. She moved to close the door.

Jasper caught it before it shut. At the sight of him, the maid's eyes goggled. "Mary, is it?"

"Yes, sir. Captain Blunt, sir." She took several steps back into the room as he entered. "You can't be in here. It's not proper."

A grand four-poster bed stood behind her. The blue damask draperies were half-drawn, concealing the bed's occupant from view.

Jasper's heart thumped hard. "No doubt. But I *am* here. I'll not leave until I see her."

Mary briefly stood in his way. Like the footman, she was a servant of middle age. A sensible servant. She didn't seem inclined to scream the house down. "You'll ruin her," she warned. "If anyone should hear of this—"

"Then best make certain they don't." Jasper walked around her.

The bedchamber wasn't as dark as the rest of the house. Sunlight glimmered through the gaps in the curtains, and a fire crackled in the grate of an ornate marble fireplace. Silk-covered walls shimmered in the light cast from the flames. The same light that illuminated the interior of the bed.

On reaching it, Jasper stopped short.

Inside the heavy draperies of the four-poster, tucked beneath a quilt, Julia Wychwood lay sleeping, half-propped against a plump pile of pillows. Her unbound hair spilled around her shoulders in a wild tangle of ebony waves.

A lump formed in his throat.

He'd never seen her with her hair down. Had never dared imagine it. Such a sight was reserved for a lady's husband.

Or her lover.

He was keenly aware he was neither.

Knowing that—accepting it—made his presence all the more unseemly.

He shouldn't be here, looking upon her in this vulnerable state. Not when she couldn't consent to it. Not when her eyes where closed, her black lashes fanning over her pale cheeks.

And she was deathly pale; her beautiful face drained and still, almost waxen in repose. The white of her prim cotton nightgown was vibrant in comparison.

"Is she—" His words failed him.

"She's resting," Mary said in a stern undertone. "Best leave her be. If Sir Eustace or Lady Wychwood were to—"

Jasper silenced the maid with a look. The footman had said Sir Eustace and his wife were in separate wings of the house. Neither would know Jasper was here. Not so long as the servants kept their heads.

"Come away, Mary," the footman said. "Let the man have a moment."

Mary gave the footman a look that would have withered an orchard. She joined him by the closed door, one eye still on her mistress as the two of them engaged in a whispered argument. Their words drifted to Jasper's ears in broken scraps.

"—by bringing him here?" the maid was demanding.

"—no romance in your soul?" the footman returned.

"—not romance. Madness. Only a fool—"

Jasper ignored them. A spoon-back chair was drawn up beside Miss Wychwood's bed. He sat down on it, scanning her face.

She showed no signs of physical distress. Nothing save the pallor of her skin and the faint sheen of perspiration on her brow, dampening the fine wisps of hair at the edge of her hairline.

It wasn't enough to reassure him.

Her arms lay outside the coverlet, one at her side and one draped loosely across her midsection. The long, ruffled sleeves of her nightgown obscured any evidence of Dr. Cordingley's treatment. But knowing it existed—that she'd been cut and hurt in such a barbaric manner—tore at Jasper's soul.

He gently took her hand. It was warm and silky soft, and so damnably small in comparison to his own. A surge of protectiveness tightened his grip.

Miss Wychwood's lashes stirred. Her eyes opened slowly. She looked up at him, brows drawn in confusion. "Captain Blunt," she murmured. "Is it really you?"

"It is," he said.

And he felt, all at once, the full impropriety of being here.

Good Lord. What must she be thinking? To wake seeing his battle-scarred face looming over her? In her bedchamber of all places. A room into which no gentleman unrelated by blood or marriage would ever dare enter. Not even if a lady was at death's door.

But she wasn't dying.

He saw that now. She was only drained and weak. Urgently in need of the restorative power of sleep, just as her maid had insisted.

And what had he done?

He'd traveled here at breakneck speed, bribing his way into her rooms like some desperate character from a penny novel.

"Forgive me," he said gruffly. "I heard you were ill. I had to come."

"I'm not ill. Just . . . tired."

"Of course. I'll leave you to rest." Rising from the chair, he loosened his grasp, expecting her to withdraw her hand. She didn't. Quite the reverse. Her fingers curled around his with a trust that entirely disarmed him.

"Please don't go," she said.

His chest constricted with emotion. He sank back into his seat. "I won't. Not if you don't wish me to."

She was quiet, lids heavy as he held her hand. He began to think she was nodding off again, when her lashes lifted and her eyes lit on something to his right.

Jasper followed her gaze to the round bedside table. It was stacked with books. Five of them altogether, bound in familiar green cloth. He might have seen them on his approach to the bed if his attention hadn't been fixed solely on Miss Wychwood.

Looking at them now, a strange sense of rightness came over him. As if the hand of destiny had reached out across time and space, bringing him to this moment. For an instant, he could almost believe in fate.

"My J. Marshland novels," she said.

"So I see." He turned back to her. Somehow, he managed a smile. "Have you finished them already?"

"Not yet. After Dr. Cordingley's visit . . . I haven't felt much like holding a book."

Jasper's expression sobered. "Why did your parents summon him?"

She lifted her shoulder in the barest suggestion of a shrug. "I said I was poorly. It wasn't serious, but . . ."

"He bled you. Twice."

"He thinks I read too many novels." She cast a rueful look at the stack of books on her bedside table. "Perhaps I do."

Jasper's temper flickered. "No one with any sense believes that reading novels promotes illness in women. Not anymore."

Granted, it had been a popular belief once. One predicated more on the fear that novel reading would take time away from a woman's household duties than on the fear that the content of the novel would do her actual harm. That hadn't stopped physicians, quacks, and writers of dubious medical tracts from attributing all manner of illnesses—both mental and physical—to the overstimulation provided by a good work of fiction.

"Dr. Cordingley believes it," she said. "And my parents would never contradict a doctor. They'd allow him to do anything he wanted to me. It wouldn't matter if I objected."

"*Did* you object?"

"Yes."

Jasper's shoulders tensed. He had to make an effort not to grip her hand even tighter.

"I'm afraid my situation has become untenable," she said. "It has been for a long while, only I was too stupid to recognize it." A frown puckered her brow. "I wish I had. I'd have had more time."

He scowled at her. "Don't talk that way. You do have time. You're not dying."

She smiled faintly. "Of course not. I only meant . . . I thought there was time before I'd have to make a decision about what I'm to do next. And I must *do* something. A lady can't spend her whole life being pulled along by the current. Not if she's to find any degree of happiness." Her eyes met his. "I do so want to be happy."

His heart ached with unrequited affection for her. It deepened his voice to a rasp. "What would make you happy?"

She didn't reply. She only looked at him.

How she looked at him.

Jasper covered her hand with both of his. He brought it to his lips. "Miss Wychwood—"

"You're in my bedchamber, Captain Blunt. My name is Julia."

Julia.

It was the greatest intimacy she'd allowed him. Almost as great as the kiss they'd shared at the ball. To call someone by their given name was to know them as only their closest friends and family knew them.

He granted her the same privilege, such that he was able. He wished it might be more. "Jasper."

"Jasper." Her mouth curved. "I didn't realize. Aside from rumors about the war, no one knows anything about you."

"Thank God for that." It was bad enough that Ridgeway should suspect the truth. Jasper couldn't afford for anyone else to do so. Not even her.

She searched his face. "But you've changed since then. For the better. You told me so yourself. You're not cruel anymore. You're not unkind."

"I try very hard not to be."

"Can you promise that? That you're a different man now?"

Jasper felt her question as much as heard it. He didn't know whether to laugh or to weep. "My dear girl, that I can promise you absolutely."

"Good," she said. "Good."

A fleeting smile tugged at his mouth. "Is my reformed character of such importance to you?"

"It is. Because it prompts me to ask you something of a more personal nature." Her fingers pressed gently around his. "I was wondering . . . Would you like to marry me?"

Jasper stared down at her. He didn't know what he'd expected her to ask, but it hadn't been *that*. The question hit him like a prizefighter's blow to the chest. He couldn't move. Couldn't speak. He could only look at her, dumbstruck, certain he must have misheard.

She went on in the same earnest voice. "I know you've a preference for Miss Throckmorton. You must think her dowry greater than mine. But it isn't. I have one hundred thousand pounds coming to me on my marriage. It's more than twice what hers is. Did you know that?"

He hadn't known. Ridgeway had said Julia was in expectation of fifty thousand pounds upon her marriage, not one hundred. Either way, it made little difference. Without her father's permission, Jasper would get none of it.

That fact should have been foremost in his mind. But sitting at Julia's bedside, her hand cradled in both of his, all he could think of was having her.

And why shouldn't he if she was offering herself to him?

She was so sweet. So beautiful. Like an enchanted princess in a fairy tale; lying there, rosy lips half-parted in expectation, waiting for true love's kiss to break the spell.

It wasn't meant to be him. She deserved someone better. Kinder, gentler. A man who could give himself to her absolutely, with no dark secrets. No sinister past.

Jasper was keenly aware that, in this story, he was the villain, not the hero. It should have stopped him. And perhaps it might have if he'd been nobler.

But he wasn't noble.

He was tired and bitter—so ungodly bitter at the injustice of it. After all he'd suffered. All he'd sacrificed. Fate couldn't be so cruel as to offer up his heart's desire and expect him to refuse it.

"Did you?" she asked again.

He didn't answer her, asking instead: "What if there were no money?"

Her brows notched. "What do you mean?"

"Just that." He refrained from going into specifics. Her father's duplicity was the last thing she needed to hear about right now. Her parents had already betrayed her enough. "What if you had no dowry at all? What if there was no means to afford servants, fine clothes, or carriages? What if there was only me?"

"Only you?" She didn't sound at all put off by the idea.

Jasper's pulse jumped on a ridiculous surge of hope. He forced it to calm. He was getting ahead of himself. "And the children," he added. "And a house that's crumbling to its foundation."

"What if? What if?" She squeezed his hand. "I don't care about the money. Not so long as I have my books to read and a safe place to lay my head. It's *that* I want. Safety. I don't ever wish to be afraid again."

"Everyone's afraid of something. It's the nature of being human."

"You're not afraid."

"Yes, I am." He was very much afraid he was going to accept her reckless proposition. "It isn't wise to tempt me, Julia. You may not like what happens next."

"I'm not a child. I shall be three and twenty soon. An old maid, too long on the shelf. And—" She faltered, lips trembling. "I don't feel safe here anymore. I would dearly like to leave."

He absorbed her words in solemn silence. It wasn't only what she said that persuaded him. It was that lip wobble. When coupled with her fingers twined around his, he was powerless to refuse her.

"Very well," he said.

She exhaled. "You'll marry me?"

"I will."

Tears started in her eyes. She made a visible effort to keep her composure. "I have conditions."

He felt a rush of tenderness for her. "Ah."

"Perhaps I should have mentioned those first?"

"You might have done." He brushed his lips to her knuckles. "What are they?"

"First, that you promise never to restrict my reading."

"Done. What else?"

"Cossack must come with me as my riding horse. And you must promise to allow me to have a cat and a dog, too. More than one each if I choose. And they may stay in the house with me. Even in my room."

"Conditions accepted. Is that all?"

Color tinged her cheeks—a delicate wash of damask pink so faint he might have missed it if he wasn't gazing at her so intently. "I-I want us to wait to consummate the marriage."

By some miracle, he kept his countenance. "For how long?"

Her embarrassment was palpable. "A month or two. Until we know each other better."

Heat crept up his neck. This wasn't a conversation to be having with a lady. Not even one's future wife. But he'd promised her she could speak plainly with him. He did her the courtesy of the same.

"It's often the best way to *get* to know each other," he said.

Her blush darkened. "I daresay it is, but I would still rather wait.

I'd like a proper courtship. And there isn't time for that. I want to be married as soon as may be."

"How soon?"

"I wish it could be today. That we could go to Gretna Green like Lord Worth and Lady Elizabeth in *The Fire Opal*."

The title wasn't among those stacked on her bedside table, but he recognized it all the same. It was another of J. Marshland's romantic novels. One of his earliest works and, by far, the most popular.

Jasper frowned. "Gretna Green doesn't perform same-day marriages any longer. What we'll need is a vicar—and a special license."

The latter was still in his pocketbook. It had been there ever since yesterday morning when he'd obtained it in Doctors' Commons. But there was no reason she need know about any of that.

"Can you—"

"I'll arrange it. But before I do . . ." He paused. "I have a few conditions of my own."

Her expression turned wary. "What sorts of conditions?"

He was matter-of-fact. Never mind that they'd just been discussing courtship and the marriage bed. "I have a past," he said. "You know some of it. The rest I prefer to keep private. You're to ask me no questions about my parents or about my time before the war."

She looked as though she wanted to ask him already. But she didn't. "I promise."

Jasper continued with brutal frankness. "There are other things I wish to keep private, too. Work I do that must remain secret. As a consequence, the door of my study on the fourth floor of the Hall remains locked at all times. You're never to enter it."

Her eyes widened. He could well imagine what she thought. That he had some exciting double life as a criminal or as a spy for the Crown.

The truth was nothing so lucrative.

"I won't," she promised. "But the work you do . . . It isn't nefarious, is it?"

"No," he said. "It hurts no one."

It helped no one, either. Not of late. But all that was going to have to change. Without a rich bride to smooth the way, the burden would, once again, be entirely on Jasper's shoulders. If he didn't make some alterations in his approach, he and his fledgling family would soon be worse off than they were now.

"Is there anything else?" she asked.

"Yes. The children. They're a bit wild. A bit . . . difficult. They may not take to you right away. And they may say things about their mother that might upset you. I haven't discouraged them from speaking of her. I wouldn't wish them to feel they couldn't."

"I would never expect them to refrain. Not on my account. I know I'm not—" She broke off, something inexplicable in her face. A brief flicker of insecurity or, perhaps, resignation. "That is, I know ours won't be a love match. I don't ask that you accord me any special treatment."

Jasper couldn't fathom what he'd said to inspire her reply. Why wouldn't he treat her specially? She was going to be his wife. The wife he was choosing for himself. The one he wanted most in all the world.

"I'll try my hardest to fit in," she went on in the same halting tone. "I hope I shall. But if I don't—"

"You'll fit." He smoothed a damp lock of hair from her brow. "You'll be mine."

Her mouth trembled again.

He couldn't resist. Leaning over her, he kissed her very softly on the lips. When he lifted his head, her blue eyes were smiling.

"I could almost imagine I was Sleeping Beauty," she confided.

"Except that you're not asleep," he said. "You're wide awake."

"Naturally, I am. I don't want to miss any of the good parts."

His mouth ticked up at one corner. "In that case . . ." He released her hand and, standing from his chair, scooped her up in his arms, quilted coverlet and all.

"Gracious!" she gasped. "What on earth—?"

"Captain Blunt!" Mary whispered sharply. "Put her down this instant."

"She's not well, sir," the footman said at the same time. "You mustn't."

Jasper ignored them. His gaze held Julia's. "You told me you don't feel safe here any longer."

"I don't." Her arms circled his neck. "But that doesn't explain what you're doing."

"Isn't it obvious? I'm rescuing you."

Sixteen

—✕—

*J*ulia pressed her face into Jasper's shoulder. He was so strong—so solid and sure—holding her in his arms as effortlessly as if she were a piece of thistledown.

She was still bleary-headed from blood loss. Her eyelids were heavy, and she couldn't focus as well as she otherwise might. Events seemed to unfold around her in a hazy romantic dream.

Jasper uttered terse commands to the servants—something about packing Julia's bags and having Cossack collected from the stables. Jenkins obeyed with all haste, dashing from the room on silent feet. Mary complied, too, eventually.

Julia suspected she knew why.

Mary had been present for Dr. Cordingley's second visit this morning. She'd stood beside the bed, lips pressed tight in disapproval. Afterward, it was she, not Mama, who had sponged Julia's brow.

"*It's not right,*" she'd muttered under her breath. "*Your own mother leaving you to that man.*"

Mary rarely criticized anything Mama and Papa did. But this time, Dr. Cordingley had gone too far, and it had been with Mama's express approval. Perhaps that was why Mary hadn't barred the door against Jasper or run to fetch Julia's parents.

Not that any of them could have stopped him.

Julia had the feeling that, once he'd made up his mind, no one on earth could stand in Jasper Blunt's way.

She tightened her arms around his neck.

"As much as you can fit," he told Mary as she stuffed clothes into a pair of carpetbags and an old leather portmanteau. "She won't have the luxury of coming back."

Jenkins returned from the stables, ducking into the bedchamber to confer with Jasper in a lowered voice.

"Miss Wychwood's horse is being led round, sir."

"Excellent." Jasper strode to the door with Julia in his arms.

Jenkins preceded them. He opened the door quietly, looking out into the hall before motioning Jasper to go through.

The next thing Julia knew, Jasper was carrying her down the stairs.

She supposed she should feel mortified. She was, after all, in her nightdress, with her hair unbound and her arms bandaged heavily beneath her sleeves. But Jasper had respected her dignity. Her quilt was wrapped around her, shielding most of her body from view as he crossed the hall.

"*I don't feel safe here anymore,*" she'd told him. "*I would dearly like to leave.*"

And he'd listened to her. He'd actually listened and understood.

He was right to say he was rescuing her. Julia didn't think she could survive another visit from Dr. Cordingley.

Jenkins trotted alongside them. "I have your gloves, sir. You left them when last you called."

"He's not interested in his gloves," Mary snapped, dragging Julia's bags down the steps. "Attend to the door. And then come and get these."

Jenkins rushed to open it, standing back as Jasper passed through with Julia in his arms.

A glossy black carriage waited in the street, with a liveried coachman on the box and a footman standing by the door. At the sight of them, he opened it and set down the steps.

In seconds, Julia was safely ensconced inside with Jasper. He cradled her on his lap, holding her firmly against his chest. His thighs beneath the thin barrier of her quilt and her cotton nightgown felt as solidly muscular as all the rest of him.

Goodness.

She looked up at him in wide-eyed astonishment. He'd actually taken her in her underclothes. Not figuratively, as she'd told Mary she wished a suitor might do, but quite literally.

"In broad daylight, too," Julia murmured. "A proper scandal."

Jasper's gray eyes shone briefly with wry humor. "You'll have to marry me now, ma'am."

"Is that where you're taking me? To a church?"

His expression became serious. He had the look of a ruthless soldier embarking on a military campaign. "No," he said. "I'm taking you to Lord Ridgeway's house."

The bedroom on the third floor of Lord Ridgeway's town house was light and airy, the curtains opened to let in the afternoon sun. Traces of lemon polish, washing soda, and beeswax lingered in the air. The fragrance was a comfort to Julia. Surely, nothing depraved could happen in a room that smelled so fresh and clean—even if it *was* a room in a bachelor's household.

A stack of pillows at her back, she sat up further in bed to better see what Mary was doing.

Jasper had ordered the maid to accompany them. Mary wasn't best pleased about it. She grumbled loudly as she reorganized Julia's clothing in her bags—folding petticoats, bodices, and underthings.

"It's all creased and rumpled," she muttered. "That's what you get for cramming things into luggage willy-nilly. If he'd given me five minutes to fold it properly—"

"We didn't have five minutes," Julia said. "We had to leave right away."

"Why? So he could bring you here? To a bachelor's establishment?" Mary snorted. "And you a well-bred girl."

"It's only temporary. Until he can procure a license."

"On a Saturday? Bah. He might have left you safe in your bed at home."

Julia gave her maid a weighted look. "Safe, was I? And what would I have done if my mother summoned Dr. Cordingley again? How would I have managed?" As it was, it would probably take her days to recover. Until then, she'd be nothing but a burden on those around her, Jasper especially.

Mary's lips flattened in a stubborn line. She was too peeved to admit Julia was right. "He didn't need to parade you through the streets in your nightclothes."

"I was covered in a blanket," Julia said. "I might have been a bundle of laundry for all anyone knew. Besides, nobody saw me."

That wasn't wholly true.

While no one save Mary, Jenkins, the coachman, and the footman had witnessed her escape from Belgrave Square, her arrival in Half Moon Street hadn't gone unremarked. As Viscount Ridgeway's carriage had rolled up outside of his town house, another carriage had stopped in front of the house next door. The occupants disembarked at the same time Jasper was carrying Julia up the stone steps to Lord Ridgeway's front door.

Julia glanced back only once, just long enough to form the impression of a bespectacled gentleman and a handsome lady with thickly plaited auburn hair. They'd been staring at Jasper quite unashamedly.

For all they knew, he was abducting some helpless young woman he'd drugged, bound, and wrapped up in a quilt. Julia had read a similar story once in a penny novel, though it had been a carpet, not a quilt. The young woman in the tale hadn't awakened until she and her seducer were halfway to Calais. By then, her fate had been sealed.

Julia was slightly more confident about her own fate.

On entering Ridgeway's house, Jasper had carried her upstairs to one of the bedchambers. He hadn't lingered long enough to debauch her. After setting her down in the bed, he'd promptly gone away, leaving her with Mary.

"It ain't proper," Mary said again. It had become her refrain. "And my being here don't make it proper."

Julia sighed. Short as the journey had been, it had overtaxed her. She was exhausted, her limbs weak and her breath shallow. "I must get dressed."

"No point in it. You may as well sleep as not." Mary removed a single light-colored French kid glove from one of the carpetbags. "Bother. I know I packed the pair of these."

Julia's brows knit in a frown. She was reminded of something. Something she hadn't fully comprehended at the time. "Mary?"

"Hmm?"

"When we were leaving the house, Jenkins tried to give Captain Blunt a pair of gloves. He said he'd left them behind on his last visit."

Mary continued rooting through the carpetbag. She pointedly didn't look up.

"Do you know anything about that?" Julia asked.

"What difference can it make? Given where you're at now—"

"Mary." Julia took a firmer tone. "Did Captain Blunt call on me in Belgrave Square before today?"

Abandoning the carpetbag, Mary grudgingly came to the bed. Her features were set. "If he did, it don't make one bit of difference. Not anymore."

"He did, then." Julia scanned her maid's face. "When?"

Mary exhaled a gust of breath. "Yesterday, while we were out at that bookshop in Charing Cross. Jenkins mentioned it in passing when we returned."

"Why didn't you tell me?"

"It's not my business. And you know how Sir Eustace feels about gossip."

"Surely, it isn't gossip to tell me I had a caller." Julia leaned back against the pillows, perplexed. "*Why* did he come?"

Mary shrugged. "To see your father. Same as the other gentlemen who've called."

A cold trickle of awareness spiked in Julia's veins. For an instant she couldn't breathe. "There have been others?"

"Now you're upset. I told you—"

"*Mary*—"

"Yes, there were others. Not many. A few over the years, that's all. Not anything to mention."

As they spoke, the front doorbell rang below, echoing through the house. A creaking tread sounded on the stairs as a servant responded to the summons. Shortly afterward, men's voices drifted up from the hall.

Julia didn't heed any of it. Her gaze never left Mary's face. "Who?"

Mary glanced at the chamber door before admitting, "An old squire from Cork, a spotty lad with a gaming habit, and two other rascals, all light of pocket and looking to acquire your fortune."

Four gentlemen altogether? Four who had come asking permission to court her?

Or had they proposed?

"Papa never told me," Julia said quietly.

"Why should he if he refused them? It would only vex you."

"I had a right to know. All this time . . . I thought no one wanted me. And all the while *you knew*—"

"They didn't want you," Mary said. "They wanted your fortune. Your father was protecting you."

Julia's stomach twisted into a knot. Was that why Jasper had agreed to elope with her? Because he'd already asked for her hand and Papa had refused?

She had no time to ponder the possibility.

There was a rap at the door. Mary leapt to answer it, clearly grateful for the interruption.

It was Jasper. But he wasn't alone. When Mary stepped back to allow him entry, he walked into the bedroom in company with a complete stranger. A woman, in fact. The same auburn-haired lady Julia had seen in the street.

She was respectable in appearance, dressed simply but elegantly in a fashionable carriage dress.

"Miss Wychwood," Jasper said, "this is Mrs. Finchley. She and her husband live next door. Mrs. Finchley? Miss Wychwood. As you can see, she's not being held against her will."

"Miss Wychwood." Mrs. Finchley seemed to take in the whole of Julia's situation at a glance. "I apologize for the intrusion. You can imagine what I thought."

Julia drew her blanket up more firmly about her waist. She wished she'd dressed, or at least taken the time to comb and plait her hair.

But there was no judgment in Mrs. Finchley's blue-green gaze, only concern.

It helped put Julia at her ease. "I did wonder if you might suspect something untoward. It was the very plot of a novel I once read. The villain was a dastardly French fellow who rolled a young heiress up in a carpet."

Mrs. Finchley approached the bed. "Is that the one where he spirited her across the Channel?"

Julia brightened. "Yes! Though, I suppose it's a common plot. In novels, heiresses are always being abducted by villains."

"Mrs. Finchley wishes to reassure herself I'm not one of them," Jasper said. "If you don't object to her presence, I'll leave the pair of you to talk while I discuss matters with her husband."

"Certainly." Julia gave Mrs. Finchley a tentative smile. "Do sit down."

Jasper regarded Thomas Finchley from across the Aubusson-carpeted parlor. He was a slim man of medium height, with brown hair and light blue eyes looking out from behind a pair of silver-framed spectacles. An unremarkable fellow.

Or so he might have one believe.

But Jasper was no fool.

He'd recognized the kind of man Finchley was on sight. The sort of fellow who reminded Jasper of the many nondescript predators he'd encountered in foreign climes. One whose outward ordinariness was nothing more than a convenient camouflage, obscuring just how dangerous the creature truly was.

"You're the solicitor, of course," Jasper said. The same solicitor he'd been planning to call on in Fleet Street. The one whose advice he required to set his mind at ease. He motioned to a chair. "Ridgeway's mentioned you."

Finchley sat, appearing perfectly at his ease. "I've heard about you, as well. It's difficult not to, given your reputation."

Jasper took a seat on the settee across from him. "I wouldn't believe everything you hear."

"I rarely do." Finchley's tone was conversational, just as it had been when Skipforth had admitted him into the hall. As if it were the most normal thing in the world to apply at the front door of a bachelor's household asking to speak to the young lady who had been carried inside wrapped in a quilt. "In my experience, the truth is often much more complex than rumor."

Jasper wondered which rumors Finchley had heard. Whispers of both Jasper's heroism and his brutality were rife in London. The former was mentioned often enough in his presence, but no one had yet dared broach the latter subject to his face.

No one except Julia.

He was painfully conscious of her presence upstairs, weak and vulnerable after her double round of bloodletting. If he could have, he'd have turned the Finchleys away at the door. But their arrival, though ill-timed, was also rather fortuitous.

Yesterday, after Sir Eustace had sent him packing, Jasper had been in no mood to make his planned visit to Fleet Street. And today, it had seemed there would be no opportunity to do so.

But Finchley was here now, by some miracle.

Jasper fully intended to make the most of his presence. "Quite complex, in fact. In both my case and Miss Wychwood's."

"I don't doubt it," Finchley said. "You can, nevertheless, understand my wife's concerns."

Jasper hadn't taken the man as a henpecked husband. "She won't be overlong, I trust. Miss Wychwood is in no fit state to be interrogated."

Finchley looked at him evenly. There was a layer of steel beneath his amiable manner. "Is she fit enough to give her consent to marriage?"

Jasper stiffened at the intimation. "Of course she is."

"You can imagine how all this looks. An unmarried lady of good family arriving as she did at a bachelor's establishment, with not one but two bachelors in residence."

"Ridgeway isn't here."

"When do you expect him back?"

"I've no idea," Jasper said. "Not anytime soon."

Julia was in no danger of encountering the viscount. If it weren't for the Finchleys, she and Jasper might have already been on their way.

It wouldn't be long before her absence from Belgrave Square was remarked. Her parents wouldn't bestir themselves, not with their ill health, but they'd likely send someone after her. Lord only knew who it would be. Servants? The magistrate? A hastily hired private inquiry agent?

Jasper was confident he could repel all comers, but the more people involved in the affair, the greater the chance of a scandal. And there would be scandal enough to contend with once the fashionable world learned he'd spirited away a vulnerable heiress.

He needed to get Julia out of London. To marry her and convey her, with all speed, to Goldfinch Hall. There, she could rest and recover her strength, if not in luxury, at least in safety; free from the dangerous influence of her parents and the oppressive attentions of Lord Gresham. Every moment spent in the parlor with Finchley was a moment wasted.

Unless Jasper could turn the conversation to matters of law.

It was difficult to do so given Finchley's suspicions.

"Is Ridgeway aware of your plans?" he asked.

"There's no plan in effect," Jasper said, "other than a desire to render Miss Wychwood assistance. She finds herself in an impossible situation."

"In such cases, marriage can provide a viable escape. I don't disapprove of it."

Jasper fixed the solicitor with an icy glare. "Your approval makes little difference. My affairs and those of Miss Wychwood are no concern of yours."

Finchley only smiled. "I concern myself with the plight of all people in impossible situations. A habit of my profession."

"Miss Wychwood isn't your client. You'd be of no use to her. What she needs is a husband. Someone to look after her—to protect her. She hasn't anyone else to do the job."

Understanding registered on Finchley's face. "You care for her."

Jasper felt a rare twinge of vulnerability. It wasn't safe to want something as much as he wanted Julia Wychwood. It threatened to make him incautious. To strip him of his carefully wrought armor, leaving him entirely exposed. "I count myself her friend," he said.

"And she feels the same about you, I gather." Finchley frowned. "I know something of her family situation. An unfortunate one, to be sure, but . . . are you certain this isn't making things worse?"

"She's not safe in Belgrave Square any longer."

"And you can make her safe?"

"I can," Jasper said. "I will." He'd never been so certain of anything in his life.

Finchley's expression turned thoughtful. "You're right, it is none of my business. However, if you'd like my advice—"

Jasper uttered a humorless huff of laughter. "I doubt I could afford it. Ridgeway tells me you count the most powerful men in London among your clients."

"Perhaps once," Finchley said. "I've recently changed the focus of my practice."

Jasper owned to a flicker of curiosity. "A crisis of conscience?"

Finchley's mouth hitched. "Something like that. Why? Are you in need of a solicitor?"

"I have a solicitor. A fellow in York who deals with estate matters." Jasper chose his next words with care. "He's not well versed in questions of criminal law."

"I see," Finchley said. There was an extended pause. "Do you require advice on a criminal matter?"

Jasper stood abruptly. He walked to the cold fireplace, setting his booted foot on the edge of the empty grate. He was silent for a long moment as he struggled with how best to convey the crux of his dilemma.

Finchley didn't press him.

Jasper sensed that the man knew a thing or two about waiting. He also sensed he could trust him.

A strange feeling.

Trust wasn't something Jasper gave easily. But Ridgeway had said Finchley was a vault of secrets. A man who kept his clients' confidences.

"That depends," Jasper said at last. "I have a question. A hypothetical. But my asking it rests on how loyal you are to your clients."

"Once they *are* my clients, my loyalty is absolute," Finchley answered. "So is my confidence."

Jasper turned. "Does that confidence extend to—"

"Everything, Captain Blunt. Providing the criminal conduct is the past." Finchley studied his face. "We *are* speaking of criminal conduct, are we not?"

Jasper thought of the children. Of Dolly's face all those years ago as she'd stood on the steps of the Hall with Daisy on her hip. "I suppose some might call it that," he said. "Others might call it justice."

Finchley's gaze lit with genuine interest behind the lenses of his spectacles. "A fascinating distinction. One I've had cause to ponder myself on more than one occasion." He nodded slowly, coming to a decision. "Very well. Consider me retained."

Seventeen

❖

$\mathcal{I}$ n the aftermath of Mrs. Finchley's visit, Julia was hard-pressed
not to close her eyes and go to sleep. She hadn't any strength left
at all. The smallest tasks defeated her. But it wouldn't do to linger in
her nightgown. Not in Lord Ridgeway's house of all places.

She was out of bed the moment Mrs. Finchley took her leave.

Mary helped her to wash and dress, muttering all the while about
the scandal and the shame of the situation.

As if Julia didn't know her reputation was hanging in the balance.

Were she not so tired, she might have been in danger of working
herself up into a state.

As it was, by the time Jasper returned, she was able to greet him
with relative calm. Clothed in a soft day dress of violet-dyed wool, her
hair brushed and rolled into a silken net at her nape, she was propped
up against the same pillows as when he'd left her.

His brows lowered. "You're even paler than you were before," he
said. "I trust Mrs. Finchley didn't vex you overmuch?"

"Not at all." Julia had found the solicitor's auburn-haired wife to be
rather nice—though the lady *had* asked quite a few pointed questions.
Understandable, Julia supposed, given the circumstances. "Have she
and her husband gone?"

"They have, thank God." Jasper's gaze drifted over her, his expression at once both protective and possessive. "You're dressed."

Heat coiled in her belly. *Goodness.* The way he looked at her.

"I rather thought I should be," she said. "I'm afraid the effort's quite worn me out."

"So I see."

Her heartbeat quickened as he approached the bed. He looked so dark and forbidding. So impervious to all sentimentality. And yet . . .

This was the same man who had kissed her so passionately in the Claverings' garden. The same man who had scooped her up in his arms and carried her away from Belgrave Square like a knight in shining armor.

He glanced at the edge of the bed. "May I?"

Her pulse accelerated. "Yes, of course."

The mattress dipped under his weight as he sat beside her. "Tell me. Are you certain this is still what you want?"

Julia was conscious of her maid hovering nearby. It didn't stop her from answering honestly. "It is."

He leaned into her, as if drawn by some hidden magnet. His voice deepened. "And am *I* still what you want?"

She stared up at him. Neither of them had made any declarations to each other. No professions of love or even affection. But yesterday morning, he'd told her that she'd been his first choice among all the other heiresses on the marriage mart.

A dubious honor. He was a fortune hunter, after all. Still, it must have cost him to admit it, knowing she was poised to elude him.

The least she could do was acknowledge her own feelings.

"You are," she said. "I wouldn't have proposed marriage to just any gentleman."

A spark of silver fire flashed in his eyes.

She would have liked to revel in it for a moment; the heat of that look. To bask in the knowledge that he was pleased—quite visibly pleased—that she wanted him.

Instead, like any earnest fool, she felt herself compelled to continue. "I only wonder why you didn't tell me you called on my father yesterday."

Just like that, the fire in his eyes flickered out. His gaze was once again as coolly unreadable as the ice over the surface of a frozen pond. Something dangerous lurked beneath. What it was, she couldn't tell. But the fact that he'd put up his guard made her draw back from him.

"Do you deny it?"

"I have no reason to deny it," he said brusquely. "It's not a secret."

Julia was no good at sparring at the best of times. Now, faint and clammy from blood loss, she felt herself even less so. She could only wait for him to explain on his own, hoping he would choose to be honest with her.

She looked at him in silent expectation.

A muscle tensed in Jasper's jaw. "I asked his permission to court you. He refused me. That's all there is to it."

"Oh." She fell quiet again.

"You don't wish to inquire after his reasons?"

"I suspect I already know them," she said.

When last she'd talked to her father, he'd remarked on the favorable location of Lord Gresham's house in reference to Belgrave Square. *"An easy distance,"* he'd called it. As if residential proximity were all that mattered in a future husband. And to him, likely it was. Naturally, he wouldn't consent to her being courted by someone who would take her away from London.

"I would have mentioned it," Jasper said, "but there's been no opportunity."

"You might have told me last night in the Claverings' garden."

"To what end?"

"It would have explained why you didn't seek me out at the start of the evening. Why you suddenly turned your attentions to Miss Throckmorton. That was the reason, wasn't it? Because my father refused your suit?"

"It was," he acknowledged.

She was vaguely disappointed. He didn't seem like the kind of man who would fall back from a challenge. "You didn't need his permission. I'm of age. I can wed whomever I choose."

"Quite so. Which brings us to where we are today." Jasper looked into her eyes. "I ask you again, do you still want to marry me?"

She bit her lip.

"Before you make your reply, I should warn you that failing to tell you about my call on your father isn't the last mistake I'll make. If you shackle your fate to mine, best prepare yourself for something less than perfection."

"I don't expect perfection." She doubted whether the quality existed either in herself or in others. "And I do still want to marry you."

The muscle in his jaw relaxed; a subtle indication of his relief.

Had he actually thought she'd change her mind? All because he hadn't told her about calling on Papa?

She wasn't so unreasonable as that.

The omission *had* hurt her a little, but it didn't change how she felt about him. He was a good man; she was sure of it.

And besides, what gentleman didn't withhold things from his wife? It was maddening, to be sure, but not at all surprising. In Julia's limited experience, married people rarely existed on terms of equality.

The most a woman could hope for was to wed a man who was kind and understanding, and who—if she was lucky—might make her heart beat faster.

Jasper had those qualities in abundance.

"What happens next?" she asked him.

In answer, he took her hand in his. His clasp was firm, but gentle. Far gentler than one might expect from a man so powerfully made. As if he held something infinitely precious in his grasp. "I have a plan," he said. "If you approve of it, we can leave directly."

She hadn't expected him to ask her approval. No one ever consulted with her about anything, least of all her own happiness. The fact that he was doing so—especially now, when things were so fraught and every second counted—moved her beyond measure.

Her fingers curved around his, just as they had when he'd taken her hand in her bedroom at Belgrave Square. "What do you have in mind?"

"There's a small church in Camden where we can be married. After that, we'll go to King's Cross. There will be a train leaving for York around four o'clock. My hope is that we can be on it." His gaze held hers. "Is that acceptable to you?"

Julia nodded. "Yes. Only . . ."

"What is it?"

She gave him an apologetic look. "I might have to lean on you a little."

His expression softened. "What do you suppose I'm here for?"

Warmth infiltrated her veins. There were a thousand things she might have said—a thousand emotions waiting to be expressed—but before she could formulate a reply, Jasper had released her hand and was up and striding toward the door.

"I'll summon the carriage," he said.

"Wait!" Julia called out anxiously. "What about Cossack?"

"He'll follow behind us along with Quintus. I'll leave instructions for Ridgeway."

She exhaled. She might have known Jasper would have a plan. "Thank you."

A hint of a smile edged his scarred mouth. "You can thank me when we're out of London." He opened the door. "Have your maid ready your things."

"I'm not coming," Mary said.

Julia's gaze jerked to her maid. She stood by the wooden washstand, her arms folded and her face set in lines of mulish resolve. Julia recognized that look. Her stomach sank. "Would you give us a moment, please?" she asked Jasper.

He frowned. "We leave in fifteen minutes."

With or without your maid.

He may as well have said it aloud. The sentiment was evident, lingering in the air as he withdrew, shutting the door behind him.

Only when he was gone did Julia give her full attention to Mary. "You don't mean it."

Mary showed no signs of being in jest. "I do. I'll not leave London."

"But why? You've come with me this far—"

"Didn't have much choice, did I? Not with Captain Blunt issuing orders as though he was our superior officer." Mary stalked to one of the carpetbags. She tucked the topmost pieces of folded clothing further inside the bag's capacious interior before fastening the clasp shut. "God forgive me for leaving you with such a man. But you've made your bed, miss, and now—"

"Don't say that," Julia objected. "It's not like you. Not when you know what my life's been like."

"You might have made a better life for yourself if you'd wed Lord Gresham. But you wouldn't listen. And now look where you are—and who you're with. It's not my place to say so, but someone must warn you. You'll be miserable with that man. Just you wait. In time, you'll see I'm right. Once he has you in his power, far away from your family and friends, you'll come to regret your choice."

Julia was stunned by her maid's words. She felt like a mortal maiden being damned by some minor goddess. Each sentence Mary uttered flayed like a knife, laying bare Julia's own private fears and insecurities.

But she'd made up her mind.

She was set on her course, and no one, not Mary or anyone else, would dissuade her from following it through.

"At least it will have been my choice," she said. "My own decision, for better or worse. Not something another person chose for me."

"There's some not capable of choosing things for themselves. Or of looking after themselves, neither." Mary stomped to the other carpetbag. She refolded a petticoat before thrusting it back inside. "How do you intend to get by without me to help you dress? To brush your hair and sponge and press your gowns?" She fastened the bag shut. "You think Captain Blunt has a lady's maid in that haunted manor of his what knows how to use turpentine to remove grease stains from a fine silk weave?"

"No," Julia admitted. "I don't think Captain Blunt has any servants at all."

Mary blanched in horror. "Lord have mercy. I've a mind to fetch your parents to bring you home. You've no notion what you're getting yourself into."

"If you came along—"

"I'll not leave London," Mary said again. "If you go with him, miss, you go alone."

It was an ultimatum if Julia ever heard one. Her spine stiffened in response to it. She wasn't helpless. Not any more than any other lady dependent on a maid to arrange her hair, lace up her corset, or fasten the hooks at the back of her gown. Nevertheless . . .

The prospect of leaving without Mary made Julia's heart quail.

Was this how it had to be? A clean break with her old life? Left to embark on her new one with no friend to stand at her side?

But Mary wasn't her friend.

Despite all her scolding, advice, and the occasional offering of a sympathetic ear, Mary was a paid servant. A skilled servant, but a servant nonetheless.

And as of this moment, she was a remnant of Julia's past, right along with the fine house, the richly made clothes, and the gleaming coach-and-four.

Julia refused to grieve for any of it.

What awaited her in Yorkshire may not be elegant or luxurious. It may not be *easy*. But it would be real. And it would be hers.

"If that's how you feel," she said, "you may go. I'll not stop you."

Mary hovered by the bed. "It's not too late for you to reconsider."

Julia didn't dignify the statement. Her mind was made up. "If you would pass me my reticule?"

Mary mutely obeyed, handing Julia the small embroidered purse with its drawstring of silken cord.

Julia opened it and withdrew several banknotes. "This should be enough to see you through while you're seeking a new position." She stretched the notes out to Mary. "If my parents refuse to give you a character, I'll provide one. You need only write to me in Yorkshire at Goldfinch Hall."

"Goldfinch Hall?" Mary's brow furrowed as she took the money. "Doesn't sound like a haunted house."

"No, it doesn't. And Mary?"

"Yes, miss?"

Julia's stomach tightened with resolve. "I won't be alone."

Eighteen

❈

$\mathcal{J}$ulia had often imagined her wedding. It was difficult not to when one was romantic-minded. The groom had been in doubt—she'd never had a specific face or figure of a man in mind—but her dream of the day itself had always been crystal clear.

There would be a church, naturally. Someplace pretty and bright with sun streaming in through tall stained glass windows. A kind vicar with rosy cheeks and a smile would stand at the end of the aisle beside Julia's nameless, faceless future husband, and she'd walk up to meet them, clothed in white satin, with a veil of Honiton lace and a bouquet of orange blossoms.

"*Like Queen Victoria,*" Anne had remarked dryly when Julia had once described it to her.

As Lord Ridgeway's carriage departed the small church in Camden, with its sagging gate and overgrown cemetery, Julia couldn't help but wonder what her best friend would have made of the slapdash ceremony Julia had just participated in.

It had been nothing like her dream.

The church had been dark and dreary, the vicar as cross as a badger at having his tea interrupted, and the ceremony itself—witnessed by two of the vicar's slatternly servants—had been less evident of romance than expedience.

Julia didn't regret any of it.

From the moment Jasper had insisted on carrying her down the stairs of Lord Ridgeway's house and into the waiting carriage, he'd been all that was solicitous. A kind and caring groom, even if he hadn't kissed her when they were pronounced man and wife, and even if he *was* presently sitting beside her, looking as cross as the vicar had as he'd read the wedding ceremony from the *Book of Common Prayer*.

She rested her head against his shoulder, crushing the cluster of lilacs that adorned the side of her fashionable leghorn bonnet.

"Are you all right?" he asked gruffly.

"I'm fine," she said. "Just dreadfully weary."

His arm came around her as the carriage rolled through the street, jostling them against each other. "We're not far from King's Cross. Once we're on the train, you can sleep all the way to York."

Julia didn't answer. It seemed too much of an effort to talk. It was only as the carriage was pulling up outside of the bustling railway station that she gave voice to a niggling doubt. "You don't think it *was* bad luck, do you?"

Jasper didn't need to ask what she meant.

When signing the register, she'd mistakenly used her new name: *Julia Blunt*. The curmudgeonly vicar had immediately stricken it out, commanding her to sign with her maiden name. Julia had done so, but not before one of the servants muttered the two damning words: *Bad luck*.

"You're not superstitious?" Jasper asked.

"Not any more than reason," she replied. "But one doesn't wish to start one's married life under a cloud."

"There are no clouds today," he said.

Julia waited in the carriage while he procured their tickets and found a porter to see to their luggage. As she gazed out the window, her heart beat like a drum. He was right. The sky was clear and cloudless, a blue so bright it almost hurt her eyes.

She wasn't going to be afraid. This was an adventure. The adventure she'd dreamed of all her life. Any doubts she had were probably only because she was so exhausted from Dr. Cordingley's treatments.

Thank heaven for Jasper.

He didn't carry her from the coach, but he kept an arm about her waist, strong as an oaken band, steadying her as they crossed the crowded smoke-filled platform to board the first-class railway carriage.

Their compartment was empty. It was also rather luxurious, paneled in gleaming polished wood, with a carpeted floor, shuttered windows, and racks fixed overhead to store their parcels.

"Do we have to share it with other passengers?" Julia asked as Jasper guided her to one of the thickly padded upholstered seats. There were four of them altogether, a pair on either side facing each other.

"I doubt it. There aren't many leaving for Yorkshire at this time of day." He sank down next to her. "Consider it a wedding gift. I don't expect we'll be traveling first-class again anytime soon."

Outside, a shrill whistle cut through the noise from the platform. The conductor shouted something unintelligible, and then, with a great heave of machinery, the train ground into motion.

Julia's stomach lurched. The fastest she'd ever gone was on a galloping horse in Hyde Park. The train was exponentially faster. It rolled out of the station in a cloud of smoke and steam, gaining speed with every second.

Soon, King's Cross was far behind them.

Jasper removed his hat and unbuttoned his coat, making himself comfortable in his seat.

Julia waited to follow suit. Only when the danger of a stranger entering their compartment seemed unlikely did she risk removing her bonnet. Her hair was pressed all out of shape, stray tendrils escaping from her silken hairnet to curl about her face. She smoothed them back from her brow with a trembling hand.

"I've never traveled first-class," she confessed. "Or any class for that matter. This is the first time I've been on a train."

Jasper frowned at her. "You never said anything."

"I assumed you knew." She turned back to the window. "I haven't ever been out of London before. So far, all my travels have been in my imagination."

Outside, the scenery whipped by at an alarming rate, the hustle and bustle of London rapidly giving way to an ever-increasing emptiness. She'd known it would to some degree. The outskirts of town, and the environs beyond it, were naturally less vibrant than the heart of the city. Nevertheless, seeing the familiar landscape slip away made her insides quaver as surely as the motion of the train.

Dropping her gaze, she withdrew a book from her reticule, anxious for the comfort of its pages.

Jasper stilled, his scarred face inscrutable. "Another Marshland novel."

Julia felt a trace of self-consciousness. She supposed a married lady shouldn't be reading a novel on her first journey alone with her husband. The pair of them were meant to be holding hands and cuddling, even kissing perhaps, taking full advantage of their private compartment.

But she and Jasper hadn't married out of any romantic attachment. He required her fortune to repair his estate, and she required his name to buy her freedom. That was the sum total of their agreement.

Never mind that he'd kissed her in the Claverings' garden. Or that he'd rushed to her bedside today, holding her hand and pressing his lips to her knuckles like a man very much in love.

He didn't love her.

And what she felt for him was likely fueled as much by her own romantic longings as reality.

She had no wish to make a fool of herself.

"You always speak his name as though you don't approve of him," she said.

Jasper's cool gray eyes were impossible to read. "I don't disapprove of him. I just wonder why you bought so many of his books all at once."

"Because I've fallen behind on reading him over the years. And because you have an interest in his work. I thought I had better catch up if you and I were to have anything to talk about."

"We have other things to talk about," Jasper said irritably, only to fall silent as she cracked open her novel and turned to the folded page that marked her spot.

She'd begun reading it last night before bed and had only got through the first few chapters. Thus far it was a poignant tale, if not a fast-paced one, filled with love, and loss, and unrequited longing. The perfect read to calm her jittery nerves.

"I thought you were going to sleep?" Jasper said after a time.

"I couldn't," she replied. "Not yet. I'm far too anxious."

An understatement.

Seated beside her new husband on a train hurtling rapidly toward her equally new life, Julia felt on the razor's edge of panic. She didn't know anything about men except what she'd read in books. She didn't know anything about being a wife or a mother.

"Bridal nerves?" Jasper's deep voice was a husky inquiry, as gentle as his touch when he'd last held her hand.

"A little," she admitted, glancing up from her book. "I hope the children will like me."

"*I* like you," he said.

She met his eyes, her heart thumping. "You're not having second thoughts?"

"If I am, they aren't about you."

She hesitated to ask. "What, then?"

His frown deepened. "Until today, I've only ever been truly selfish once in my life. Things didn't go quite the way I expected them to."

Julia didn't understand. "Are you saying that marrying me was selfish?"

"Of course it was," he answered. "I told you. I *like* you, Mrs. Blunt. The children will like you, too, once they get to know you."

Some of the tension in her spine eased. He hadn't previously addressed her by her married name. It was rather reassuring.

Belgrave Square hadn't been warm or welcoming—it hadn't been safe—but it had still been her home. Leaving it made her feel like a boat cut loose from its mooring, set adrift on a turbulent sea.

But she wasn't adrift at all.

She belonged to Jasper now. He was her husband. Her anchor. Even if they weren't madly in love, she was still safe and wanted.

"I like you, too," she said earnestly. "More than any gentleman I've ever known."

He flashed a brief lopsided smile. Except for his scar, it might almost have been boyish. The sort of smile to make a lady's heart turn over. "Convenient," he said, "seeing as how we're married."

Her heart swelled. Seated side by side, they were already close, her arm pressed to his and her skirts bunched against his leg, the hem pooling intimately over one of his booted feet. She drew closer still as she read, taking comfort from the muscular strength of his large presence.

He slipped his arm around her, drawing her against him. His attention was still fixed on her book. "Why do you have so many of Marshland's novels to catch up on?"

"I stopped reading him for a time."

"Any particular reason?"

"I don't know," she said. "One drifts away from authors occasionally." It was inevitable given the sheer number of novels available. There was always something new to try—a new writer, a new story. But with Marshland, it had been something specific that had made her stray. "I think it had to do with the last book of his I read. The one released when I was eighteen. *The Missing Heir*, I believe it was called."

"What was wrong with it?"

"It wasn't anything specific. More of a feeling. It was different than Marshland's previous work—serious and even a little sad. I suppose, at the time, I preferred stories that were more thrilling."

"And now? You liked *The Garden of Valor* well enough."

"Yes. It was exceedingly poignant." She turned the page of her book. "It made me wish I'd never strayed. I'd forgotten how different Marshland is from other authors."

"Different how?"

"For one thing, he's not anywhere near as prolific. His novels used to come out with some frequency, but in the last several years, his publications have slowed to a trickle. They've changed as well. *The Missing Heir* and *The Garden of Valor* are nothing like his earlier works, the ones I read as a girl."

"Perhaps he's grown up."

"Perhaps. It may be why I stopped reading him for a time. I do love his style, but when compared to Mrs. Braddon and Mrs. Trent-Watkinson, his stories seem to lack something."

Jasper was quiet a moment before asking, "Such as?"

"I don't know. I haven't made a thorough study of it. But I think that perhaps Marshland's stories lack adventure."

"*The Garden of Valor* is about a knight on a quest. That's not adventurous?"

"It's too realistic. People don't read sensation novels for realism. They want thrills and danger."

Jasper's mouth hitched. "Murderous lady bigamists pushing people down wells?"

"Something like that." Julia turned another page. "I will say Marshland's romantic sentiment far exceeds any other author I've read of late."

"I'm pleased he can do something right," Jasper said dryly.

"The speeches Sir Richard made to Lady Elaine in *The Garden of Valor* were so beautiful. In this novel, too, the hero, Colonel Lawrence, expresses himself in the most heart-stirring terms." She glanced up at him again, temporarily diverted. "Do you suppose Marshland says such things to his own wife?"

Jasper's gaze held hers. "Is that the sort of thing a wife wants to hear?"

Heat bloomed in her cheeks. "I daresay she does, if a husband means it. And we were speaking about Mr. Marshland, not about you and me."

"Quite." He drew her closer. "As to that, doubtless the poor fool saves it for his novels."

"I hope not. What a waste it would be to keep such things to himself. If he does feel that way, I mean. And if he is married. He may well be a grumpy old bachelor."

"Speaking of marriage . . ." His hand stroked over her arm in a soothing caress. "How are your bridal nerves?"

"Better." An uneasy thought occurred to her. "Is that why you've been indulging all my senseless chatter?"

"It's not senseless," he said. "Your opinions are perfectly sound. I'm grateful to hear them on any subject."

It was by far one of the most wonderfully romantic things anyone had ever said to her. Almost as romantic as when he'd told her she was a beautiful soul. Or when he'd kissed her or held her hand. Indeed, it seemed that within the short time she'd known him, he'd gifted her with a half dozen romantic moments—a smile, a touch, a gruffly expressed sentiment. Like so many jewels, each of them more precious than the last.

She settled against his shoulder with a sigh, her novel still open on her lap.

The train rolled on, the rhythm of the wheels and the regular shriek of the metal and steam lulling her ever closer toward sleep.

Time must have passed because, eventually, she felt Jasper close her book. The gold-stamped title and author name on the cloth cover blurred before her weary gaze.

The Hero's Return by J. Marshland

It was the last thing she saw before her eyes drifted shut. "I wonder what the J stands for," she murmured.

Jasper didn't answer her. At least, she didn't think he did. But as exhaustion wrapped itself around her mind and body, dragging her down into oblivion, she was certain she heard him whisper a reply very softly against her ear.

"It stands for James."

Nineteen

✦

As promised, Jasper let his new bride sleep all the way to York. He might have slept, too, if he didn't feel so damned protective of her. It wasn't a new sensation. He'd been experiencing it ever since he'd rushed to her bedside in Belgrave Square. This urge to shelter and defend her. To keep her safe. He wouldn't have thought it could get any stronger.

More fool him.

When the ill-humored vicar at the little church in Camden had pronounced them man and wife, he may as well have uttered a magical incantation. The words had had a startling and immediate effect, not only deepening the strength of Jasper's feelings for his new bride, but seeming to alter the very alchemy of his soul.

Seated beside her in their first-class compartment, cradling her in the crook of his arm and feeling the precious weight of her head resting on his shoulder, he was conscious of the great responsibility he owed her.

She was his now completely, in law as well as in spirit. His own selfish choice. One that had nothing at all to do with the estate or the children or anything else that had come either before or after the war.

No matter that it hadn't started that way. That it had been her dowry—not her kindness or her sweetness or even her taste in novels—that had first inspired his interest.

They were long past that now.

When they arrived in York, he gentled her awake just long enough to change trains. She was still pale and weak. He expected it would take several days for her to regain her pallor after her ordeal. In the meanwhile, she was content to lean on him and he was glad, quite shamelessly glad, to assist her in dozens of little ways—tying the ribbons of her bonnet beneath her chin, holding her hand, and encircling her waist as he guided her to their new compartment.

It was nightfall by the time they reached Malton, far too late to continue any further. Hardholme had no platform halt. The remainder of their journey would have to be made by coach—a long and arduous drive at the best of times. One best not attempted after sunset, especially when there was no full moon to light the way.

Foul weather greeted them at the station, cloudless blue skies replaced by darkness and driving rain.

Jasper found them a carriage at the cabstand. "We'll put up for the night," he said as he helped Julia into it. "Somewhere close."

"We needn't stop," she said. "I'm strong enough to go on."

"I'm not." He climbed in after her, shutting the door behind him. He thumped on the roof to give the coachman the office to start. "The road to Hardholme can be treacherous. Better to start fresh in the morning."

"Will we stay at a hotel?"

"Nothing so luxurious as that. There's a coaching inn outside of town, just along the highway. I've stayed there once before. It's clean and they serve a decent meal."

It was a minor economy, but a necessary one. He'd already spent more than he should on their rail tickets. He didn't regret the decision. Traveling first-class had enabled Julia to rest in the comfort and privacy of their own compartment. But going forward, he'd have to tighten the purse strings.

He hoped she wasn't too disappointed. If she was, he couldn't tell. The interior of the carriage was dark and there was no lamp to light her face.

With the weather, it took the driver a good half hour to reach the inn. Rain poured down in buckets, making a marshy stew of the un-characteristically busy yard. Jasper's boots squelched in the mud as he jumped down from the carriage.

He didn't attempt to guide Julia through it. Instead, as she stepped out of the cab, he swept her up in his arms and carried her into the building.

Julia clung to his neck. "So much for a cloudless sky."

The unspoken sentiment was clear: *Perhaps we're in for some bad luck after all.*

Setting her feet down in the smoke-filled front passage, Jasper won-dered if she might not be right. The inn was teeming with people; a chaos of voices and clinking glass drifting out from the small dining room.

When the innkeeper finally deigned to make an appearance, it was to inform Jasper they were full up.

"The rain came so unexpected like, travelers come straight in off the road," the man explained in a thick Yorkshire drawl. "We've only got the one spare room in the attic, and it ain't fit for any but a single guest."

Julia's teeth were chattering.

"We'll take it," Jasper said.

He arranged for their baggage to be carried up, and ordered dinner to be sent in to them in a half hour's time. Julia was in no state to sit up in the dining room, and he had no wish to expose her to such a rowdy group of people.

That didn't prevent her from being curious. Cleaving to Jasper's side as he spoke with the innkeeper, she gazed about in round-eyed wonder.

"*I haven't ever been out of London before*," she'd told him.

He couldn't imagine how all this must seem to her. First the rail-way journey and the carriage drive, and now this. A busy coaching inn on the edge of a remote North Yorkshire highway.

Add to that the fact that she now had a husband, and he wouldn't blame her if she fell into a fit of the vapors.

But she didn't.

She was being extraordinarily good-spirited about the whole thing.

"Jasper," she said as the innkeeper fetched them a key.

He bent his head to hers. "What is it?"

Her voice dropped to a bashful murmur. "I'm not certain I'm able to climb four flights of stairs."

"There's no question of you doing so."

She bit her lip. "But surely you can't—"

"Here you are, sir," the innkeeper said. "The boy's lit the fire and brought in your bags. All's in readiness for you."

Jasper accepted the key, and then, once again, picked his new bride up in his arms. She made a muffled sound of protest, burying her face into the curve of his neck as he carried her up the stairs.

"Hush," he whispered to her. "It's no hardship on my part, I assure you. Quite the contrary."

"I'm mortified," Julia whispered back. "What must everyone think?"

"They'll think I'm an eager husband with a very fetching new bride."

She groaned in embarrassment.

He wasn't merely being gallant. It was no effort to convey her up the stairs to their attic room. Reaching the fourth floor, he found a single door at the end of a short passageway. He had to duck to carry her through it, knocking off his hat in the process. Only when they were safe inside, the door shut and locked behind them, did he set her down.

The room, though tidy, was ludicrously small, even by the standards of a modest coaching inn. Shadows cast by the flames from the newly prepared fire shifted over the slatted floor, the worn armchair by the hearth, and the washstand in the corner topped by a chipped porcelain bowl and pitcher.

A bed in an old iron frame stood at the center of the room. Made up with clean sheets and a patchwork quilt, it was barely big enough for one large-sized man, let alone that man and his wife. Unless, that is, the couple slept together with a particular degree of familiarity.

A frown notched Jasper's brow.

Bloody hell. This was his wedding night. A night he was meant to spend in that bed deflowering his new bride.

It wasn't going to happen. Not yet. He'd promised her that. Nevertheless . . .

The bed was there, an almost taunting reminder.

Julia hadn't noticed it yet. After being set down, she stood against him for a moment to get her bearings, head bent and gloved hands flat on his chest. Her bosom rose and fell rapidly, as if she had been the one to climb the stairs and not him.

Blood loss made one short of breath. Jasper recalled that much from his own experience. The saber cut to his face had bled like the dickens. In the aftermath of the skirmish, packed onto a ship with hundreds of other injured and dying soldiers, he'd made the brief voyage from Sebastopol to Constantinople, breathless and weak, falling in and out of consciousness, only to awaken boiling with fever in a bed at Scutari Hospital.

He didn't know how much blood the doctor had taken from Julia, but he could well imagine how she must be feeling.

"Easy," he murmured as he untied her bonnet. Removing it from her head, he tossed it onto the bed alongside his hat. Her cloak followed, then her gloves. She submitted to his ministrations without a word. "Would you like to sit down or lie down?"

"Sit down," she said. "And then lie down."

A smile tugged at his mouth. "Both, then."

The chair was only a few steps away, but Julia made no move to go to it. She seemed reluctant to leave him.

He smoothed a hand over her rumpled hair, brushing it back from her face. It was one of the dozens of minor liberties he'd already taken with her—as tender as it was proprietary.

It should have been enough.

But this was the first time they'd ever been alone. Truly alone.

There were no servants about. No riders on Rotten Row or party guests smoking on a balcony or encroaching at the edges of a darkened garden. For the first time, he had her all to himself, inside a bedchamber, behind a securely locked door.

And she was his wife.

He dropped his hand from her hair to cup her face, tipping it up to his. Her skin was satiny warm, her blue eyes burning bright in the firelight. "Julia." His voice went gruff. "I mean to keep my promise to you about waiting to consummate our marriage. But it is our wedding night, and . . ."

A wash of rosy pink crept up her throat and into her face. "Yes?"

He moved the pad of his thumb over the slope of her blushing cheek in a slow caress. "I'd like to kiss you."

Her lips trembled. She didn't give him permission. Not with her words. But her arms slid up to wrap about his neck.

Heat surged through his veins as he felt the soft curve of her hand on the bare skin at his nape. She coaxed him to her. He needed little enough encouragement. Bending his head, he caught her mouth in a fiercely passionate kiss.

Her fingers slid into his hair, twining tightly.

And everything within him—from his heart to his lungs to his very soul, now bound for eternity with hers—contracted with a pleasure so keen it was almost too much to bear.

He wrapped his arms around her, one at her waist and one about her shoulders, holding her small body against his from her bosom to her knees. Her skirts tangled about his legs, crinoline and petticoats pushed all out of shape.

Alarm bells went off at the back of his mind, warning him to be careful with her, not to crush her with his size or overwhelm her with the strength of his passion.

But Julia showed no signs of being put off by his ardor. Standing on the toes of her boots, she strained up to meet him. Their breath mingled as she returned his kiss with soft, half-parted lips, her mouth yielding beneath his in the same blood-stirring fashion it had when he'd kissed her in the Claverings' garden.

Though untutored, she was not unskilled. There was a natural sensuality in the way she touched him. The way her lips moved on his with a sweetly seeking pressure.

It was an agony to break the kiss. Even when he did, he still held her in the same crushing embrace, his lips sliding along her jaw and cheek and temple.

"My darling girl," he murmured roughly. "You must tell me if I'm hurting you."

Her fingers loosened from his hair. "You're not hurting me."

"Are you certain?"

"Quite certain." She slid her hands to his shoulders. "I wish you could hold me like this forever."

A husky laugh rose up in his throat. It might have been a groan. He rested his cheek against her brow. "Don't tempt me."

For once, Julia was grateful to be exhausted. If she wasn't burnt to the socket, she might have expired from repressed embarrassment.

Illuminated by a glass oil lamp standing on the bedside table, the bed itself seemed to fill the whole of their small attic room. Everywhere she looked, there it was. There was no avoiding it, or the dilemma that would face them when it was time to retire.

Were they going to sleep together? Or would Jasper sleep on the floor? And after that kiss . . .

Good heavens.

She hadn't unwittingly changed the terms of their agreement, had she? In kissing him so passionately, she hadn't given him permission for more?

Not that he needed her permission.

A wife belonged to a husband in every regard. Her money wasn't her own. Her body wasn't her own. Even her children—if she ever had them—wouldn't be hers. Not in the eyes of the law. Once married, a husband and wife became one person. According to the law, that person was the husband.

For all intents and purposes, the moment she'd said *I will* at the little church in Camden, Julia had ceased to exist.

She could only imagine what Anne might have to say about it. Indeed, Anne's voice was echoing in Julia's mind with increasing frequency.

What have you done? Did you not stop to think for a moment that you might be leaping out of the frying pan and straight into the fire?

It was difficult not to think it now, despite how kind Julia's new husband was being.

They ate dinner alone in their room at a small table set up in front of the fire. Though solicitous about serving her meat and refilling her glass, Jasper was—for the most part—silent. Julia was equally so. The memory of their kiss was a palpable presence. A veritable third guest at their table, preventing any hope of normal conversation.

At last, the tension could be borne no longer.

She set down her fork. "Jasper—"

"I wonder," he said, "if we might not have progressed past the point of names."

Her attention was momentarily diverted. "You don't wish me to call you Jasper?"

He shrugged. A deceptively casual gesture.

Julia couldn't help feeling his remark was anything but. "What would you like me to call you?"

"The possibilities are limitless." He methodically folded his napkin, setting it down beside his plate. "How do your parents address each other?"

"They don't," she said frankly. "Not if they can help it. And when they do it's rarely directly." She hesitated before continuing. "My father refers to my mother as 'your poor dear mama' and my mother refers to him as 'your poor father.' That would hardly suit in our case."

Jasper's mouth tipped up at one corner. "Not yet anyway."

A blush threatened. But she wouldn't be distracted. "Don't you like my name?"

"Your name is beautiful. I like it very much."

Her brows knit. "Then . . . is it *your* name you don't like?"

"I confess, I don't. I'd rather you call me something else."

Her expression turned quizzical. "An endearment, do you mean? Or should I choose a different name altogether?"

"An endearment will suffice." He loosened his black cravat. He'd already removed his coat when they sat down. Another reminder of their newly minted intimacy. Clad in his shirtsleeves, his black waistcoat buttoned over his trim midsection, he appeared even larger and more powerful than ever.

"Is there one you'd prefer?" she asked.

"I'd like you to choose." Again, that deceptively casual tone. As if his request meant nothing at all. As if it was merely a whim.

Julia didn't understand him. "A name is important. I've realized that recently. It's part of a person's identity. You can't simply take it away from them and turn them into someone else."

His fingers stilled on the knot of his cravat. He looked at her intently.

"My parents renamed all our servants," she explained. "That's not fair, is it, to call a girl Jane when her name is Florence? It may seem like nothing very much, but if someone takes away your identity what do you have left?"

"I thought you were fascinated by the idea of people reinventing themselves."

"Only if they choose to do it freely."

"It *is* my choice," he said. "And it's not a reinvention. It's a privilege of being married." He finished removing his cravat. The collar of his white linen shirt gaped open, revealing a glimpse of the strong column of his throat.

Her eyes fell briefly to that exposed piece of bare skin. Like his face, it was gilded bronze by the firelight. When her gaze lifted back to his, it was to find him watching her. She moistened her lips. "I suppose, if you don't object to it too strenuously, I could refer to you as *my dear* or *dearest.*"

His gaze didn't waver, but his throat bobbed on a swallow.

"Is that all right?" she asked.

"For now," he said.

She brightened. "What will you call me?"

"I haven't decided yet. I might have to experiment to see what best suits you."

"You may keep calling me Julia if you wish. I have no objection. Unlike you, I rather like my name." She failed to stifle a yawn. Her hand flew to her mouth. "Oh, I do beg your pardon!"

He smiled. "You should have been in bed hours ago. Are you finished eating?"

"I am." Her eyes once again drifted to the bed. She must have stolen three dozen glances at the dratted thing since she and Jasper first sat down. Even while eating, it had been there, looming large at the edge of her vision.

His deep voice recalled her attention. "You were going to say something before I interrupted you?"

Julia gave him a rueful look. "There's only one bed."

"There is," he agreed solemnly. "You'll take it, of course."

"Where will you sleep?"

"On the floor. Or perhaps in this chair."

Neither appeared very inviting. The floor was hard wood, the rug all but threadbare. The chair was little better. Its upholstery was faded, and the springs and cushioning seemed to have long given up the ghost.

"You'll be dreadfully uncomfortable," she said.

"I've slept in worse places." He stood. "And no. I'm not going to discuss where." He came around the table and offered her his hand.

She slid her fingers into his large grasp. His skin was warm and faintly calloused from work, abrading her palm in the most delicious way. It sent a delicate thrill through her core.

Good gracious. He was her *husband.* They were *married.*

As he assisted her from her chair, a perilous thought occurred to her. "We could share it."

Jasper's hand tightened reflexively on hers. It was the only sign that he was affected by her words. There was no other indication—not in his voice or in his expression. His tone was entirely calm. "My dear, are you suggesting that we sleep together?"

Twenty

⚜

*J*asper knew the answer before she gave it. He couldn't think why he'd bothered to ask. She obviously hadn't been proposing they consummate their marriage. Even if she *had* suggested it, he wouldn't have obliged her. Not when she was so weak with exhaustion she could scarcely keep her eyes open.

"I could do little else in this state," she responded ingenuously. "And I'm a sound sleeper. You needn't worry about disturbing me."

"Plainly, it's only me who's going to be disturbed this evening," he said.

"Because the bed's so small? I don't expect it will be too unpleasant. Not in comparison to sleeping on the floor."

"'Unpleasant' isn't the word I'd use to describe it." He frowned at her for a moment. "Very well," he said at last. If he was going to torture himself, he may as well fully commit to the business. "Shall I leave you to change?"

"As to that . . ." Her cheeks pinkened with embarrassment. "I'm afraid I've never undressed without a maid to assist me. Not since I started wearing a corset."

Jasper's blood stirred with warmth.

So, this was what marriage was like. Standing in a tiny room at an inn with his bride, listening to her reference the difficulties of disrobing. It was a topic no lady would ever broach in mixed company. And yet, a few muttered words from the vicar and here Jasper and Julia were, husband and wife, on terms of the greatest intimacy.

It was difficult not to be affected by it.

"Would you like me to assist you?" he asked.

Her blush deepened. "If you wouldn't mind."

"You'll have to direct me." He attempted to keep his voice light and failed miserably. It sounded as raspy as the devil. "I'm not accustomed to undressing fine ladies."

She touched the front of her bodice with unsteady fingers. Her condition had already been weakened when they departed London, but after the rigors of their long journey, her remaining strength had faded to a shadow. She wouldn't last much longer.

"There are interior hooks all the way down," she said. "I can unfasten them myself, but—"

"Let me." He gently brushed aside her hands. "It will be quicker."

It wasn't.

Indeed, it took him an abominable length of time. His large hands kept fumbling over the delicate little closures. He was distracted by the lushly feminine shape of her. By the way every unfastened hook spread the two violet-dyed halves of her bodice open a little further, revealing another glimpse of the voluptuous swell of her bosom, confined behind a lace-trimmed cambric chemise and matching corset cover.

By the time he finally finished, he was perspiring.

Good God. There was torture and there was *torture.*

He nevertheless soldiered on, slipping her bodice from her shoulders and tugging her sleeves down over her arms. It was then he saw them—the twin bandages wound tight around her forearms.

A rush of concern swept through him like wildfire, burning away every other emotion. It was accompanied by something very like rage.

She tucked her arms behind her back. "It isn't as bad as it looks."

"Let me see." Jasper held out his hand. He was relieved when she took it, however reluctantly. "I won't hurt you."

"I know that." She permitted him to draw her right arm out to inspect it. "But you needn't fuss over me. I'd really rather you didn't."

"Naturally, I'm going to fuss over you. You're my wife." He examined her bandages. "What did the villain use? A lancet?"

"A scarificator."

Jasper made a soft sound of disgust as he took her left arm. It was bandaged even more heavily than her right. He glanced up at her in question.

"It wouldn't stop bleeding," she said.

He clenched his jaw, so angry on her behalf he could scarcely get the words out without snarling them. "Where were your parents?"

"They'd gone to their rooms by then. It was only Mary and me. And Dr. Cordingley."

Jasper couldn't understand how her mother and father could have allowed her to be subjected to such an outrage. "You must have been very ill for them to summon the man."

"I wasn't ill," Julia said quietly. It was the same thing she'd said in her bedroom at Belgrave Square.

He gave her a sharp look. "What?"

"I wasn't ill. I only needed some time alone, by myself, with my books. The only way I'm permitted any privacy is if I'm in poor health. So . . . I said that I was. That's why Dr. Cordingley was summoned."

Understanding sank in. Jasper didn't know if he should be amused or appalled. "You've done this before."

"Sometimes." Her color heightened. "Often," she amended. "It isn't as bad as it sounds."

"You let him bleed you so you could stay in bed reading a novel?"

"You make it sound quite unreasonable."

"Julia—" He broke off. "My God."

She tugged her hand from his grasp. "And I don't *let* Dr. Cordingley do anything. I never ask for him to come. My parents are the ones who summon him. It's the price I must pay to be left alone. In the past, it's seemed to be worth it."

"Not today, obviously."

"No. Not today."

Jasper was poised to say more on the subject, but Julia was in no state to hear it. Her face, in the firelight, was as bloodless and pale as it had been when he'd called on her in Belgrave Square.

He came to an instant decision.

Sweeping her up in his arms, he carried her to the bed. She opened her mouth to object, but he silenced her with a look as he set her down on the edge of the mattress. "I should have known this would be too fatiguing for you. Had I been thinking clearly when we arrived, I'd have ordered you straight to bed."

"Ordered me," she scoffed. "Really, Jasper."

He gave her a dark glance as he crouched down to untie her boots.

"My dear," she said, correcting herself.

"That's better." He removed her boots, and then, reaching up beneath her skirts, he found the satin ribbon garter tied above her right knee.

Julia sucked in a scandalized breath. *"What are you doing?"*

"I'm removing your stockings."

"You mustn't." She pushed against his shoulders. "I mean it. I can do that part myself."

His fingers curved around the back of her silk-clad knee. "Let me," he said. "Please."

She held his gaze, brows knit in indecision. "Very well." She lay back on the bed with a sigh of maidenly resignation. "If you insist."

Jasper suppressed a smile. One might think he was on the verge of ravishing her.

It wasn't at all the case.

He *did* want her. How he could not? She'd permitted him to kiss her—deeply, passionately—and she'd kissed him back in full measure. But it hadn't changed the terms of their agreement.

He didn't want her this way. Not when she was weak and vulnerable. Not when the whole of her life had been turned upside down. In this room, in this moment, she didn't need him to seduce her. She needed him to be steady and reliable. She needed to know he was going to look after her.

"Tell me something," he said as he rolled her stocking down her shapely right leg. "What did your lady's maid do to help you each evening? Did she remove all your clothes?"

"Not all of them." Julia's voice quavered as he continued to undress her. "I can do most of it myself. Everything except the hard-to-reach buttons and hooks."

"Not tonight you can't."

"No," she acknowledged. "But most nights I can. Mary only helped with the difficult bits."

Jasper stripped off her other stocking. It took an effort not to linger. Her calves were muscled from riding, her ankles so narrow he could encircle them with his fingers. And her feet, delicately arched and pale, and small enough to cradle in his hand.

He cleared his throat. "Is that all?"

"She brushed my hair."

"You couldn't brush it yourself?"

"It wasn't like that. It was a ritual we had—one of my favorite parts of the day." She inhaled another sharp breath as his arms came around her, fingers moving to the fastenings at the back of her skirts.

"Describe it to me," he said, endeavoring to distract her.

"I-I would sit in front of my dressing table. Mary would unpin my hair and start brushing. One hundred strokes, she liked to say, but it wasn't ever as many as that." Julia was quiet for a moment before admitting, "I'll miss that part of my old life the most."

"Why?"

"It made me feel as though someone cared for me. And it always helped soothe me to sleep."

As she spoke, Jasper removed her skirt, petticoats, and crinoline, tugging them down over her hips and legs. Her corset cover came next, then the corset itself with its row of strong metal hooks at the front of her midriff.

Her breath came faster as he stripped it away.

His own breath wasn't coming at all. It was dammed up in his chest, his pulse throbbing with stifled longing. Thus far, he'd remained purposeful. Respectful. But by God, he wasn't made of stone.

By the time he was finished, she was clothed in nothing but her short-sleeved cambric chemise and matching cambric drawers. It was a modest enough ensemble, though doubtless, she was feeling more exposed than she had in her life.

"Do you wish to sleep as you are?" he asked, scarcely recognizing the sound of his own voice. "Or would you prefer a nightgown?"

"A nightgown, if you please. There's one in the brown carpetbag."

He retrieved it for her. It was the same nightgown she'd been wearing when he'd rescued her. A ruffled white cotton garment, as primly virginal in its construction as anything he'd ever beheld.

"You can leave now," she said as she took it from him. "Or at least . . . turn around."

He obliged her. As he stood facing the fire, he heard the frantic rustle of soft garments coupled with the sound of her quickening breath. "Are you certain you don't need my help?"

"No, thank you."

He waited awhile longer before inquiring again.

"Yes, yes," she said. "I'm finished now."

He turned back to her. He'd seen her in her nightgown before. But she hadn't only changed her clothes. She'd taken down her hair. It tumbled loose over one shoulder in a thick ebony spill.

Regarding her from across the room, Jasper felt a disconcerting mix of emotions. Not only desire for a beautiful woman, but affection, compassion, and a deep thread of masculine possessiveness.

"Would you like me to brush it for you?" he asked impulsively.

She blinked. "Would you?"

His mouth hitched in a sudden smile. "Why not?"

As Julia angled herself on the edge of the bed, a cashmere shawl wrapped around her in lieu of a dressing gown, it occurred to her that having her new husband brush her hair was very different than having her maid do it.

For one thing, she hadn't anticipated how trembly and breathless it would make her feel. And she was already quite trembly and breathless enough after Jasper had helped to undress her.

He'd removed her corset, for heaven's sake. And he'd touched her bare legs and even her naked feet.

Butterflies rampaged in her stomach to recall it.

In other circumstances, the whole experience might have left her mortified beyond permission, but Jasper had done nothing to exacerbate her embarrassment. He'd been both gentle and ruthlessly efficient. Just as he was being now.

As he sat next to her, running her brush through the length of her hair, Julia was plagued by a gnawing sense of guilt.

Her new husband might be a fortune hunter, and theirs might be a marriage of convenience, but he was still a man, and this was still his wedding night. Doubtless he hadn't expected to spend it caring for an invalid bride.

"I'm not always this frail," she informed him.

Jasper continued plying the hairbrush. "I realize that."

"In a day or two, I shall be myself again."

"I trust you will, providing you get enough rest."

She glanced back at him, struck by a sudden suspicion. "You aren't going to insist I remain in bed, are you?"

His countenance was stern. "If that's what it takes to recover yourself."

It wasn't the answer she'd wanted.

"It won't be." She bent her head, allowing him to continue brushing. "By tomorrow I'll be much stronger. You'll see."

He gathered a section of her hair in his hand. His fingers skimmed the shell of her ear.

The contact made Julia's pulse quicken.

He was sitting at an angle beside her. All she need do was lean back against his chest. And then . . .

If she was lucky, he would take her in his arms and hold her as he had in those moments before they'd sat down to dine. A crushing, all-consuming embrace. It had made her feel so safe. So wanted.

It was a feeling she longed to repeat.

"There's no hurry," he said.

Her heart missed a beat. For an instant she thought he'd read her mind. *Foolish.* He was talking about her recovery. "There is," she replied. "I don't want the children to know I've been ill."

"Why not?"

"Because I want to make a good first impression." They were going to be her family now. She had a keen desire not to disappoint them. "I'd like them all to think well of me."

"Julia . . ." The brush stilled on her hair. "If you're expecting a warm welcome . . ."

She looked back at him once more. "Shouldn't I be?"

Jasper's scarred face was shadowed in the dim glow cast by the oil lamp on the bedside table. "I told you the children were wild. They can be quite a handful. Especially the boys."

"Charlie and Alfred." She recalled him mentioning their names at Lady Holland's dinner. "Charlie's twelve, didn't you say?"

"He is. Alfred's one year younger."

She dipped her chin as he resumed brushing. "I don't know much about boys that age. None of my friends have brothers except for Miss Hobhouse. And hers is older than her, not younger."

"Boys aren't so complicated. Not if you can overlook their surliness and bad manners."

"How can they have bad manners with you as their father? I'd have thought you'd have molded them into perfect little soldiers."

He huffed. "Hardly. My experiences in the Crimea carry no weight with Charlie and Alfred."

"What about Daisy?"

"She's wild, too, in her way." Jasper patiently untangled a knot in Julia's tresses before brushing it through. "All the children are in want of civilizing."

Julia had a troubling thought. "You don't expect *me* to civilize them, do you?"

A wry smile sounded in his voice. "You can but try."

"I'd rather be a friend to them."

"I hope you will be," he said.

She gradually relaxed under his ministration, sighing with contentment as the brush moved over her hair. He had a stronger stroke than Mary. It was exceedingly pleasurable.

"You're very good at this," she observed.

"I'm glad you think so."

"Have you done it before?"

"Often. I frequently assist in readying Daisy for bed or in helping her to dress in the morning. She's not as fond of having her hair brushed as other ladies I've known."

Her mind latched on to a single phrase. "*Have* there been others?"

He was silent.

"Have there?" she asked again.

He stopped brushing. It was answer enough.

A stab of jealousy took Julia unaware. She turned to look at him. And something in his face told her that there hadn't been others; there had been only one. Another woman he'd been intimate with in this exact same way.

Hurt warred with curiosity within her breast. "Who was she?" she asked. But she feared she already knew the answer. It was his mistress, of course. The mother of his three children. Judging by their ages, Jasper had been with the woman for years.

He neither confirmed her suspicions nor denied them. Instead, he set aside her hairbrush and, rising from the bed, crossed the room to stand in front of the fire.

Worse and worse.

"You can tell me," she said. "I won't be jealous." It was a lie. She was already jealous.

He faced her from across the short distance, the flames at his back. "You have no reason to be. It was a long time ago."

She studied him in the firelight. "Did you care for her very much?"

"I did," he admitted. "I loved her."

Julia's stomach clenched. Well. There it was. He'd been in love with his mistress. Perhaps he still loved her.

It served Julia right for asking.

A shiver went through her. She drew her shawl more firmly about her shoulders. If she had any sense, she wouldn't ask him anything more. But as always, her inquisitiveness got the better of her. "What happened?"

He shrugged. "She died."

Any relief Julia might have felt at the revelation was overshadowed by a genuine and immediate sympathy. "Oh, my dear," she said softly. "I *am* sorry."

Something flickered in his eyes. An emotion she couldn't interpret. "Don't be," he said. "I told you, it was a long time ago."

"I'm still sorry. If you loved her—"

"It's in the past. I shouldn't have mentioned it." He came toward her. "You're cold."

She stood; the ends of her shawl twined in her fingers. "I am, rather. It's past time I went to bed."

He reached out to her.

"No, no." She drew back from him. "I can manage. You must attend to yourself. I daresay you're as tired as I am."

She didn't give him an opportunity to object. Hastily pulling back the coverlet, she clambered into bed and slid clumsily beneath the sheets. The faded pillow slip was soft on her cheek as she burrowed her face into the pillow, determined not to look as Jasper disrobed.

If he *was* disrobing.

The room had gone silent, save for the intermittent crackle of the fire. She sensed his presence near the bed, still standing there, as if on the verge of saying something.

Or doing something.

Anxiety bubbled within her. The mattress was indeed small. And Jasper Blunt was a large man. He outstripped her in height by nearly a foot. And he was easily more than six stone heavier than she was. She knew that much for a certainty. Only moments ago, she'd felt every inch of his powerfully muscled frame as he'd held her in his arms and kissed her.

And now he was going to be sleeping beside her.

Goodness.

Goodness.

She waited for him to speak, but he never did. He withdrew to the other side of the room, the floorboards creaking beneath his feet. In time, she heard the sound of clothing being removed. First his boots, then everything else—or so she imagined.

But when he at last came to join her in bed, she opened her eyes to discover him still wearing his shirt and trousers. She caught a glimpse of his untucked linen shirt before he turned down the oil lamp.

"You're still dressed," she said with some chagrin.

"I am." He climbed in beside her. The already sagging mattress sagged still further under his weight.

Julia had to grip her side of the bed to keep from rolling against him. A futile effort. In seconds, they were as close as they'd been when he'd embraced her.

They faced each other in the firelit darkness, practically nose to nose.

Her heart hammered so hard it stole her breath. "Won't you be uncomfortable?"

"I'll be uncomfortable regardless."

"Then why—"

"I mean to keep my promises to you—one way or another."

She offered him an uncertain smile. "Am I that hard to resist?"

"Sweetheart," he said gravely, "you have no idea."

Twenty-One

—◆◆◆—

$\mathcal{P}$ushing back the curtain, Julia peered out the rain-streaked window of the hired carriage. It was still pouring outside, the lonely Yorkshire landscape a blurry expanse of stormy skies and eerily empty countryside. They'd been on the road for nearly three hours—a distance of more than fifteen miles from the roadside inn outside of Malton.

"Is it much further now?" she asked.

"Another hour," Jasper said. Dressed in a sober black suit, with an equally sober expression on his face, he was seated across from her in the carriage, not beside her. Indeed, since they'd left the inn, he'd seemed resolved to put a bit of distance between them.

Julia couldn't think why. Had she said something? Done something? Or was it only that he was brooding about returning home with a new wife in tow?

She was anxious, too. Though her anxiety had nothing to do with regrets about their marriage. Last night, tucked beside him in their narrow attic bed, she'd slept more soundly than she ever had in her life.

It had been an entirely new experience—and not only because he was a man. She'd never shared a bed with anyone before. Even as a little girl, none of her ever-changing roster of nurses had slept beside her. And Julia had never been permitted to have any of her friends stay over, or to stay over with them in return.

Sleeping with Jasper had felt scandalous at the start. He was too big—too male. It was impossible to move an inch without touching him. But exhaustion quickly overtook any thought of shyness or embarrassment. She'd drifted off as soon as she closed her eyes.

After that, she couldn't remember much of anything about the experience. But she could readily recollect the feelings it had engendered. She'd been wonderfully warm and utterly and completely safe.

At dawn, she'd awakened to an empty bed. Her new husband was an early riser. He was already up and half-dressed, standing in front of the washstand, shaving himself. She'd watched him for a moment from the warmth of the tangled bedcovers, fascinated to witness such a private masculine ritual.

Her spying hadn't lasted long.

He'd caught her gaze in his shaving mirror. His razor had stilled on his jaw. Taut seconds passed, and then: "*I've ordered breakfast,*" he'd said. "*If you're equal to it, I'd like to be on the road within the hour.*"

She'd pushed her tousled hair back from her face, feeling suddenly self-conscious as she registered the change in his mood. "*Of course. It won't take me long to wash and dress.*"

As the poorly sprung carriage rattled through the mud, jolting her in her seat, Julia again wondered what had happened to alter his manner toward her.

Perhaps it was only now sinking in that he was stuck with her. That he hadn't only gained her fortune, but her as well—until death would they part.

She reminded herself once more that she hadn't married him for romance. She'd married him to free herself from the oppressiveness of London, and from an inevitable betrothal to Lord Gresham. Jasper's isolated estate would be a sanctuary for her. A place where she could finally breathe.

All that was required was that she get along with the children—and that she exhibit a minimal competence in household management. It was the least expected of a wife.

Dropping her hand from the curtain, Julia settled back in her seat. She'd dressed on her own this morning and even managed to arrange her hair. Hopefully, the children would find her good enough to pass muster.

"Are you certain they'll know we're coming?" she asked.

"They should," Jasper said. "I had Ridgeway's butler send a wire to Hardholme. With luck, Beecham will have received it by now."

"How far is the village from the Hall?"

"Five miles of bad road. Carriage travel is difficult, but a horse and rider can manage it, even in this weather. Mr. McCready at the telegraph office will have sent someone."

"Five miles isn't such a great distance," she said. "I'm surprised you've been unable to find any servants."

"It isn't only the distance that dissuades people from accepting regular employment at the Hall."

Her brows lifted in question.

"There's my reputation, for one," he said. "And the children's lack of legitimacy. And then there's the house itself."

She waited for him to continue, but he once again fell silent. He was in a grumpy, brooding frame of mind, more content to frown at her from across the carriage than he was to indulge her curiosity.

In the early days of their acquaintance, it might have put her off. Then, she'd been disposed to shrink from him the moment he looked in her direction. But not anymore. Not now she knew something of the man lurking beneath the beastly exterior.

"Lady Arundell claims it's haunted," she informed him. "And she's not the only one who's said so."

A scowl darkened his brow.

Julia was undeterred. "Is it true?"

"It's true that the Hall has a reputation."

She looked at him expectantly.

He grudgingly continued, "It was originally owned by a family of Royalists who were executed during the Civil War. According to local superstition, some of them still walk the grounds."

"Have you ever seen them?"

"Are you asking me if there are ghosts living at the Hall?"

Her mouth tipped at one corner. "Are there?"

Jasper surprised her with his answer. "Goldfinch Hall *is* haunted. But not by the kind of ghosts you imagine."

Her attention was captured as surely as if he'd unveiled a new chapter in a serialized sensation novel. "What do you mean? What kinds of ghosts?"

"Old sins cast long shadows," he said. "If the atmosphere at the Hall is unsettling, you can attribute it to that, not to any spectral presence."

Her rapt expression faded. He wasn't tempting her with a ghost story. His bleak sentiments were all too real. She regarded him with bewilderment. "You make it sound as though you're unhappy there."

He looked back at her steadily, his stern countenance belied by a gruff admission: "I'm not unhappy. Not now you're coming home with me."

His words settled inside her breast, glowing warm and bright, like a coal fresh from the fire.

Her smile returned slowly. "I do believe you mean that."

"You *can* believe it," he said. "If nothing else."

"It isn't only my dowry, then?"

He gave a humorless laugh. "If it were, we wouldn't be here."

"Wouldn't we?" Julia's smile turned quizzical. "I thought that was the most important quality in your prospective wife—the size of her dowry."

"The size matters little if your father refuses to grant it to me."

She stared at him. "My father *refused* you?"

"I told you he did. We discussed it yesterday." He scanned her face, frowning with concern. "Don't you remember?"

"Of course, I remember." She hadn't been *that* ill. "You didn't say anything about my dowry."

"I assumed it was obvious. Without your father's permission, there's no money at all. *'Not a farthing,'* I believe is the way he put it." Jasper grimaced. "Not the most flattering experience of my life. But his meaning was quite clear."

Julia recalled Jasper's question to her yesterday as she'd lain propped up in her bed. "*What if there were no money?*" he'd asked. "*What if there was only me?*"

She hadn't taken him seriously. She'd long accepted that she had nothing but her dowry to recommend her. That she wasn't good enough or worthy enough on her own. It had seemed an incontrovertible fact. In response to it, she'd constructed three failed seasons' worth of defenses.

The truth finally began to penetrate them.

She didn't dare believe it. "Do you mean to say that . . . you married me with no hope of receiving my fortune?"

"I did."

"But what about the house? The children? You need money for repairs and—"

He shrugged. "I shall find another way. It won't be easy, I know, but . . ." A rueful smile touched his scarred lips. "I had to have you."

Julia shook her head in disbelief. She was too stunned to speak. Too altogether astonished by the revelation, and all its various implications, to move or even to breathe.

He had truly taken her in her underclothes. Not only undressed, but penniless as well. Her fortune had had nothing to do with it. It was only her. Because he'd wanted her. Because he'd chosen her for herself alone.

A great swell of emotion clogged her throat.

"Oh." The word emerged in a broken whisper. "Oh, I had no idea. I thought . . . I thought you only wanted my money."

His brows lowered. "Why the devil would you think that?"

"You said so yourself. That you must needs marry an heiress. I knew once you learned my dowry was greater than Miss Throckmorton's you would renew your addresses. It's why I mentioned it when I proposed to you."

Jasper looked vaguely appalled. And worse. He seemed to have gone a trifle pale.

All at once, he surged up from his seat. The floor of the carriage rocked beneath his booted feet as he crossed the small space to sink down at her side. He caught her gloved hand tight in both of his. "Julia . . ." He stared down at her intently. "Don't say you thought we were going to be rich."

"We *are* rich."

He brought her hand to his lips, pressing a hard kiss to the leather-clad crease of her thumb. "Yes," he admitted grudgingly, "I suppose we are. Rich in blessings. And we have our health and—"

"I was talking about the money," she said. "We're rich in money."

Jasper went still as stone, even as his gaze sharpened to a razor's edge.

"My dowry is one hundred thousand pounds altogether," she informed him, "but only fifty thousand of that comes from my parents." Her chin lifted with a hint of pride. "The other fifty thousand belongs to me."

Jasper had had no idea. Not even the smallest suspicion. Not even when he'd noticed the discrepancy between the amount Julia was reported to be worth and the amount she'd claimed to be worth herself.

A fifty-thousand-pound discrepancy.

He felt as though she'd struck a blow straight to his solar plexus. As devastating a hit as when she'd proposed to him. Indeed, for all she was sweet and dainty, his new bride had the lethal repertoire of a bare-knuckle boxer.

It occurred to him that he may have misunderstood. It wouldn't be at all surprising, not after the restless night he'd had. With Julia next to him, he'd scarcely managed to sleep a wink.

Though blushingly shy when awake, his wife was a menace while sleeping. No sooner had she nodded off, than she was pressing herself against him, seeking his warmth. At various times throughout the night, her arm had been flung around him, her head burrowed in his chest, and once, much to his alarm, her leg had even insinuated itself between both of his.

She was a soft, feminine armful. All voluptuous curves, silken hair, and delicately perfumed skin.

He'd spent most of the night so painfully aroused he couldn't think straight.

Rising at dawn, he'd found himself in a devil of a mood. Keeping his promise to her was never going to be easy. But after *that* experience, it would be well-nigh impossible. He wanted her like mad—physically, emotionally. In every way he could have her.

And yet, as close as she'd been to him, as close as he still hoped they might be, there were pieces of himself he could never share. He knew, with a miserable certainty, that in every way that mattered, he was destined to be a stranger to her.

Recognizing that fact had made him as cross as a wounded bear.

And now this.

"Did you say *fifty thousand pounds*?" he asked.

She nodded. "My great-aunt Elinore left it to me. She was widowed young, and had no children of her own. I believe she felt sorry for me."

"Fifty thousand pounds," he repeated, rather stupidly.

"She felt *very* sorry for me," Julia amended. "When I was a little girl, she came to stay with us for a short time. My parents had me in bed with leeches and mustard plasters for the whole of her visit. Aunt Elinore had words with them about it. I never saw her again. She died the following year. That's when I learned she'd left me all her money. I keep it in Hoares Bank in Fleet Street, the same place my father keeps his accounts. It's how I bought Cossack. How I buy all the things that are important to me."

He continued to stare at her, still holding her hand in both of his. Would she never cease surprising him? "Julia . . ."

"It isn't as much as one hundred thousand pounds, I know. But it's still sizable. There are other young ladies on the marriage mart with dowries no larger than ten or twenty thousand, and they're considered great catches. But fifty—"

"It's enormous," he said.

A faint line of worry creased her brow. "Is it enough for your purposes?"

He kissed her hand once again, holding it to his lips. "You're enough for my purposes. Even without the money."

Her expression softened. Lifting her hand from his, she reached up to gently touch his cheek.

The shy caress sent a jolt of heat straight through his vitals.

Her eyes searched his. "A moment ago, I wouldn't have believed you. But you truly mean it, don't you?"

"I mean it," he said huskily.

"You did want me for myself alone."

"I still want you." He lowered his head to hers, seizing her lips.

Her fingers slid into his hair as he kissed her with fierce tenderness—softly, deeply, and all too briefly.

The carriage shuddered, careening over a stone in the muddy road.

Julia gave a breathless laugh as they broke apart. "I fear this vehicle is too poorly sprung to support such activities."

"A shame." He smoothed a stray lock of hair from her face, tucking it back into the crepe-lined interior of her fashionable straw bonnet. "We shall have to postpone our kisses until this evening."

Her cheeks turned pink. "I meant to ask you about that."

He put his arm around her, drawing her close. "About kissing each other?"

"No. Not that exactly." She snuggled against his side. "I was wondering if we're going to share a bedchamber?"

The question ignited his already smoldering blood. It took an effort to answer with any degree of equanimity. "Ah." He affected to consider the matter. "Would you like to share a room with me?"

She didn't hesitate. "Yes."

"Most ladies would rather have their privacy."

"I do enjoy my privacy. And I hope I shall have plenty of it. But at night . . ." She slid an arm around his midsection. "I slept so soundly with you next to me, dearest."

Dearest.

His heart clenched hard.

Julia continued on, oblivious to the havoc she was wreaking in his breast. "More soundly than I ever have. I can't think why, except that you make me feel so safe. Rather like a lamb in company with a very large sheepdog."

He choked on a hoarse laugh. "Good God."

"I didn't know it was possible to ever feel that way. I shouldn't like to give the feeling up, not so soon after I've found it."

"Very well," he said. "If that's what you want."

"You don't mind it?"

To sleep with her every night and not to have her? He minded it like the devil. But at the moment, he had the besotted notion that he'd give her anything she desired. Anything—even his very life, if she asked for it. Even all his secrets, though it may destroy him in the process.

"I don't mind," he said. "I want it, too."

An hour later, amid a pounding rain that fell sideways as much as downward, they passed Hardholme. Another five miles, jolted in the carriage as the wheels rolled over the deserted scrap of uneven road that cut through the North York Moors, and the tall iron gates of Goldfinch Hall appeared in the distance.

Jasper drew back the curtain for his wife to see. "There. Is that gothic enough for your romantic sensibilities?"

Julia leaned across him to get a better look, bracing one hand on his thigh. "Gracious. How sinister they look! And they're standing open, too." She glanced back at him. "Do you suppose that means Mr. Beecham and the children are waiting for us at the house?"

"Possibly." Or it might mean that the last person to go through them had failed to shut them. The Hall housed a veritable collection of savages—Daisy among them. For all Jasper knew, the gates had been standing open for the entirety of his absence.

She sat back in her seat. Her face was anxious. "I wish I'd had time to buy gifts for the children."

"Your presence will be gift enough," he said gallantly.

She gave him an amused look. "If that's what you think, you must not remember your own childhood very well. A new toy or a book means the world to a child."

"They have books," he said.

If only she knew how many.

A part of him was eager as a lad to show her. To share it all with her—this remote, ramshackle place that would soon be her home. A place where she would remain, to be his own and to live with him for the rest of his life.

"You can never have too many books," she said. "That's a fact."

He refrained from comment.

Julia didn't notice his lack of reply. She was too busy straightening her skirts and smoothing her hair.

He watched her with possessive attention, learning all her various fidgets and idiosyncrasies. Committing them to memory.

She had nothing to be concerned about. Wearing a carriage dress of lobelia blue silk, her ebony hair swept back in a black velvet–trimmed net, she looked beautiful, just as she always did. It was a beauty that shone out of her like a beacon, irrespective of outward trappings, warming whoever was fortunate enough to fall within its proximity.

It warmed him, even now. Even though he was fully aware of what was to come.

But there was no prolonging his pleasure.

Inevitably, the carriage turned the familiar corner, advancing up the sloping drive. The same corner Jasper had turned six years ago, the future stretched before him, seemingly endless with possibility.

He pulled back the curtain once more. The great stone house loomed ahead against a slate-gray sky, as hateful to him now as any fairy-tale castle might be to the creature cursed to exist within its walls.

"There it is," he said grimly. "Goldfinch Hall."

Twenty-Two

❖

$\mathcal{J}$ulia held tight to Jasper's hand as he assisted her out of the carriage. It took an effort not to gape at the house.

The monstrous edifice was built of granite that had severely weathered in places, giving the surface a look of perpetual shadow. A mad tangle of heavily thorned wild roses climbed the high walls, encroaching on the arched windows and doorways in an oddly sinister fashion. Only a few rain-battered blooms were evident among all the prickly leaves and spikes, their overblown petals as red as freshly spilled blood.

No wonder people said it was haunted. With its imposing facade and air of derelict grandeur, it appeared like something from a gothic story. All gloom and decay and lingering mystery. A castle under an evil fairy's curse. *Heavens*. There was even a tower!

Stepping down onto the muddy drive, she took Jasper's arm. He shepherded her through the rain and up the moss-covered stone front steps. An aged gentleman awaited them at the top, sheltered beneath a stone outcropping. His eyes were keen with intelligence; his gleaming bald head complemented by a profuse white beard.

A boy stood next to him—young and slim, with a mop of black hair, and a scowl etched so deeply into his narrow face it might have been carved there with a chisel.

"My dear," Jasper said, "this is Mr. Beecham. And this young man is Charlie." He set a hand at the small of Julia's back. "Beecham, Charlie. This is my wife. I trust you'll make her welcome."

"Mrs. Blunt." Mr. Beecham bowed. "Welcome to Goldfinch Hall."

"Mr. Beecham." Julia inclined her head. "I'm glad to make your acquaintance." She turned a smile on Charlie. "And I'm very pleased to meet you, sir. Your father's told me so much about you."

The boy's features hardened. "He's told us nothing about you."

"*Charlie.*" Jasper's voice held an unmistakable note of warning.

Charlie didn't heed it. Without another word, he bolted off into the house.

Jasper's muscles tensed as if he might follow him.

Julia squeezed his arm. "It's all right."

Jasper's jaw tightened. It plainly wasn't all right. Not as far as he was concerned. "Where are Alfred and Daisy?"

Mr. Beecham was shamefaced. "Run off, sir. I haven't seen either of them since breakfast."

Jasper's already somber expression darkened. Without another word, he ushered Julia through the arched front door. Made of weather-beaten wood, it swung back on creaking iron hinges, opening into a slate-tiled hall.

Mr. Beecham accompanied them inside. "We've not had a chance to get anyone out to patch the leak in the nursery yet," he said to Jasper in a low voice. "I only received your letter yesterday evening. McCready's boy delivered it along with your telegraph. You could have knocked me over with a feather. I told Charlie he wasn't to trouble you while you were in town."

"Daisy's not still sleeping in the nursery?"

"I've moved her to the adjoining room. It's dry there, with less of the damp. She might do well to remain there permanently. Even with the money you sent, the repairs will—"

"We can discuss it later," Jasper said.

"Yes, indeed," Mr. Beecham replied. "You'll be tired after your journey and wanting some refreshment."

Julia's gaze drifted over the entrance hall as the two men spoke.

An unnervingly steep staircase rose to the right, curving up to the floors above. To the left was a carved stone archway, leading into a sort of drawing room. After divesting her of her bonnet, cloak, and gloves—and removing his own rain-spattered outer garments—Jasper escorted her there, guiding her in front of a cavernous marble fireplace.

Sunk deep into the wall, it was as wide as it was tall. The largest fireplace Julia had ever seen. The roaring fire within its fathomless depths took the chill out of her limbs in record time.

The rest of the room was less imposing. To be sure, there was nothing very gothic about it. It was furnished neatly, if not lavishly, with a plain rug, upholstered sofas and chairs, and heavy draperies shrouding the tall windows.

"I've set out a small repast for you," Mr. Beecham said, following after them. He gestured to a low wooden table in front of the sofa. A tray had been arrayed there, containing a plate of sandwiches, mismatched porcelain teacups, a silver sugar bowl, and a ceramic pitcher of milk. "I'll fetch the tea from the kitchen. And there's a cake that should be done soon."

Julia sank down on the sofa, grateful for the chance to rest. "Do you bake, sir?"

"Aye, I do, Mrs. Blunt," Mr. Beecham said. "It's a pleasure of mine, it is. Though there's little enough time for it when I'm looking after the children."

Jasper remained standing in front of the fire. His hair was damp, the silver strands at his temples cast into prominence by the bright light of the flames at his back. "They should be helping you."

"They do help when they've a mind to," Beecham said. "Though I confess 'twere easier when the boys were in school."

Julia gave Jasper an inquiring look. "They don't attend school any longer?"

Jasper's frown deepened. "They did up until three months ago. The schoolmaster's recently asked that they not return."

"I'll fetch the hot water," Beecham said, ducking out of the room.

Julia hardly noticed his departure. She continued to look at Jasper, brows lifted in question. "Why? Did something happen?"

Jasper heaved a sigh. Moving from the fireplace, he came to sit beside her. "I'd hoped we would have a few hours reprieve before having to deal with all this misery. I might have known that was too much to ask."

"We needn't talk about it now if you don't wish to."

"I don't wish to," he said. "But you're bound to hear of it eventually—among other misdeeds. The boys have a penchant for getting into trouble, and the schoolmaster, Mr. Filbert, is something of a martinet. At the beginning of last term, Charlie painted a layer of glue on the man's chair."

"Oh no," Julia said.

"Oh yes. And that's not the worst of it. Filbert sat down unaware during a long lesson. When at last he stood, the seat of his trousers ripped off."

She pressed her lips together hard to keep herself from laughing. A choked noise emerged nonetheless.

"Don't." Jasper's eyes briefly reflected her merriment. "We *cannot* be amused by this sort of behavior."

"No, indeed," she said soberly.

The humor in Jasper's expression faded. "It's bad enough that Charlie should greet you as he did." He ran a hand over his hair. "Good God. I could box his ears."

"Should you go and find him?" she asked.

"I will, once he's cooled off."

"He seemed dreadfully upset."

"No more than usual."

"He must be very angry about you marrying me."

"It has nothing to do with you," Jasper said. "It's about me. I warned you about the past casting long shadows."

Julia waited for him to elaborate, to explain what events from the past had made Charlie so angry at him, but Jasper didn't offer anything more. "Another secret you'd like to have a reprieve from?"

His mouth hitched in a wry smile. "Something like that."

"I can wait," she said. "After all, we have the whole of our lives."

His gaze lingered on her face. "We do, don't we?" Lifting his hand, he stroked his knuckles along the edge of her jaw. It was an infinitely gentle caress. Almost as gentle as the words that followed. "How are you, sweetheart?" he asked. "If you're feeling weary, you must tell me so."

She was disarmed by his touch, just as she always was. "I *am* weary," she admitted. The hours-long carriage ride from Malton had been arduous, and she was still weak after her bloodletting.

"Would you like to retire to bed?"

"At this time of the morning? No, no," she said. "A cup of tea and some cake will soon put me right."

"I know something else that might do so." His eyes glimmered with a flash of devilry. "Shall I wait to share it with you until after you've eaten something?"

Her interest was instantly piqued. "On no account," she said. "What is it? Tell me."

"It isn't something for me to tell you. It's something for me to show you." He stood and offered his hand.

She took it, permitting him to assist her to her feet. She'd never seen him look so pleased with himself. It lent a boyishness to his stern features. A trace of vulnerability that fairly stole her heart away.

Weary or no, in that moment, she believed she'd follow him to the ends of the earth.

Luckily, he asked her to accompany him no further than back out into the hall. From there, he guided her down a corridor toward the rear of the house, through a double set of stone archways that led to a large wooden door.

He pushed it open.

A familiar fragrance assailed her. *Books.* She recognized it immediately—which rather spoiled his surprise.

Or so she thought.

But when Jasper nudged her across the threshold and into the room, the sight that greeted Julia wasn't just a bookroom or a library. It was something else entirely.

It was paradise.

"Oh," she whispered. "Oh my."

Bookshelves lined the walls, stretching two stories high, every one of them packed full to bursting. But not with the large, leather-bound tomes one usually found in a well-stocked private library. Not with expensive books on art or classical history, or dry volumes on agriculture, animal husbandry, or economics.

"They're novels," she said in wonder. "They're all novels."

Jasper stood behind her as her eyes skimmed the shelves. "Not all of them. That would be impossible in a library of this size. But a fair number of them are. Six-shilling novels and penny serials, mostly."

Julia was in awe. "However did you acquire so many?"

"They're inexpensive to accumulate. I started buying them when I was a lad. It was how I spent all my pocket money. When I inherited the estate, I discovered my uncle had shared a similar passion—though his tastes veered more toward the horrid than the adventurous or romantic. His novels account for the greater part of the collection."

In the dim light filtering through the library windows, Julia caught glimpses of titles she recognized, and many others she didn't.

"Have you read them all?" she asked.

"Most of them, and some of them twice over." Jasper's arm came around her waist, his breath warm at her temple. "What do you think?"

She covered his arm with both of hers, leaning back against the hard wall of his chest. "I think," she said in all solemnity, "I'm very much in danger of falling in love with you."

Jasper's eyes squeezed shut briefly at her words. She was jesting, he knew. It was about the books. Those were what she loved, not him. He nevertheless allowed the warmth of the sentiment to penetrate into his soul. For one fleeting moment, it filled up the emptiness inside of him, making him whole.

It didn't last.

Julia stepped out of his arms almost immediately to inspect the bookshelves. "I wish Anne and Stella could see this. And Evelyn, too. We all of us adore novels."

"Perhaps one day you can invite them for a visit."

She glanced back at him over her shoulder. "You wouldn't object?"

He shrugged. "Not if they don't."

A frown marred her brow as she resumed perusing the shelves.

Jasper wondered if it had occurred to her yet that her friends might not wish to visit her here. That, in marrying him, she'd ostracized herself from their society as surely as she had from her parents and every other fashionable connection in London.

She traced the spines on a row of books, her expression distracted. "I must write to Anne. She'll be arriving back in London this evening. Heaven only knows what she might hear."

Jasper could easily imagine.

By this time, Sir Eustace and Lady Wychwood would be aware of their daughter's flight. Soon, news would filter throughout the fashionable world. There would be no keeping it secret, not when the Wychwoods' servants and Ridgeway's staff had all been privy to Julia's abduction.

Doubtless her maid, Mary, had divulged the whole of it on returning to Belgrave Square.

Jasper fully expected that within a fortnight, he would have to contend with the consequences. The only question in his mind was how those consequences might present themselves.

He followed behind Julia at a distance. "There's paper and ink in the desk. Write to whomever you like. I'll see it's posted."

That seemed to alleviate her concerns—for the moment, at least. "Thank you," she said.

"Of course."

She resumed investigating his collection, stopping to withdraw a novel from one of the shelves. "*The Cursed Veil.*"

"A gruesome tale about a new bride kept prisoner in a haunted ruin." He plucked the book from her fingers, returning it to the shelf. "Not the best story to begin your new life here."

She gave him a speaking glance. A silent reminder that he'd promised not to restrict her reading.

"I didn't say you *couldn't* read it," he said. "Only that it might not be an auspicious beginning."

Julia wandered onward. She'd gone no further than the next shelf when she came to an abrupt halt, her attention riveted by a long row of books—fifteen altogether, of similar size and shape. "These are J. Marshland novels."

Jasper stilled. "Er, yes. They are."

Her gaze scanned the shelf. "But . . . you have titles of his I've never even heard of." She extracted a novel from the front of the row, opening it to examine the frontispiece. "This one was published in 1848."

"Marshland's first novel, I believe."

She met his eyes. "Do you have *all* his novels?"

"That surprises you?"

"A little. I knew you'd read him, and that you have decided opinions about his style, but I never thought you a particular admirer of his work."

"I wouldn't call myself an admirer. No more than I admire the works of Mrs. Braddon or Mr. Collins. It's reading I enjoy, and if an author can tell a good story . . ." He shrugged.

"Do you have all Mrs. Braddon's novels?"

"No," he admitted.

"What about Mr. Collins's? Or Mr. Dickens's?"

Jasper fell quiet. A part of him began to question the wisdom of having brought her here. "I'm afraid," he said carefully, "their novels don't come as cheaply as Marshland's do."

The answer appeared to satisfy her.

"I suppose not." Returning the first novel to the shelf, she reached for another.

He gently stopped her hand. "You wouldn't wish your tea to get cold."

"But there's so much more to see!"

"Tea first." He tucked her hand in his arm, leading her away. "These novels aren't going anywhere."

After tea, Jasper carried their bags up to their bedchamber. Julia accompanied him, looking around the room with vivid interest as he brought in first her two carpetbags, then the rest of their luggage.

It was a comfortable enough space, even for a wife. Jasper had made certain of that. Since taking possession of the Hall, the bulk of his small income had gone toward making the family apartments hospitable. His own bedroom and those belonging to the boys, Daisy, and Beecham were all well-appointed, with new mattresses, draperies, linens, and fresh coats of paint.

The furnishings themselves were the same as in Erasmus Blunt's day. Great mahogany chests, wardrobes, and—in Jasper's chamber—a magnificent four-poster bed carved with what, he suspected, had once been the figures of angels and cherubs. Their features had long been worn away, giving the blank faces and writhing limbs that adorned the bedposts the appearance of creatures screaming in agony.

Julia examined the carvings with something like alarm.

"We can replace the bed," Jasper said.

"I don't mind it. Only . . ." She traced one of the angels with a curious fingertip. "Is this poor man being tortured?"

"I daresay he's meant to be in religious ecstasy."

Her brows lifted. "Gracious. It doesn't seem at all pleasant."

Jasper hoisted her carpetbags and portmanteau onto the bench at the foot of the bed. He felt a twinge of guilt that she had no maid to assist her in unpacking them. She shouldn't be exerting herself.

"I must find the children," he said. "But afterward, I'll help you get settled."

Her hand fell from the post. She turned to him, her hip leaning against the mattress, causing the wide skirts of her blue carriage gown to swell out to one side. "Where do you suppose they've got to?"

"In this weather? Somewhere in the house, very likely. Once I round them up, I'll bring them to you for a proper introduction."

"Or you could let them come to me on their own."

"I'd prefer to start as we mean to go on. Besides," he added irritably, "if we waited on their initiative, we might well be waiting 'til Judgment Day."

Her gaze tipped briefly to something behind him. Her mouth curved in a sudden smile. "Very well," she said. "I *am* anxious to meet them properly. Daisy, especially."

"I'll find her for you," he promised.

With that, he took his leave, striding off down the empty stone corridor.

He hadn't anticipated having to play truant officer the very day he arrived home with his new bride. No doubt he should have done. Though the children had known why he'd gone to London, none of them had seemed particularly keen on his mission. Too many books with evil stepmothers, he'd wager.

Ridgeway would say it was his own fault for insisting the children learn to read.

Jasper trusted that, in his absence, their knowledge hadn't extended to reading anything in his study.

It was the foremost thought in his mind as he made his way up the circular stone staircase that led to the fourth-floor tower. A heavily bolted door stood at the top of the steps. A door to which only Jasper held the key.

Sliding his key into the lock, he opened it with a grating scrape of metal. The door swung open before him, revealing the shadow-kissed room where he'd spent the majority of his six years at the Hall.

Inside, things looked much as he'd left them. There was a sturdy wooden desk stacked with ledgers, a set of glass inkpots in a brass holder, and a sheaf of papers weighted down with a stone he'd found while walking on the moors.

None of the books that lined the walls were out of place. And none of the locked desk drawers had been forced open.

Thus far, the children had respected the sanctity of his study. Nevertheless, it was always the first place Jasper checked whenever he returned from a visit to Malton or York, never entirely confident he wouldn't find it ransacked, all his secrets laid bare.

But not this time.

He'd been exceedingly careful. Before leaving for London, he'd locked his most private papers away in the desk. The study was neat and tidy, absent its usual whirlwind of clutter—the stray pages covered edge to edge in scrawled script, the stacks of dog-eared novels, and piles of correspondence.

Satisfied, Jasper withdrew, locking the door behind him.

Charlie and Alfred were probably hiding in the east wing. And Daisy was either battened down with them or tucked away in a cupboard somewhere.

Jasper set out to find them.

"You can come out now," Julia said.

The door of the large mahogany wardrobe slowly creaked open. A small head emerged, followed by an equally small body clothed in a stained cotton pinafore. It was a little girl, with plaited hair as black as Charlie's, and a face just as narrow. She gave Julia a frank look of appraisal.

"You must be Daisy," Julia said. "How do you do?"

The little girl didn't speak. She merely edged closer, examining Julia's face and dress, as if drawn by an overwhelming curiosity.

"Have you been in there long?" Julia asked.

"Since the coach arrived," Daisy said. There was a grave matter-of-factness to her words, reminiscent of the tone Jasper so often took. As if she'd modeled herself on him—the same solemn speech and manner.

"It can't have been comfortable," Julia observed.

Daisy shrugged. Another gesture of Jasper's, all the way down to the dry expression on her dirt-smudged face. "I like small spaces."

Julia couldn't help but be charmed by the girl. "Do you often hide in wardrobes?"

"Sometimes." Daisy moved closer still, sidling up to the bed. "Did you come from London?"

"I did. Your father and I traveled all the way here on a train. It was terribly exciting."

Daisy didn't appear at all impressed. "Are you going to live here now? In father's room?"

"I am," Julia said. "Is that all right?"

Daisy set a hand on the counterpane. Her thin brows beetled in a frown. "You're *not* my mother."

Julia's smile dimmed. "No. No, indeed. I'm not. I would never presume—"

"My mother had golden hair," Daisy informed her.

"Did she? How lovely." Julia could think of nothing else to say in reply.

She hadn't met many children in her life. In London society, the youngest of them were kept separate, never permitted to intrude at meals or at parties. During the journey to Yorkshire, Julia had fretted over how Jasper's children would receive her.

At the time, she'd been optimistic. Confident that kindness would carry the day.

That confidence was waning by the second.

"She *was* lovely," Daisy said. "Father loved her very much."

Julia's smile threatened to vanish completely. She forced it to remain through sheer strength of will. Jasper had warned her that the children spoke freely of their mother. Julia refused to be hurt by the fact.

But it *did* hurt, all the same.

Of course he'd loved their mother. He'd said so only last night. And even if he hadn't admitted to it, the evidence of his regard for her was present in all his actions. Why else would he have taken on the care of the three illegitimate children she'd borne him? Why else would he plan to leave them the whole of his estate?

For love, obviously. Love of his beautiful golden-haired mistress.

"I'm sure he did," Julia said. "I'm sure he still does."

"He does," Daisy said confidently. She touched one of the carpet-bags. Her small fingers tugged at a stray thread. "I can show her to you."

Julia blinked. "Your *mother*?"

Daisy nodded, as solemn as a little judge. "She's here."

The fine hairs rose on Julia's nape. She felt, for an instant, as if a goose had walked over her grave. "I don't understand—"

"She's outside," Daisy said. "Sleeping in the garden."

Twenty-Three

Jasper found Charlie and Alfred in the east wing of the Hall in what had once been the servants' quarters. The damp set of rooms boasted peeling walls, rotting floorboards, and mildewed furnishings covered in dust-covered sheets long yellowed with age.

Jasper didn't dare venture over the threshold. The flooring couldn't support anything greater than a child's weight. It was precisely why the boys chose the room.

"Your hiding places are beginning to lack creativity," Jasper said, propping one shoulder against the doorframe. "This is the first place I looked."

Charlie and Alfred were perched in the deep-set window embrasure, a stack of playing cards set between them.

"Not the first place," Charlie said under his breath.

Jasper ignored the remark. The boys were aware that, when it came to his study, he trusted no one. He always made it his first stop on returning from his travels, even if he'd ventured no further than Hardholme. "I suppose Daisy is in one of the kitchen cupboards?"

Alfred's lips twitched.

"No?" Jasper made an effort to mask his impatience. "Where, then?"

"She's in the wardrobe in your bedchamber," Alfred said.

Jasper stiffened. *Good God.* What was the little devil playing at? Did she intend to leap out and scare Julia half to death?

But no.

He recalled the fleeting glance Julia had cast over his shoulder and the smile that had followed soon after it. She must have observed Daisy spying on them. No wonder Julia had emphasized how much she wanted to meet the little girl.

Knowing all the children's whereabouts should have set Jasper's mind at ease.

It didn't.

The boys were notorious for their ill-advised remarks. And Daisy was no better. Lord only knew what horrors she was relating to her new stepmother.

"Is there anything else you'd like to confess?" Jasper asked the boys. "Any other surprises in the offing?"

The boys resumed their card game in mutinous silence.

"If this is another battle of wills," Jasper said, "may I say it's poorly timed."

Charlie slapped down a card. "What care we what *she* thinks."

Jasper wasn't wholly unsympathetic to his feelings. As a boy, Charlie had been abandoned by his own mother, left to languish in the workhouse. The betrayal had hurt him deeply. Even now, after six years in Jasper's care, Charlie would still rather reject someone outright than risk the chance of, ultimately, being hurt or rejected himself.

"You don't know her," Jasper said. "If you did, I suspect you'd like her."

Charlie only snorted, but Alfred chanced a cautious glance in Jasper's direction.

One year younger, Alfred was often led by his older brother. Often, but not always.

"She's an excellent horsewoman," Jasper went on. "Her gelding will arrive within the week. I'm relying on the pair of you to assist me in that regard."

"How?" Alfred asked.

"When I'm too busy to accompany her," Jasper said, "it will fall to one of you to escort her on her rides."

"On who? Musket?" Charlie gave another derisive snort. Musket was the aged gelding they kept to pull the dogcart. He rarely exerted himself to go faster than a jog.

"Musket couldn't keep up," Jasper said.

"You'd let us ride Quintus?" Alfred abandoned any pretense of being interested in the card game.

"Naturally," Jasper said. "In company with my wife—providing you can manage to be civil to her."

Charlie scowled. "Who wants to ride that big lummox?"

"I might," Alfred said. "If I can gallop him."

"That all depends on your behavior." Jasper straightened from the doorframe. "I expect both of you downstairs in the drawing room before dinner—washed, dressed, and well-behaved." He met Charlie's eyes across the distance, his own gaze implacable. "You and I will address your temporary lapse after dinner."

Having said his piece, Jasper withdrew, leaving the boys to mutter among themselves about his unrelenting high-handedness. Let them do so. It was preferable to them thinking he was undependable.

From the beginning, he'd striven to be steady with them. A man they could rely on—the same on one day as on the next. It was that which they needed, not an outpouring of affection or a torrent of discipline. They needed to feel safe and secure.

It was the same thing Julia required of him. Not his love, but his protection. His steadfastness and strength.

Returning to their shared bedchamber, he found her standing in front of the open wardrobe, placing a folded skirt onto a high shelf. Several articles of her clothing had already been carefully put away. They lined the lower shelves in colorful stacks of silk, wool, and muslin.

He scanned the room. "Is Daisy not here?"

Julia glanced at him, her expression peculiarly blank. "She *was* here."

"Where did she go?"

"Downstairs, I believe." Her tone was as opaque as her countenance.

Jasper had a sinking feeling. He entered the room, shutting the door behind him. "I suppose she said something untoward."

Julia turned to face him. "Nothing you didn't warn me about."

"She spoke of her mother?"

"She did." Julia walked to the window. Framed by folds of heavy leaf-patterned damask drapery, it boasted a deep-set seat much like the one the boys were taking advantage of in the servants' quarters. She sat down upon it, rain drumming on the glass behind her. "What was her name?"

His sinking feeling swiftly transformed into a leaden weight in his chest.

This wasn't a conversation he'd anticipated having so soon after their arrival. But like much in his cursed postwar existence, the unpleasant reality of it was unavoidable. The best he could hope for was that, in divulging some semblance of the truth, he wouldn't hurt Julia in the process.

He approached her slowly, conscious of the fact that it may be too late. That she may already be hurt. "Her name was Dolly Carvel."

"Is she buried in your garden?"

Bloody hell. Is that what Daisy had told her?

Not that it wasn't the truth.

"She is," Jasper said.

"I see."

He sat next to her in the window seat, far enough away that he could look her in the eye. "You don't," he assured her. "There's no way you possibly could."

It was the wrong thing to say. That much was evident immediately.

Julia's beautiful face hardened, twin spots of color rising in her cheeks. "I'm not entirely ignorant, you know. Even though I've never been anywhere or done anything. Even though you're the first gentleman I've kissed."

"That isn't what I—"

"You loved her. You told me so last night at the inn."

What?

Jasper opened his mouth to deny it, only to close it again. He belatedly recalled his admission to her as he'd brushed her hair. *Good God.* She'd assumed he was talking about his mistress.

Of course she had.

He'd been too caught up in his own painful memories to recognize it. And now it was too late. There was no way to correct her misapprehension. Not without divulging more than he was able. But he had to say something.

"I never meant—"

"What I hadn't realized," Julia went on, heedless of his protestations, "was that it was the kind of grand passion Heathcliff had for Cathy. Something that transcends a person's death."

Jasper choked back what would have been an exceedingly ill-timed laugh. "This isn't *Wuthering Heights*. If it were any novel, it would be . . ." He struggled to come up with a comparable title and failed. "Blast it all, Julia, this is real life! There's nothing romantic about it."

"How well I know it." She folded her arms, leaning back into the window seat as if to put an even greater distance between them. "You still might have prepared me. The very idea—"

"I warned you the children would say things," he said. "And you promised—you *promised*—you wouldn't ask me about my past. It was part of our agreement."

Her blue eyes glistened with injury. "I'm not *asking* you anything."

He scrubbed a hand over his jaw, bitterly conflicted, torn between six years' worth of secrets and the powerful urge to alleviate the look of hurt in her gaze. A look that told him she was no longer certain of her place here, in his home—or in his heart.

But it wasn't only that.

The truth was, he wanted to tell her. He wanted to tell her so damned much. Frustration welled within him, driving out the last vestiges of caution.

"Very well," he said at last. "If you want to know about Dolly, I'll tell you about Dolly."

Julia's stomach trembled with anxiety as she waited for Jasper to speak. It was all she could do not to pepper him with questions. But she recognized the danger in his mood.

Though it took an effort, she held her tongue.

At length, he began: "Six years ago, when I returned from the Crimea, I came here with the intention of settling down. I was still recovering from my injuries, and, ah, not entirely myself. Beecham was here. He had the management of the place. Other than that, I was alone. Until one day, a month after my arrival, Dolly appeared at my door, with a ten-month-old infant in her arms. She told me . . ."

Julia waited for him to continue, but he didn't. He didn't seem to know how. "Why do you hesitate?"

"Because," he said, "what I'm about to tell you is going to make me sound more monstrous than anything you've heard about my reputation thus far."

A stab of apprehension quickened her pulse. "It can't be any worse than what I heard from Lady Heatherton."

"It's worse," he said.

Raindrops streamed over the window glass in rivulets, obscuring the view of the overgrown garden below. A garden where, according to Daisy, the grave of Jasper's much-beloved mistress was marked with a white marble angel.

He went on in a harsh undertone, as if he were admitting to something too shameful to express. "Dolly told me she'd surrendered Charlie and Alfred to the workhouse the previous year and that she'd be sending Daisy there, too, now she was weaned."

The workhouse?

Julia's blood went cold. "I don't understand."

"Dolly had been supporting herself and the children with her earnings from . . . from prostitution. That all came to an end when she contracted consumption. By the time she arrived here, she'd largely wasted away."

Julia paled.

"She asked me to retrieve Charlie and Alfred," Jasper said. "And she asked me to take Daisy in as well. So, I did. Dolly stayed here, too, for a time. It would have been cruel to deny the children her presence so close to the end. She was dead within a month. The church in Hardholme refused to bury her. They're a pious lot in the village. Not overly keen on fallen women. Which is why I buried her here."

Julia stared at him, her head spinning at the implications of what he'd confessed. Her heart was in similar turmoil. "How did she find herself in such circumstances? Your relationship with her was one of long standing. And recent, too, if Daisy's age is any indication. Did you not provide for them?"

"I did not."

"Why not?" She tried and failed to keep the edge of accusation from her words. "You're their father."

"Many gentlemen fail to provide for the children they sire outside of marriage. It's no excuse, but . . ." A muscle worked in his jaw. "I was of a different mindset before the war. A different man."

So he had told her in the Claverings' garden. And so Julia had believed. She still wanted to believe it, quite desperately.

She searched his face. "And yet . . . when you returned, you didn't seek them out. Dolly had to come to you. If you'd truly changed, why did you not go to her and set things right?"

A frown darkened his brow. His gaze dropped from hers. "I wasn't well for a time. I was . . . confused."

"And all the while the boys were in a workhouse? And Dolly was dying of consumption?" Julia's chest ached with muted anguish. The truth did indeed make her new husband sound monstrous. "Oh, Jasper."

He winced. Only this morning, she'd called him dearest.

"You can't forgive me," he said flatly. It wasn't a question.

"I haven't any right to forgive you. It's not me you wronged. It was your children. It's to them you must make amends."

He looked at her again, his frost-gray eyes burning with a furious light. "I *am* making amends. I've been trying to set things right from the moment Dolly appeared on my doorstep. Sometimes it seems as though I'll spend the rest of my life atoning. You can ask Beecham if you don't believe me."

"I do believe you."

He exhaled. "Well. That's something, at least."

Julia felt a flicker of guilt. Had she overreacted? Been too harsh in her judgment? The past was the past, after all. She had no right to censure him for it, not when he was so clearly doing his utmost to repair the damage.

And he was right, of course.

Gentlemen didn't make a habit of taking care of their by-blows. Not that Julia was aware. It was the very thing that had scandalized London society about Jasper's behavior—his desire to clothe and house Charlie, Alfred, and Daisy as openly as if they were his legitimate children. It wasn't done. Not by respectable people anyway.

But Jasper had been doing it for six years. Out of love for his mistress, Julia had thought. Admirable as it was, it had pained her to recognize it.

But *had* he loved Dolly?

He'd claimed he had, but his past conduct indicated not. If he'd loved her, he wouldn't have abandoned her to such a fate. He wouldn't have abandoned his children.

It was all too awful.

Julia couldn't reconcile any of it with the man she knew today. A man who had come to her rescue, marrying her and whisking her away with no hope of ever obtaining her dowry. A man who had brushed her hair last night, who had held her and kissed her with such passionate tenderness. A man who read novels, for heaven's sake.

This wasn't a man who could have done the cruel things Lady Heatherton had described. The even crueler things Jasper had just confessed to.

Julia rubbed her temple. Her head was beginning to ache.

"You're tired," he said.

She blinked up at him. How long had she been sitting there, engaged in her grim ruminations? "I'm sorry. My thoughts are running wild. I can't stop wondering—"

"No more talk of the past," he said firmly. "Nothing good can come of it. From this moment on, we adhere to our agreement."

She balked at his directive. How was she to refrain from talking about the past when it permeated the whole of their lives here?

But it was what she'd agreed to when she married him. That she wouldn't ask him about his time before the war. And that she'd never enter his study. They weren't unreasonable restrictions. Not any more than the restrictions Bluebeard imposed on his newest wife.

A disturbing thought. And an unjust one, too.

Jasper wasn't Bluebeard, surely. And she'd *promised* him. One couldn't start a marriage by breaking one's word.

She gave a reluctant nod. "Very well."

He stood. "Would you like to lie down? There's plenty of time before dinner."

"Perhaps I shall." She *was* rather fatigued from the journey. Troubles always seemed worse when one was battling exhaustion. In times like this, bed and a good book were generally the best prescription for her own peace of mind.

She rose from the window seat, smoothing her skirts with an anxious hand. Her unfinished Marshland novel, *The Hero's Return*, beckoned to her from the bedside table.

"Do you need help undressing?" Jasper asked as she walked past him to the bed.

She moved out of his reach. "No, thank you," she said quickly. "I-I can manage."

His manner was instantly formal. "Of course." He bowed to her. "I'll leave you to it."

He was gone before Julia could say anything more. She was left standing beside the gruesomely carved four-poster bed, painfully aware that a chasm had opened up between her and her new husband.

It would be up to her to bridge the gap. Jasper was too decent a man to force the issue.

Decent. Honorable. Heroic.

Nothing like the Captain Blunt of six years ago.

Could war really change a person to that degree? Could it truly turn a man from a villain into a hero?

She wanted to believe it.

She *had* to believe it.

Twenty-Four

—✦—

Jasper spent the next several hours going over the accounts with Beecham. A depressing activity at the best of times. It wasn't how he'd envisioned spending his first day home. He'd thought he would pass the time in Julia's company. But it wasn't to be. Not now she knew the truth about Dolly and the children.

It wasn't the whole truth, naturally, but enough of it to paint Jasper in a thoroughly despicable light. He wasn't only a whoremonger who had sired three children on his mistress; he was a villain who had left those children to starve. An unconscionable monster who, through his base neglect, had allowed them to be relegated to the workhouse.

They were unpardonable crimes. Jasper had known Julia would eventually hear of them. With the children in residence, it was inevitable. What he hadn't expected was that he'd be constrained, on the very day of their arrival, to lay the sordid details out for her himself.

No matter how long he lived, he'd never forget the expression of horrified disappointment on her face. As if every romantic daydream she'd cherished about him had been crushed underfoot, replaced by something akin to disgust.

Jasper felt sick to recall it.

And what of how she'd shrunk from him when he'd offered to help her undress? As though she couldn't bear the thought of him touching her?

Her reaction had reduced him to formality. Good God, he'd actually bowed to her before taking his leave. A stiff, militaristic gesture, at odds with the intimacy that had been building between them.

Is this how it was to be from now on? A coldly polite marital relationship absent any semblance of affection?

She was in their bedchamber now, presumably asleep. He didn't begrudge her the rest. If not for his reluctance to play the overbearing husband, he'd have insisted upon it. After her ordeal, she needed as much rest as she could get.

And *he* needed to focus.

Closeted in the steward's office with Beecham, the unrelenting rain beating against the window, Jasper managed to draft a timeline for implementing the first of the major repairs. He intended to discuss his plans with Julia, but not today. Not tomorrow, either.

It was going to take time and patience to earn back her trust. The same patience he'd been obliged to exercise with the boys. He was becoming a master at it.

At half four, Beecham withdrew to begin preparations for dinner. Jasper remained in the steward's office, finishing a letter to his solicitor in York. He was writing out Piggott's direction on the envelope when Daisy poked her head into the room. She was garbed in a pinafore, her black hair arranged in a single frazzled plait.

Setting down his pen, Jasper turned in his chair. "Come here."

Daisy crossed the small room to stand in front of him—a penitent position she'd taken dozens of times before.

He regarded her with a frown. "You've been making mischief, I hear."

"I haven't."

"Hiding in the wardrobe instead of coming to greet your new stepmother in a civilized manner?"

"I haven't," she protested again. "I only wanted to show her mother's grave."

Only. As if it were a matter of no consequence.

"Did you not think that might upset her?"

"It didn't upset her. She *wants* to see it. She said she'll come with me when the rain stops."

Jasper inwardly grimaced. He didn't like to think of Julia visiting Dolly's grave. And she *would* visit it, he knew. She'd do anything to endear herself to the children.

"What else did you tell her?" he asked.

"Only that mother was beautiful. And that she had golden hair. And that you loved her better than anyone."

Jasper sighed. "Daisy . . . What am I to do with you?"

"But it's true, isn't it?" Her brow puckered. "You loved mother best."

"We don't need to love anyone better than anyone else," Jasper said. "Love is big enough to encompass everyone."

It was something his father had used to say from the pulpit. A hypocritical statement, given the man's treatment of his own family, but a statement that had stuck with Jasper, nonetheless.

"That includes your new stepmother," he added.

Daisy's expression turned sullen. "She's very pretty." It might almost have been an accusation.

"She's kind," Jasper replied. "Kindness is more important than prettiness." He smoothed his hand over Daisy's hair, giving an affectionate tug to her plait. "Much more important."

"Is that why you married her?"

"It is," he said. "When I went to London, I was determined to find the kindest, sweetest lady in all the world. And when I found her, I married her straightaway and brought her here to you."

"She isn't my mother."

"No. But she'll be a friend to you. And she'll care for you very much if you let her. I believe she was made to care for people like you and me."

Daisy appeared to cautiously take this in. Though raised by Jasper, with Beecham's not inconsequential assistance, she was often as hesitant to trust people as her brothers were.

"Do *you* care for her?" she asked.

"I do. I'm exceedingly fond of her, just as I am of you. And I'm happy the two of you are going to get on so well together."

Daisy's lower lip wobbled. "She didn't like me."

And there it was. The crux of her fears.

Jasper drew her to him, enfolding her small body in the circle of his arms. She leaned against him, one tiny hand clutching at his waistcoat.

She wasn't a handsome child, nor one of respectable pedigree. She was odd. An outcast, like the boys were. Indeed, on their rare trips into Hardholme, the female villagers had been more apt to look on Daisy with disdain than to pinch her cheeks and offer her a boiled sweet.

Jasper had done his best to make up for it. But he was only a man, and one who was as little welcomed in village society as the children were themselves.

What Daisy needed was a mother.

"Give her a chance," he said into her ear. "That's all I ask of you."

Daisy's reply was a muffled and very reluctant whisper. "I'll try, Papa."

Seated at the splintering oak table in Goldfinch Hall's cavernous dining room, Julia applied herself to cutting the piece of mutton on her plate. The overcooked meat defied every effort.

"Permit me," Jasper said from his chair beside her. Taking her plate, he quickly cut her mutton into bite-sized morsels, just as he'd done for Daisy at the beginning of their meal.

Julia murmured a polite word of thanks. He'd been excessively civil to her since she'd emerged from their chamber this evening. Almost too civil. As if he was wary of presuming too much. The result was a meal that was coldly formal.

The children's presence did nothing to thaw the chilly atmosphere. Dressed in clean clothing, with freshly scrubbed faces, they sat quiet in their seats, focused entirely on their respective plates of mutton, potatoes, and boiled vegetables.

Was it Julia's presence that had rendered them mute? Or were they always like this at meals?

She had nothing to compare it to. She'd never dined with children before. She didn't know quite how to behave. It was all so strange and new. Even the dining room, with its water-stained paper hangings and smoking fireplace, left her feeling distinctly out of place.

Anxiety had been plaguing her ever since she'd come downstairs. The same uneasy panic she experienced when attending a fashionable dinner party. No longer anchored by Jasper, she was unmoored again and drifting, desperate for any safe harbor.

At the moment, their bedchamber seemed a tempting port in the storm.

But she wouldn't run away this time. She couldn't stomach the thought of what the children might think if she did. It wouldn't do for them to believe their stepmother a scared little mouse of a woman, ready to dart back into her mouse hole at the first sign of discomfort.

Julia was determined to be braver than that.

"I begin to think you have the only sharp knife at the table," she remarked lightly as Jasper passed her plate back to her. It seemed an innocuous statement, one she made with an effort at cheerfulness, meant to break the uncomfortable silence.

The effect it had on the table was instantaneous.

Jasper frowned. Mr. Beecham paled. Daisy's eyes goggled. And both boys immediately sat to attention.

"Forgive the oversight, ma'am," Mr. Beecham said. "I should have given you one of the sharpened ones, but I'm that used to setting out cutlery for the children."

"You don't permit the boys to handle sharp knives?" she asked.

"Not anymore," Charlie said before Jasper or Mr. Beecham could answer. "They were all locked away after our knife-throwing competition last year."

Alfred pointed proudly to a white line on his earlobe. "I still have a scar from it."

Julia's brows shot up. "Your brother threw a *knife* at you?"

"They threw knives at each other," Jasper said. "An unfortunate occurrence."

She looked between the two boys. "But . . . why?"

"We read it in a penny novel," Alfred explained. "A champion knife thrower and his rival had a contest."

"The first to draw blood was the loser," Charlie said.

Alfred smiled gleefully. "Which means I won."

Mr. Beecham shuddered at the memory. "My heart nearly failed me when I saw what they were up to. Captain Blunt had to summon the doctor from Hardholme."

"For Alfred *and* for Beecham." Charlie shoved a forkful of potatoes into his mouth. "They were both laid out flat."

Alfred nodded. "Beecham had apoplexy. He nearly *died*."

"That's quite enough," Jasper said. "We needn't relive it."

Julia had no idea managing young boys could be so fraught. "What a frightening event."

"One of many." Jasper locked eyes with the boys. "We're not proud of ourselves, are we?"

"No, sir," Alfred and Charlie replied in unison. Their answer was swift, if not entirely convincing.

"You don't get into trouble, do you, Daisy?" Julia asked the little girl.

Daisy paused in the act of lifting her goblet to her lips with both hands. She carefully set it back on the table, her eyes seeking Jasper's, as if asking his permission to speak candidly.

He gave her a slight nod.

She sat a little taller in her seat. "I tore my new dress climbing a tree."

"Goodness," Julia said. "I hope you could repair it?"

"Mr. Beecham sewed it."

"Did he? That was clever of him." Julia cast a glance at Jasper, as nervous about saying the wrong thing as Daisy was. But unlike with his daughter, Jasper offered Julia no guidance on how to proceed next. Indeed, he was regarding her with one of his indecipherable looks.

"Do you like to sew yourself?" she asked Daisy.

"No," Daisy said.

"What do you like to do?" Julia included the boys in her question. "How do you pass the time now you're not in school?"

Charlie stabbed a piece of mutton with his fork. "There's plenty to do when it's not raining."

"We go out on the moors," Alfred said. "And we have a pond, too. It's as big as a lake. You can swim for hours."

"I should like to see it," Julia said.

Charlie's gaze narrowed with skepticism. "Can you swim?"

"No," she confessed. "I don't know how, I'm afraid. I've never lived in the country."

"I'll teach you," Jasper said.

Their eyes met and held. And Julia felt a spark of . . . something. The anxious trembling in her stomach transformed into the delicate flutter of butterfly wings.

"Thank you," she said. "I'd like that. That is . . . if it isn't too much trouble."

"It would be my pleasure," he replied.

Julia had the distinct sensation that he meant it. A blush crept into her cheeks. She had to make an effort not to prolong the moment.

She turned her attention back to the children. "I hope we'll spend a lot of time out of doors together when the weather clears."

"It's not all fun and games here at the Hall, ma'am. Not even when the sun's shining." Mr. Beecham refilled his glass from the carafe of watered wine on the table. "The boys have lessons in the mornings. We're reading Plato, aren't we, lads?"

"It's better than Mr. Filbert making us read the dratted Bible every day," Charlie grumbled.

"Charlie," Jasper warned.

"He *did* make us," Alfred said. "Charlie and me more than any of the others. He *hated* us."

"Filbert's a strict fellow," Mr. Beecham said. "He'd have done better as a clergyman than a schoolmaster, but he doesn't have the learning for it."

Julia offered her glass for Mr. Beecham to refill. "He sounds like my old nurse, Nanny Plum. Whenever I was in her black books, she'd make me sit in the corner of the nursery and read from an old Bible for hours on end. She thought it a punishment."

"It *is* a punishment," Charlie declared.

"Not at all," Julia said. "The Bible can be as exciting as a novel if you know where to look. It's filled with countless exciting tales."

Alfred was skeptical. "I never read any."

"Oh yes," Julia went on. "Let me see. There's the story of Daniel in the lion's den. And the one about Samson and Delilah—though it paints ladies in rather a poor light. Then there's the story of Joseph and his coat of many colors. That's my own favorite. It's filled with injustice, revenge, hidden identities, and a spectacular triumph at the end. There are even prophetic dreams. Quite thrilling, I must say."

Charlie scrunched his nose in disbelief. "Those stories are in the *Bible*?"

"They are, and plenty more besides. I can show you if you like. And then, if ever anyone again attempts to use reading the Bible as a punishment, you shall have the last laugh."

Alfred's mouth quirked. "Mr. Filbert wouldn't like that."

Julia smiled at him as she resumed her dinner.

Jasper gave her an odd look. "'*Hours on end?*'" he repeated. "How old were you?"

"Not much older than Daisy." Julia cut herself another piece of boiled carrot with her dull knife. "And Nanny Plum wasn't the worst of them. One day"—she gave the children a portentous look—"I shall tell you about Nanny Bracegirdle."

"Was she unkind to you?" Daisy asked.

"Not unkind, no." Julia dropped her voice to a confiding whisper. "But she did have a mustache."

The boys exploded into peals of laughter.

"Ladies don't have mustaches, do they, Papa?" Daisy asked Jasper.

Jasper choked on his wine.

"Would anyone care for cake?" Mr. Beecham inquired before Jasper could answer. "There's plenty left over from tea."

Daisy's attention was instantly diverted. "I would! Can I have cream, too?"

"May I," Jasper said quietly.

"May I have cream?" Daisy amended.

"Don't see why you shouldn't." Beecham's chair scraped back on the stone floor as he got to his feet. "There's enough for everyone."

Later that evening, while Jasper bid good night to the children, Julia washed and changed into her nightgown. She was already in bed, sitting up against a pile of pillows, when he returned.

He hesitated for a moment on the threshold, watching her plait her hair. "You don't wish me to brush it for you?"

Her hands stilled on the three sections she was twining together. Her heart performed a queer little somersault. "You needn't."

"You told me it was the thing you'd miss most about your old life, having your maid brush your hair each evening."

"You're not my maid," she pointed out.

"No, indeed. I'm your husband." He stripped off his coat and unknotted his cravat.

Heat rose up Julia's throat. She wasn't as tired as she'd been last night at the inn. Then, she'd been too exhausted from travel and blood loss to fully appreciate the intimacy of a man disrobing in front of her.

But not tonight.

Tonight, she was wide awake and attuned to Jasper's every movement.

After removing his cravat, he unthreaded his pocket watch from his waistcoat and placed it on the brass-cornered mahogany chest of drawers by the window. His cuff links followed, making a decisive clink against the wood as he set them down. His waistcoat was next—tossed over the back of the same wingback chair where he'd draped his coat—leaving him in nothing but his shirtsleeves and a pair of black wool trousers.

Her mouth went dry as he removed his boots.

It was her own fault. She was the one who had asked if they could share a room.

She reminded herself that he'd wanted it, too. Whatever had happened in the intervening hours, he still seemed to want it.

He retrieved her hairbrush from the dressing table. *His* dressing table. Earlier, when she'd unpacked, it had felt a trifle presumptuous to put her things there.

What few things she had.

Mary hadn't packed everything. The carpetbags and portmanteau had been stuffed full to bursting, but with Julia's clothes, hats, and shoes, not with any less-essential luxuries.

She had no lotions or powders. No perfumes, save a bottle of lavender water.

It was rather dispiriting.

Jasper arched a brow at her as he approached the bed. He held up the brush. "Well?"

In answer, she abandoned her efforts at plaiting her hair and angled herself on the bed to make room for him.

The mattress springs creaked under his weight as he sat behind her. He was dangerously close. Closer even than he'd been last night. And this time there was no cashmere shawl to act as a barrier between them. There was only him—large and warm at her back.

He gathered her hair in his hand, pausing to run his fingers through it. She heard him take a deep breath. "How beautiful it is."

She didn't reply. Not because she had nothing to say, but because it seemed he was on the verge of saying something more himself.

But he didn't speak again. He simply brushed her hair.

Her eyes closed with pleasure at the sensation. "Thank you."

"For the compliment?"

"Yes. And for the service. It feels divine."

"Thank *you*," he said. "You made a splendid effort with the children this evening. I'm grateful for it."

"I hope I wasn't too silly, telling them about Nanny Plum and Nanny Bracegirdle."

"Not at all. It amused them greatly."

But not him, it seemed. Julia sensed an underlying tension in his frame. As if something about their dinner conversation had troubled him.

"Have you always escaped into stories?" he asked.

"For as long as I can remember," she said. "What is it you called novels at Lady Clifford's musicale? 'An inexpensive escape from the realities of life'?"

It's what they'd been for her. An escape. A gateway to another world. Somewhere she could experience romance and adventure without anxiousness or fear—even if that experience was only in her imagination.

"I did," he said. "But that's not *all* they are."

"What else?"

He ran the brush through her hair—one long, deep stroke from her roots to the end of her thick tresses. Julia's limbs turned to treacle under his ministrations. Mary's brushing had never had this effect. It had never made Julia feel so warm and languorous, as if she might melt with every sweep of the bristles.

"Stories like the ones we read in novels help us understand the human condition," he said. "They teach us empathy. In that way, they're more than an escape *from* the world. They're an aid for living *in* the world. For being better, more compassionate people."

Julia frowned. She hadn't thought of it in those terms before. "Is that what novel reading has done for you? Made you more empathetic?"

"It has." He ran the brush through her hair for another long stroke. "And you as well, I suspect. Perhaps that's why you're so unlike your parents." His deep voice tickled her ear. "It wasn't them who raised you. It was romances and fairy tales."

She smiled, even as a shiver traced down her spine at the huskiness of his words. "One could just as easily say I was raised by penny dreadfuls. And what kind of parent would Varney the Vampire make? Or Sweeney Todd?"

He chuckled. "Fair point."

Her smile faded as he continued brushing. "Speaking of empathy . . . Is Mr. Beecham responsible for *all* the household chores?"

"God no. He's too old for any of the heavy work. He attends only to the cooking and light housekeeping. And to tutoring the boys now they're out of school."

"What about the laundry?"

"I do the laundry."

She cast him a startled look. "*You?*"

"Why not? It's generally too taxing for Beecham—all that bending and scrubbing. And it isn't as though I've no experience with the job. Any good soldier knows how to wash and press his clothes."

Her brows knit. "Goodness. I never considered it."

He gave her a wry smile. "I've found it's better to be self-sufficient. It doesn't pay to rely on people too much. You never know when they might be gone and you'll be left on your own."

Julia dipped her chin again so he could resume brushing. She hoped he wasn't referencing her own plight. She didn't think he was. Jasper wasn't the kind of man for cutting remarks or innuendo.

No, she realized. He was talking about himself.

Had he been disappointed by the people in his life? Left without anyone to help him or support him?

She had the feeling he had. That he was used to being alone, though not entirely content in that state. What had he said to her in the carriage?

"I'm not unhappy. Not now you're coming home with me."

She recalled his words with a pang of sadness. Whatever his past—

whatever he'd done—he didn't deserve to be consigned to this remote place, lonely and friendless.

But she refused to feel guilty over it. She'd done nothing to cause his fate. His suffering was of his own making.

"Do you look after the stable, too?" she asked.

"We don't keep a stable," he said. "Not formally. We've no coach horses or carriage. There's only Quintus and Musket."

"And now Cossack," she reminded him. "When do you think Lord Ridgeway will send them?"

"Within the week, I trust. Until then, we must rely on Musket and the dogcart. Beecham can drive them into Hardholme tomorrow to post your letter to Lady Anne, and to collect anything else we require from Taggert's Market."

"I must write to my bank in London, too," Julia said. "I daresay I should have done so already. You'll need access to my funds as soon as may be."

"Let's not think of that at present."

"Have we something more important to think of?"

"Yes," he answered. "Us."

She turned to face him on the bed. Their eyes met just as they had at dinner. Except now she was in her nightgown and he was in his shirtsleeves; exposed and vulnerable. An electric charge seemed to pass between them. She felt it in her soul—an alarming quake of longing.

"I mean to court you," he said. "Just as you asked me to do before we married."

She shook her head, flustered. "I didn't—"

"You did. You said you wanted a month or two in order to know me better. You said you wanted to be courted." Casting aside her hairbrush, he reached to cup her face. His large hand engulfed her cheek and jaw. "That's what I mean to do," he said. "I mean to woo you and win you, and when you're sufficiently amenable to the act, I mean for us to consummate our marriage, here, in this bed."

A scalding blush swept through her body. "That's . . . That's all very

well, but after what you told me today about Dolly and the children . . .
I'm not certain I can bring myself to—"

His hand tightened on her cheek. "I know that," he said roughly.
"You're disposed to think me a monster. But I promise you—"

"Not a monster, no. Just . . . not the gentleman I thought you were."

He stared down at her. "Did you truly believe me someone better?"

"Yes," she said. "*Yes.*" She looked deep into his eyes, past the frost-
covered surface to the fathomless warmth beneath. "When I look at
you like this, the man I see isn't a man who could have done any of
those things. I see someone else. Someone who's honorable and good.
That's the man I wanted to share a first kiss with. The man with whom
I could, eventually, share a bed."

A spasm of emotion passed over his face. It was gone before Julia
could grasp it. "I am that man," he said.

"Jasper—"

"I *am* that man." He bent his head to hers, his voice gone gruff.
"And I will win back your trust, however long it takes."

Her resolve cracked at the deep thread of sincerity in his words. She
wished she could succumb. That she could forget everything he'd confessed to. But she couldn't. No decent lady could.

"It might take a long while," she said frankly.

"I can wait." A grim smile edged his scarred mouth. "I've had a
great deal of practice."

Twenty-Five

~*~

*H*unched over his desk, head resting in one hand, Jasper stared down at the script-covered sheet of paper in front of him. Scowling, he crossed out another sentence. The nib of his quill pen dripped a spatter of ink across the page. *Blast it.* This was the third time he'd used the same phrase to describe something.

He was becoming careless.

It had been three days since they'd returned to Yorkshire. Three long days of working alone in his study during the morning hours and courting his wife in the afternoon and evening. It was the latter that had thrown all his cautious habits out of balance.

Thoughts of Julia permeated his every waking hour. And most of his non-waking hours, too. Lying beside her in their bed, attempting to maintain some semblance of detachment as she snuggled against him in her sleep, he was fast approaching a permanent state of distraction.

This morning, anxious to leave before she awoke in his arms, he'd washed and dressed so quickly, it wasn't until he was downstairs, halfway through his breakfast, that he'd realized he'd forgotten both his pocket watch and his study key in the bedroom.

Obliged to go back and retrieve them, he'd ended up walking in on Julia sponging herself in front of the basin.

She'd looked up at him with a start, her ruffled nightgown drawn partway to her waist and the wet sponge dripping in her hand.

Jasper had frozen on the threshold as the door snicked shut behind him, standing there like a great bewildered lummox who'd just received a blow to the head.

The moment he'd regained his wits, he'd averted his eyes. "Forgive me. I should have knocked, but . . ." He'd willed himself not to look as she righted her clothing. "I didn't wish to wake you."

"Do you require something of me?" she'd asked.

"No. Nothing like that." Regaining some small measure of composure, he'd stalked to the chest of drawers, sweeping his pocket watch and key up in his hand, aware all the while that she was watching him. "Forgive me," he'd muttered again before taking his leave. And then— rather lamely: "I'll procure a screen."

Jasper had been replaying the encounter over and over in his head all morning. *I'll procure a screen.* Good God.

A screen wasn't going to solve his problem. Nothing would except for having her. And he was a fair way from attaining his goal.

The most he'd achieved was that she was giving him a chance. An opportunity to court her. To show her who he really was, even if he couldn't tell her.

And he'd been trying to show her in dozens of different ways. Talking to her and listening to her, accompanying her out on the grounds with the children every afternoon and brushing her long raven tresses every night.

Setting down his quill, he raked both hands through his hair.

How was he to convince a gently bred lady to give herself to a monster? To vouchsafe her heart—and her body—to a man whose reputation was as black and irredeemable as that of Hades himself?

A true villain would simply have taken her. Affection could come later. Perhaps even love.

But Jasper didn't believe it would. Not with Julia. Real life wasn't, after all, a myth or a fairy tale.

Rising from his chair, he went to the high, narrow tower window.

The rectangular sliver provided no view of the grounds, only of the sky. It was clear outside today, the sun burning as brilliantly as it had since Monday. There was no longer any sign of the fog and the damp that had greeted them when they'd arrived on Sunday.

A glance at his pocket watch revealed the time: half past twelve. The boys should be done with their lessons soon.

He exited his study and, locking the door behind him, made his way downstairs.

Julia emerged from the drawing room at the same moment he stepped down into the hall. Catching sight of him, she stopped where she stood, blushing to the roots of her hair.

An answering heat crept up from beneath his collar and cravat, sneaking its way into his face.

Bloody hell.

He wasn't some raw lad. He was a man in his thirty-second year. A man who should be well past the point of blushing.

But she was his wife. A wife whose lushly curved body he'd held while she slept. One who he'd seen, not four hours ago, in a blood-stirring state of undress, her nightgown at her hips and her bosom bare, as perfectly proportioned as any sculpture of a Grecian goddess.

He swallowed hard. "Er, good morning."

"Good morning." She clasped her hands in front of her. "Or, rather, good afternoon. It's nearly one o'clock."

"So it is." He crossed the hall to join her. She looked unbearably pretty in her plain white frock with its violet ribbon sash at her waist. Soft and touchable. He suspected she wasn't wearing her corset.

Without a lady's maid to assist her, she'd been managing her own morning toilette. Of necessity, some components had gradually fallen by the wayside. The result was a softer, simpler style of dress that suited her far better than the overly constricted silhouettes of her days in London. Even her hair was lovelier than it had been in town. No longer pinned into submission, it was swept back into loose chignons or haphazardly tucked into silken nets.

Imperfection became her. Made her even more beguiling. Like a wild rose blooming in a hedgerow.

Noticing his regard, she smoothed her hands over her skirts. "I'm rather rumpled, I know. Mary used to press my gowns. I don't know how to do it myself. Not yet."

"I'd be pleased to do it for you."

"Oh no," she objected quickly. "I couldn't ask that. You have too much to do already." She didn't specify what.

So far, his work had remained a mystery to her. True to their agreement, Julia never asked him what he was doing every morning in the tower—though she was plainly curious.

She'd referenced it only once in passing, and he'd responded vaguely, muttering something about estate business. It was true enough in a general way. Whatever he earned from his labors would go toward maintaining the estate.

If he ever earned anything again.

After this morning's work, he had plenty of cause to doubt his abilities.

"I shall simply have to learn how to look after my clothes myself," Julia said. "Not only how to press them, but how to treat the stains. It's that which may prove difficult."

The solution was obvious. "You require a new maid."

"Perhaps a housekeeper-cook might suffice?" she suggested. "And a parlor maid to assist her with the housework?"

"You've been giving it some thought, I see." He wasn't surprised. There were only so many days a baronet's daughter could spend at the Hall without feeling the profound lack of staff. It impacted everything from their meals to the delivery of the water she'd been washing with this morning.

"I have," she said. "Surely, we can afford it now?"

"It's not only a matter of money. The servants you have in mind would first have to be persuaded to work here. That's not as easy as you might think, given the house's reputation—and my own."

"It's not impossible, either. Not now you're respectably married."

"Speaking of my recent marriage . . ." He came closer, his large frame looming over her small one. He was conscious of her every change in breath. "How have you been occupying yourself today?"

"I finished *The Hero's Return*," she said.

"Ah. And your verdict?"

"It wasn't as adventurous as I'd have liked. But it was rich with sympathetic characters, and really quite romantic." A pensive frown touched her lips. "There was only one part that troubled me."

Jasper was instantly alert. "Which part?"

"The part where Colonel Fulham's body was loaded into a cart with other wounded men."

"What about it?"

"I wonder how he could have been mistaken for a common soldier."

The answer was obvious enough to Jasper. "He was grievously injured, and all was in chaos. Without his horse or his coat—"

"I'm still not certain it's believable. Not when you consider his rank."

"Believable or not, it's based in fact," he said. "Many mistakes are made in the aftermath of a battle."

Julia frowned. "Is that how it was after the fall of Sebastopol?"

"It was worse. You could scarcely tell us apart. We all had enormous beards."

Her mouth tilted up at one corner. "You as well?"

"Everyone, to a man." He gave her an amused look. "Did you never see any of the soldiers returning home?"

"A few," she said. "Their whiskers *were* substantial, but I didn't know it was a feature of the breed. I thought it merely a personal preference."

"It was a necessity. Crimean winters are cold as the devil. And shaving soap was difficult to come by. '*Let nature be your valet.*' That's what one of my superior officers used to say. We all of us were glad to do so. Facial hair keeps a man warm."

She examined his countenance. "I can't imagine you with a beard."

His blood warmed under her regard. "I don't much like having one."

"I'm glad." A faint blush colored her cheeks. "I don't care for them, either."

He gazed down at her, wanting to kiss her so badly in that moment it was all he could do to draw back a step. He cleared his throat. "Is Daisy about?"

"She's gone down to the barn. It seems she requires a certain amount of time to herself each day. I'm trying to give it to her."

"I try to do the same," he said. "Within reason. Too much time on her own isn't good for a child of her disposition."

"She needs a playmate," Julia said. "Someone close to her age. Her brothers are too old to include her. They have their own games."

"Not today they don't. Today we're all going to the pond."

Julia's face lit with delight. "Now?"

"As soon as Beecham packs us something for luncheon. We'll eat and we'll swim."

"Oh, splendid. But . . ." A note of uncertainty seeped into her voice. "Are you certain you won't find it tedious to teach me?"

"Tedious? Lord no." He took her hand. "I've been looking forward to it all morning."

Julia had often read stories in magazines about ladies bathing at the fashionable seaside resorts of Margate or Scarborough. The women depicted wore heavy woolen bathing costumes, lace-up canvas slippers, and oilskin caps over their hair. Wheeled out into the ocean in wooden bathing machines, they emerged beneath the cover of a canopy to climb down into the water.

It was all done modestly, far from the view of anyone of the opposite sex.

Not so today.

For one thing, the pond at the edge of the moors was nothing like the sketches she'd seen of the seaside. It was wild and remote, surrounded by encroaching trees and a profusion of wavy hair grass with delicate flower heads trembling in the rippling breeze.

For another, Julia had no bathing costume. Jasper had said she didn't require one. She would swim in her chemise and drawers, as Daisy did.

And there would be no question of separating the sexes. They were all going to swim together, with Jasper and the boys wearing even less than she and Daisy wore. Indeed, they were no sooner in view of the pond than Charlie and Alfred took off running for the water, stripping down to their drawers as they went.

Julia averted her gaze.

"You needn't be shy," Jasper said. He walked along at her side, the hamper containing their picnic lunch hoisted on one broad shoulder.

His black three-piece suit was gone. In its place were Bedford cord breeches, a loose linen shirt, and a pair of old top boots. If not for the fearsomeness of his scar and the proud, upright carriage of his frame— a posture that loudly proclaimed his years in the military—he might almost have resembled a country squire.

Almost.

Daisy trotted off after her brothers to the water's edge. She was clad in a clean pinafore, her dark hair pinned up in a crown of plaits.

"It feels indecent," Julia said when the little girl was out of earshot. "Being undressed like that in company."

"You're not in company," Jasper replied. "You're with your family. And this is the country. People don't fret about such things out here. Who would do so? There are no strangers to see."

Her family.

They were, weren't they? Jasper, Charlie, Alfred, and Daisy. Even Mr. Beecham, whose role was more that of an old friend than a put-upon servant.

Julia had passed three days in their company, her confidence building by slow degrees.

At first, she'd been overwhelmed. Not only did she have to look after herself now, without benefit of a maid or a proper laundress, she had the burden of being mistress of Goldfinch Hall.

Some mistress.

She knew nothing about managing a household. Certainly not one without any staff. How was she to distinguish herself?

But the household seemed to chug along without her guiding hand. The men were surprisingly self-sufficient. The children were self-sufficient, too.

The boys still hadn't fully accepted her. She consoled herself that they didn't appear to have fully accepted Jasper, either. Only Daisy genuinely looked on him as a father. She even called him Papa on occasion, when she deigned to speak at all. She was a quiet, watchful child, content to keep her own counsel.

Charlie and Alfred were the exact opposite. They were loud and boisterous, capable of trying the patience of a saint.

Of the two, Charlie was the more difficult. He was a moody boy, angry and sullen at times, behaving as though he hated Jasper. Other times, he was civil, even playful, laughing at a jest or grinning over a story from their mutual past.

Jasper bore it all with an impressive degree of patience.

But then, he'd said he was a patient man.

He was waiting for her, wasn't he? Courting her.

Julia couldn't fail to notice his diligence. He never pressed her. And he hadn't tried to kiss her again. Not since the day they'd arrived at the Hall. But he was there—kind and solicitous and wanting her so much. She could feel it, the desire he had for her. It was a physical sensation. A connection between them that was stretched even tighter after the events of this morning.

She shivered to think of it.

The way he'd looked at her as she'd stood at the basin, half-undressed in front of him. In that moment, it had felt as though all the oxygen had been leeched from the room. As though she couldn't expand her lungs for want of breath.

She'd been embarrassed. Of course she had. But, alarmingly, that hadn't been her only emotion. Something else had chased after it. A warm, delicious thrill that had made her belly clench and gooseflesh rise on her naked skin.

If he'd kissed her then, she had the ridiculous notion she might have burst into flames.

Up ahead of them, the boys leapt into the pond with a resounding splash. Alfred disappeared beneath the shimmering surface, only to reemerge a few yards away. Charlie swam after him, his arms cutting through the water in a confident arc.

"Did you teach them to swim?" Julia asked Jasper.

"I did."

"Who taught you?"

He hesitated before answering. "My father."

Julia knew better than to ask anything more. His parents were off-limits. That's what he'd said before accepting her proposal.

"You're to ask me no questions about my parents or about my time before the war."

Perhaps he hadn't got along with his mother and father. Perhaps the memory of them was as distasteful to him as his experiences in the Crimea.

"If you can call it teaching," he added grimly.

She glanced up at him, surprised he was willing to say anything else on the subject. "What do you mean?"

"When I was a boy, he threw me off of the village pier. Sink or swim, that was his philosophy. There was no instruction connected with it." Jasper stopped to set down their hamper on a shady patch of grass beneath one of the trees that curved toward the water. "Pity. The current was quite strong that day."

"What did you do?"

"I nearly drowned. And then, after swallowing most of the lake, I managed to save myself." A rueful smile quirked his mouth. "Sorry. That's rather a poor tale to start your first day in the water."

That wasn't the reason she was frowning at him. "I thought you didn't want to talk about your past."

"I don't." His brows notched. "That is, I ought not. But sometimes, when we're together . . . I have the urge to tell you things I shouldn't."

"Why shouldn't you if you want to? No harm can come from confiding our secrets to each other."

His smile broadened. "Do you have secrets, sweetheart?"

"Some," she replied, on her dignity. "Every lady does. Though not as many as *you* have, I'd wager."

"Not all my secrets are mine to tell." At that, he shouted to Daisy, "Don't go into the water in your boots!"

"I'm not!" Daisy stepped away from the water's edge. "They're only a little wet."

"Come and change," Jasper said. "Show your stepmama there's nothing to be afraid of."

Daisy ran back to them. "*Are* you afraid?"

"Not so long as I have you and your papa nearby," Julia said.

"There's nothing at all to be afraid of here," Jasper said. "The pond is quite safe."

"I saw a snake in there once." Daisy expanded her arms. "He was this big."

Julia blanched. "There aren't snakes in the water, are there?"

"There are not." Jasper gave Daisy a stern look. "No more tall tales."

"But I did see one," Daisy insisted as Jasper helped her out of her pinafore and dress. She rested a hand on his shoulder as he crouched to remove her tiny boots. "And a frog, and a lizard. And once a great big crocodile."

"A crocodile? In North Yorkshire?" Julia's brows lifted. "My goodness. I wonder how he made it here all the way from the Egyptian Nile?"

"By steamer ship, of course," Jasper said. "Then by rail."

"By rail!" Daisy echoed gleefully.

Julia's mouth tugged into a smile. The little girl's laughter was contagious.

If that wasn't enough to warm her heart, there was the way Jasper interacted with his daughter. He was steady and patient. Stern at times, but ultimately kind. The same way he was with all his children. A man they could rely on.

A *good* man.

Julia had daily evidence of that fact. She never failed to notice it.

Jasper stood. "All right," he said, gazing down at Daisy. "No more foolery. Swimming is a serious business. You know the rules. Stay close to your brothers and venture no further than the blackened oak. Is that understood?"

"Yes, Papa."

He pivoted her small body toward the pond. "Go on."

She burst into a run the second he released her, leaping into the water with as much exuberance as the boys had. They greeted her as she paddled out to them, splashing and cheering her in equal measure.

Jasper raised his voice. "Charlie, Alfred, look after your sister!"

The boys answered in unison: "Yes, sir!"

Julia observed the interaction as she unfastened the hidden hooks at the front of her bodice.

Jasper turned back to her. "She has a vivid imagination. I don't usually discourage it."

"*An imagination is nothing to apologize for*,'" she quoted back to him. "You told me that at Lady Holland's dinner. Do you remember?"

"I remember everything we've ever said to each other."

Her cheeks warmed. "That's very flattering."

He shrugged. "It's the truth." His gaze dropped briefly to the front of her bodice. She'd unfastened it almost to the waist. "Do you need help?"

"No, thank you. I can manage." She focused on removing her own clothing, first endeavoring to ignore the intensity of his regard, then attempting to ignore the fact that he was disrobing, too.

As she stepped out of her skirts and petticoats, she cast him a cautious glance through her lashes.

He'd already removed his top boots and stripped off his shirt.

Her breath caught in her throat. She'd never seen him shirtless before—or any gentleman, come to that.

He was impossibly large and powerful. All broad shoulders, hard muscles, and sun-burnished skin. A picture of raw masculine power, rather like the Grecian friezes and sculptures in the British Museum.

One of them in particular: the reclining Dionysos. She remembered admiring it once in company with Anne, the two of them staring wide-eyed at the god's nude torso, every plane and groove of his chest chiseled in perfect relief.

Jasper's naked chest was as mightily defined as the sculpture, but there the similarities ended. Unlike the marble flesh of Dionysos, her new husband's skin was riddled with scars. Raised scars that resembled the slash on his face, and other scars, too—small and puckered, as if he'd been scorched or burned.

"Bullet wounds," he said.

Her gaze leapt to his, her face flaming with mortification. She'd been staring at him like some silly schoolgirl. "You were shot?"

"Several times." His hands were at the front of his breeches, unbuttoning them as if it were the veriest commonplace. "It's been my misfortune to always find myself in the way of stray bullets. Luckily, none have penetrated so deeply that the surgeons couldn't remove them."

"Was this in the Crimea?"

"It was. All of these scars—" He stopped. "Forgive me. I realize it isn't pleasing to look at."

"No. It's . . . You're . . ." She moistened lips that were suddenly dry. "It pleases me very much."

His mouth hitched in a lopsided smile. One of his boyish smiles— as rare as it was potent.

The impact on her constitution was immediate. Her stomach fluttered and her heart turned over, leaving her flustered and breathless and wanting nothing more than to throw herself straight into his arms.

A foolish notion.

The children were within view, and she was in no state to be embracing anyone. Indeed, wearing nothing but her chemise and drawers, the sun warming her skin through the thin layers of cambric, she felt positively naked.

"Don't forget your boots and stockings," Jasper said.

"I haven't forgotten them." She bent to unlace her half boots, heedless of her chemise gaping open at her neck. It took her longer than usual. She was all thumbs. By the time her legs and feet were bare, she'd been bent over for heaven knows how long.

Straightening, she found Jasper staring at her. A dull red flush was evident high on his cheekbones.

A surge of self-consciousness made her hesitate. "What is it?"

His throat worked on a swallow. "Nothing."

Her gaze flicked briefly downward. He'd already removed his breeches and was wearing nothing save a pair of flannel drawers. She expected to be scandalized, but the garment wasn't at all indecent. In fact, they were rather utilitarian in appearance, falling partway to his knees, with an overlapping front secured with small buttons.

She bit her lower lip.

To think just a week ago he'd been a stranger to her. And now, here they were. Not only married, but standing out of doors together in their knickers. She didn't know whether to laugh or to swoon.

"Are you ready?" he asked.

"I think so." She walked alongside him down to the bank of the pond. The children splashed nearby, oblivious to any shyness or discomfort Julia might be feeling. "Is the water very cold?"

"Let's see." Jasper stepped into it ahead of her.

And that's when she saw it. A sight that stopped her heart from flip-flopping and her stomach from trembling. It was his back—broad and lean and muscular as all the rest of him. It was scarred, too. But not with cuts like the one on his face and chest, and not with bullet wounds. These scars were uniform, one laid down after the other as if made with the same implement over and over again.

Julia had never seen anything like it, but some part of her recognized it for what it was. He'd been beaten. Flogged.

She couldn't comprehend it.

Who on earth would have had the temerity to flog the notorious Captain Blunt?

Twenty-Six

—✕—

The water rose up around Jasper, first to his waist, then to his chest, hiding his scars from view. He turned back to Julia.

"Your turn now," he said. "The temperature's perfect."

It was all she could do to keep her countenance. "I'm coming."

She dipped a toe into the water. It was cool, but not unbearably so. She walked into it as he had, slowly and deliberately submerging herself as she made her way out to where he stood. Her teeth chattered, all thoughts of the whip marks on his back forgotten. "It's freezing!"

"It won't be for long," he said. "Not once you start moving."

She took another few steps. The uneven bed of the pond was slippery beneath her feet. As she walked deeper, the hem of her chemise floated up from her body. She slapped a hand down over it. "Oh, this is dreadful," she muttered. "I don't think I like it at all."

"You're not even swimming yet." His large hands closed around her waist. He drew her toward him as he stepped back further into the pond. "Here. Come deeper with me."

She clutched at his shoulders. "I can't feel the bottom anymore!"

"I have you. I'll not let you sink."

"You had better not," she warned him. "If I drown in this pond—"

"You'll not drown."

"—I shall come back to haunt you."

He gave her a fleeting grin. "*"Be with me always—take any form—drive me mad.""*

Her fingers dug into his muscles. "You said this wasn't like *Wuthering Heights.*"

"Thank God for that. I much prefer you alive." He spun her in a slow circle, taking her even deeper.

Some of the chill dissipated as she acclimated to the water. It was actually quite comfortable. The perfect temperature, just as he'd said. Gleaming rays of sunlight reflected on the pond's dark surface in sparkling glints, warming her damp hair and face. She moved her legs, feeling strangely weightless.

"You're floating," Jasper said.

"I'm not. You're holding me up."

His hands loosened at her waist. "It's you, not me. See? The human body is buoyant in the water."

She held on to him even tighter. "If that's the case, how do you account for so many people drowning in the sea?"

"You're not going to drown," he said again. "So long as you remember not to panic."

Further down the pond, the boys were splashing each other and shouting. Daisy was encouraging them with piercing shrieks of laughter.

The sight of them heartened Julia. If they weren't afraid, what right had she to be frightened?

She gradually eased her grip on Jaspers shoulders.

He was a patient teacher, showing her how to kick her legs and to move her arms, and how to float on her back when she was weary. In time, he moved away and she was able to paddle a short distance to him. On reaching him, she clutched at his shoulders, laughing.

His arms came around her waist. His hair was wet, and water droplets clung to his face. He was smiling at her, proud of her small accomplishment.

She clung to him, breathing heavily. "Jasper . . ."

His smiled faded. Every time she used his given name it was a reminder of the distance between them.

She couldn't help it. It would have been disingenuous to call him *my dear* or *dearest* so soon after the revelations about his past. Certainly not now, when Julia had the unhappy premonition there were even more revelations to come.

"How did you get those scars on your back?" she asked.

His expression shuttered. But he didn't dissemble. "I was flogged."

"In the Crimea?" She searched his eyes. "But . . . who would dare?"

A flicker of wry humor crossed his face at her naivete. "Everyone has a superior."

"I can't imagine you having one. Not one brave enough to flog you."

"Bravery had nothing to do with it. Floggings are a part of life in the army. During my time in the Crimea, they were administered with frequency, often for the smallest infractions."

She hesitated before reminding him, "You administered quite a few yourself."

He didn't deny it. "There are many who consider the conduct justifiable."

Julia didn't doubt it. It was why Jasper hadn't been blackballed from polite society. Why he'd been welcomed to London as a hero, despite his rumored history of cruelty. She nevertheless inquired, "Who thinks so?"

"Old soldiers and politicians, mostly. Ask any of them about floggings and brandings, and they'll say such punishments are necessary to keep order in the ranks. They may be right. I don't know anymore."

"Why were you flogged?" she asked.

"Insubordination."

"Who did it? Was it some major or colonel or somebody?"

"It was an evil man, irrespective of his rank. Probably the evilest man I've ever had the misfortune to encounter."

"Who—"

"No more questions." Jasper gave her a look as stern as the one he'd given Daisy before she went into the pond. "I mean it. My past is a poison. There's enough of it here in Yorkshire already. I don't fancy any more of it."

Her hands slid to the nape of his neck, smoothing over his wet hair in unspoken apology. "I'm sorry. I know I promised not to ask. But that was before."

"Before what?"

"Before you were mine," she said.

His brows notched in a troubled frown. As if she'd expressed something he didn't quite know what to do with. "Julia . . ."

She stroked his nape with gentle fingers. "I want to know everything about you."

He bowed his head to hers, submitting to her soft caresses in much the way a very large lion might submit to his mate. "Can this not be enough?"

"Perhaps it can," she said. "Eventually." And then she surprised them both by pressing her damp lips to his.

His arms tightened at her waist.

"They're kissing!" Daisy cried.

The boys whooped with laughter.

Julia broke the kiss almost immediately on a self-conscious laugh of her own. "I forgot we have an audience."

Jasper didn't seem to care. His gaze was riveted to hers. "What was that for?"

Her mouth curved in a faint smile. "I suppose I was reminding you."

"Of what?"

"That you're mine, of course."

He gave a husky laugh. "I'm not likely to forget." His fingers flexed at her waist. "But please, do remind me again whenever the mood takes you."

"Is Father already in his study?" Alfred asked when Julia entered the dining room the next morning. He and Charlie were seated at the table eating their breakfast. A teapot and teacups were arrayed next to them, along with the jam pot and a half-empty rack of toast.

Julia crossed to the sideboard and retrieved a plate for herself. It was Mr. Beecham's habit to set out the hot food in silver chafing dishes. There was no specific time the household was expected to breakfast, but if one waited too long, one was inevitably left with cold eggs and congealed porridge.

As a result, Julia had been acclimating herself to rising before half past eight, merely so she might enjoy the benefit of a hot meal. It was a vastly different experience than she'd had at Belgrave Square, where breakfast had been brought to her in bed each morning on a tray.

"I believe he is," she said as she filled her plate. "He starts his work very early, doesn't he?"

Indeed, she'd not seen her new husband even once in the morning since they'd arrived. He was always gone from their bed—and their room—when she awoke. In more vulnerable moments, she sometimes suspected he didn't wish to prolong his time in her company.

"*Work,*" Charlie echoed with a snort. "If you can call it that."

"What else?" Julia carried her plate to the table.

"He's a forger," Charlie said.

A forger?

Julia froze in the act of pulling out her chair. "Why on earth would you say that?"

"Because it's true." Charlie continued eating. "What else is he doing in the tower all day with the door locked? It must be something against the law."

"It's the truth," Alfred agreed. "Everyone says so."

Julia sat down. "Who?" she demanded.

"The boys at school," Charlie said.

"And some of the people in the village," Alfred added.

Julia felt a hot surge of anger at the villagers' ignorance. She made an effort to contain her temper. "Your father isn't a forger. And you shouldn't listen to slanderous things other people say. Particularly when what they're saying is about your own family."

The boys clammed up, resuming their meal, but not before exchanging knowing looks with each other.

Later that morning, trudging along at Daisy's side through the overgrown garden that lay at the back of the house, Julia reflected on the conversation with a distinct sense of unease.

A forger indeed.

If that were true, Jasper wouldn't have needed to marry an heiress. His criminal skills would have sufficed to repair his fortunes.

Besides, he'd told her when she proposed to him that he wasn't involved in anything nefarious. He'd said that his secret occupation hurt no one.

That didn't mean she'd ceased wondering about it.

He was in the tower every morning, often until well past noon. What in heaven was he doing that required such solitude? Such secrecy?

Perhaps he was a spy in the service of Queen Victoria.

Or perhaps his tower study housed laboratory equipment and he was engaged in important scientific research.

Julia had thought of every possibility, up to and including the likelihood that he may be locking himself away each morning simply to read uninterrupted. If that was the case, she could hardly fault him. She'd been known to go to extremes for a little uninterrupted reading time herself.

"It's there behind those trees," Daisy said, skipping ahead. "Do you see the angel's wings?"

Julia raised a hand to shadow her eyes. The sun was shining as brightly today as it had on the previous three days. The ideal weather for a visit to Goldfinch Hall's informal graveyard.

Or so Daisy had claimed when Julia had gone to fetch her from her room after breakfast.

Julia had had little choice but to acquiesce to the excursion. In truth, she was in no mood to pay homage to the final resting place of Dolly Carvel. She didn't think she ever would be. But Dolly had been more than Jasper's longtime mistress. She was also the children's mother, and, therefore, a very important person, alive or dead.

"Yes," Julia said. "I see."

At the bottom of the garden, where the land was flat, Dolly's grave lay beneath the trunk of an alder tree. The branches provided a natural shelter over the marble angel with its outstretched wings.

"He's watching over her." Daisy's voice was quiet with reverence. "Isn't that nice?"

"It is." Julia followed Daisy to the grave. The ground was still soggy in places from the heavy rains that had come on Saturday and Sunday. Julia was conscious of the grass staining the box-pleated hem of her silk poplin skirts as she passed through it.

She'd complained about her laundry woes in the letter she'd written to Anne. It had been a long letter—more than four pages front and back—though not an overly intimate one. Julia had refrained from mentioning anything about her burgeoning feelings for Jasper. And she hadn't written a word about the Bluebeard-like restrictions he'd imposed on her movements in the house.

Anne wouldn't understand. She'd never liked Jasper to begin with. And she'd have no patience with the agreement Julia had made with him.

What is he hiding? Anne would ask. *What's so horrible he must keep it secret from you?*

Julia consoled herself that Anne didn't know anything about husbands. In five days of marriage, Julia had learned precious little herself. Still, she was leagues ahead of her unmarried friends.

She knew what it was to kiss a gentleman. To sleep with him every night in bed, and to feel his strength pressed up against her softness as he held her in a powerful embrace. She knew what it was to belong to a gentleman, and to feel that he belonged to her absolutely—regardless of his past or his secrets or any of the doubts she might still have about him.

And there were more than a few to plague her.

The children weren't helping in that regard. Between the boys' remarks about Jasper being a forger and Daisy's constant avowal that Jasper had loved her mother more than anyone in the world, Julia was finding it a trifle difficult to get her footing.

"She's sleeping all the time now," Daisy said, standing over Dolly's grave.

Julia glanced at her. "Did your mother sleep a great deal before?"

Daisy nodded bleakly.

Julia didn't press her on the subject. Jasper had said that Dolly had been desperately ill in her final month. That she'd largely wasted away. Naturally, she must have spent a great amount of time in bed asleep. Though how Daisy knew of it, Julia hadn't the slightest notion. The little girl had been barely a year old at the time of her mother's death.

Kneeling down, Daisy removed the broken branches and stray leaves that had gathered over the burial mound.

Casting one last rueful look at her clean skirts, Julia knelt down on the grass beside her. She helped to clear away the debris.

"My mother was the nicest, kindest, most beautiful lady in the world," Daisy informed her—not for the first time. "She loved me very much."

"I'm sure she did."

"Did your mother love you?"

Julia brushed the dried mud from the chiseled placard at the base of the angel. It was inscribed with Dolly's name and the date of her death. "I don't know," she answered honestly.

"Is she dead, too?" Daisy asked.

"No, indeed. She lives in London."

Daisy's face scrunched in a frown. "Do you miss her?"

"I don't, I'm afraid. My mother wasn't very nice to me. She wasn't at all like the kind of mother you had."

Daisy's eyes dropped to Dolly's grave. "Charlie says she wasn't nice."

Julia stilled. "Oh?"

"She pinched me and hurt my arm. Charlie said I had a bruise this big." Daisy indicated a large spot near her elbow. "I cried and cried."

"I'm sorry to hear it." Julia chose her next words with care. "Perhaps your mother was having a bad day?"

The idea seemed to give Daisy comfort. "She *was* very ill." She paused. "Do you pinch people when you're poorly?"

"I don't pinch people at all. I would rather hug them and kiss them if they let me."

Daisy's lower lip gave a faint wobble.

Julia slipped her arm around Daisy's narrow shoulders, drawing her close. She gave the little girl a brief but heartfelt hug. "There," she said, pressing a kiss to her forehead before releasing her. "That's the worst you can expect from me."

Daisy clutched Julia's hand, holding on to it for the remainder of the time they knelt at the grave.

Julia was touched. "Would you like to go back to the house for some tea?"

Daisy shook her head.

"Shall we stay awhile longer, then? We can find some flowers for your mama. I saw roses by the arbor."

Again, Daisy shook her head. She tugged Julia close to whisper in her ear. "I have a secret."

Julia widened her eyes. "Do you? How thrilling."

"I can show you," Daisy offered, scrambling to her feet.

"If you like." Julia stood, permitting the little girl to draw her away, back through the garden and down the drive that curved around in front of the crumbling stone stable block.

She wasn't wholly convinced this wouldn't be another unpleasant variety of surprise. Something akin to the invitation to visit Dolly's grave. But she was resolved to be cheerful about it—even when Daisy pulled her into the darkened barn.

If any place at Goldfinch Hall was haunted, surely it was this one. There was a strange coolness to the air, and a scent of lingering decay even more pronounced than in the rotting east wing of the Hall.

Sunlight streamed through holes in the roof, revealing a floor strewn with antiquated straw. Several empty loose boxes were situated under the portion of the ceiling that was still intact. There was no sign of Musket. He must be out in the pasture somewhere.

"It's back here." Daisy quickened her pace. "In the hayloft."

Julia reluctantly followed her. As they stepped up to the rickety wooden ladder, a soft mewling emanated from the loft above.

Julia's fear of ghosts evaporated. "Oh my goodness," she whispered. "Kittens!"

Twenty-Seven

◆

*J*asper entered the abandoned stables to find his wife standing atop what was surely the most antiquated ladder in Christendom. Daisy remained safely on the ground, clutching the ladder's teetering legs.

"There's six of them altogether," Julia called down. "Three striped ones, two black ones, and one with orange patches on her fur."

"That one's going to be mine!" Daisy called back, shaking the ladder in her enthusiasm. The ancient wood gave out an ominous groan.

Julia's foot slipped from the rung. "Oh!"

Jasper was at her side an instant before she fell. He caught her neatly in his arms.

She clung to his neck, gazing up at him in amazement. "Jasper! Thank heaven. For a moment I feared I was about to do myself an injury."

Jasper glowered at her, his heart threatening to beat straight out of his chest. If she had fallen—if she had hurt herself—

The prospect was enough to make his temper boil over.

"What do you mean by climbing up there?" he barked at her. "Can't you see how dangerous it is? You might have broken your blasted neck!"

Daisy's face drained of excitement. "It was my fault. I told her to climb it."

"It's not Daisy's fault," Julia said. "I went up the ladder of my own accord. There are kittens up there. Did you know that?" Her hands slid to his shoulders. "Oh, do put me down. And stop scowling. Nothing happened. I'm quite safe."

He unwillingly set her feet down on the straw-covered floor. The mewling of kittens punctuated the silence, as if in explanation of her reckless behavior.

"Kittens?" he ground out. "We don't even own a cat."

"She's wild," Daisy said. "From the moors. Julia says we can tame her."

"*Julia?*"

Daisy flushed. "She said I could call her that."

"I did." Julia set a reassuring hand on Daisy's narrow back. "And we'll *try* to tame them. I can't promise it will work."

"We'll use cheese and milk, won't we?" Daisy gave Julia an expectant look. "Then the mama cat and her kittens will be ours to keep."

"I hope they will," Julia said. "Your papa doesn't object, does he?"

Jasper ran a hand through his hair. "What I object to is the pair of you climbing up a rotting ladder into a rotting hayloft. The whole of this stable may come crashing down at any given moment."

"It can't be that dangerous," Julia said. "You keep Quintus here, don't you?"

"Of course not. He's stabled in an outbuilding on the other side of the Hall. Cossack will be kept there as well. That's what I was coming to tell you." He marched them out of the stables and back into the yard. "The horses have arrived."

Julia's face lit up. "What? When?"

"Just now. Ridgeway's man has brought them. He's been on the road since Sunday, traveling in stages." Jasper addressed Daisy. "Run up to the Hall and tell your brothers. They can come out as soon as their lessons are done."

Daisy was off like a shot.

Julia moved to follow after her.

Jasper caught her hand, bringing her to a halt in front of him.

She gave him a puzzled look.

"Don't scare me like that again," he said.

Her expression softened. "I didn't mean to scare you. All I could think of was seeing the kittens."

"Clearly. You forgot everything I've told you about being careful." He reminded her again, "There are parts of this estate that need to be torn down and built anew. Until they are, you must take care to avoid them. If anything happened to you—"

"I'm fine. Even if I *had* fallen—"

"Don't," he said gruffly. "You've no idea what it does to me to think of losing you."

Understanding registered on Julia's face. "I really did scare you, didn't I?" She twined her fingers through his. "I'm sorry, my dear. I'll be more careful in future, I promise."

My dear.

She hadn't called him that since their wedding night. He'd been trying to earn back the privilege ever since. At last, it seemed he had.

He brought her hand to his mouth and pressed a rough kiss to her knuckles. He'd have rather kissed her lips. But this was neither the time nor the place for such intimacies. "See that you are," he said. "I'm trusting you to look after yourself—and Daisy."

"Daisy's in no danger. She knows the whole of the estate backward and forward. She's been showing it to me."

"Anyplace in particular?" he asked as he offered her his arm.

Julia took it, accompanying him back up the uneven dirt drive at a leisurely pace. "We visited her mother's grave."

"Of course you did." Jasper couldn't prevent a surge of bitterness from coloring his words. It seemed that every inch of progress he made with his new bride was doomed to be undone by constant reminders of the past. "I suppose Daisy gave you an earful."

"She did." Julia walked with him in silence for several steps before asking, "Was the children's mother not good to them?"

"Not in the usual way of mothers. She had her own survival to think of. Everything else was an afterthought."

"I'm not asking if she was neglectful. I'm asking if she was cruel."

Ah. Daisy *had* been talking.

Jasper gave Julia a thoughtful look. "You must have made quite an impression on Daisy for her to confide in you."

"I like her," she said. "I truly do. I very much want her to like me."

"She does. She thinks you extraordinarily beautiful." His mouth twisted in a fleeting smile. "She's not the only one."

Julia squeezed his arm in acknowledgment of the compliment. But she wouldn't be distracted. "*Was* their mother cruel?"

Up ahead, the drive divided into two separate branches. The first led up to the front of the Hall. The second curved around to the opposite side, a distance away, toward the outbuildings that were presently housing the horses.

Jasper guided Julia down the second path, his mouth set in a grim line. "At times," he said. "Near the end, especially. She blamed them for a great deal that had gone wrong in her life. I did my best to keep them clear of her."

Julia frowned. "And yet you've buried her here with all reverence, as though she were a saint."

Good Lord. Is that how it appeared?

Dolly Carvel had been no saint. When she'd first appeared at the Hall six years ago, Jasper had been disposed to think her a devil. It was true, he *had* buried her here, and he *had* marked her grave with an angel. But it hadn't been for her benefit. It had been for Charlie, Alfred, and Daisy.

"What purpose would it serve to tear down the children's memory of her?" he asked.

"A false memory, it would seem," Julia said.

Jasper couldn't dispute the fact. "If the children wish to reflect on Dolly's petty cruelties, they may do so in their own time. I'll not be the one to remind them of her faults."

"You'd rather they make a fiction out of her?"

"If that's what they prefer," he said. "No doubt it's better that way."

Julia's wide silk skirts brushed his leg. "Can a lie ever be better than the truth?"

He inwardly flinched. "Sometimes, yes. I believe it can. If it's in a good cause."

"It's still a lie," she said. "I'm not convinced that lies are ever a good idea. Not even when a person means well." She paused. "But it's none of my business, is it?"

"You're my wife. Naturally, it's your business. On this subject, however, I trust you'll defer to me."

"You needn't worry. I'd never presume to criticize the children's mother to them. It's obvious they revere her. I know you cared for her, too. You must have done to have been with her for so many years."

Bloody hell. How did they get on this subject?

There was nothing Jasper could say that wouldn't make him out a villain. If he told the truth, that he'd never cared for Dolly at all, he sounded like a cad. And if he lied and said he had, he'd sound as though he was betraying his feelings for his wife. Either way, Julia would be hurt.

"Must we be forever talking about the past?" he asked with a scowl.

"I can't simply pretend you didn't have a life before."

No, indeed. How could she with the children in residence and Dolly buried at the bottom of the garden? Every corner Julia turned on the estate held a reminder of the sordid history of the infamous Captain Blunt. And Jasper could do nothing about it.

The only solution was to go forward.

"I'm more concerned with the life I have now," he said. "We should be talking about the future."

"Very well." She cast him a guarded glance. "What about it?"

In that moment, he could have told her anything. Spoken about his feelings or about what he hoped for their marriage. But the time wasn't right. Not when they'd just been discussing his relationship with Dolly.

"I've been, ah, thinking of the tenants' cottages," he said instead.

"The tenants' cottages?"

"They require a great deal of work. New roofs to start. I thought we might begin with them once we have your fifty thousand pounds in hand."

She lifted her skirts out of the way as they left the dirt path to cross the grass. "You haven't mentioned my money since the day we arrived here."

He grimaced. "I've thought of it enough," he admitted. "It's tempting to want to improve everything at once. But we must be strategic. After the tenants' cottages are repaired, we can take people on to look after the fields and the livestock. They'll bring us an income, eventually. As for the house, we must have builders in to assess the rot, and to repair the roof. Once that's completed—"

"You keep speaking of *us* and *we*. As if you wish my opinion on the matter."

"I do," he said solemnly. "It's your home now. I want you to be happy here."

The swell of her bosom brushed his arm as she walked at his side. "I think I can be."

His pulse quickened. It was his private dream. That she'd find contentment here with him. That she wouldn't come to regret their marriage. "Can you, sweet?"

Her cheeks took on a familiar rosy glow. The same diffuse watercolor blush that appeared whenever they spoke of intimate matters. "I believe so," she said. "I'm still anxious about things more than I'd like, but it's nothing to how I felt in town."

"What things?" he asked.

"Disappointing the children. Disappointing *you*."

He uttered a husky laugh. "You couldn't if you tried."

She gave him a speaking glance. "I know *that* isn't true. If it was, you wouldn't leave our bed with such haste every morning."

His gaze shot to hers.

What the devil?

Did she truly believe he was leaving her at break of dawn every day because he was *disappointed* in her in some way? The idea was so ludicrous—so ridiculously far from the truth—he'd have laughed if he wasn't so stunned.

They were but a few yards from the outbuilding, still unable to see it clearly from around the corner of the house. Only a few seconds of privacy remained.

"Julia," he began. "I—"

The shrill whinny of a horse cut through his words.

Julia eyes brightened with recognition. She released his arm. "It's Cossack!" she cried. Hoisting her voluminous skirts in her hands, she took off at a sprint.

Julia cradled Cossack's large head in her hands, pressing kisses to his velvety nose. He appeared in good health, none the worse for wear after his long journey from London. He whickered softly to her, nostrils quivering, as she murmured to him about how much she'd missed him.

The groom who had delivered the horses stood outside the outbuilding that was serving as their temporary stables. He was a genial fellow approaching middle age, with sandy hair and a broad, muscular frame. "He were a good traveler, ma'am," he said. "Never put up a fuss, not at any of the coaching inns we stopped at along the way."

"He's always been very good." Julia hugged Cossack's neck, vaguely conscious that, in doing so, she was soiling the bodice of her gown. "Ever since he was young."

"Not like that one." The groom cast a pointed look at Quintus. Jasper's enormous black stallion had already been set loose in a paddock nearby and was rolling in the grass, rubbing his neck and head as if to scratch an itch he couldn't quite reach. "That one were a handful."

"He has a delicate temperament," Jasper said. "Like all oversized brutes."

Julia smiled at her husband. "He's glad to be home."

"Undoubtedly. Except for the occasional ride into Hardholme, he's left to do as he pleases here." Jasper set his hand on Julia's back as he addressed the groom. "You'll be wanting to get back there before sunset, once your team's rested."

The groom had driven to the Hall in a four-wheeled open carriage pulled by a pair of chestnuts. They were nothing very fancy, but they were solid horses, obviously chosen with care.

"As to that, sir, Lord Ridgeway said as how I was to give you this." The groom retrieved a rumpled letter from the inside of his brown cloth coat. He gave it to Jasper.

Frowning, Jasper broke open the wax seal and began to read. As he did so, Charlie, Alfred, and Daisy trotted down to join them.

"Famous!" Alfred exclaimed on seeing Cossack. "He's nearly as big as Quintus!"

"May I pet him?" Daisy asked.

"You may," Julia said. "Charlie? Would you take charge of him for me? I'm sure he'd like to graze while you all get to know him."

Charlie stood a little straighter. Taking the lead rope from Julia's hand, he walked Cossack further out on the grass. Alfred and Daisy went with him, Alfred chattering all the while.

Julia turned her attention back to Jasper. The expression on his face sparked a flicker of apprehension in her veins. "What is it?"

He passed her the letter. "It seems Ridgeway has made us a wedding present."

Julia quickly read the brief note for herself.

Blunt,

I've entrusted your horses to Plimstock for the journey. He's a decent fellow and a competent groom, though not suited for London at present. His wages have been paid for the year. Please accept him, along with the carriage and matched pair, as a wedding gift.

Yours, etc.
Ridgeway

Julia looked to the groom—Plimstock, apparently—and the two chestnuts who were grazing in a paddock next door to the one where Quintus was cavorting.

"Is there a particular reason you wish to remove from London?" Jasper asked the man.

"Aye, sir," Plimstock said. "I'm Yorkshire born. My young lady resides in Malton. She's in service to the squire there. We plan to marry as soon as we can settle our living arrangements. Lord Ridgeway said as how you might be in the way of giving us a cottage."

Jasper's frown deepened. "Did he, indeed."

Julia waited until they were alone again to ask, "Are you displeased with Lord Ridgeway?"

Jasper walked alongside her up the drive to the house. The sun gleamed in the thick raven-black threads of his hair. He wasn't wearing a hat, nor even a coat. Clad in black trousers and a plain black waistcoat, his shirtsleeves rolled up to reveal the sinewy muscles of his bronzed forearms, his appearance suggested he'd come straight from his work in the tower.

Whatever work that might be.

"No more than usual," he said. "He's been exceptionally generous. And I can't claim we wouldn't benefit from an extra pair of hands about the place—and an extra pair of horses."

"What is it, then?"

"If we're to house and feed them all, we can't delay in getting access to your inheritance."

She nodded in agreement. Thus far, her letter to the bank had gone unanswered. It was an ominous sign. She'd been anticipating the need for further action. "How do you plan to go about it?"

"I'll speak to a solicitor," he said. "I have a man in York. Mr. Piggott. He isn't my first choice, but he'll have to do for now."

"Is there someone else you'd prefer?"

"Mr. Finchley in London seemed exceedingly competent. Ruthless, too. If any problems should arise, we'll need a solicitor with teeth."

"Do you anticipate difficulties?"

"Given your bank's silence? Yes, I do. Your father didn't strike me as a man who enjoys being thwarted."

"No. He isn't." Not that Julia had ever disobeyed before. There had been no reason to do so. Her own fears and insecurities had kept her a prisoner in Belgrave Square as surely as any rules her parents had set down. At the time, defying them would have meant defying her own inclinations.

She'd been too scared, too uncertain of her own value, to assert her right to happiness. Until Jasper, the only happily-ever-afters she'd ever contemplated had been the kind in novels.

Since leaving London, she hadn't thought of her parents overmuch. She'd been too focused on regaining her strength and on acclimating to her new life. But she thought of them now—Papa wrapped in his blanket cocoon and Mama with her eyes streaming from camphor oil.

She felt a sharp twinge of guilt for abandoning them. It was all tangled together with her feelings of anger and hurt at how they'd treated her.

"I'll have to go into York," Jasper said as they approached the front steps of the Hall.

"When?"

"Sooner rather than later." He didn't look pleased at the idea. "If I leave first thing in the morning, I can catch the early train from Malton. I'll be back by nightfall. Possibly sooner."

Julia climbed up the moss-covered steps alongside him. "You must take as long as you require."

"And leave you alone here overnight?" He flashed her a dark glance. "I don't think so."

"I won't be alone. I'll have Mr. Beecham and the children. And now Mr. Plimstock. I'll be perfectly safe."

He held the front door open for her, and she preceded him inside. It was darker and cooler in the entrance hall, the shadows drifting over their faces as the door shut behind them.

Jasper gazed down at her. "You'll be alone," he said. "In our bed."

A shiver of awareness went through her. She took an unconscious step back; unaware she'd done so until she felt the stone wall behind her. "For only one night."

"One night is too long to be without you." He loomed over her, so close that the swell of her petticoats and skirts was pressed back against her legs. "You're wrong, you know."

"About what?"

"I don't leave you each morning because I'm unhappy with you. I leave because I haven't the strength to last a second longer. Any more time spent in our bed and you'd awaken to me doing this." Bending his head, he caught her mouth in a scorching kiss.

Julia knees weakened. She reached for him instinctively, only to be swept up in his arms in a crushing embrace. "Oh," she murmured. "Oh, I didn't know."

She felt him smile, his scarred lips moving over the curve of her own with delicious friction.

"Now you do," he said, kissing her again.

She wrapped her arms around his neck, her mouth yielding to his on a sigh of pleasure.

Was there anything more glorious than being held and kissed by Jasper Blunt? If there was, she couldn't think of it. Couldn't even dream of it. He'd exceeded all her wildest imaginings.

And this was but a glimpse of marital intimacy.

There was more still to come. All she need do was say the word and he would take her. Have her. Make her his in every way.

The only obstacle was her own conscience.

It was no minor impediment. If she submitted to her desires, she'd have to live with the fact that she'd given herself to a man with a notoriously evil past. A man who still had secrets he wouldn't share. Worse secrets, perhaps.

Would it be worth it? Risking her heart and her principles, her very future, for a few moments of pleasure in his arms?

He deepened their kiss, and for one smoldering moment, she almost believed it would be.

But no.

Her fingers twined tight into his hair. "Wait," she breathed. "Wait, wait."

His mouth stilled on hers. There was a taut pause, as if he were marshaling his senses, then gradually—reluctantly—he straightened, loosening his grip on her. "Forgive me. I forget what a great big brute I am." He looked down at her with genuine concern. "Did I hurt you?"

"No, no. I'm not that fragile." A blush burned in her face. She sunk her voice, admitting, "I like it when you hold me and kiss me so fiercely."

His gray eyes gleamed. "Do you?"

"It's terribly exciting." She smoothed her hands down the front of his waistcoat, feeling a tad possessive of him. "Perhaps I shouldn't admit to that."

"On the contrary." He bowed his head to hers, his deep voice dropping to a confiding murmur. "You must tell me everything that pleases you."

Her stomach clenched.

She reminded herself that they were in the entrance hall, not their bedchamber, and that this was the middle of the day, not the dark of night.

As for her other qualms, she needed no reminding.

"It would please me," she said carefully, "if we could have fewer secrets between each other."

Twenty-Eight

◆◆

Jasper's body had been poised for action, his blood warm and his muscles tight with burgeoning arousal. He'd wanted to kiss Julia again. Indeed, given the chance, he'd have picked her up and carried her to bed and shown her just how little disappointed he was in his choice of bride.

But not now.

Her words were as effective at dampening his ardor as a bucket of cold water.

He stared down at her. "*No more secrets?* Julia, you promised me—"

"I didn't say no more," she corrected him. "I said fewer. There's a difference."

"We agreed—"

"I know what we agreed. But surely, you can't object to sharing *some* of your secrets with me. Not now we're married."

A flare of anger took him unaware. He might have backed away from her if she didn't have such a relentless grip on his waistcoat. "What secrets of mine did you have in mind?" he asked. "And which of your own conditions are you willing to relinquish in exchange? Shall I forbid you from keeping those kittens? Or perhaps I'll restrict your reading, or—"

"Don't be absurd. You know which of my conditions I'm willing to give up." She listed closer, confessing to him despite her blushes. "I want to *be* with you."

His chest constricted. Just like that the anger evaporated. In its place was a swell of longing so acute it closed his throat. He covered her hands with his, squeezing them tight. "Then *be* with me. Never mind my secrets. They've nothing to do with how we feel about each other."

"But they do," she insisted in the same softly earnest voice. "I can't give myself to you if I don't know who you truly are."

Jasper recoiled. Cold water be damned. This time, he felt as though she'd struck him with the bucket itself.

His hands fell from hers as his blood turned to ice. "You know who I am. You know the very worst of me."

"I don't know what you're doing in the tower all day." She straightened her fingers on his chest, smoothing the wrinkles she'd created in his waistcoat. "Some of the villagers have been putting it about that you're a forger."

"What?"

"The boys have heard their schoolmates say so. And they're inclined to believe them. They've no other explanation for your being cloistered in the tower every morning."

Jasper scowled. "Hardholme is populated by fools with nothing but baseless gossip to entertain them. The boys know better than to believe anything they hear there." He pulled away from her. It took all his strength to do so.

Her eyes followed him, a stricken expression in her gaze. "Now you're angry with me."

"I'm not angry." He raked his hand through his hair. "If you must know . . . I'm bloody tempted to give you want you want." He glared at her, wanting her so much it hurt to look at her. "Tell me, is this the only secret you demand of me? Some proof that I'm not forging documents up there?"

"I don't believe you're a forger," she said. "And I don't *demand* anything."

He scoffed. If she were any other lady, he'd accuse her of attempting a variety of blackmail. One of his secrets in exchange for the right to bed her? An unscrupulous bargain.

But Julia wasn't some calculating Delilah. She was his wife. His sweet, vulnerable—and quite virginal—romantic-minded little wife. A lady who, having heard about his history in the Crimea and his even worse history with Dolly and the children, had every right to suspect him of continued villainy.

And her suspicions weren't far wrong.

But perhaps . . .

Perhaps there was a way he could satisfy her without putting anything else at risk. Another portion of the truth, whittled to suit the situation, carved clean of the darker truth to which it belonged.

Jasper didn't like it. He didn't like any of it. But what other choice had he?

"I can't think," he said. "Not with this visit to York hanging over my head."

Her face fell. "Of course. That must come first."

He stalked back to her with a growl, framing her face in his hands. "*You* come first," he informed her. "*You.*" He kissed her hard on the mouth. "As for all the rest of it . . . we shall discuss it when I return tomorrow evening."

When Julia woke in the morning, Jasper was already gone. She wasn't surprised. Nothing had been resolved yesterday. She rather suspected she'd made the situation worse.

Rising from bed, she went to the marble-topped mahogany washstand. Water was still in the porcelain pitcher from Jasper's morning ablutions. It was no longer hot.

She sighed. It was either wash with cold or summon Mr. Beecham or one of the children to fetch hot water for her from the kitchen. Given those choices, she'd rather shiver a little than make a nuisance of herself.

The sun streamed in through the patterned damask draperies as she filled the basin. A glint of something metallic twinkled at the corner of her eye. Returning the pitcher to its place, she turned to look, and was alarmed to see Jasper's keys and pocket watch sitting on the chest of drawers by the window. In his haste to leave, he'd forgotten them. It wasn't the first time he'd done so.

As if she needed more evidence of his eagerness to quit her presence!

But no. He wasn't leaving her so abruptly because he found her company distasteful. It was the opposite. He'd admitted as much yesterday. He was finding her increasingly hard to resist.

Any other man might have simply broken his promise. Either that, or endeavored to persuade her to change her mind.

Jasper had done neither.

It was yet more evidence of his being a good and decent man. A man who was doing his utmost to adhere to the conditions she'd given him.

She finished washing and dressing, and after arranging her hair in an invisible net, she made her way downstairs to the dining room.

Charlie and Alfred were seated at the table with Mr. Beecham, their plates already heaped high with steaming eggs, toast, and sausages. Daisy was there as well, a bowl of porridge and cream in front of her.

Mr. Beecham stood as Julia entered, his linen napkin clutched in his hand. "Mrs. Blunt. Good morning."

"Good morning, Mr. Beecham. Charlie, Alfred." Julia smiled at Daisy. "You're up early today, my dear."

"I wanted to see father leave," Daisy said.

"And did you?" Julia helped herself to a plate at the sideboard.

"No," Daisy admitted glumly. "He was gone when I woke."

"He'll be back this evening." Mr. Beecham resumed his seat. "Perhaps earlier if his business in York is resolved quickly."

Julia spooned a serving of eggs onto her plate. "I confess, it will be quite strange without him here, even for a day. Though I expect we all have enough to keep us busy."

"Quite right, ma'am." Mr. Beecham spread his napkin back over his lap. "The boys and I have lessons to occupy us, don't we, lads? And Miss Daisy will be joining us again today with her primer."

It wasn't uncommon for Daisy to do so. In lieu of a governess or nurse, she often attached herself to the boys' lessons, reading along from her primer as they worked with Mr. Beecham on more difficult subjects.

"We shouldn't have lessons this morning," Charlie said.

Julia glanced back at him as she selected a sausage. "Why not?"

"We have a carriage now," Charlie replied.

What seemed to be a non sequitur was at once explained by Alfred. "We should go into Hardholme. There's sweets at Taggert's Market."

Daisy perked up immediately. "I want sweets!"

Returning to the table, Julia exchanged a look with Mr. Beecham. "Would Captain Blunt object to our driving into Hardholme?"

Mr. Beecham frowned. "I don't rightly know, ma'am."

"Does he often take the children into the village?" she asked, sitting down in her chair.

"Not regularly, no."

"He didn't need to take us," Charlie said. "We boarded there during the school term."

"You stayed at the school?" Julia reached for the teapot. "I didn't realize."

"Mr. Filbert takes on boarders from the outlying estates," Mr. Beecham explained. "It was easier for the boys to stay on rather than have them traveling ten miles in the dogcart every day. Musket wouldn't have tolerated it."

"But we have a carriage now," Charlie said again. "With two sound horses."

Alfred nodded eagerly. "*And* a coachman. He can drive us."

Julia's brows knit with indecision. She hadn't envisioned going into the village anytime soon. Certainly not without Jasper's escort. The prospect of meeting strangers—of being stared at and whispered over—was enough to make her stomach tremble with anxiety.

But she wasn't the same person she'd been in London.

She wasn't Julia Wychwood anymore. She was Mrs. Julia Blunt. A different creature altogether.

Hadn't that always been a dream of hers? To go to a new place and start afresh? To reinvent herself as someone new—someone confident? It had been an appealing fantasy.

Not so much in reality.

Even so . . .

"It may be nice to do a little shopping," she conceded. "Is there a draper in Hardholme?"

"There's a *shop*," Mr. Beecham replied. "Orrick's Emporium. It's run by Mr. Orrick and his wife. They've silks and woolens, and a selection of gloves and ribbons and such like."

"It's Taggert's that has sweets," Alfred reiterated. "Peppermints kept in jars on the counter."

"What about a tailor or dressmaker?" Julia asked.

Charlie's expression darkened with suspicion. "What need have we of those?"

Julia cast a meaningful glance at his and Alfred's clothing. Their little coats were too short at the sleeves and their trousers were too short at the ankles. Daisy was in no better trim. She'd stained or torn nearly every garment in her possession.

"When did the three of you last have new clothes?" Julia asked.

Beecham answered in their stead: "It was last autumn, ma'am. Captain Blunt saw to it himself. It's not his fault the boys are growing like weeds."

"It's no one's fault, except mother nature's, I daresay." Julia sipped her tea. She had a goodly amount of money tucked away in her reticule. More than enough to outfit the children—and herself—with a few necessities. "Very well," she said. "We'll go into the village, and I'll even purchase you each some sweets, but you must agree to be fitted for new garments."

Alfred's excitement dimmed. "At Orrick's Emporium?"

"Of course, at Orrick's," Charlie retorted.

"They don't like us in the village," Daisy said in a small voice.

"Oh, don't they?" Julia's indecision hardened into firm resolve. "We shall see about that."

The village of Hardholme was as dreary as its name suggested. Situated on the edge of the moors, it consisted primarily of a single main street flanked by a handful of shops, most of which had plainly seen better days. Among them, Orrick's Emporium appeared the most prosperous. It boasted an elaborate painted sign and a large front window in which a display of ruffled parasols, dyed-leather gloves, and two jauntily trimmed straw bonnets had been arranged on stacks of pink and green hatboxes.

Mr. Plimstock helped Julia down from the carriage. She shook out her blue silk skirts. Before leaving the Hall, she'd changed into one of her carriage gowns. She'd even managed to put on her corset, determined that her appearance would be beyond reproach.

The children climbed out after her—Charlie and Alfred eager, and Daisy looking anxious.

"We won't be overlong," Julia informed Plimstock as she took Daisy's hand.

Plimstock stood at the horses' heads. "I'll be waiting, Mrs. Blunt, don't you worry."

Taggert's Market was two shops down from Orrick's Emporium. A village woman in a drab dress and bonnet was exiting with her shopping.

Julia extracted a few pennies from her reticule and gave them to the boys. "Run ahead and get yourselves some sweets. Daisy and I will be at the Emporium. You can join us there directly."

Charlie and Alfred bolted off to the market. The door of the shop jangled as they entered, swinging shut behind them.

Julia took a moment to reassure Daisy. "You needn't distress yourself. I won't let anyone be unkind to you here."

Daisy's eyes were doubtful.

"Shopping can be extraordinary fun," Julia promised. "Just you wait and see."

She'd no sooner got the words out than the door to Taggert's Market jangled open again with a crash. Alfred and Charlie tumbled out into the street. Their arms flailed as they staggered to keep from falling down.

A large man filled the doorway behind them, his hair and mustache glistening with pomade. Both his manner and the apron tied at his waist proclaimed his identity as the shop's owner, Mr. Taggert.

"And stay out, you ruffians!" he bellowed. "I've told you before, I won't have you in my shop making trouble."

Julia stared at the shopkeeper in outrage. "I *beg* your pardon." She strode toward him, pulling Daisy along behind her. "What's the meaning of this?"

The shopkeeper looked at her, startled. He immediately recovered himself, seeming to register the ladylike refinement of her accents and the elegance of her London-made clothes.

He sketched an apologetic bow. "Forgive the disruption, ma'am. These guttersnipes will make a nuisance of themselves. Why, only last month—" He broke off as his eyes lit on Daisy. His genial expression vanished. "I say, is that another of Blunt's—"

"How *dare* you?" Julia had never confronted a person in her life. She'd never had the courage. No matter the injustice, her nerves had always got the better of her. But not today. A fiery indignation tore through her. "Who do you think you are, sir, to lay hands on my children?"

He gaped. "*Your* children?"

"You heard me." Julia stretched out her hand to the boys. "Charlie, Alfred. Come here."

Charlie and Alfred flew to her side, permitting her to enfold them in the protection of her arm. Their faces were as blank as professional card sharps. One wouldn't know they'd just been unceremoniously tossed into the street.

A beady-eyed woman in an apron appeared from behind the shopkeeper. She addressed Julia in scathing tones. "And who might you be, madam?"

Julia drew herself up to her full height. It wasn't much. Not more than five feet and three inches. But in that moment, she felt as commanding as Lady Arundell herself. "*I* am Mrs. Blunt, and these children are in *my* charge. How dare this man presume to lay hands on them?"

The woman's eyes goggled. "I told you Captain Blunt took a wife," she hissed at Mr. Taggert.

Mr. Taggert shushed her with a wave of his hand. "I ask your pardon, Mrs. Blunt," he said to Julia. "But if you knew these boys as I do—"

"I know them quite well, thank you. And if their coin isn't good enough to be spent in your shop, mine will certainly be spent elsewhere." Julia turned the children back toward the carriage.

It was only then she realized they'd garnered an audience of gawking villagers. The woman with her bag of shopping stood staring on the side of the street, now in company with another woman. A shopkeeper had emerged from his store to join them. Up ahead, a man in a suit was standing outside the door of Orrick's Emporium. Another shopkeeper. Perhaps Mr. Orrick himself.

Julia's stomach sank. She hadn't intended to make a spectacle of herself on her first visit into the village. On the contrary, she'd hoped to make a good impression.

The man in front of the Emporium regarded her warily.

She stiffened her spine. "Mr. Orrick, I presume?"

He bowed. "Mrs. Blunt."

Steeling herself, Julia affected the same lofty tones she might use in a Mayfair drawing room. "I trust the service at your Emporium is more in line with what I'm accustomed to in London."

"*London!*" one of the bystanders echoed in an awed undertone.

Mr. Orrick bowed again, even lower than before. "I endeavor to please, ma'am." And stepping back, he held open the door so she and the children could enter his shop.

Several hours later, Julia and the children arrived back at the Hall, their arms filled with more boxes than they could carry. The boys were still in high spirits over how Julia had routed their tormentor. Even Daisy was beaming, awash with pleasure at the colorful fabrics, ribbons, and dainty little parasol Julia had purchased for her.

"Where do I put these?" Charlie asked, using his chin to steady the stack of boxes he was carrying.

"You may take them upstairs," Julia said to the boys as she followed them into the entrance hall. She removed her hat and gloves. "Put them in my bedchamber for now. I'll sort through them after we've had our tea."

Alfred traipsed up the stairs after his brother, struggling to contain two hatboxes and a chin-high stack of fabrics wrapped in paper and twine.

Mr. Beecham passed the boys on the staircase as he was descending. "Upon my word. Did you buy out the whole of the Emporium?"

"Hardly," Julia said. "But the children have all got new undergarments, stockings, and gloves, and we selected a great deal of fabric for their new clothes. All that remains is to find a good tailor and dressmaker." Julia removed Daisy's bonnet for her before ushering her into the drawing room. "We're exhausted, aren't we, Daisy?"

Daisy gave Mr. Beecham a broad smile, revealing her missing baby teeth. "I have a new parasol and a new nightgown. And Julia bought me a new hairbrush, too."

"Did she, now? That was grand of her." Mr. Beecham opened the drawing room drapes. "You'll be wanting your tea."

Julia sat down on the sofa. "If it isn't too much trouble."

"Not at all, ma'am." Mr. Beecham departed. He returned shortly with the tea tray. There was bread and jam, along with savory rolls.

Alfred joined them a quarter of an hour later, a guilty expression on his face. He plumped down in a chair next to Mr. Beecham as Julia poured his tea.

"Where's Charlie?" she asked.

Alfred took the teacup, avoiding her gaze. "Upstairs."

"He's not attempting to put things away, is he?"

Alfred shrugged. "I don't know."

Julia frowned. She knew Charlie was famished. He'd complained enough about it on the journey back from Hardholme. She couldn't imagine him delaying his tea in order to unpack their purchases. "I hope he isn't," she said. "He wouldn't like his tea to get cold."

When another quarter of an hour passed and Charlie still hadn't joined them, Julia began to have an uneasy feeling. Returning her teacup to the tray, she rose from her seat. "I'll just go up and see what's keeping him."

Alfred's anxious gaze followed her as she exited the drawing room. It did nothing to quell Julia's suspicions.

Climbing the stairs to her bedchamber, she couldn't help feeling disappointed. After their trip into the village, she'd thought the boys had begun to accept her. But perhaps it was still too soon for that.

Reaching her room, she found the door ajar. All the boxes from their shopping were heaped rather untidily on the bed.

"Charlie?" Julia called out as she entered.

There was no answer.

Her gaze swept over the room. A glimmer caught her eye, just as it had this morning—the sun shining through the windows to twinkle on Jasper's pocket watch. She gave it a distracted glance.

And then she froze.

The pocket watch was still lying on the brass-cornered chest of drawers. Except now it was alone.

Jasper's keys were gone.

Twenty-Nine

—✦—

$\mathcal{J}$ ulia raced up the spiral stone staircase that led to Jasper's study, her skirts clutched in her hands lest she trip over her hem. The location was unfamiliar to her. Despite her curiosity, she'd never before climbed the stairs to the tower. She hadn't dared defy the condition Jasper had made on their marriage.

"The door of my study on the fourth floor of the Hall remains locked at all times. You're never to enter it."

Images of Bluebeard's castle danced across her mind as she reached the door at the top of the stairs. Like the door to her bedchamber, it stood open. Her pulse skittered wildly as she crossed the threshold, expecting she knew not what.

But no gruesome sight was there to greet her. Nothing like the one that had awaited Bluebeard's wife.

It was only a shadowy, sparsely furnished room, containing a large wooden desk, a leather-upholstered chair, and a wall of bookcases. The drawers of the desk had been wrenched open. Papers were strewn about over its surface.

Charlie stood in front of the desk, holding one of the papers in his hand, struggling to read it in the light filtering through a high window.

"Charlie! Put that down!" Julia went to him in a rush. "You know you can't be in here!"

He looked up at her. "It's nothing private. Just some rubbish about a chap called Colonel Dryden and a nurse named Eloise."

Julia tugged the paper from his hand, careful not to tear it. "Out," she said. "I'll not have your father find you here."

"Are they people he knew in the war?" Charlie asked.

"If they are, it's none of our business." She gave Charlie a little push toward the door. "My goodness, the mess you've made. What on earth did you hope to find here?"

"Whatever it was he's been keeping secret. I thought it must be something terrible." Charlie flashed a disgusted glare at the heaps of paper on the desk. "But all this time, he's only been writing his stupid memoirs!"

"Yes, yes, it's very deflating." Julia attempted to console him, even as she felt an overwhelming wave of private relief. "Life isn't like a penny novel, you know," she said, as much for Charlie's benefit as for her own. "Sometimes people's secrets are really quite ordinary and uncomplicated."

"I thought he was a criminal."

"I know you did." She gave him a look of gentle reproof. "Your father isn't the same man he was before the war. It may be hard to trust that, but after all these years, I would hope you could at least give him a chance."

"Is that why you married him? Because you think he's changed?"

"I believe he has. People can, if they have a mind to. Sometimes all it wants is time. You're wise to be skeptical, but it's all right to have a bit of faith now and then." She urged Charlie out of the room. "Go and have your tea. I'll join you after I tidy up here."

Charlie stopped on the threshold. His face was drawn with a sudden worry. "You're not going to tell him, are you?"

"I daresay I should."

"He'll probably beat me."

Julia doubted that. If anything, Jasper would be disappointed. Charlie had broken his trust. It was unfortunate. Their relationship didn't need any additional strain put on it. "Perhaps he doesn't need to know," she said. "You've done no real harm, not as far as I can tell."

Charlie shoulders sagged with relief. "Thank you. I'm . . . I'm sorry, I—"

"Go and have your tea, dear," Julia said again. "Go on."

He flashed her a rare smile before darting off down the steps. His footfalls faded into the distance.

Julia returned to Jasper's desk with a sigh. His memoirs. That's all it was. Pages and pages of reminiscences about the war, written edge to edge in Jasper's characteristic scrawl.

She gathered them up, trying her best not to read them. Sentence fragments nevertheless caught her eye as she organized the pages. There were mentions of Colonel Dryden and Eloise. References to cannon smoke and a corpse-strewn battlefield in Belgium.

Waterloo.

The single word jumped out at her from the page. That's what Jasper was describing. Not the Crimean War, but the Napoleonic Wars.

It made no sense. The Battle of Waterloo was nearly fifty years ago, long before Jasper was even born.

She permitted herself to read a little more, her gaze flicking over one paragraph, then another. There weren't only descriptions of the aftermath of the battle, there was dialogue, too. *Romantic* dialogue.

Good heavens. These weren't Jasper's memoirs at all. This was a novel!

She sank down in his leather chair, continuing to read.

She felt a strange sense of recognition. Something about the narrative structure. The way the sentences flowed together in elegant harmony. It was almost lyrical in its beauty. And the emotions described! They were poignant and heartfelt—and exceedingly familiar.

A slow-dawning realization came over her.

Setting aside the loose pages, she retrieved the full manuscript from the open drawer of the desk. She riffled through it, heart beating swiftly in anticipation of what she might find.

And there it was at last, tucked out of order amid the rest of the papers, a cover sheet written in Jasper's own hand.

Reunion at Waterloo
by
J. Marshland

The truth crashed through her with an impact that stole her breath. *Good gracious.*

Jasper *was* James Marshland.

The remaining evidence was easy to find. Indeed, it was right there along with the manuscript. Correspondence between Jasper and Mr. Bloxham. References to advances, royalties, and dwindling sales numbers.

Julia didn't know how long she sat there, reading it and putting it all together.

She was amazed she hadn't done so before.

In hindsight it was all glaringly obvious, beginning with Jasper's visit to Bloxham's Books, where she'd overheard him ask to see Mr. Bloxham, and ending with his questions to her about Marshland's novels themselves.

She shuddered to remember the things she'd said. The criticisms she'd levied against Marshland. Good Lord. What must Jasper have been thinking?

Julia had no sooner pondered the question than a creak sounded on the threshold. Jasper's deep voice followed, sending a jolt of alarm through her.

"Care to tell me what you're doing in here?"

Jasper already knew what she was doing. It was abundantly clear. She was reading his blasted unfinished manuscript. A novel that was due to Bloxham on the first of next month.

And not one of Jasper's better efforts, either.

He was in no mood for a confrontation. Not tonight. Not when he hadn't yet washed and changed his clothes. There had been no opportunity. On returning to Goldfinch Hall this evening, tired and irritable from his journey to York, he'd found his family in the drawing room, lingering over the cold remnants of their tea.

Only Julia had been absent.

It hadn't taken much for Alfred to blurt out her whereabouts. "She's in the tower."

As if that revelation hadn't shocked Jasper enough, Charlie had then proceeded to shock him even more by confessing his own part in the break-in.

"It's my fault," he'd said. "I took the key and went in on my own. You can't blame Julia. She only stayed to clean up the mess I made of your papers."

But that wasn't all she'd been doing up here.

She faced him now, blue eyes wide as saucers. "Jasper. You're back."

"As you see." He entered the room, shutting the door behind him. "You didn't answer my question."

"Ah yes. As to that . . ." She moistened her lips. "Forgive me. I know I'm not supposed to be here, but you left your keys behind and I'm afraid my curiosity—"

"There's no point in protecting Charlie," Jasper said crossly. "He's already confessed to what happened."

She blinked. "Did he? How brave of him."

"Yes, it was, rather. I suspect he was trying to protect you from me." Jasper scowled at the very notion of it. As if he was some unreasonable brute who might harm his own wife! "But that's beside the point."

Her brows lifted in question. "Which is?"

"*You're* still here," he said. "And you're not putting away Charlie's mess. You're reading my private papers."

Rising from her chair, Julia set the papers in her hands down on the desk in a neat stack. Her movements were precise, as if she was taking time to formulate the right words.

He waited for her to speak, his heart beating like a bass drum. *She* was the one in the wrong. She'd broken his rules. Violated his trust. But it was Jasper who felt as though he'd committed a crime.

He'd kept something important from her. Something as intrinsically a part of him as she was becoming herself.

"Why didn't you tell me your pen name was James Marshland?" she asked.

His pen name.

Of course that's what she would think.

Perhaps the situation wasn't as dire as he'd feared.

He ran a hand over the back of his neck. He was covered in soot from the railway station at Malton. The platform had been filthy with it, and now so was he. He felt himself at a distinct disadvantage.

"It's complicated," he said.

"No more than it is for any romance novelist, surely. Most ladies who write novels do so using a pen name. I wouldn't think it was any different with a gentleman. Certainly not one with your reputation. But that isn't what I asked." She held his gaze. "I asked why you didn't tell *me*."

He exhaled a heavy breath. "I was going to tell you."

She looked doubtful.

"It's the truth." This was to have been his concession. The secret he gave up to her in order to make something normal of their marriage. He'd spent most of the railway journey back from York determining how best to explain it to her.

Not that any of that mattered now.

"Why didn't you?" she asked. "You might have done so the day we married. We were talking about your novels on the train. You could have told me easily."

"There's nothing easy about it," he said. "My writing is personal to me. Something private that's mine alone." He moved to his desk, gathering up the rest of his manuscript and returning it to the drawer. He slammed the drawer shut. "I've been doing it since I was a lad. It's not anything I've ever wished to share with anyone."

"I see."

He turned back to her. "You don't. I can tell by your face. You're hurt."

"Not hurt, no, but . . . I wish you hadn't let me run on giving my opinions about your books as if we were talking about a stranger. When I think of all I said—"

"I told you. I value your opinions."

"I would that you'd valued my confidence a little more," she said. "That you'd trusted me."

He leaned back against his desk, half sitting on the edge of it. He regarded her with a frown, uncertain of what he could say to make things right. In real life, he was rarely as eloquent as the heroes in his novels. The more deeply he felt something, the less he could articulate it. With Julia, he'd increasingly found himself reduced to grunts and growls.

"Does anyone else know?" she asked.

"No one," he said.

"Mr. Bloxham must. It's why you were at his shop that day, wasn't it? To discuss something about your novels?"

"It was." He'd managed to get fifty pounds out of the man in unpaid royalties for *The Fire Opal*. "But you're wrong. He doesn't know they're my books. To him, I'm merely the author's proxy."

Julia's expression of doubt lingered. "He doesn't know you're James Marshland?"

Jasper shook his head. "When he bought my first book, we corresponded by post. It was the same with my subsequent novels. I only visited him in person after I returned from the war."

He'd had no choice. There had been no other way to arrange for payment on his previous works, or to negotiate sales of future ones.

Julia came to stand in front of him. Her full skirts bowed against his legs. "Are you ashamed of the stories you write?"

"No."

"You shouldn't be. Your writing is beautiful. And I'm not just saying that because I'm your wife. I told you as much before I knew Marshland's novels were really yours."

"Yes, you did." Hearing it now, he felt the same ridiculous surge of pleasure he'd felt then. "You have no idea what it meant to me."

"Yet still you kept it secret?" Her eyes searched his. "Why? I wouldn't have judged you for it. Indeed, it would have made me care for you even more."

She did care for him, then.

On some level, he'd already known it. It was there, evident in the way she held his arm when they walked together. The way she looked to him for guidance and approval. The way she melted into his embrace.

He reached for her hands. She let him take them, let him hold them gently in his grasp. A tremor of connection passed between them, stirring his blood. He had a vivid recollection of how he'd kissed her yesterday in the downstairs hall.

But he didn't want her kisses now. He wanted something else. Something more.

He wanted her to know him.

A futile impulse.

There was too much risk associated with it, and not only to him. He *knew* that. His spirit nevertheless railed against the constraint.

He drew her to stand between his booted feet. His voice roughened with repressed emotion. "My father didn't approve of novels. I had to hide my writing from him. It's always been a secret to me. The most private part of myself. I've never had the urge to share it."

"You do share it. There are countless readers who adore your stories. They'd be glad to know you. Indeed, you could be as celebrated as any famous author if you wished."

"I don't. It's the writing I love, not the notoriety. Not the lifestyle. I've never been interested in holding court in coffee shops or giving talks at lecture halls. I prefer anonymity."

"Even from those you love?"

He huffed. "That hasn't been much of a concern until now."

Until now.

The two words hung between them. He hadn't intended to utter them. But once spoken, he could no more deny the truth of them than he could all the rest of it. It was simply a fact.

He was no longer alone—a cursed character in another man's story. He had someone of his own now. A wife who, somewhere between Belgrave Square and Yorkshire, he'd fallen deeply and irrevocably in love with.

The realization of it squeezed at his heart and lungs so he could scarcely breathe.

"I don't want to be a stranger to you," he said.

"Then don't be." Her slim fingers slid through his in an intimate clasp. "Let me into your life just a little. Let me share some of your secrets."

He bowed his head to hers. "Everything I have—everything I am—is yours."

Thirty

—✦—

$\mathcal{J}$t wasn't many hours until it was time to retire, but every moment seemed to drag on forever. Julia's gaze kept tangling with Jasper's, all through dinner, and the long hours that followed after as they dutifully repaired to the drawing room to drink tea and talk with the children about the events of the day.

Julia couldn't focus on any of it. Not Jasper's visit to Mr. Piggott or her own less-than-ideal trip into Hardholme. Her thoughts were entirely consumed by the simmering tension. The thrilling shimmer of knowledge that when they finally withdrew to their chamber, Jasper was going to take her to bed and make her his own.

His confession to her in the tower had all but assured her of it. Before he'd left for York, she'd given him her conditions. And now he'd met them. He'd told her his secrets. There was no more reason to delay their being together as husband and wife.

When the children were put to bed, she accompanied Jasper to bid the boys good night and to tuck Daisy in. Then, heart thumping hard, Julia allowed him to guide her to their own room.

Once inside, he wasted no time in taking her in his arms.

She clung to him, fingers threading into his hair as his mouth covered hers. His lips were hot and seeking, tasting her as much as kissing her. A heady sensation. It made her insides melt and her knees buckle.

His arms tightened around her in a powerful embrace.

And she didn't feel nervous any longer. She felt boneless. Breathless. Incapable of doing anything but holding him and kissing him back.

If this is what it was like to be intimate, she had nothing to be afraid of. Jasper was strong and sure of himself. Completely in command of the situation.

Or so she thought.

Only a moment later, it was he who broke the kiss, his breath coming in harsh rasps. He gazed down at her, his gray eyes brilliant with heat.

She brought her hand to cradle his jaw.

He turned his face into her palm, pressing a kiss there.

It was a small gesture. Almost courtly in comparison to the kisses they'd been sharing. The sweetness of it resonated within her, flooding her with a peculiar warmth. Everything at once felt too tight and constrictive. Her corset. Her gown. Her own skin. She was as restless as a wild bird.

He bent his head to hers, nuzzling her cheek, and pressing soft kisses to her lips to soothe her. "You said you wanted to be with me. Is that still true?"

"Yes."

"I want it, too." He moved one large hand over the curve of her spine. "But there's time. We needn't rush anything."

"I don't feel rushed. I feel impatient."

His mouth tugged into a faint smile. "What would you like me to do about it?"

She flashed him a disgruntled glance. "You don't know?"

A husky laugh rumbled in his chest. "I do," he assured her. "Do you?"

She stiffened. Was she supposed to know something? None of the other young ladies of her acquaintance did. Not that she was aware. It was information meant to be imparted by one's mother—at least, that's what Mary had claimed. Julia doubted whether her own mama would have taken the trouble. Likely, she'd have left the matter to Julia's future husband.

Julia felt a rush of relief that it was Jasper she was having this conversation with and not the Earl of Gresham. "I haven't been given the particulars," she said. "Though my maid did mention—" She stopped abruptly, too embarrassed to continue.

"What did she say?" Jasper's lips brushed her temple. "Whisper it to me in my ear, sweetheart."

Julia sank her voice, a blush burning her face. "She mentioned a minute or two of discomfort."

Jasper's hand stilled on her back. "Ah. That."

She pulled back to look at him, her senses alert. "Is it true?"

He frowned, seeming to consider his words. "The first time may not be entirely comfortable for you."

"Why not? Is it because of our difference in size?"

"God no. It isn't . . . That is, it shouldn't . . ." A red flush crept up his neck, barely visible in the glow of the oil lamp. "What I'm trying to say is . . . I'm going to be careful with you. Gentle. You know that, don't you? I wouldn't hurt you for the world."

Some of the tension eased in Julia's limbs. "I know," she said. "I trust you."

It was the right thing to say. A tacit permission for Jasper to take charge.

And he did.

He gathered her close and kissed her again. He kept kissing her, kept touching her, until she forgot her shyness. Forgot her concerns about his past and her worries about the future. Until she was warm and pliant in his arms.

By the time they were both unclothed and he'd taken her to their bed, her body was awash with passionate sensation. Any discomfort was fast replaced by a feeling of infinite closeness. As if they shared the same breath, the same heartbeat. He had become a part of her.

It wasn't at all unpleasant. It wasn't entirely comfortable, either. It was raw and elemental—a moment so powerful in its connection it made tears smart in her eyes.

Never in her life had she been so vulnerable with another person. So totally open and exposed. And Jasper was there with her all the way, just as vulnerable as she was, and as much in need of tender reassurance.

She gave it to him instinctively. Kissing him, holding him, and cradling his big body with her own.

A long while later, as they lay sated in each other's arms, Julia could think of nothing to say that would do the experience justice.

Jasper had no such difficulty. "I love you."

Her gaze jerked to his in the waning light. "What?"

"I said that I love you," he repeated. "You're not obliged to say it back."

Emotion closed her throat. She swallowed hard. "Jasper—" She felt him flinch.

Drat it. She'd forgotten his unaccountable dislike of his Christian name.

It was a pity. In that moment, it felt right to call him Jasper. What could be more intimate? More personal? A name was important. She'd told him that herself.

"I realize you aren't ready," he said. "How can you be, given what you've learned of my past? But I want you to know, despite your reticence . . ." He smoothed a damp strand of hair back from her face. "You have my heart, utterly."

If she hadn't already been aglow from his lovemaking, his words would have made her so. "Did I seem reticent?"

"No, you didn't. But physical passion is easy. Love is something else altogether."

"'*An ever-fixed mark that looks on tempests and is never shaken,*'" she quoted to him from one of her favorite of Shakespeare's sonnets. "Yes, I know what love is."

"From personal experience?" He asked the question casually. *Too* casually.

"No, indeed. I've never been in love before. I've only ever imagined it."

"What did you imagine?"

"Little things. Flowers and chocolates. A gentleman sending me a Valentine or writing me a poem."

"A poem."

"You don't like poetry?"

"Enough to know I shouldn't be writing it myself."

Julia smiled as she settled back into his arms. He gathered her close, resting his chin on her head.

In that moment, she could easily believe herself in love with him.

She was tempted to tell him so, not only for her own sake, but for his. She didn't like him to think he was unworthy, or that she was punishing him for his past.

But she didn't tell him.

The truth was, she didn't know *what* she felt.

Lying with him this way, twined in his arms, her emotions were as tangled as their limbs.

And worse.

She couldn't help but think that he'd lain this way before, with Dolly Carvel. And not only once, but many, many times.

A depressing recollection. It threatened to eat away at the edges of Julia's happiness. She refused to let it. No matter Jasper's past, in this moment, he belonged to her.

Julia awoke sometime later to the mattress creaking as Jasper climbed out of bed. When he didn't return, she sat up, pushing her hair from her eyes. The room was cold and dark, raising gooseflesh on her naked skin.

Good gracious. She wasn't wearing a nightgown.

A rush of self-consciousness had her pulling the coverlet over her bosom. "What time is it?"

"Nearly midnight." Jasper stood from lighting the fire. The flames caught quickly, illuminating him in the darkness. He was in his dressing gown, his black hair disheveled. "This room gets a fearful draft when the weather turns. I didn't wish you to be cold."

"I wouldn't be cold if you hadn't got up," she said. "Come back to bed."

"In a moment." He crossed the room to where his coat was draped over the back of a chair. Reaching into an interior pocket, he withdrew a thickly stuffed envelope. "In all the excitement of the evening, I completely forgot. I have a letter for you."

"From the solicitor?"

He returned to their bed. "From Lady Anne."

"Anne has written?" Julia was wide awake now. She took the envelope from him.

Jasper lit their bedside oil lamp. "It was waiting at the post office. It appears to have been misdirected at first."

Julia examined the envelope. It was postmarked from London, not two days after they'd wed. "She must have written immediately on hearing the news of our marriage."

Which meant Anne had sent it before receiving Julia's own letter.

A glimmer of anxiety made her hesitate before breaking the seal. Anne wasn't above scolding her, and in the most severe terms if she felt they were warranted. As excited as Julia was to hear from her friend, she didn't relish the thought of Anne's rebuke.

Jasper climbed in bed beside her. He pressed a kiss to her bare shoulder. "Go ahead and read it. I don't mind."

"I suppose I may as well." Securing the bedsheet more firmly under her arms, Julia opened the letter and began to read.

My dearest Julia,

You nonsensical little goose. What have you got yourself into? I called on you in Belgrave Square this morning only to be informed by your ailing father that you'd eloped, not two days ago, with the infamous Hero of the Crimea. Can it be true? Have you really married the man and in such a hurly-burly fashion?

I should have known this might happen. He's been pursuing you ever since he arrived in London. We all saw it. I blame myself for not intervening sooner. Had I confronted him, I might have prevented it, but even I—with all my suspicions—underestimated the fellow. Who could have guessed he would be so ruthless as to carry you away? And you on your sickbed!

Your father says you are in North Yorkshire by now, living among the savages. I dare not believe it. You are altogether too good to be exposed to such villainy. I fear the effect it might have on your consti-tution. I cannot even be sure you will see this letter. Captain Blunt is likely reading your post, discarding anything that might encourage your will to escape him. It's in his interest to keep you feeling as though you were alone and friendless.

Take heart, my dear. You're not friendless. You have me, and Stella, and Evie. And though we may not have much power at our disposal to see things right, trust that I shall make every effort to do so. I have several ideas up my sleeve. In the meanwhile, please write to me at once and assure me of your safety.

With affection,
Anne

"Unpleasant news?" Jasper asked.

Julia cast him a rueful glance. "She thinks you abducted me."

Jasper didn't appear surprised. "Is that all?"

Julia slowly refolded the pages of the letter and returned them to the envelope. "She's worried about me. I shall have to write her again to reassure her. She seems to believe I'll shatter like glass at the first sign of difficulty."

"Perhaps she doesn't know you as well as she thinks she does."

"She knows who I was in London." A scared little mouse with her nose in a book. A young lady unwilling to defy her parents, even if obedience to them meant she must give up her dreams, her desires, her very life.

Julia was ashamed to recall it.

It wasn't as if her parents had beat her or locked her in her room without any food or water. She'd had no good reason not to stand up to them. None save her own anxiousness and lack of self-worth.

"You're not that person anymore," Jasper said.

"I don't feel as though I am," she said. "Perhaps it's simply that things are easier in the country?"

"Easier? Here?" A glint of wry humor flashed in his eyes. "You can suggest that after the day you've had?"

Julia suppressed a grimace. At dinner, she and the children had told Jasper about their tumultuous visit to Hardholme. "It's easy to be brave on someone else's behalf."

"No, it isn't," he said. "It's easier to do nothing. To turn a blind eye. Many people do, even the biggest and strongest of us."

"I could hardly do so when someone was mistreating the children. They were relying on me to protect them."

"You did. And admirably so."

"I'd rather I hadn't made such a scene. I'd promised Daisy a lovely day shopping." Her gaze drifted guiltily to the stack of boxes teetering on the bench at the end of the bed. She still hadn't unpacked them. "I fear I may have bought too much trying to make up for it."

"I meant to ask . . . Did you put it on my account?"

She bit her lip. They'd had no opportunity to discuss finances earlier, nor to talk about Jasper's visit to the solicitor. At their first moment of privacy, they'd been in each other's arms, all thoughts of money forgotten.

But not now.

Now, the reality of their situation all came crashing back.

"Some of it," she said. It was always more respectable to pay with credit than cash. "The rest I bought with money from my reticule."

His brows lifted in question.

"I'm accustomed to keeping a large quantity tucked away for books and hair ribbons and things," she explained.

"Not so large now, I'd wager."

"No, indeed. It's diminishing by the day." She hesitated to ask, "Did Mr. Piggott tell you when we might expect the rest of my funds?"

"He's setting things in motion."

"How?"

"Sending a telegraph to the bank to start, with a formal letter to follow. I gave him a copy of our marriage lines, and I instructed him to contact Mr. Finchley if there should be any difficulties."

She nodded, praying there wouldn't be any difficulties to speak of. "Should I do anything?"

"Not a thing." He bent his head to nuzzle her ear. "Except . . ."

A delicate shiver of pleasure traced down her spine. "What?"

He kissed her neck. "I wonder if you'd be willing to read my manuscript?"

Julia's face spread into a smile.

He'd called his writing the most private part of himself. And now he was offering to share it with her. As gestures went, it felt almost as important as him telling her he loved her.

"I would be honored," she said. "When would you like me to start?"

"Not at this precise moment."

Warmth ignited in her veins. "Do you have something else in mind?"

He took her in his arms. "As a matter of fact," he said, "I do."

Thirty-One

━━✦━━

The next three days passed in a whirlwind of activity. In the mornings, while the children were at their lessons, Julia repaired to Jasper's tower room to pore over the pages of his manuscript. Jasper came with her, pacing in front of the bookshelves as she read, as restive as a caged lion.

On the afternoon of the third day, reading still unfinished, Julia was obliged to carry the manuscript out to the garden. There, settled on an old blanket beneath an alder tree, she continued reading as Jasper supervised the children's riding lesson with Plimstock.

Alfred was mounted on Quintus, and Daisy was perched atop Cossack, acclimating herself to Julia's sidesaddle. Charlie led the black gelding back and forth along the edge of the overgrown garden, encouraging his little sister to stop fidgeting and sit up straight.

Jasper eventually left the three of them in the groom's charge. Crossing the garden, he came to join Julia. "Haven't you finished yet?"

"Unfortunately not." She moved her full skirts out of the way, making room for him on the blanket.

He sank down beside her. He was in his shirtsleeves, his collar open at the neck. Her gaze flitted over the column of his throat. She'd kissed him there last night as he made love to her.

But he wouldn't be distracted by memories of their marital intimacies.

"In London you claimed you could finish a book in but a few hours," he said.

"I can," she replied, "if I'm left alone uninterrupted."

That hadn't been possible these past days. Not with the children and all the demands of the household. She'd had Cossack to exercise, letters to write, and kittens to visit with Daisy. Indeed, at any given moment, Julia's attention was pulled in a dozen different directions.

Jasper was jealous of every moment she spent away from him.

It took an effort not to distract her. Not to touch her as often as he would have liked. Indeed, since they'd consummated their marriage, he couldn't seem to stop touching her, in their bed as well as out of it.

He was becoming insatiable.

Becoming. As if he wasn't already a lovestruck madman. A besotted fool who, at any given moment, was stroking his wife's cheek, kissing her hand, or tucking a stray lock of her hair back into her coiffure.

"*I love you,*" he'd told her after he'd taken her for the first time. "*You're not obliged to say it back.*"

But he longed for her to say it. He wanted her love as much as he wanted all the rest of her—her friendship, her respect, her approval.

Why else had he asked her to read his bloody manuscript?

When she at last turned over the final page, he went still, bracing for the worst. "Well?"

She lifted her gaze to his. "It's quite good."

Quite good. It was faint praise. She might as well have said it was rubbish.

"But not as good as *The Fire Opal*," he concluded. It had been his bestselling work. It was also one of his oldest, written before the war.

"It's different," she said. "A bit more serious."

"Ah."

"That isn't bad."

"No. But it's the very thing you said about *The Garden of Valor*. And we both know how well that's sold." Jasper stood from the blanket.

"Is it only the sales you're concerned about?" she asked.

"Frankly? Yes." He was dependent on his royalties. Along with his soldier's pension, it was his only source of income.

Granted, it wasn't enough to repair the roof or to rebuild the rotting east wing, the tenants' cottages, or the stables, but it was enough to feed and clothe them. To pay Beecham's modest salary, and to patch the cracks as they appeared.

Never mind that Jasper was in expectation of Julia's fifty thousand pounds. He didn't wish to rely on it. Not after his meeting with Piggott.

The old solicitor hadn't exactly instilled Jasper with confidence. In discussing their course of action, Piggott had been as uncertain of the outcome as Jasper was himself.

"*Sir Eustace could, naturally, cause a substantial delay if he takes a mind to,*" Piggott had said. "*As the girl's father, and a resident of London in good standing in fashionable society, the bank and the courts will be favorably disposed to him.*"

Jasper had departed York in a foul mood. These past days with Julia had done much to improve his frame of mind, but in moments such as these, when confronted by the fact he might have another literary failure on his hands, his spirits once again plummeted.

"If this manuscript performs as badly as *The Garden of Valor*, not only will I lose out on potential royalties, I may lose my publisher altogether." He extended his hand to Julia.

Gathering his manuscript under one arm, she permitted him to help her up. "Mr. Bloxham has published all your books thus far. I see no reason he'd give up on you now."

"He's not running a charitable institution. He expects the novels he publishes to sell. If enough of mine don't, he has no reason to keep printing my books. It doesn't matter how much money I've made for him in the past."

She gave a huff of disapproval. "One would think he'd show some loyalty."

An unwilling smile tugged at Jasper's mouth. She was on his side. She'd *always* be on his side. That much he'd learned about her since their marriage. He may not have her love, not yet, but he had her loyalty absolutely.

He slid his arm around her waist as they walked back to the house. She was soft and pliant, with no corset to constrain her. "Even you abandoned my books for a time, sweetheart," he reminded her.

"I was very young."

He turned his face into her hair. Pulled back in a plaited chignon, it was sleek and sweet-smelling. As fragrant as it had been last night when it was unbound, a wild tangle of ebony waves about her bare shoulders. "You're still very young."

"Don't tease me. You know that once I came back to your novels, I was sorry I'd ever given them up."

"The rest of my readers aren't so enlightened. When they abandon my books, they simply move on to the next better thing."

Julia covered his hand at her waist. "There's no one better than you."

His heart squeezed. "I shall remind you of that one day."

"I won't need reminding," she said.

He brushed a kiss to her temple. The unruly hedges at the edge of the garden all but shielded them from view. One of the rare benefits of being unable to afford a gardener.

She leaned into him, his manuscript clutched protectively to her bosom. "I'm not a writer myself, but I've read more novels than I can count. If you like, I could offer some general advice."

"I'd prefer the specific kind."

"You won't take offense?"

"How could I? I already know you think my stories lack excitement." He flashed her a wry look. "Even the ones with actual knights. Or the ones that take place on smoking Belgian battlefields."

"There's excitement and there's *excitement*," she said. "The history in your latest stories *is* fascinating, but these are novels, not history books. Most of us shopping at places like Bloxham's aren't looking to be educated. We're looking to be thrilled."

"Yes, I know. Falsified deaths, bigamy, and murder." He shook his head. "Such subjects fail to inspire my interest."

"They did once. Your old novels are all exceedingly thrilling."

"Perhaps I'm past the point of providing thrills."

Julia gave him a speaking glance. "I doubt that very much."

He grinned. "Very well," he said. "Tell me what it is about this story that you suggest I change."

Thirty-Two

❖

The week that followed was the most idyllic in Julia's memory. When she wasn't in company with the children or Mr. Beecham—attending to the house, riding Cossack, or visiting the kittens—she was closeted with Jasper, talking to him about his novel.

He seemed to value her opinions no matter how unhinged some of them might sound. And they *were* unhinged; even she recognized that.

She had a lifetime of reading to draw upon. Everything from sensation romances to horror stories, adventure novels, and gothics. She shared it all with him, delighting in the conversations they had together, often punctuated by kisses and embraces, and once—though she blushed to recall it—an instance of lovemaking in his tower study.

"*How can we?*" she'd asked naively as he'd taken her in his arms. "*There's not even a bed.*"

"*It doesn't require a bed,*" he'd told her. "*Let me show you.*"

Thinking of it now, as she sat primly coiffed and clad in the library, Julia feared she was becoming a wanton. Only this morning, she'd lingered in bed with her husband so long that the two of them had missed breakfast. Surely, the entire household was aware of what they were doing.

She'd mentioned as much to Jasper as he'd helped her dress. In response, he'd only twined his fingers in her hair and kissed her deeply.

Infuriating man.

He was seated at the library desk, head propped in his hand as he wrote. His quill pen scratched over the page.

It wasn't his custom to work in the library. He preferred the privacy of his study. But the heat was oppressive today, and the tower, with its high, narrow window, wasn't best disposed for elevated temperatures.

The library was more comfortable. Its line of windows faced out over the garden, providing a view of the children at play. Free from their morning lessons, the boys were clacking sticks in a mock battle while Daisy hovered around them, wringing her hands and looking mournful.

"I believe she's pretending to be the heroine in their little play," Julia remarked. "And the boys are two rivals dueling for her favor."

Jasper glanced up, frowning. "They what?"

"Nothing," she said. "Forgive me. I didn't mean to disturb you." Jasper required silence to write. Julia was forever having to remind herself not to be a nuisance to him.

She was obliged to remind the children, too, and even Mr. Beecham. Since she and Jasper had come downstairs, it seemed one of them had rapped at the library door every ten minutes—the boys asking about taking the horses out, Daisy inquiring about whether she could go swimming, and Mr. Beecham offering to bring them refreshment.

No wonder Jasper preferred the tower.

The thought had just crossed her mind when another knock came to disrupt her husband's peace.

Mr. Beecham poked his head in. "Excuse me, Captain Blunt. Could I have a private word, sir?"

"Can it not wait?" Jasper asked.

"I don't believe so."

Jasper set down his quill pen with a sigh. He stood from his desk, casting Julia an apologetic glance as he walked to the door. "I won't be a moment."

Mr. Beecham withdrew, taking Jasper with him. The door clicked shut behind them.

There was still much about the workings of the estate Julia didn't know. All the little crises that happened on a daily basis. At any given instant, something was always demanding Jasper's attention.

What was it now?

It couldn't be the children. They were still playing outside. And it couldn't be the roof, not now the rain had stopped.

Likely it was something to do with money.

Julia didn't like to think of it. Not when her own fortune was tied up in London with no means of her getting hold of it at present.

Jasper never reproached her with the fact, but she knew it was the impetus for him revising his latest novel. He was determined it would outsell his previous book.

She hadn't read any of his changes yet. She didn't even know what suggestions of hers—if any—he'd decided to implement. He wouldn't permit her to look at it until it was finished.

Julia nevertheless had every confidence in her husband's work. She only hoped critics like Mr. Bilgewater wouldn't savage it in the press before the public had a chance to judge it for themselves.

When Jasper wasn't back in another five minutes, she got up from her chair and strolled to the bookshelf that held the entirety of his novels. She trailed her finger along the spines, wondering, not for the first time, how a man who had written something as breathlessly exciting as *The Fire Opal* could have written books like *The Garden of Valor* and *Reunion at Waterloo*.

On their railway journey from London, she'd pointed it out to Jasper, the fact that Marshland's novels had changed.

"Perhaps he's grown up," he'd said.

She supposed it was possible. Still . . . it was difficult to reconcile. Not only that.

Sometimes she found it hard to believe that the same man who had abandoned his children and who had been so cruel to the soldiers serving under him could have secretly been writing novels. Novels rife with romance, heroism, and adventure, where love won the day and good ultimately triumphed over evil.

But bad men often wrote good books, didn't they? Only look at Mr. Dickens, who had treated his wife so abominably that she'd been obliged to leave him. And yet his books were beloved by many.

Perhaps Jasper's books were the same. At his wickedest, he'd written stories filled with goodness. Stories she still loved, despite knowing the worst of his past.

She was just withdrawing one of them to look at it when the library door opened. She smiled, returning the novel to its shelf. "At last. I thought Mr. Beecham would never be through with you." She turned to find Jasper standing in the doorway. His scarred countenance was as unreadable as it had often been in London. Her smile faded. "What's wrong? Has something happened?"

He shut the door behind him. "Plimstock's been to the post office in Hardholme. He brought back a letter from my solicitor."

Her pulse jumped. "Mr. Piggott's written? Does he have news of my money?"

"He does. But it isn't—" Jasper broke off. He ran a hand over his hair. "It's not good, I'm afraid."

She might have guessed that from his lack of expression. It didn't make it any more comfortable to hear it uttered aloud. "What did he say?"

Jasper didn't mince words. "The bank has put a hold on your funds while your father investigates the legality of our marriage."

Julia stared at him. She couldn't have heard him correctly. It didn't make any sense. "What does that mean? Of course we're married. You gave Mr. Piggott our marriage lines, didn't you?"

"I did."

"Then what seems to be the difficulty?"

Jasper didn't answer for a long moment.

A moment during which Julia's already strained nerves began to fray even further. She moved away from the bookcase, resting her hand on the back of a nearby chair to steady herself. "You're making me very anxious."

"I'm sorry. I don't mean to." He crossed the library to her, only to stop short—too far away to touch her. "Perhaps you should sit down."

She didn't hesitate to obey him. Her knees felt like jelly. "What else did Mr. Piggott say? If my father refuses to accept the validity of our marriage—"

"He isn't refusing." Jasper came to stand in front of the cold fireplace. He turned to face her. His jaw was rigid with tension. "Not outright."

"I don't understand."

"He'll accept it. He's even agreed to convey your fifty thousand pounds to me without delay. On one condition."

Her mouth was so dry she could scarcely formulate a reply. "Which is?"

"You must return to London. You must resume living with your parents in their house in Belgrave Square. If you refuse, he's vowed to delve into my past, to expose me as a villain and a reprobate. To make various arguments about fraud or deceit on my part—and lack of capacity on yours. In other words, he plans to slander us both, and tie up your fortune in perpetuity. Worse than that, he intends for us to expend an additional fortune in fighting his charges in the courts. A fortune he knows I do not have."

Julia's stomach was shaking out of control. For a moment, she feared she would be sick. "I see."

A muscle ticked in Jasper's cheek. "Yes, I believe you do."

Her parents wanted her back. Back in that house and in that room. Back at their beck and call. Not because they loved her or valued her, but because Papa was too spoiled and querulous to accept her defection with good grace. She felt a fool to have ever thought he might.

"My father hasn't any right to interfere with my money," she said.

"Your money is in your father's bank."

"He doesn't own the bank."

"He's one of their largest depositors. They have reason to oblige him. And it isn't as if he's making these accusations in a vacuum. He's employed a respected firm of solicitors to do it for him—Birchall, Crawley, and Micklethwait. Piggott says they've a reputation for tying matters up in the courts for years. By the time a case is resolved, the money in dispute has been entirely expended in fees."

"Like in Mr. Dickens's *Bleak House*," she said faintly. "*Jarndyce and Jarndyce.*"

"Something like that." Jasper's gray eyes had gone the color of hoarfrost. Julia had no idea what he was thinking. Every last vestige of warmth was gone.

She clasped her hands in her lap to stop their trembling. "What do you propose we do?"

"I would have thought it obvious."

It wasn't, not to her. "You're not suggesting I return home?"

Jasper's gaze locked with hers. And he no longer looked cold and remote. He looked furious. "*This* is your home."

"But my fortune—"

"To hell with your fortune." He came to her, sinking down on his haunches in front of her chair. "If it must come between having you and having your fifty thousand pounds, my choice is clear. Let your father have the money and be damned."

His words should have reassured her.

They didn't.

"What about *my* choice?" she asked.

Mr. Piggott's letter had unsettled Jasper deeply. Standing in the drawing room, poring over its contents, he'd recognized at once the very real danger to their lives here. The legitimate risk to the children, and to himself.

And not just to them.

He had a wife to think of now. The mere idea of losing her—of giving her up—was enough to make his blood run cold. By the time he'd finished reading the solicitor's words, the paper those words were written on had been crumpled in Jasper's fist. It had taken a herculean effort to bring his anger under control.

And now this.

He stared at Julia, unable to comprehend her meaning. "What choice?"

"It's *my* fifty thousand pounds," she said. "I won't relinquish it to my father."

"Do you think I want you to?" he replied. "It's Piggott who advises it. He believes it's the only way to get your father to leave us alone. If we don't let him have the money, he'll make a nuisance of himself, digging around in our private affairs until—"

"Let him."

"What?"

"Let him," she said again. "What care we for his slander? I already know the worst of your history. And it isn't as though the children will be surprised by it."

He shook his head. She didn't understand. She never would, not without knowing the whole of it. And that was something he couldn't share with her. Not now. Not ever.

"No," he said. "It's out of the question."

"My aunt Elinore left that money to me, not to my father. And we need it, don't we? We have our plans for the roof and for the tenants' cottages—"

"None of that matters now. Not when—"

"How can you say that when it's the whole of the reason you came to London? You were in need of an heiress."

"I married you believing you penniless."

"Yes, but—"

"And it's all beside the point!" He surged to his feet. "If your father insists on delving into my past, no amount of money in the world will be enough to hold on to any of this."

Her eyes widened. He'd never before raised his voice to her.

He turned from her to move back to the fireplace, feeling like the veriest brute. "Listen to me." He made an effort to moderate his tone. "I don't propose this lightly. I know what that money could mean. But no amount is equal to the well-being of our family. If we make a legal dispute out of this, it could ruin us."

Indeed, it could ruin everything.

He'd known that from the beginning. It was the reason he'd restricted his search for a wife to ladies whose relatives would ask no questions. Ridgeway had claimed the Wychwoods were such a family. Invalids anxious to marry off their wallflower daughter to any respectable gentleman who would have her.

But that wasn't the case at all.

Nothing about Julia had been what it seemed, least of all her sickly parents, who—it transpired—wanted nothing more than to keep their daughter as close to them as possible, even at the sacrifice of her own happiness.

"Will it truly be so expensive?" she asked. "To have Mr. Piggott oppose my father's attempts?"

"Piggott doesn't stand a chance against Birchall, Crawley, and Micklethwait. We'd have to hire someone better. Someone more expensive."

"What about Mr. Finchley? You told me he'd be your first choice if—"

"It isn't an option," Jasper said. "Not just because of the money. Because of the notoriety it would bring. I won't subject the children to it. I'm sorry, but that must be my final word on the subject."

Hurt flashed in her eyes. It took her a moment to rally. "Naturally, I don't wish to expose the children to anything unpleasant, but . . . I have my rights. I can't permit someone to take them away from me. Not my father." She paused before adding, "And not you, either."

Jasper's jaw hardened. He rested his fist on the mantelpiece, hating himself for what he must do. "How do you propose to go about securing those rights?" he asked. "You haven't the means to hire a solicitor of your own, and I've no intention of providing you with them."

She stiffened in her chair. In the space of but a few words they'd gone from allies to combatants. "I shall start by writing to Hoares Bank again, and this time in the most severe terms."

"Yes, that should solve things," he said dryly. "A strongly worded letter."

She continued, undeterred, "I shall write to my father as well. I can't believe he'd stoop to causing a scandal. He deplores the very idea of gossip. Besides, he doesn't need my fortune. If we relinquish it, there's no guarantee he'll alter his course."

"No, there isn't," Jasper acknowledged. "But if the alternative is allowing his inquiry agents to rake up the past—"

A knock sounded on the library window, arresting his speech. Charlie was standing outside the glass, with Alfred and Daisy hovering behind him.

Jasper strode to the window and unlatched it. "What is it?"

"There's someone coming up the drive," Charlie said. "A great big coach-and-four."

Julia stood, pressing a hand to her midriff as she came to join them. It was the only sign of how unsettled she was by their previous conversation. "Is it someone from the village? The vicar or—"

"It's not the vicar," Alfred said. "He drives a green gig."

"And he never comes to call," Charlie added.

Daisy wasn't taking any chances. At the first mention of the village's dour clergyman, she was off and running toward the trees at the bottom of the garden.

Alfred hesitated but a moment before haring off after her.

"Good God," Jasper muttered. "One would think we'd never had proper callers."

"You'll remain, won't you, Charlie?" Julia asked. "Mr. Beecham might bring in tea."

Charlie snorted. "I'm not going to take tea with some stranger. I don't care who they are." With that, he ran off to join his siblings.

Jasper looked to Julia. "It appears we're on our own." He offered her his arm.

She took it silently, and a trifle stiffly.

As he walked with her out into the hall to greet their unexpected guests, he felt a sharp stab of remorse. Keeping his secrets—and keeping her in the long run—meant hurting her in the short term. He didn't like it one bit, but it was better than the alternative.

"Pray don't be unhappy with me," he said to her in a low voice.

"I'm not unhappy," she said. "I'm angry."

Jasper gave her an alert look. *Angry?*

But she was. He saw it in her eyes. He'd not only injured her feelings, he'd done the impossible. He'd riled her temper.

If he wasn't the one on the receiving end of her ire, he'd have marveled at it. Julia in a temper was a thing to behold.

He had no time to reply to her. Beecham was already ahead of them, throwing open the front door of the Hall.

A hired coach-and-four rolled up at the bottom of the moss-covered stone steps. The door opened the instant it stopped, and a lady in a black velvet traveling gown alighted unassisted. She tilted her head up to look at them, her aristocratic features framed by a black mourning bonnet and hair the color of spun gold.

Julia's hand slid from Jasper's arm. "Anne!"

Thirty-Three

✦

Julia met Anne halfway down the steps, enfolding her friend in a fierce embrace. "You've come! But how—"

"Forgive me," Anne murmured, squeezing her tightly a moment before releasing her. "There was no other way."

Julia at once discerned the crime for which her best friend begged forgiveness.

Anne hadn't come alone.

A tall, handsome gentleman in a plaid suit followed her out of the coach—Mr. Hartford of all people! More surprising still was the black crepe–clad lady he handed down from the carriage.

It was Anne's mother, the Countess of Arundell.

Julia sank into a curtsy. "Lady Arundell."

Widow of the Earl of Arundell, the Countess was a formidable dark-haired lady with a slight double chin and a magnificent bosom. A leader of fashionable London society, and well-known devotee of spiritualism, she was famous for her various eccentricities, among which was a propensity to wear mourning clothes, and to insist that her unmarried daughter do the same.

"Miss Wychwood. Or should I say Mrs. Blunt?" Her ladyship's gaze swept over Julia dismissively before moving to the house behind her. "So, this is Goldfinch Hall. An ill-suited name for a place of such reputed power. When the tragedy struck, I believe it was known locally as Edgemoor House."

Rising from her brief curtsy, Julia flashed a bewildered glance at Anne.

Anne gave a stiff shake of her head. *Later*, it seemed to say.

Mr. Hartford greeted Julia with a bow. Though his features were soberly disposed, his eyes flickered with their usual expression of private mirth, as if he found the whole situation devilishly amusing. "Mrs. Blunt. Captain. Felicitations on your marriage."

Jasper had come down the steps to stand at Julia's back. "Hartford. Ladies." His voice was as glacial as his countenance. "To what do we owe this unexpected pleasure?"

Lady Arundell leveled her gaze at him, appalled by his ignorance. "Mr. Drinkwater's bimonthly column. Don't say you haven't read it yet?"

"Mr. Drinkwater?" Julia echoed, feeling completely at sea.

"Mr. Drinkwater writes for the *Spiritualist Herald*," Anne explained. "He's lately received intelligence that the veil will be at its thinnest this week between the spirit realm and sites of spiritual significance in the northern counties. His most recent column makes specific reference to Edgemoor House."

Julia glanced at Jasper. His face was a studied blank. "Goldfinch Hall was once Edgemoor House?"

"In the seventeenth century," he said. "It's been rebuilt since, and renamed. Nothing of the original structure remains."

"Nothing save a portion of the old stable block," Mr. Beecham volunteered from his place at the top of the steps. He gave Jasper a look of apology. "Your uncle mentioned it on occasion."

"Your manservant knows more of this place's history than you do, Captain Blunt," Lady Arundell said. "I shall speak with him after tea."

Julia gathered her wits. "Of course. Please come in. Mr. Beecham? If you would bring a tray into the drawing room?"

Not fifteen minutes later, they were all seated comfortably as Julia poured out their tea. She was conscious of her duty as hostess. She'd played the role often enough in her parents' house. But this was no typical afternoon call. Whatever Lady Arundell's and Mr. Hartford's motivations, it was plain that Anne had come solely out of concern.

"We've taken rooms at the inn in the village," Lady Arundell informed them.

"If you can call it an inn," Mr. Hartford said.

Jasper's brows lifted a fraction. "You intend to stay?"

"Not above two nights." Mr. Hartford accepted a cup of tea from Julia with a murmured word of thanks. "I'm needed back in London by Friday."

"I'm amazed you're here at all," Jasper said.

Mr. Hartford's mouth quirked as he brought his cup to his lips. "I'm quite amazed myself."

Anne flashed him a repressive glare. "My mother won't travel without a gentleman to make the way smooth. As Miss Maltravers's uncle, Mr. Fielding, was unavailable at present, we were obliged to look elsewhere for an escort."

Julia was beginning to understand.

It seemed that Anne had compelled her mother to visit by holding out the haunted history of Goldfinch Hall as a lure. And she'd managed to convince Mr. Hartford of all people to accompany them here.

How she'd arranged it all, Julia couldn't fathom, but Anne must think the situation dire indeed to ask aid from a man she'd been at odds with since girlhood.

"Have you received word from Miss Maltravers?" Julia asked.

"Only a letter thus far," Anne said. "She's longing to hear from you. Miss Hobhouse is as well. We were astonished to learn of your marriage."

"Yes. As to that . . ." Julia added some sugar to her tea, the spoon clinking on the edge of the cup as she stirred. "It all happened rather quickly."

Anne's lips compressed. "Rather conveniently, too. And now here you are, in the wilds of North Yorkshire, far out of reach of your friends."

"Not so out of reach," Jasper said. "You've managed to find her."

Anne opened her mouth to respond, but Mr. Hartford forestalled her.

"This is a fine room. With a fine prospect of your park. You must spend a good deal of time here."

Julia raised her cup to her lips. "Either here or in the library. Or out of doors when the weather permits. We have much to occupy us."

"I sense no vibrations here," Lady Arundell remarked. "You've made this room over, I take it."

"I have," Jasper said. "The renovations were done some years ago. They were necessary to make it livable."

Lady Arundell didn't hesitate to voice her displeasure. "You'd have done well to leave it in its natural state. All the better to commune with any lingering spirits."

"I don't expect Captain Blunt wishes to commune with the dead," Mr. Hartford said.

"Why not?" Lady Arundell demanded. "We have much to learn from the past. Who better to convey the truth of it than those who lived in it?"

Anne was seated beside her mother on the sofa, her attention fixed on Julia as Lady Arundell and the others talked. "I understand Cossack is with you."

Julia smiled. "He is. He's stabled with Captain Blunt's stallion, Quintus. They're very happy together."

"Happiness is a state greatly to be desired." Anne's sherry-brown gaze was weighted with meaning. "For human beings as well as horses."

"Happiness has little to do with marriage," Lady Arundell said. "There are more important concerns, best left to a girl's parents to sort out." She looked to Julia. "*Your* parents might have done so, my girl, had you but heeded their counsel."

"Mama," Anne said under her breath. "You promised."

"Indeed. Remonstrances are best left for another time." Lady Arundell returned her teacup to the tray. "We have greater matters to occupy us. Where is that manservant of yours, Blunt?"

Mr. Beecham was summoned back, and Lady Arundell occupied herself in questioning him about the house's history. In short order, he agreed to escort her out on the grounds to have a look at the old stable block.

Julia and the others accompanied them. They'd gone no further than the front steps when Anne hung back, taking hold of Julia's arm.

Jasper came to a halt along with them.

"I have a wedding gift for you," Anne said to Julia. "Several, in fact. They're of a private nature. I trust your husband won't object to us having a moment to ourselves?"

"Not at all," Jasper said.

Julia chanced a look at his face. His countenance was still cold and forbidding—a look that had once made her quail in London. But she knew him now. She could see he was annoyed by the intrusion, by the presence of strangers wandering on the property, and by Anne's prior claim on Julia's affection.

She met his eyes, having to remind herself that she was still angry with him. "Please don't let them disturb the kittens," she said softly.

He inclined his head in a rigid bow to her before striding off with the others.

Anne's eyes sparkled with laughter. "*Kittens?*"

"Their mother is wild," Julia said. "Daisy and I have been attempting to tame them, but Jasper—that is, Captain Blunt—doesn't like us going into the old barn. It's not safe there."

"Jasper, is it? And Daisy? Who is that? One of the children, I suppose." Anne heaved a sigh as she linked her arm with Julia's. "My dear, you've caused me no end of worry. The things I've done to get to you. The evil bargains I've been constrained to make on your behalf. And now I see, rather than planning your escape from the notorious Hero of the Crimea, you've been setting up your nest in his home like a contented little hen."

Julia's mouthed curved up. "You came to rescue me?"

"That was my original plan. It was only when I received your two letters that I began to have an idea which way the wind was blowing. By then it was too late. My scheme was already in motion. Mama couldn't be dissuaded. Nor could Mr. Hartford—the odious man. Did you note the plaid monstrosity he's wearing? He chose it purely to vex me, I'm sure of it."

"How does it come about that he's here with you?" Julia asked.

Anne's expression tightened, just as it always did when someone broached the subject of her relationship with Mr. Hartford. Whatever had happened to make them enemies, it was a secret she refused to share.

"Mama counts him a friend of the family," she said. "She's known his grandfather, the Earl of March, for ages. And Hartford is always hanging about making a nuisance of himself. It was natural for him to offer his escort. It isn't as though he had any other pressing engagements. The man's as idle as the day is long."

"I think he must like you very much," Julia said.

Anne gave an unladylike snort. "Bah. Enough about him. I didn't travel hundreds of miles in the wretch's company only to speak of him on arriving here. I came to talk about *you*. What possessed you to take such a leap? And with Captain Blunt of all people."

Julia gave her friend an abridged version of the events leading up to her marriage, telling her about Lord Gresham, Dr. Cordingley's visit, and how she'd proposed to Jasper from her sickbed.

"It was the best thing I've ever done," she said sincerely. "He's made me so very happy."

Anne's gaze softened. "I suspected as much. I can only regret I didn't see it myself. I was that set against him. Evie was more open-minded. She ran into him at Hatchards once when he was purchasing a novel. That was enough to merit her good opinion. Mine is more difficult to earn."

"Even now?"

"I'm warming to the man. Anyone who makes you this happy must have some redeeming qualities. Mind you, I still think he's too big for you, and far too dour."

"Indeed he is not," Julia objected. "We suit each other perfectly."

"Hmm." Anne was doubtful. "What about this old ruin? Can you really be content here? There appear to be no servants of quality. And the grounds—I don't mean to criticize, but I'm sure you'd agree they're a little shabby."

"They're grand," Julia said. "All of it—the children and the estate and my husband. I *am* happy here, truly. I promise you."

Anne studied her face for a long while before nodding her head. "In that case, I suppose I had better give you your gifts and wish you joy."

Releasing Julia's arm, Anne returned to the carriage. A footman assisted her in removing a large book-shaped package from inside. "Is there somewhere we can go?" she asked. "Somewhere out of doors? I've had enough of closed spaces to last me a lifetime."

Julia took her friend's hand. "I know just the place."

There was an old arbor in the garden, all overgrown with wildflowers and vines. Julia led Anne there, and the two of them sat side by side in the shady embrace of the leaves.

Julia tore open the wrappings on her package, revealing the enormous book inside. She read the title aloud: *"Beeton's Book of Household Management."*

"It was published only last year, written by a lady who knows everything in the world about managing a household. She even has a section on treating stains." Anne examined the pages along with Julia as she flipped through them. "You shall learn it all, I have no doubt. In the meanwhile, I've brought my lady's maid, Jeanette, with me from London. Well, not *with* me. She's at the inn now, making things comfortable in our rooms. But I shall bring her when we visit tomorrow morning, and she'll clean and press all your gowns for you."

Tears of gratitude sprang to Julia's eyes. She embraced her friend tightly. "Thank you."

"It's my second wedding gift to you," Anne said when they broke apart. "And this is the third." Opening the black velvet reticule that hung at her wrist, she extracted a folded piece of paper. "I confess, I went in search of it with the intention of exposing Captain Blunt as a villain. Now I know you have feelings for the man, I'm relieved I didn't succeed."

Julia eyed the paper with apprehension. "What is it?"

"It's an old clipping from an 1855 edition of the *London Courant*. The most thorough report I could find on what actually happened all those years ago in the Crimea." Anne smiled at Julia's hesitance. "You needn't look so anxious. The report says he was a hero. Here, take it. Read it for yourself."

A HERO OF THE CRIMEA

Success has at length crowned the endeavors of France and England in the Crimea; the mighty fortress of Sebastopol is in the possession of the allied armies. The victory has come with a fearful cost. While gallant hearts were toiling outside of its walls, there were brave defenders inside, who staked everything upon the issue. Among them, Capt. J. Blunt of the 10th Royal Hussars will surely be remembered as one of the conflict's greatest heroes. Along with a scouting party of four of his valiant men, Capt. Blunt came under fire from an enemy sharpshooter during the fall of the city. Lieut. J. Marshland, son of the late Rev. Marshland, Vicar of Caden-ham, was killed instantly. Blunt's remaining men, Lieut. R. Grainger, brother of Viscount Ridgeway, and Lieutenants T. Akers, son of Mr. L. Akers of Wimbledon, and W. Vaughn, son of Mr. M. Vaughn of Newcastle, succumbed to a hail of bullets. Severely injured himself, Capt. Blunt disabled the sharpshooter, and when an enemy patrol descended and might have made away with valuable intelligence secreted on Lt. Marshland's body, Capt. Blunt single-handedly dispatched the enemy at great cost to his own life. Blunt is recuperating from grievous wounds at Scutari Hospital. He is being considered for a special medal of bravery to be awarded by Queen Victoria.

The blood drained from Julia's face as she read. By the time she'd finished, she felt clammy and faint, much like she had after a visit from Dr. Cordingley and his scarificator.

"There, you see," Anne said triumphantly. "Your husband *was* a hero. I misjudged the man; I freely admit it."

"Yes, I see," Julie answered.

But it wasn't all she'd seen.

A name had leapt out at her from the newspaper article: *Lieutenant J. Marshland.*

Jasper had lied to her. J. Marshland wasn't his pen name. J. Marshland wasn't anyone's pen name. He'd been one of Jasper's men. A soldier serving under him. The son of a country vicar.

"He was a dreamer. He loved novels—reading them and writing them." Jasper's words in the Claverings' garden echoed back to her.

No wonder the style of James Marshland's books had changed after the war. It was because James Marshland was no longer writing them.

Thirty-Four

——✦——

Jasper stood back as Lady Arundell investigated the dark interior of the stable. He was well aware of Goldfinch Hall's haunted reputation. Rumors had plagued the estate long before he'd arrived and would no doubt linger long after he was gone.

It was nonsense, of course.

There were no ghosts at the Hall. No spirits cursed to wander the earth. Only rot and decay—the lingering effects of all-too-human neglect.

"I feel it here quite strongly," Lady Arundell declared, coming to a halt in front of the empty loose boxes. "There's a cold shaft coming through. A presence."

"The floor has rotted away," Jasper said. "So has the roof. What you're feeling is the damp."

"Do you mean to repair it?" Hartford asked. "I assume you will now you've married."

Jasper shot him an irritated look. Whatever the man's motivations for being here, he was making a damned nuisance of himself. "Eventually, yes." He stepped forward. "My lady? If you will? The structure isn't safe."

Lady Arundell reluctantly withdrew with them back out to the empty stable yard. "Have you considered holding a séance? I'm not acquainted with any practitioners in this part of the country, but I daresay you could get a party together with some of the locals."

"I wouldn't advise it," Hartford said. "The people in that drab little village don't look particularly enlightened. According to history, it was they who strung up the house's original inhabitants."

"It was a political execution." Jasper escorted them back to the house. "One of many during the Civil War."

"I'm not interested in the history of Roundheads and Cavaliers," Lady Arundell retorted. "I'm concerned with spiritual matters. And this house is a reputed hotbed of spiritual activity."

"I have lived here six years, ma'am," Jasper said, "and never encountered a ghost."

Hartford grinned. "You've probably scared them away. You're not a very welcoming presence."

Jasper didn't dispute the fact. He had no interest in welcoming anyone here. Not spirits. Not human beings. He wanted to be left alone with his family.

A family that was presently nowhere to be seen.

Nearly an hour had passed since Julia had gone off with Lady Anne. She hadn't come back, nor had the children.

Jasper ushered Hartford and Lady Arundell back into the drawing room. He sent Beecham to the kitchens for more tea.

It was another quarter of an hour before Julia and Lady Anne returned. Lady Anne was determinedly cheerful, talking about some housekeeping book she'd given to Julia as a gift, but Julia was silent, her face nearly as pale as it had been in the aftermath of her bloodletting.

Jasper was instantly on his feet. "Is everything all right?"

"Excellent," Lady Anne answered, sitting beside her mother. Her tone was bracing, but her attention lingered on Julia with thinly veiled concern. "We've had a lovely visit, haven't we, my dear?"

"Yes. Lovely." Julia sat down, her posture straight as a ramrod in her chair. She avoided Jasper's gaze as she freshened everyone's tea.

He watched her with a growing sense of unease. There was something strangely detached about her movements. It put him in mind of the way she'd looked when he'd seen her dancing with Lord Gresham at the Claverings' ball. As if she'd withdrawn into herself.

By some miracle, he got through the next hour without drawing her aside to interrogate her. He walked with her to see their guests out, stood silent as she hugged Lady Anne goodbye and waved off the carriage.

Only when the coach had disappeared out of sight down the drive, when Beecham had withdrawn into the house, and Jasper and Julia were alone on the steps, did Jasper finally speak freely.

"What happened?" he asked. "And pray don't insult me by saying nothing is wrong. You're clearly upset."

She smoothed the skirts of her gown, still avoiding his gaze. "I am upset. I've already told you so."

"This isn't about your fortune. Lady Anne must have said something—"

"Yes. Quite." Julia looked at him at last. Her sapphire eyes were accusing, her countenance as hard as a piece of Sèvres porcelain about to crack.

His breath stopped.

But she didn't accuse him of anything.

"I must change into my riding habit," she said abruptly. "I'm taking Cossack out for a gallop on the moors."

He scowled. "Now?"

"Yes now. You're free to come if you like." With that, she turned and strode back into the house.

The North York Moors were bleak and barren. As bleak as Julia was currently feeling inside. She gave Cossack a gentle nudge with her heel. He lengthened his stride, galloping over the treeless landscape toward the low heather-covered hills in the distance.

She already felt braver—stronger—just being on Cossack's back. It was why she'd insisted on taking him out. If she and Jasper must have this conversation at all, better it was had while she was at her strongest.

He cantered behind her on Quintus. He was holding the stallion back, letting Cossack take the lead. Letting *her* take the lead.

And not only on horseback.

It was a stratagem, no doubt.

Jasper would say nothing—confess to nothing—until he knew exactly what it was he was being accused of.

They finally slowed to a walk as they approached the hills. It was colder here, wind whipping through the scattered trees and over the large piles of sandstone that littered the uneven ground.

Jasper rode up alongside her on Quintus, still silent.

She forced herself to meet his eyes. Her heart ached with the pain of his dishonesty. "The vicar's son—the one you flogged when he tried to give bread to a dying man—the one who loved reading and writing novels. Was his name James Marshland?"

Jasper recoiled from her words as if she'd struck him.

It was answer enough, but Julia wouldn't be satisfied until he admitted it in his own words. "Was it?" she asked again.

His face went pale, the raised ridge of his scar standing out in stark relief. "Yes," he said hoarsely. "How—?"

"Anne brought a clipping from an old newspaper. She meant to show me how heroic you were during the war. It said you were the sole survivor of a brutal attack, where you dispatched a patrol of enemy soldiers and rescued vital intelligence. It also said that the first to die during the attack was your lieutenant, a vicar's son named J. Marshland." Her fingers tightened on Cossack's reins. "It's not your pen name, is it?"

"No. It isn't." Quintus stamped restlessly beneath him, tossing his head with impatience. Jasper made no move to quiet him. His attention was riveted to Julia's face.

She was amazed at the steadiness of her own voice. "James Marshland truly did write all those books, didn't he?"

"He did."

"*The Fire Opal* and all the others I loved so much. All of them, right up until he died. Then you took over."

Jasper's gaze sharpened. Something flickered at the back of his frost-gray eyes, as if he understood a crucial fact he hadn't before. It altered his demeanor. The color gradually returned to his face as he brought Quintus under sharp control.

"It's why the style has changed," she said. "You stole his name after the war. For money, I suppose."

"Is that what you believe?"

"I can come to no other conclusion."

Jasper was silent for a moment, as if calculating his response. "Would it be a crime?"

Julia's lips curled in disgust. That he even had to ask! "To take advantage of a man who died serving under you? A man you treated abominably?"

"He *was* treated abominably," Jasper said.

"By *you*," Julia snapped back. "*You're* the one who mistreated him. You said you regretted the past. That you were making amends for it. But you haven't changed at all, have you? If you had, you'd never have stolen his work."

"I've stolen nothing from him."

"You've already confessed that you have. That the books were written by him. Now you're passing them off as your own—and collecting his royalties, too! Have you no thought for his family?"

"Marshland had no family," Jasper said. "He had no one on this earth."

"Everybody has someone."

"He didn't. As for his royalties . . . there's little enough to speak of. Hardly worth the grand deception you're accusing me of."

"It *is* a deception."

"If it is, it harms no one."

Julia could no longer keep her countenance. "It harms *me*! Can't you see that? *I'm* the one you've deceived." She trembled with hurt and anger. "What else have you lied to me about?"

Jasper didn't answer. He only looked at her, his brows drawn in a brooding frown.

She averted her face, very much afraid there were tears in her eyes. "That's how it is, then? I must wait for the truth to be revealed to me as it comes? Never knowing what evil surprise might lurk around the next corner and the next?"

Jasper moved Quintus closer to Cossack. "Julia—"

"Another mistress, perhaps? More children? Some additional cruelty you perpetrated against a soldier who couldn't defend himself?"

"Good God. Is that what you're afraid of? I don't have any other mistresses or children. And I was never—" He broke off with a muttered oath. "Damnation, Julia, don't make me have this conversation with you. You won't like how it ends."

Julia continued to stare out over the moors, refusing to look at him. Her throat was tight. She dashed her gloved hand over her cheek, brushing away a rogue tear.

Jasper made a husky sound of anguish. "Please don't cry."

She hardened her heart. She had to protect herself from being hurt.

Feeling Quintus edging closer, she was possessed by the urge to give Cossack a kick. To gallop away as fast as she could. She wasn't crying, not yet, but if Jasper dared touch her, she feared the dam of her emotions would burst and she'd lose what little was left of her dignity.

He must have sensed her intention. In one decisive movement, he caught hold of Cossack's reins.

She turned on him, lips parted in outrage. "How dare you—"

"You're not going to run away from me," he said gruffly. "Not here." He dismounted from Quintus in one fluid movement and, catching her round the waist, lifted her from her sidesaddle. "Your horse would trip and you'd dash your head on the stones, then where would I be?" He set her feet down on the uneven ground, gripping her hard. "Don't you know by now that I can't live without you?"

Tears filled her eyes. "I wouldn't fall off. I'm an excellent rider."

"So am I," he said gravely, his hands tight at her waist. "An excellent writer, that is."

She stared at him.

He looked steadily back at her. He was white about the mouth. "You wanted the truth. There it is. J. Marshland isn't my pen name. It's my real name."

She blinked. "*What?*"

"It was Captain Blunt who died at the fall of Sebastopol," he said. "Captain Blunt who perished from a rifle shot to the face. *I* was the sole survivor of the skirmish—the man who routed the patrol of Russians. I had no one waiting for me at home. No one in this world. Neither had Blunt, or so he said. But he had something else. He had an estate. A remote property in Yorkshire he'd inherited, where he meant to retire after the war. A refuge, he called it."

Julia shook her head in disbelief. It couldn't be true.

Jasper went on relentlessly. "I told you when we married that I'd been selfish once before. It was the day I decided to take Blunt's estate as my own. We were of a similar height and build, both of us with black hair and light eyes and great big Crimean beards. When I woke up in Scutari Hospital, they believed I was him. They spent the first weeks addressing me by his name. And I thought . . . why not? There was no one to stop me. No one who would be harmed. If Blunt died, the estate would revert to the Crown. So after I recovered and was fit enough to make the journey, I came back to England, I traveled here to Yorkshire, and I claimed Goldfinch Hall as my own."

Her legs sagged beneath her.

He maneuvered her to one of the standing stones. It was the approximate height of a chair.

Julia sank down on it numbly. Her thoughts were in chaos. She had the vague notion that she *had* fallen. That she'd suffered a blow to the head.

Jasper briefly stepped away from her to secure the horses to a nearby tree. "I convinced myself I deserved it," he said as he tied off their reins. "That it was the least Blunt owed to me for all the violence and misery I'd endured at his hands."

"The marks on your back . . ." She didn't recognize the sound of her own voice. "It was Captain Blunt who flogged you?"

"Mercilessly." Jasper returned to stand in front of her. His face was taut, as if he was resolved to continue his tale, no matter the cost. "He was a merciless man, to me and to everyone within his power. We were already in a wretched state. It was freezing—we had to thaw our ink to write. And our clothing wasn't suited for the elements. We were emaciated and starving. What food we were allotted wasn't fit for consumption. But Blunt made it worse. He cut our rations for the smallest infractions. He flogged men for insubordination who were already dying of dysentery and exposure. I took pity on one of them and gave him my bread. When Blunt found out, he made an example of me."

Her throat convulsed on a swallow. She recalled Jasper's words to her in the Claverings' garden. The way he'd described the vicar's son who had been flogged.

"He was a brave lad, too. Noble, you might say. All the same, he wasn't made for soldiering."

He'd been describing himself. *He* was the noble young soldier who had given bread to a dying prisoner. The bookish son of a country vicar. A lad who hadn't been made for soldiering.

"I was confined to the guardroom for the night," Jasper continued. "My wounds were left untreated. I was unable to sleep or even to move. Blunt sat with me until the wee hours, drinking and talking and drinking some more. It's when he told me about his estate. He said he was the last of his name. That he had no one waiting for him. Imagine my dismay when, a few weeks after I arrived at the Hall, Dolly Carvel turned up at the door with Daisy in her arms."

It was the faintest shadow of a silver lining. Julia clutched at it with both hands. "She wasn't your mistress."

"Of course she wasn't. I've never had a mistress. I've never—" He broke off again, scrubbing at his jaw. "Dolly was something wholly out of my experience. As I was to her, I have no doubt. She'd heard Blunt had taken up residence at the Hall and had used the last of her coin to make the journey, hoping he'd do something for her and the children. But she was no innocent. She recognized my game as soon as she clapped eyes on me. It took her less than five minutes to resort to blackmail."

"Blackmail?" Julia struggled to marshal her racing thoughts. "What did she want from you?"

"She wanted me to fetch the boys from the workhouse, and to care for the children after she was gone. If I refused, she intended to expose me. She was the sole person who could do so. Blunt spent most of his life serving in remote parts of the world. He hadn't any friends. He was too volatile to maintain relationships. Dolly was the only one who knew him for any length of time. He gave her money when he visited her, but he'd provided nothing for the children's long-term support."

"You could have left. You could have gone away somewhere."

"I could have," he acknowledged. "Indeed, I planned to after I retrieved the boys from the workhouse. But Dolly was dying. And Daisy was so small and helpless. They had nowhere else to go and no one to look after them. I couldn't bear the thought of Blunt's cruelty claiming any more victims. Not if I could do something to help them."

"They don't know?" she asked.

"No one does." He paused, a frown flattening his mouth. "Ridgeway suspects, but he's not likely to share his suspicions. As for everyone else . . . I've been careful. I've had to be. If anyone found out the truth, it would mean losing the children. They're the reason I stayed. The reason I've done all of this. I care for them now as if they were my own. It's why I came to London to find a wealthy wife. It seemed the only way to save the estate and secure their futures. But I didn't find what I was looking for. I found something else—something better. I found you."

She blinked rapidly against an onslaught of tears.

He sank down in front of her, just as he had earlier in the library, except now there was a burning intensity in his gaze. "I didn't marry you for the children or the estate or for anything to do with Blunt," he said. "I married you for myself. My *true* self. I married you because I love you. That much you must believe."

Julia looked back at him, her heart in her throat. *"Are* we married?"

Thirty-Five

—✦—

J asper flinched. He'd anticipated the question. That didn't make it any easier to hear it. Crouched in front of Julia on the desolate moor, alone with her amid the rocky sandstone and the biting wind, he felt a building sense of desperation.

She was too quiet. Too stoic. Though tears brimmed in her eyes, she wasn't crying and she wasn't raging at him.

His deception had hurt her badly. He was only now beginning to realize how much.

"Of course we're married," he replied roughly. "You're my wife."

"I married Captain Blunt," she said.

"Which is who I am now. Who I must be for all time."

"But you're not Captain Blunt. You're James Marshland."

Jasper's chest contracted painfully. Many a time as he'd kissed her or made love to her, he'd have sold his soul to hear her utter his name. To call him James just once.

But not now.

Now it felt like an indictment.

"In spirit, perhaps," he said, "but not in law."

She shook her head. "Our marriage can't be legal."

"It *is*. I made certain of that."

"How?"

He hesitated to explain, aware of how cold-blooded it would make him sound. "I made confidential inquiries before we married."

She gave him a sharp look. "Inquiries of whom?"

He was quiet for a moment before admitting, "I consulted with Mr. Finchley the day he came to Ridgeway's house."

Her bosom rose and fell on an unsteady breath. "He knew the truth, then."

"Not entirely. I presented the issue to him as a hypothetical. He knew only enough to render counsel."

"What did he say?"

"He said, if the marriage was by license, it didn't matter if a man used a false name. So long as his bride, the vicar, and the witnesses had no knowledge of his true identity—so long as they all acted in good faith—the marriage would be legal."

She didn't appear reassured by the information. "We didn't only marry in law. We married in a church. We made each other promises—vows before God."

"I meant everything I promised you," he said. "None of that was a lie."

"It was built on a lie. Our entire life here is. Yours, mine, and the children's—"

"Would you have me tell them the truth? To salve my conscience at their expense? What purpose could it possibly serve except to make them doubt their place in the world? To make them live in fear of one day having all this taken away?"

Her eyes shimmered with tears. "You should have told *me*."

He leaned into her, aching to banish the injured look from her face. His voice sank with a desperate sincerity. "I wanted to. So many times."

The urge had struck him on the train from London, and then again in the tower when she'd discovered his manuscript. It had been there the first time he'd made love to her, and every night since as he'd held her in his arms.

But he wouldn't unload his burdens onto her shoulders. He knew too well the cost of carrying them. The nagging guilt that had plagued him in those early days. The nights spent wrestling with his conscience, wondering if there could, indeed, be virtue in living a lie.

He'd long ago come to terms with the necessity of it.

The truth was all well and good from a moral standpoint. A noble conceit, to be sure. But there were things in life that were far nobler. There was duty and self-sacrifice.

There was love.

"Then why didn't you?" she asked. "Did you fear I wouldn't keep your secret?"

"It's not about keeping the secret. It's about bearing it. Besides," he added, "it wasn't my secret to tell. It still isn't. The risk to the children is too great. And the children *must* come first. They're depending on me. If I fail them . . ." He shook his head, refusing to countenance the possibility. "I can't. I won't. Not if I must play the part of Captain Blunt for the remainder of my life."

"Where do I fit into this charade?" she asked. "We've already established I'm a secondary concern."

His brows lowered. "That isn't what I meant and you know it. They come first because they're children. *My* children. It doesn't matter who their parents were. Family isn't solely determined by blood. And we *are* a family. All of us—you included. I know you care for them, too. I've seen it for myself."

"I do care for them. I can even understand why—" Her words were lost on a stifled sob as her composure finally cracked. Tears spilled down her cheeks. She rose from the stone, swiping at her face as she moved to walk away from him. "You may think me selfish, but just once, *I* want to come first in someone's heart. *I* want to be important enough—"

Standing to block her way, Jasper caught her by the arms, forcing her to face him. "You're first in my heart. In *mine*, Julia. James Marshland. You're the only person on this earth who's truly mine."

She bowed her head, weeping. "James Marshland is dead."

Or at least, that's what it sounded like she said. She was weeping too heavily for him to fully understand her.

His hands tightened on her arms. "*Look at me.*" He stared down at her, willing her to see him for who he really was. "You told me once that when you looked into my eyes you saw a different man. A better man. *That's* who I am. Not Blunt, but me. I've been here all along."

"Please let me go."

"I won't ever let you go." Pulling her hard against him, Jasper covered her mouth with his.

Julia struggled with him for a moment before succumbing to his kiss. It wasn't a wholehearted capitulation. She still strained to be free of him. Only her lips softened, yielding briefly beneath his in unwilling surrender.

She was damp and salty with tears, her tremulous breath mingling with his on a gasping sob.

He kissed her fiercely, desperately, so afraid of losing her that his own eyes smarted with the sting of it. "I love you," he rasped against her mouth. "*I love you.* That's the truth. The only truth that matters."

"And I love you," she admitted.

A tremor went through him. He closed his eyes, clinging to her tear-clogged words as if they were a lifeline on a stormy sea. His grip on her tightened so that he feared he might crush her.

It would be all right now. If she loved him, *everything* would be all right.

But it wasn't all right.

Her body remained stiff in his arms.

"I love you," she said again. "If I didn't, perhaps all this would be easier to forgive."

His eyes opened as understanding sank in. An unsettling chill stole the warmth from his blood. "Julia—"

"Let me go," she said softly. "Please. I can't think clearly when you're near me."

He reluctantly loosened his hold. When she withdrew from his arms, he felt a sickening sense of loss. She was slipping away from him and there was nothing he could do about it.

She stood out of his reach. Her habit was rumpled from his embrace, her ebony hair half falling from its pins. She looked as though she'd been mauled by a tiger.

Jasper regarded her with a brooding frown as she put herself to rights. "What can I do?"

"You can leave me alone," she said.

He flinched.

"I need time to think."

"How much time?" he asked.

She tucked her hair back into its silken net. Her hands were trembling. "The rest of the day for a start."

"And then what?"

"I don't know," she answered. "That's why I need time."

It went against Jasper's every instinct to allow it. He didn't want to leave her alone—to give her a chance to formulate an even more damning opinion of his conduct. He wanted to hold her tighter. To overwhelm her with the strength of his feelings for her. To kiss her and make love to her and compel her forgiveness.

But forgiveness didn't work that way.

It wasn't something he could demand. It had to be given of Julia's own free will—if it was given at all.

"Very well," he said. "If time is what you require, time is what you shall have." *So long as you don't leave me*, he wanted to add.

But he didn't.

He merely assisted her onto Cossack, and then, mounting Quintus, he rode away, back to Goldfinch Hall.

Alone.

Julia didn't return to the Hall until the early evening. Jasper wasn't at the stables waiting for her. There was only Plimstock. Leaving Cossack in the groom's care, Julia made her way to the house.

Jasper wasn't there, either—not on the steps, impatiently anticipating her arrival, and not in the entrance hall to ask what had taken her so long.

The house felt quite empty.

She supposed everyone was readying for dinner. She hadn't much appetite herself. What she wanted was a book, a bath, and then her bed. If Jasper truly meant to honor her request to be left alone, perhaps he'd arrange to sleep elsewhere tonight?

The thought provided no comfort.

Sagging with weariness, she walked down the corridor to the library. There were only J. Marshland novels in her bedchamber, and at the moment, she had no wish to read any of those. What she needed was something else—something with less meaning attached to it.

She found the library door half-open. The low hum of conversation drifted out into the corridor. It was Jasper and Daisy.

Julia hesitated on the threshold, uncertain whether to go in.

"Then what happened, Papa?" Daisy was asking.

Jasper's deep voice murmured in answer, "After the happily-ever-after? It doesn't say. These kinds of stories never do."

"But you must know."

"I daresay it all depends on one's definition of happily-ever-after." He paused. "What do you suppose it means?"

"That they had babies," she said.

"Ah." There was the sound of a book being closed and returned to a shelf.

"What do *you* think it means?" Daisy asked.

"I don't know," he said. "Perhaps that they cared for each other, and looked after each other, and that they were never lonely again."

"I like being alone," Daisy said.

"Being alone isn't the same as being lonely," Jasper replied.

Julia's heart clenched. It was the same thing she'd told him at Lady Clifford's musicale. It seemed a lifetime ago. And yet he'd remembered.

Of course he had. He loved her. She knew that beyond all doubt.

It didn't change the fact that he'd lied to her.

Pushing open the door, she entered the library. Jasper stood at the bookcase in his shirtsleeves, his hair disheveled, as if he'd been raking his fingers through it. Daisy was seated nearby, her pinafore smudged and her plaited hair frayed in an ebony halo around her face.

"Julia!" She leapt from her chair. "You're back!"

Jasper turned to the door. A faint expression of relief flickered in his eyes, then was gone.

Julia vividly recalled how he'd kissed her so desperately on the moor. He hadn't wanted to leave her there, but he had in the end—obviously against his own better judgment. He must have been dreadfully worried.

"Good evening," she said. "I don't mean to interrupt."

"You're not interrupting. Daisy was just leaving to wash for dinner."

Daisy hurried to Julia's side, grabbing her sleeve in entreaty. "Will you arrange my hair?"

"I will." Julia smoothed a hand over Daisy's perpetually frazzled head. "Go ahead and wash. I'll be up directly." She watched the little girl depart, shutting the door behind her. Only then did she turn her attention back to Jasper.

He was regarding her with a frown. He seemed reluctant to speak. Julia felt rather at a loss for words herself.

"You look as though you're feeling a little better," he offered at last.

"I am," she said. "I've had time to come to a decision."

A muscle worked in his jaw, belying the calmness of his tone. "Anything you'd care to share with me?"

Julia replied carefully, conscious of the step she was taking. "Tomorrow, when Anne and her mother return to London, I intend to go with them."

Jasper's face turned ashen.

"I'm not leaving you," she said. "Though I'd be justified in doing so."

He held her gaze, his gray eyes gleaming with a strange light.

She had the impression that his self-control was poised on a knife's edge. She moistened her lips. "The fact is, I've been too happy here to give any of it up. Happy with the children and the house, and . . . and with you." Heat rose in her cheeks. "I won't pretend I haven't been."

"Then why—"

"Several reasons." She folded her arms, wandering closer to him as she formulated her thoughts. "I want to speak with Mr. Finchley for myself." Given Jasper's dishonesty, it would be foolish to rely on his assurances about the legality of their marriage. "And I must see my parents."

He shook his head. "You can't—"

"After everything you've admitted to, I have even more reason to fight for my fortune. But I see now why it can't be a fight in law. Which is why I must go back to Belgrave Square." Julia felt sick to contemplate it, but she'd made up her mind. "It's the only way."

"What is it exactly you plan to do?"

"I don't know." She studied his face. It occurred to her that she knew nothing about him. At least, nothing about the man he'd been before he became Jasper Blunt. "I don't even know what to call you anymore."

"I suppose an endearment is out of the question."

She huffed a humorless laugh, comprehending now why he'd objected so strongly to her using his given name in their more intimate moments. He hadn't been Jasper when he was kissing her and holding her. He'd been James, the bookish son of a country vicar. A man who loved reading and writing novels. A man not made for soldiering.

And yet he'd been a war hero. The *true* Hero of the Crimea. A young lieutenant whose spectacular act of bravery had served not to bolster his own reputation, but to redeem the reputation of the very man who had flogged him so mercilessly.

It was part of the price he'd paid in taking on Captain Blunt's identity.

A price he was still paying, for the children's sake.

"Why did you go away to war?" she asked abruptly.

His frown deepened. He rested a hand on the bookshelf behind him. His fingers curled into a fist. "Because my mother died and I was too angry with my father to remain in the same house with him."

Julia moved closer. "Angry about what?"

"He was a pious, miserable old hypocrite. He saved the best of himself for the pulpit, and the worst for my mother and me. He didn't know what kindness was. When my mother became ill . . . he made her last months a misery."

"Were you close with her?"

"I loved her," he said. "I tried to make her comfortable—brushing her hair and sponging her brow, but—"

Julia gave him a startled look. "That was your *mother*? I thought—"

His brows knit. "What?"

She shook her head, realizing her mistake. "I thought it was Dolly whose hair you brushed when she was ill. On our wedding night you said that you loved her. But . . . you weren't talking about her at all, were you? You were talking about your mother."

Julia felt the urge to sit down. It was all too overwhelming, this recalibration of everything she'd believed until now. It shifted by the second, making her realize how much she'd misunderstood about him.

"I shouldn't have mentioned her," he said. "Certainly not on our first night together. But I wanted to confide in you, even then. I wanted you to know me for who I truly was."

"It hasn't all been a lie, surely."

"No. Not all of it. Only my name and the truth about my past—what there was of it." He grimaced. "My mother was ill for nearly a year. Our house took on the air of a sickroom, not too dissimilar from your parents' house. The curtains were always drawn and the fires stoked, even in the summer. The village doctor said it was likely cancer. He recommended she be taken to London for an operation, but my father refused. There was no swaying him. It caused an irreparable breach between us. After the funeral, I stored away my personal belongings—my collection of novels and a few mementos of my childhood—and joined the army. It was done less out of a desire to fight than a desire to punish my father."

"The newspaper report said he'd died as well."

"He did. I received word of it not long after I left. He took a chill while out walking and was gone in a fortnight. Rather ironic, really."

"I'm sorry," she said. "All that loss—"

"Don't be. It's ancient history now. If I think about it at all, it's only because occasionally something happens that I wish I could share with my mother." A regretful smile ghosted over his lips. "I would have liked her to have met you."

"Do you suppose she would have approved of me?"

"She would have adored you," he said. "She was a gentle lady, with a romantic spirit. It was she who first encouraged me to write when I was a lad."

Julia edged closer to him. "Did you intend to give it up? Your writing, I mean? When you went away to war?"

"I didn't think about my writing at all. Not for a long time. When I finally returned to it . . ." His expression sobered. "You asked me why the style of my novels changed. It's because *I* changed. I had to become someone else. I understood then that there was nothing thrilling about falsified deaths and secret identities. There was only loneliness. And I had enough of that to contend with in my new life. I had no desire to write about it."

She was near enough now to touch him, her shoulder brushing the bookshelf as they stood face-to-face. "I wish I had known you before," she said. "The real you."

"You do know the real me," he replied gruffly. He took a step toward her. "Promise you won't leave me."

Her pulse quickened. "I told you I wouldn't."

"Yet you insist upon returning to London." He loomed over her. "I could forbid you going."

She stood her ground. "You could," she acknowledged. "But you won't."

He stared down at her with palpable frustration.

"I'm leaving tomorrow," she said. "I intend to stay in London for however long it takes to resolve things."

"And then?"

"And then . . . we'll see."

Thirty-Six

❦

Julia didn't know where Mr. Finchley's offices were. She'd only ever encountered him at his home in Half Moon Street. So, the morning after arriving back in London, Half Moon Street is precisely where she went.

Anne had offered to accompany her on her errand. Julia had politely declined. The less Anne knew about Julia's true reasons for returning to London the better. Thus far, Julia had only confided her intention to regain control of her funds. It was enough to explain her visit to a solicitor.

The Finchleys' housekeeper showed her into a small room off the entrance hall. It was furnished with a mahogany desk and a pair of carved chairs with seats covered in green morocco leather.

Julia remained standing, smoothing her carriage dress as she waited. She wasn't obliged to wait long.

Within minutes, Mrs. Finchley appeared, accompanied by her husband.

"Mrs. Blunt," she said, smiling. She was clad in a fashionable cambric morning dress, her magnificent auburn hair caught up in a plaited roll at her nape. "This is indeed a surprise."

"Mrs. Blunt." Mr. Finchley bowed. Like his wife, he was informally dressed, wearing a loose-fitting sack coat and trousers of light gray cloth.

Julia greeted them both, smiling woodenly as they traded pleasantries. All the while, she was conscious of Mr. Finchley's attention. His eyes were remarkably keen behind his spectacles. She had the impression he'd been expecting her.

"Forgive me," she said at last. "This isn't a social call. It's about a legal matter. I'm afraid I didn't know where to find your offices."

"Not at all," Mr. Finchley said. "These days I'm at home more than I'm at my office."

"You can blame me for that." Mrs. Finchley exchanged a private smile with her husband before withdrawing. "Shall I send in tea?"

"Oh no," Julia said. "I won't be staying long."

Mrs. Finchley seemed to understand. Professing herself to be available if either of them should have need of her, she exited the room in a rustle of fabric.

Mr. Finchley motioned for Julia to sit down.

She took a seat in one of the carved chairs, folding her hands in her lap as he sat across from her.

"How can I help you, ma'am?" he asked.

Repressed anxiety made Julia's stomach tremble. It was difficult enough being back in London, but to have ventured out on her own— entirely alone—with no maid or anyone else to support her had taken a level of courage she hadn't known she possessed.

She was driven by the same compulsion that had prompted her to challenge the shopkeeper in Hardholme—a deep desire to protect her family. She wanted to protect herself, too. To reassure herself that she *was* married, in law as well as in spirit.

"My husband recently told me that he consulted with you before our marriage," she said. "He mentioned having asked your advice on a hypothetical question."

Mr. Finchley neither confirmed nor denied it.

Julia pressed on in spite of his silence. "I wondered if I might consult with you on the same subject?"

A glint of sympathy flickered in Mr. Finchley's gaze. "You may ask me whatever you like, of course. I'll advise you if I can."

"Very well." She cleared her throat. "Could you please tell me . . . If a person—a man—married someone under a false name, would that marriage be legal?"

Mr. Finchley didn't bat an eye. "That depends. Were the banns published?"

"Does it matter?"

"Very much so. The object of publication is publicity. If a false name is used when calling the banns, it defeats the entire purpose of the exercise. A marriage in those circumstances would be invalid." He paused. "Now, if it were a marriage by license . . ."

"Yes?" She leaned forward in her seat.

"A license isn't a matter of public notoriety. If one of the parties used a false name to obtain it, the marriage might still be held valid, providing certain criteria are met."

"What criteria?"

"That depends," he said again. "Did the man's wife know it was a false name at the time they wed?"

"She did not."

"And did the vicar? Or any of the witnesses?"

"No, indeed."

"Then yes, the marriage would be legal."

Julia's brows knit. It was too convenient. Almost too good to be true. She didn't dare trust it. "How can it be? Surely, it's fraud or some other crime?"

"On the husband's part? Probably. But the husband's crime does nothing to invalidate the marriage. When you wed, you marry a person, not a name."

A person, not a name.

She wanted desperately to believe it. "You're certain of this?"

"I am," he said. "Providing the license and all the other preliminaries were in order, the woman would be the man's wife."

Her hands tightened in her lap. "And any children arising from their marriage?"

"They would be legitimate."

Relief coursed through her. But her conscience wasn't satisfied. Not yet. "What if . . . What if the name the husband used wasn't only false? What if it belonged to another?"

"Many people share the same name, Mrs. Blunt," Mr. Finchley said gently. "A name isn't unique."

"Yes, but . . . what if, in taking the name, he'd also taken the other man's property?"

"And deprived the man of it?"

"No. That is . . . the man whose name he took is dead."

"So, he's deprived the man's heirs?"

"Quite the opposite." Julia thought of Charlie, Alfred, and Daisy. Of what might have happened to them if James Marshland hadn't assumed the identity of Jasper Blunt. "In taking the man's name, he's made right a great wrong. Even so, if something is against the law—"

"The law is a strange beast," Mr. Finchley said. "We must respect it and abide by it. Our society couldn't function if we didn't. But laws aren't synonymous with justice."

"You believe there's a distinction?"

"I know there is." His expression was solemn. "Laws are made by men and, therefore, fallible. Justice is something greater. Most of us— the poorest and the weakest—won't see it on this side of the grave. But sometimes, on rare occasions, someone manages to balance the scales. It can be difficult to reconcile it with the law. That doesn't negate the rightness of it."

She frowned. "You don't oppose it, then? Someone taking matters into their own hands?"

"In the scenario you've proposed? I can see no harm in it. That doesn't mean there aren't circumstances that would alter my opinion." He smiled. "For that, however, I'd have to know the whole of the facts."

Julia had no intention of sharing the facts with anyone. She was too protective of Jasper and the children to risk exposing them.

She stood. "You've been very helpful, sir."

Mr. Finchley rose from his chair. "I trust I've managed to set your mind at ease."

"You have." She fumbled with her reticule. "Please allow me to—"

He stayed her hand. "That won't be necessary. I don't charge for consultations. Certainly not hypothetical ones."

Julia smiled in gratitude. Her heart felt lighter after speaking with him. He was so kind and competent. So very knowledgeable. She resisted the urge to lay even more of her troubles at his door.

Or *tried* to resist.

He'd no sooner inquired if there was anything else he might assist her with, than she found herself blurting out the difficulty she was having with obtaining her funds from Hoares.

"It's my parents, you see," she explained. "My father's exerted pressure on the bank. He's even hired a firm of solicitors to argue the issue."

"Do you know who he's retained?" Mr. Finchley asked.

"Birchall, Crawley, and Micklethwait," she said. "I don't suppose you've heard of them?"

Mr. Finchley's gaze sharpened. "Indeed." He gestured to the chair. "Perhaps you should sit back down?"

"When is Julia coming home?" Charlie demanded from the door of the tower.

Jasper looked up from his manuscript with a distracted frown. Seated at his desk, he was reviewing the final chapter of *Reunion at Waterloo* for what must be the twentieth time. He'd thought he had locked the door before beginning his work.

Clearly not.

It wasn't the first mistake he'd made since Julia had gone. In her absence, he couldn't seem to keep anything straight. His thoughts were in turmoil.

"She only left yesterday," he said.

"I know when she left." Charlie stalked into the room, his narrow face set in a scowl. "I asked when she was coming back."

Not soon enough, Jasper thought grimly.

He'd already spent one night in their bed alone. It was one night too many. From the moment Julia had gone—disappearing down the drive in the Arundells' carriage—he'd ached for her. Longed for her. And he could do nothing about it. He had to respect her wishes.

"*Is* she coming back?" Charlie asked.

Jasper's heart was a leaden lump in his chest. She'd promised she wasn't leaving him, but he couldn't entirely believe it. Not after how he'd hurt her.

Good God.

The very idea of her returning to London—to that house where she'd been so unhappy.

He should be there with her. Not to fight her battles for her, but to stand at her side. To offer her his strength, the support of his proximity, just as he once had standing beside her on Lady Holland's balcony.

"Is she?" Charlie asked again.

"She is," Jasper said.

"How do you know?"

"Because she told me so." And because her horse was here and most of her clothes. She'd have to return for them, at least.

"When will she be home?"

"A week. Possibly a month. However long it takes." It was too long. Jasper knew that as well as Charlie.

"I still don't know why she left in the first place," Charlie grumbled.

"She needed time to think," Jasper said. "And she had matters to attend to in London."

"Alone."

"She's not alone. She's staying with Lady Arundell and Lady Anne." Charlie came to a halt beside the desk. "*You're* not there."

"No." Jasper pushed his fingers through the hair at his brow. "No, I'm not." But he should be. He *should* be.

Thrusting his manuscript into the drawer of the desk, he stood, too restless to remain seated. He paced to the narrow tower window.

Charlie trailed after him, as persistent as a gnat. "How much time does thinking take?"

Jasper exhaled heavily. "I don't know."

"Only an hour or two," Charlie said. "Not a whole week. Not a *month*."

Jasper cast him a beleaguered look.

"Sometimes you can think too much," Charlie pointed out.

A shaft of sunshine drifted in through the window. Jasper stopped to stand in its warmth. "I daresay that's true."

"It is," Charlie said. "I don't reckon she wanted to go anyway. She looked sad when she left."

Sad. Yes, she had, hadn't she?

She'd parted from the children yesterday morning with all due care, hugging each of them in turn and asking them to be on their best behavior in her absence.

"*Be good for your father,*" she'd said. "*And for Mr. Beecham. And mind you be careful when you're swimming and riding. I couldn't bear it if anything were to happen to you.*"

A lump formed in Jasper's throat to recall it.

She'd had no such exhortations for him. Holding his hand as he'd assisted her into the carriage, she'd bidden him goodbye with the same level of formality she might use when taking leave of an acquaintance at a house party.

He'd borne it because he had to. Because he deserved it. She wasn't being cruel; she was protecting herself from being hurt by him.

Time was what she'd asked for, and time is what he'd given her. But perhaps Charlie was right. Too much time could be a detriment.

"You should go and fetch her home," Charlie said.

Jasper heaved another sigh. "Charlie—"

"Daisy misses her. She wants her to come back."

A brief smile edged Jasper's mouth. "Only Daisy?"

Charlie glowered, refusing to admit to any vulnerability.

But Jasper knew it was there—the soft, secret part of him that Julia had touched with her kindness.

"It isn't unmanly to admit you want her back," Jasper said. "That you've grown fond of her."

"I don't need her," Charlie replied. "I'm not a baby like Daisy and Alfred."

Jasper set a hand on the boy's shoulder. "Of course you need her. We all do. Me most of all." He squeezed gently before releasing him. "I trust you'll help Beecham look after your brother and sister while I'm gone."

Charlie's head jerked up. "You're going after her?"

Jasper collected his coat from the back of the chair. "As a matter of fact," he said, "I am."

Thirty-Seven

❦

*J*ulia stared up at the imposing facade of her parents' house in Belgrave Square. It had been less than a month since Jasper had carried her out in his arms. Only a few weeks spent in the country, living as his wife, and stepmother to his children. Not much time, really, and yet . . .

It had altered her completely.

A shimmer of anxiety still fizzed in her veins, but it didn't overpower her. Alone on the front step, she raised her hand and knocked firmly on the door.

It was opened by a footman she didn't recognize. Jenkins Five, presumably, hired to take the place of Jenkins Four.

His gaze flitted over her. "Madam?"

She smoothed her hands over her lobelia blue silk carriage dress. Thanks to Anne's maid, Jeanette, it was freshly sponged and pressed. Jeanette had seen to all Julia's gowns on their final day in Yorkshire. It was a reminder of how invaluable a trained lady's maid could be.

Julia was resolved to hire a new one for herself while in London. Perhaps, when visiting the employment agency, she could inquire about a governess for Daisy, and a tutor for the boys.

First, however, she had to regain control of her fortune.

"Please inform Sir Eustace and Lady Wychwood that Mrs. Blunt is here to see them," she said.

The footman betrayed a flash of recognition at the name. No doubt he'd heard of her elopement. For all that Papa abhorred gossip, there was no way to stamp it out completely.

"Mrs. Blunt." He bowed. "This way if you please."

Julia followed him upstairs to the morning room. The curtains were drawn shut, and the remains of a fire crackled in the hearth. Papa must have been in earlier to meet with someone. Hicks, possibly. Or else he'd had a consultation with someone from his new firm of solicitors.

The thought of it put steel in Julia's spine.

"What is your name, sir?" she asked the footman.

"Jenkins, ma'am."

"Your *real* name."

He tugged at his collar. "It's, er, Cedric."

"Cedric," she said, "you may tell my parents that, if they wish to see me, they can do so here in the morning room."

"Ma'am?"

"Here," she repeated. "*Not* in their bedchambers."

"Yes, ma'am." The footman beat a hasty retreat.

Julia stood a moment in the darkness and suffocating heat before impatience spurred her into action. She first removed her bonnet and her gloves, and then one by one, pulled the curtains back from the tall windows, letting the sun shine fully into the room.

Whether her parents would agree to bestir themselves, she didn't know. Part of her hoped they would, and the other part—a remnant of the girl who had grown up here, shy and frightened—prayed they would not. She didn't relish a confrontation with them.

But there was more at stake than her own fears.

She waited by the window as the clock ticked down the minutes. At length, a familiar tread sounded outside the door.

"Oh ho!" Her father's thin voice rang with vindictive glee as he entered the room. "Look who's come crawling back." He was in his banyan and house slippers, with a muffler at his throat. "Didn't I tell you she would soon repent her recklessness?"

Her mother was behind him. She wore a quilted dressing gown, her hair covered by a muslin cap bordered in guipure lace. She clutched a handkerchief in her hand. "And for this I must be summoned from my bed?" Her watery eyes squinted into the sunlight. "Who opened these curtains?"

"I did," Julia said. "We're going to speak candidly, and I'd rather the conversation not be had in darkness."

"We're going to speak candidly?" Mama echoed. "What about, pray?" She sank onto the settee. "Coming here and making demands, as if you were in any position to do so. Were I stronger, I'd slap your face for such impertinence."

Papa sat down in a chair, drawing a blanket over his knees. "Your poor dear mama would be within her rights to chastise you. No one would dare stop her."

"I would stop her," Julia said quietly.

"You what?" Papa looked up with a start. "What did she say?"

"She says *she* would stop me." Mama's eyes kindled. "You've no right to put on airs, my girl. You've shamed us, and made Lord Gresham a laughingstock. He's turned his attentions to Bingham's daughter—the silly little chit. She'll be his countess now. And you, wed to an ex-soldier of dubious fame, with no money or connections to recommend him. An alliance doomed from the start. I could have told you it wouldn't last. Count yourself lucky we're willing to have you back."

Julia sat down, facing her parents. "You've mistaken me," she said. "I haven't come back."

Papa chuckled. "I expect Captain Blunt will have something to say about that. He knows my terms. He won't get a penny if he doesn't relinquish you to us."

"My husband has no intention of relinquishing me. Not ever." Julia felt the truth of it to her marrow. Jasper would never let her go. He'd scarcely been willing to allow her to leave Yorkshire with Anne. Only his guilt had kept him from forbidding her departure.

"We'll see about that," Papa said. "With your money tangled up for years on end, he'll soon—"

"He has no interest in my fortune. You must know that. You told him he wouldn't get a farthing. Yet still he married me." Julia managed a smile. "We're doing very well together, by the way. The air in Yorkshire is exceedingly fresh. I've been riding and walking and have even gone swimming."

"Foolish child," Mama said. "Dr. Cordingley warned you about exerting yourself."

"There's nothing wrong with me," Julia said. "Except that I've been miserable for more years than I can count."

"Bah," Papa said. "You don't know misery. If you'd suffered what I suffer—"

"I'm sorry for your suffering, Papa," Julia said. "And for yours, Mama. But I have suffered, too."

Mama sniffed. "You have been spoiled."

"Yes. You did much for me in terms of material comfort. I'm very grateful for it. But a girl requires more than expensive things. She needs love and acceptance. She needs to know she has value." Julia forced herself to continue, though her parents blustered with outrage. "I never felt as though I had your love. And you reminded me often enough that I had no value except to look after you both in your infirmity."

Her father shook his head in denial. "You're our daughter. You have a duty—"

"Being your daughter made me into a shadow," Julia said. "Much longer and I fear I'd have vanished altogether. Is that what you wanted? A frightened, cringing ghost of a person to wait on you for the remainder of your lives?"

Her mother's nostrils quivered with indignation. "You take no responsibility? You who have had the best of everything? Who have been coddled and indulged—"

"I do take responsibility," Julia said. "You both made me small, but I made myself even smaller, trying to shield myself from hurt and disappointment. It wasn't in my nature to fight for my happiness. Not then. Indeed, the only happiness I ever had in this house was in the pages of a novel."

"And there it is," Mama pronounced in ominous tones. "The root of the problem, just as Dr. Cordingley said. You've polluted your mind reading that drivel. Now you are home, we shall dispose of every last one of those hateful books."

"This isn't my home," Julia said. "My home is in Yorkshire with my husband. I've only come back to tell you that I won't permit you to take the money I inherited from Aunt Elinore."

"What do you intend to do about it?" Papa asked. "Hmm? If you fight the issue, you'll end up with nothing. Worse than nothing. Blunt will be ruined and you'll be a pauper. My solicitors will see to that."

"There's nothing she *can* do," Mama said.

Julia stood, disappointed it had come to this. "Indeed there is."

Her parents stared up at her.

"If you don't inform the bank that they can release my funds—if you don't cease your meddling and call off your solicitors—you shall never see me again."

Mama scoffed. "Nonsense."

"I mean it." Julia looked at each of them in turn. "I won't see you or speak with you for the remainder of my life. Nor will my children. You will be deprived of knowing my daughters. My sons."

Papa stilled. "Did she say sons?"

Mama silenced him with a wave of her handkerchief.

"Worse than that," Julia went on, "in my absence, you'll be left to the care of nurses and attendants who will gossip about you and take advantage of you. Strangers who will whisper your affairs in the street."

Papa's face drained of color.

"It's inevitable, I'm afraid." Julia tugged on her gloves. "I shall be sorry for it, but I won't be a part of your lives any longer. I won't be at liberty to intervene on your behalf."

"Your father's solicitors have matters well in hand," Mama said. "These threats of yours will soon come to nothing when your money is permanently out of your reach."

Julia collected her bonnet. "About your solicitors, Papa . . ."

Her father was still white as a sheet at the dual prospect of being deprived of a grandson and of being an invalid in the care of gossiping servants. "What about them?"

"I've lately discovered that Mr. Micklethwait's name will soon be published in relation to an action for divorce," she said. "And not as a solicitor, but as a named party."

"*What?*" Papa's enraged bellow shook the glass in the morning room windows.

Julia calmly related the intelligence that Mr. Finchley had provided to her yesterday. "The scandal will doubtless make all the papers. Gossip will be unceasing. Only imagine."

Papa's face went from white to blood red. He moved to rise. "The treacherous dog!"

"Eustace," Mama warned. "Your heart."

Papa didn't heed her. He was too caught up in Mr. Micklethwait's betrayal. "The man assured me his firm's reputation was beyond reproach. To think that he would expose me to gossip by association—"

"Quite." Julia advanced on her father. "Which is why you're going to cease employing them to meddle in my affairs. You're going to write out a letter to Hoares this very instant, instructing them to release my funds."

"Impudent girl!" Mama cried.

"Or you can accompany me there yourself," Julia said, undaunted. "It's up to you, Papa."

Her father at last seemed to register the sincerity in her voice. To understand she would not bend or break. That she would not be bullied.

He sank back into his chair with a rattling sigh. "Would that I'd had a son," he muttered impotently. And then: "Tell the maid to fetch me my writing box."

A half hour later, Julia emerged victorious from the morning room, her bonnet in hand and her father's letter to the bank tucked safely in her reticule.

Triumph surged within her breast.

She'd done it. She'd actually won. And she hadn't needed Anne or Jasper or even Mr. Finchley to do it for her. She'd faced it herself, and she'd prevailed.

Though she hadn't been completely alone. Not in spirit.

She'd been strengthened by the support of her friends, and by the love of her husband. People who cared for her and accepted her exactly as she was—an odd, anxious, romantic-minded bluestocking who preferred the safety of novels to the uncertainty of real life.

At least, she had done.

But not anymore. Now, she longed for a happily-ever-after of her own. It didn't matter that Jasper had deceived her about his past. Or rather, it did, but it wasn't the sum total of her feelings for him.

Real life was more complicated than that. And real love was more complex still. It wasn't faint or feeble. It was rich and nuanced and strong. So relentlessly strong. It had to be. Human beings were fallible. They stumbled and fell. They made mistakes. Love didn't crumble in the face of those errors. It held fast and true.

An ever-fixed mark that looks on tempests and is never shaken.

Julia couldn't articulate it as well as Shakespeare, not even to herself. She wasn't the writer in the family. For that, she needed her husband. He would understand precisely what she was feeling in this moment. She desperately wished he was here.

And miraculously . . . there he was.

As she approached the top of the curving oak staircase, she saw him standing in the entrance hall below—tall, dark, and menacing—looming over the unfortunate footman who had answered the door. "I ask you again," he growled, *"where is my wife?"*

Julia's heart soared.

Good heavens.

He'd come for her. And directly from the railway station if the leather Gladstone bag in his hand was any indication. He looked tired and rumpled and so extraordinarily dear.

And she didn't think. She didn't hesitate. Hurtling down the stairs, she ran to him and threw herself straight into his arms. "Oh, my darling love. It really is you!"

Thirty-Eight

—◆—

Jasper's arms closed around her, dropping his bag as he lifted her straight up off her feet. She clung to his neck, her full skirts frothing against his legs. "This is a far warmer welcome than I'd anticipated," he murmured gruffly against her ear. "Mind you, I'm not complaining."

The footman tactfully receded from the hall, leaving the front door standing open to the square.

Julia hardly noticed. Tears of joy blurred her vision. "I was certain I must be dreaming."

Jasper turned his face into her neck, his breath warm on her bare skin. "Don't cry, love."

"I'm not crying. I'm just so glad to see you. I've missed you dreadfully."

"I should have been here with you." His voice deepened to a husky rasp. "I should never have let you go in the first place."

"You're here now. That's all that matters." She smoothed her hands over his nape. "When did you arrive in London?"

"An hour ago. I traveled straight from Malton without stopping. Forgive me. I'm a bit worse for wear."

She drew back to look at his face. He was indeed a little haggard. Lines of weariness etched his features, as if he hadn't been sleeping well. "How did you find me?"

"I went to Lady Anne's house. She told me you were calling on your parents today." He rested his forehead against hers. "I wish I'd got here in time."

"In time for what?"

"To accompany you into the lion's den."

She laughed.

Jasper seemed to find no humor in the situation. "Have you so quickly forgotten? On the last occasion you left this house, I had to carry you out in my arms."

"Yes." Her smile softened. "You were very heroic. Everything a young lady could wish for."

His brows lowered with concern. "Are you all right?"

"I'm in exceedingly good spirits. Put me down and I shall show you."

He obliged her, setting her feet back on the hall floor. But though he loosened his arms, he didn't let her go completely. His large hands remained at her corseted waist, stroking over her back and sides, squeezing tightly.

She reached for her reticule, only to stop, belatedly registering the activity in the square. A barouche was passing in the street, its fashionable occupants blatantly staring.

They weren't the only ones.

There was a nurse lingering by the green with her three young charges, and two well-to-do gentlemen strolling along who had slowed to look.

Flushing with embarrassment, Julia backed out of Jasper's grasp. "We shouldn't be embracing in front of an open door."

"No. You're right." He looked outside, frowning. "Is that Lady Arundell's carriage?"

"It is. Anne loaned it to me for the afternoon."

"Generous of her." Jasper picked up his bag. "Shall we?"

"Yes, of course."

Setting his hand at her back, he guided her out the door and down the front steps to the waiting carriage. The footman looked straight ahead as he opened the door for them and set down the step. Jasper assisted Julia in himself before climbing in after her to sit at her side. He dropped his bag onto the floor.

"Back to Grosvenor Square?" the footman asked.

"By way of Hyde Park," Jasper said. "And take your time."

"Yes, sir." The footman shut the door.

Julia's pulse quickened as the carriage sprang into motion, rolling away from Belgrave Square.

Jasper met her inquiring gaze. "I need to say a few things. And I don't expect we'd have any privacy at Lady Anne's house."

"Probably not," Julia conceded.

She loved her friend, but between Anne and her mother, privacy at the late Earl of Arundell's residence could be difficult to come by. Julia had scarcely been alone except for on her visits to see Mr. Finchley and her parents.

But she was alone now. Alone with her husband.

The air between them crackled with a palpable tension.

She had to remind herself to breathe. "What is it you wish to say to me?"

Jasper devoured her with his gaze. The thought of seeing her again had spurred him on for miles on end, by rail and hired coach, all the way from North Yorkshire to Mayfair. He was tired and irritable and fully aware that his suit was in need of pressing. But none of that mattered now he was with her.

Her skirts were bunched against his legs as the two of them sat side by side on the upholstered seat, angled to face each other. Sunlight shone through the cracks in the curtains that covered the carriage windows, glinting in her blue eyes and over her ebony hair.

His heart clenched with love for her. "First? That I've missed you, too, quite desperately. Nothing has been right since you left me."

"I didn't leave you. I told you—"

"You *left* me. And with good reason. I kept something important from you, when what I ought to have done was tell you everything the moment we decided to marry."

"You couldn't take the risk. I understand. The children—"

"Yes, the children. They were the root of it. But I can't pretend I wasn't motivated by other impulses. The fact is, I wanted you badly. I didn't dare take a chance that the truth would drive you away."

She searched his face. "Have you told me the whole of it?"

"I have," he said. "God help me. The secret's not easy to bear. I would have spared you the burden of it if I could."

"*You're* bearing it," she said. "Indeed, it seems to me that since you took on Captain Blunt's identity you've been a veritable Atlas. Don't you ever rail against having to atone for the man's crimes? You're not, after all, the one who committed them."

"No, I didn't. But I'm rarely called to account anymore, except occasionally by Charlie." He paused, his mouth hitching ruefully. "And by you."

The carriage rolled through the street, bouncing gently as the coachman expertly navigated the afternoon traffic on the way to the park.

"I should have known none of it was true," she said. "That it wasn't the real you." Her brows knit in an elegant line. "I think I *did* know. It never made sense that *The Fire Opal* could have been written by a man so cruel and brutal. Only a dreamer could have imagined that story. Someone with a romantic heart and a heroic spirit."

Heat crept up his neck. "I was young when I wrote it. Full of idealistic notions. I'd seen nothing of the world outside of my village."

"You were like me?"

"Yes, I suppose I was," he said, though he privately thought that no one was like her. No one on this earth. She was utterly unique. The only lady he'd ever loved. That he *could* ever love. A beautiful soul who had, by some miracle, been fashioned just for him.

Good Lord. What if he'd never come to London all those months ago? What if he'd never found her?

"I saw Mr. Finchley yesterday," she said. "You were right. We *are* married."

"Yes," he replied gravely. "We are."

Julia leaned into him, sweet with the fragrance of lavender water and starched petticoats. An intoxicating scent. It stirred his senses, setting his heart to thumping in an erratic rhythm.

She reached to touch his cheek. "You must promise never to lie to me again."

He covered her hand. "I promise."

"And you must swear not to withhold things from me. Even if you think it's for my own good. It's no different from lying."

"I swear it. From now on, I'll tell you everything." Drawing her hand from his face, he tugged off her kid glove, needing to feel the silky softness of her skin. When her hand was bare, he pressed a kiss to her palm before lifting it back to his cheek.

Her fingers curled to cradle his face. "I want it all," she said. "The good and the bad, for better or worse, just like we vowed to each other in church."

"It's yours," he said. "I'm yours."

She held his gaze, her blue eyes luminous with warmth. "I love you, James."

James.

His heart stopped, only to start again, beating stronger and steadier than before. He gathered her in his arms, bending his head to hers. "Julia—my dearest girl—I love you more than life."

Her hand slid to curve around his neck. She tugged him closer, stretching up to him as their lips met.

It was a gentle kiss that swiftly transformed into something fiercer and deeper. An affirmation of their love for each other. Of their trust and unconditional acceptance.

One kiss led to another and another, each dissolving into the next, punctuated by murmured words of praise and affection.

"Come home with me," Jasper said.

She stilled. "Right this minute?"

He smiled against her mouth. "Do you have somewhere else to be?"

"Actually, yes." She pulled back from him to fumble for her reticule. "I never finished telling you what happened at my parents' house. My father has written a letter to the bank, you see, and—"

He kissed her again.

She laughed. "Don't you even care about the money?"

"I care about you. I'm so proud of you, sweetheart."

"I'm rather proud of myself," she admitted. "I was frightened to go back there, but I did it anyway. Now we can repair the Hall, and hire a governess for Daisy, and a tutor for the boys. Servants to do the cooking and cleaning—*and* the washing. You shall have more time to write."

"Ah. As to that." Reluctantly releasing her, he reached for his Gladstone bag. He opened it and withdrew his manuscript. "I've finished my book."

"Did you?" She gave him an uncertain look. "And . . . ?"

"I incorporated some of your suggestions," he said. "I also made a few changes of my own devising."

"Such as what?"

He smiled dryly. "Colonel Dryden is now presumed dead for the last quarter of the story, Eloise is the natural daughter of a duke, and there's a fortune in jewels sewn into the coat of the soldier Eloise nurses when she's at the convent in Brussels."

"She's in a convent? But why?" Her eyes widened. "Oh, goodness! She's not a nun, is she?"

"Do you want me to spoil it?"

"No, no," Julia said hastily. She took the manuscript from him. "I shall read it myself."

He regarded her with sudden solemnity. "It's not a poem, I realize. But it's for you, nonetheless. I trust it's romantic enough as gestures go."

Her eyes glistened. "It's romantic enough."

He gathered her back into his arms. She came willingly, eagerly, melting into his embrace.

"I do love you," she said. "So very much."

"And I love you," he whispered in return, capturing her mouth with his.

Daisy had asked him what happened after the happily-ever-after. He hadn't known then. Not for certain. But now he did.

It was this.

And more of this.

Epilogue

YORKSHIRE, ENGLAND
OCTOBER 1862

*J*ulia leapt up from the drawing room sofa. "Is that the post?"

The silver salver in Mr. Beecham's hand held a small stack of letters, along with what looked to be a literary journal. "It is, ma'am. Plimstock's just returned with it from the village."

"I'll take it," Jasper said. Though better at hiding it, he was as anxious for news as Julia was herself. Clad in his shirtsleeves, his black cravat tugged loose at his throat, he'd been pacing the room all morning.

It had been over a fortnight since the release of *Reunion at Waterloo*. Mr. Bloxham had been so excited by the novel he'd rushed it to print, promising a letter by the fifteenth of the month to report its performance. And today was the fifteenth.

"Shall I bring up the champagne?" Mr. Beecham asked. Julia had instructed him to keep a bottle iced and at the ready.

"Not yet," Jasper said grimly. "There may be no need of it."

"As you say, sir." Mr. Beecham tactfully withdrew.

Julia fluttered around her husband as he rifled through the post. One of the envelopes was addressed in bold script to the care of Capt. J. Blunt. "Is that it?"

"It is." Jasper stared at it for a moment before flipping through the remaining envelopes. "The rest are for you. Letters from Lady Anne,

Miss Maltravers, and Miss Hobhouse." He passed them to Julia. "One from your father as well."

Julia took them, vowing to give them her full attention later. But not now. Now her mind was wholly fixed on Mr. Bloxham's letter—and on the literary journal still in Jasper's hands. "That must be my copy of the *Weekly Heliosphere*."

Jasper surveyed it with a frown as he handed it to her. "I can't think why you insist on subscribing to it. Bilgewater's never had a kind word about any romantic novels, mine least of all."

"Aren't you at all curious?" she asked.

"I'm more interested in what Bloxham has to say." Jasper tore open the letter from his publisher. "It's this I've been waiting for, not the opinion of some reviewer."

"I daresay you're right." Julia flipped through the journal, scanning for Mr. Bilgewater's column. "As for myself, I own to an insatiable curiosity. After everything he said about *The Garden of Valor*—"

"He's a fool," Jasper remarked as he read his letter. "An anonymous fool. Had he the power of his literary convictions, he'd use his real name."

"Perhaps Bilgewater *is* his real name."

"I doubt it. Water-related pseudonyms are popular at the moment. There's one in every . . ." he trailed off. "*Good Lord.*"

Julia glanced up sharply. Her husband's countenance, formerly taut with apprehension, had transformed into an expression of amazement. "What is it?" she asked anxiously. "What does he say?"

A smile spread over Jasper's face—first touching his scarred mouth and then reaching all the way to his eyes. He looked at Julia with a lopsided grin. "You'll never credit it. *Reunion at Waterloo* has sold out its first printing."

"*What?*" Julia surged toward him.

"Here. See for yourself." He gave her Bloxham's letter.

She read it swiftly, her heart racing with excitement.

"It's a success," Jasper said. "If sales continue as they have been, Bloxham predicts they may eventually surpass those of *The Fire Opal*."

"*The reading public is clamoring for more stories in this vein,*" Julia read aloud. "*I trust you haven't exhausted your supply of them.*" Her own smile grew to mirror Jasper's. "Oh, my love. You did it." She flung her arms around his neck, Bloxham's letter crumpling in her hand. "I knew you would."

Jasper held her tightly. "*We* did it." He pressed a fierce kiss to her temple. "You and I together."

"Yes, well . . ." Julia drew back to look in his eyes. "I must concede we make an exceptional team." She smoothed his thick hair from his brow. "All of us. You and I, and the children." She cast a brief glance out the drawing room windows. The curtains were open, revealing an unimpeded view of the damp gardens below. "I hope they haven't ventured too far. The rain's only just stopped."

"Daisy's riding Musket. There's only so far they can go."

It was true enough. Even when in company with Quintus and Cossack, the old gelding rarely exceeded a lethargic trot.

"She'll need a pony of her own soon," Julia said. "Perhaps a little mare to help build her confidence?"

"Her confidence *is* building," Jasper replied. "Thanks to you."

Julia beamed. She was proud of her success with the children. Charlie, Alfred, and Daisy hadn't only accepted her, they'd come to care for her, too. Almost as much as she cared for them.

She wished they could share in Jasper's good news, but the children knew nothing of their father's secret profession. All they knew was that life, of late, had been exceptionally good. The five of them were a family. A *happy* family.

The addition of a few more servants hadn't hurt. Thanks to Julia's inheritance, they'd managed to employ a small household staff. They'd also hired workers to start on the tenants' cottages and to repair the leaking roof of the Hall.

It was only the beginning.

Releasing her from his embrace, Jasper plucked the copy of the *Weekly Heliosphere* from her fingers. "No need to read this now."

She snatched it back from him. "And why not?"

"It's the sales that matter, not the critical acclaim."

She moved out of his grasp, taking the journal with her. "I won't share it with you if that's what you're afraid of."

His mouth quirked. "I survived the fall of Sebastopol. I think I can handle a scathing review." He paused, adding, "It's not me I'm concerned about."

Julia wasn't listening. She was too busy flipping through the pages. "Tripe and treacle indeed," she muttered. "The man deserves a firm clout on the head. And if he's said a single unjust word about *Reunion at Waterloo*, I've a mind to— Ah. Here it is." A puzzled frown creased her brow. "But . . . it's not a review at all."

"No? What is it?"

"It seems to be a farewell." She read the short passage to him:

> To my esteemed readers: I bid you adieu and good fortune on your literary travels. Alas, I can no longer vouchsafe my services as your guide. The siren song of connubial bliss compels me to give up my weekly column and turn my attention to pursuits matrimonial. As Goethe once wrote—

Julia broke off. "The ridiculous man. Quoting Goethe of all people." She tossed the journal onto a nearby table in disgust.

Jasper picked it up, briefly skimming the page. Laughter shone in his eyes. "*The Sorrows of Young Werther*? Perhaps Bilgewater was more of a romantic than he let on. Pity he's retiring."

"Good riddance to him, I say," Julia retorted. "Though, I confess, I was rather looking forward to your latest novel proving his opinions wrong."

"I don't care what he thinks," Jasper said. "I don't care what anyone thinks." His arm slid around her waist, drawing her near. "No one except you."

Julia leaned into him. Four months of marriage had only made their union stronger. It was more than a love match. It was a friend-ship, a partnership, all wrapped up with bonds of loyalty and mutual respect.

And passion, of course. A passion that still made her heart thrill whenever she looked at him.

Captain Blunt or James Marshland, he was hers. *All* hers.

And she was his.

"Shall we call for the champagne now?" she asked.

"Yes, let's." He held her close. "We have a great deal to celebrate."

Author's Note

✦✦

When writing *The Belle of Belgrave Square*, I found inspiration from a variety of sources. As always, I first turned to Victorian history. My research included Victorian views on the dangers of novel reading, the efficacy of bloodletting, the legalities of marrying under a false name, and the appalling conditions soldiers endured during the Siege of Sebastopol. I was also heavily inspired by myths and fairy tales—and by my own girlhood struggle with shyness, which often had me retreating to the safety of my bed to lose myself in the pages of a good book. For more info, see my notes below.

Literary Inspiration

The love story of Julia Wychwood and Captain Blunt owes a lot to myths and fairy tales, particularly the stories of Hades and Persephone, Beauty and the Beast, Sleeping Beauty, and the tale of Bluebeard's wife. In addition, I drew inspiration from three historical novels: *The Law and the Lady* by Wilkie Collins (1875); *Lady Audley's Secret* by Mary Elizabeth Braddon (1862); and *The Blue Castle* by L. M. Montgomery (1926).

If you've read *The Law and the Lady*, you'll have recognized my easter egg for it in chapter 18. There, Julia mentions having accidentally signed the wedding register with her married name instead of her maiden name, thus incurring bad luck for her new marriage. This is a direct reference to an incident at Valeria Brinton's wedding to Eustace Woodville in *The Law and the Lady*. As Valeria relates:

> The last ceremony left to be performed was, as usual, the signing of the marriage register. In the confusion of the moment (and in the absence of any information to guide me) I committed a mistake—ominous, in my aunt Starkweather's opinion, of evil to come. I signed my married instead of my maiden name.

This mistake does indeed foreshadow worse things to come. Like Julia, Valeria later learns that her husband has married her under a false name.

My references to *Lady Audley's Secret* similarly foreshadow hidden identities, as well as illustrating the popularity of sensation novels. Chock-full of bigamy, murder, and madness, *Lady Audley's Secret* was an enormous success with the novel-reading Victorian public. They devoured the story—and many others like it. As a novel reader herself, Julia would have been well aware of this trend. It's why she encourages Jasper to revise *Reunion at Waterloo*, ultimately helping to make it a hit.

My nods to *The Blue Castle* are a little more straightforward. Like Julia, Montgomery's heroine, Valancy Stirling, proposes marriage to a man with a bad reputation in order to escape her family. Barney Snaith agrees to marry her on the condition that she never enter the locked lean-to on his property. At the end of the novel, Valancy finally disobeys him, only to discover that Barney is the author of some of her favorite books.

I'd always intended to make Jasper a secret romance author, but the Bluebeard element—along with the *Blue Castle* connection—is what compelled me to give him a locked writing room in the tower of Goldfinch Hall. The vague rumors that Jasper is a forger are also an allusion to Montgomery's novel.

Victorian Views on Novel Reading and Bloodletting

The views on novel reading espoused by Dr. Cordingley and Lady Wychwood aren't as outlandish as they may sound. At the time, the effects of novel reading were often compared to that of drugs or strong spirits. For example, *Books and Reading* by Noah Porter (1871) refers to "excessive novel reading" as "intellectual opium eating," while *The Local Preachers' Magazine and Christian Family Record* (1875) calls it "mental gin drinking."

Some of Dr. Cordingley's quotes are paraphrased from an editorial in *The Mother's and Young Lady's Annual* (1853) that claimed reading novels tended to "inflame the passions, pollute the imagination, and corrupt the heart," that morality was weakened by "the false sentiments" that novels provoked, and that "in young ladies, especially, do the sensibilities and imagination need to be repressed rather than stimulated."

When blood was believed to be overstimulated or polluted, Victorian physicians often resorted to bleeding a patient to calm the inflammation and rebalance the humors. Bloodletting was considered a viable treatment in the 1860s, with physicians employing either leeches, a lancet, or the mechanized scarificator that Dr. Cordingley uses on Julia. As the century progressed and new scientific methods were introduced, the practice gradually began to fall from favor.

False Names, Marriage, and the Law

In the Victorian era, there were many cases of people marrying under false names. The courts generally found these marriages to be valid—providing the marriage was by license and not through the calling of the banns. Mr. Finchley's explanation of this distinction was inspired by an article in Charles Dickens's weekly journal *All the Year Round* (January 21, 1860), which states:

> The very object to be gained by publication of the banns being publicity, this purpose, should the publication be made in false names, is utterly defeated. On the other hand, a license not being a matter of public notoriety, is granted by the ordinary upon such evidence as he may be content to receive.

As a result, if a marriage license was obtained under a false name, the subsequent marriage could still survive legal scrutiny. *A Digest of the Law Relating to the Relief of the Poor* by Henry Walter Parker, Esq. (1849), reports several cases of this variety, including:

> A marriage under a license, in which one of the parties was described by a false Christian and surname held to be valid. (*Cope v. Burt*, 1 *Hag.* 434: *S.C. on appeal*, 1 *Phil.* 224.)

> A marriage by license not in the man's real name, but in the name which he had assumed because he had deserted, he being known by that name only in the place where he lodged and was married, and where he had resided sixteen weeks, was held a valid marriage. (*R. v. Burton-upon-Trent*, 3 *M & S.* 538.)

Even in Victorian fiction, this sort of marriage was upheld. In *The Law and the Lady*, Valeria Brinton consults a solicitor on the very subject.

> At my request Benjamin put my case to the lawyer as the case of a friend in whom I was interested. The answer was

given without hesitation. I had married, honestly believing my husband's name to be the name under which I had known him. The witnesses to my marriage—my uncle, my aunt, and Benjamin—had acted, as I had acted, in perfect good faith. Under those circumstances, there was no doubt about the law. I was legally married.

Does that mean James Marshland wouldn't have been guilty of some other crime for impersonating the deceased Captain Blunt? As with most legal questions, the answer is that it depends. In *Belle*, I chose to focus on the basic legality of the marriage—and on the moral justification for the hero's actions—rather than delve deeper into other issues of criminality.

The Fall of Sebastopol

The Siege of Sebastopol lasted nearly a full year, from October 1854 to September 1855. Jasper's account of the conditions he and his fellow soldiers suffered in the lead-up to the fall of the city was taken, in part, from an officer's letter printed in the *Reading Mercury* (January 27, 1855). The officer writes:

> I have thawed my ink to write, with the hope of saving life . . . [Your soldiers] have been left to die from starvation. For the last six weeks the rations issued have not been of a kind nor of a quantity to support strength or health. The clothing has not been sufficient to maintain the necessary vigour of the circulation . . . The men are now so sickly from dysentery and diarrhea, from emaciation and debility from disease marking the advent of scurvy and dropsy, not to mention affections of the feet and fingers that we cannot send them away from camp fast enough.

Similarly, a few of the lines of the newspaper article Julia reads from the fictional *London Courant* were partially excerpted from an actual report in *Bell's Weekly Messenger* (September 15, 1855). The report, titled "The Fall of Sebastopol," both declares the allied victory and laments the loss of all the "noble lives" sacrificed in achieving it.

Acknowledgments

——⊹×⊹——

D uring a difficult year, writing has been, at times, both a blessing and a burden to me. While it's provided a much-needed escape from the grim realities of life, it's also required a degree of focus that I was hard-pressed to maintain. In order to finish this story, I relied so much on the people in my life who left me alone when I needed to work, distracted me when I needed a break, and encouraged me when I felt too disheartened to go on.

Chief among them were my parents, to whom I owe my endless gratitude. To my mom, for tea services, medication management, pet maintenance, and for always being in my corner, even when she insists on playing devil's advocate. And to my dad, for bookkeeping, tech support, and for limitless patience and positivity, even when his own health was at its worst.

I'm also exceedingly grateful to my publishing family. To my amazing agent, Sarah Hershman. Thank you for listening to me and sticking with me. To my brilliant editor, Sarah Blumenstock. Thank you for believing in my stories and helping to make them the very best they can be. To Yazmine Hassan, Jessica Plummer, Farjana Yazmin, Marianne Aguiar, and everyone at Berkley and Penguin Random House who do such great work to get my books out into the world and into the hands of readers. Thank you for your diligence, creativity, and enthusiasm.

Additional thanks to Rel Mollet, who is as invaluable as a friend as she is an assistant. To Flora, Dana, Alissa, Rachel, and Renee, for reading early drafts of this story and offering such helpful feedback. And to my animal family—Stella, Jet, Tavi, and Bijou—for emotional support and writerly companionship.

Lastly, to Asteria, my new Andalusian filly. She came into my life in the months after my Andalusian gelding, Centelleo, passed away. A solemn little foal with a grave expression, she seemed to know she was destined to fill some pretty big horseshoes. Her name means "starry one," and aptly so. She's been a bright light in a dark time. I'm so thankful for her.

The Belle of Belgrave Square

MIMI MATTHEWS

Discussion Questions

1. Julia Wychwood manages her anxiety by either riding her horse or losing herself in a novel. Given the expectations of her parents and of Victorian society in general, how successful are her coping strategies? What other methods might she have employed to deal with her condition?

2. Julia often pretends illness in order to be left alone, even if it means undergoing a course of bloodletting as a consequence. Is this a fair trade-off? What other trade-offs might Victorian women in Julia's position make in order to maintain some degree of privacy and autonomy?

3. Captain Jasper Blunt has come to London to find a wealthy bride. Considering the many secrets he's keeping, is marrying an heiress the wisest course? What else might he have done to improve his family's fortunes?

4. Dr. Cordingley blames novels for inflaming Julia's passions. Was reading romantic novels truly dangerous for impressionable Victorian girls? Did it negatively impact their ability to be happy with their lots in life? Or did it encourage them to strive for something more? How does reading impact your life?

5. Julia proposes to Captain Blunt as a way of escaping an untenable situation. Was marriage to a stranger better or worse than remaining in her parents' care?

6. Captain Blunt guards his true identity both to protect his children and to save them—and Julia—from carrying the burden of his secrets. Is this a noble course of action? Or is he unnecessarily shouldering the burden alone?

7. Why might Julia find it easier to speak up on behalf of the children than she does on behalf of herself? Does advocating for the children help to strengthen her self-confidence? How does that influence her future behavior? Have you been in a situation where you found it easier to champion others over yourself?

8. What motivated Captain Blunt to stay on at Goldfinch Hall after returning from the Crimea? Was it sensible of him to remain? Or would it have been better to leave Dolly and the children to their fates?

9. Why might Victorian novel readers have preferred sensation novels (melodramatic stories with elements of romance, crime, and an emphasis on hidden secrets and identities, like *Lady Audley's Secret* by Mary Elizabeth Braddon or *The Woman in White* by Wilkie Collins) to those that were more historically accurate? Do you think those reasons are still relevant to fiction today?

10. What facets of Captain Blunt's life mirrored those of a Victorian sensation novel? How might these elements have served to further attract Julia?

11. Why is it important for Julia to face her parents? Why does she ultimately insist on confronting them alone?

12. Should Julia have remained angry with Captain Blunt for keeping secrets from her? Or was she right to forgive him?

Keep reading for a preview of
the next Belles of London romance

The Lily of Ludgate Hill

Coming soon from Berkley Romance!

London, England
June 1862

*L*ady Anne Deveril flattered herself that she had many outstanding qualities. Chief among them was her willingness to do anything for a friend. And Julia Wychwood was her best friend in the whole world. She had been thus ever since the pair of them had endured a first season together; two unwilling wallflowers—one in unrelieved black and one in over-flounced blue—left to languish, unadmired, at the back of every fashionable ball, society musicale, and amateur theatrical on offer.

One disappointing season had followed another in rapid succession. Three altogether. It had only served to strengthen the bond Anne and Julia shared. No longer wallflowers, they were comrades in arms. Fellow horsewomen. Sisters.

Yes, for Julia, Anne would do anything, even face the devil himself.

Tucking her folded copy of the *Spiritualist Herald* more firmly under her arm, she marched up the freshly swept stone steps of the Earl of March's stately town house in Arlington Street and firmly applied the brass knocker to the painted door.

Lord March was no devil, but he was currently housing one.

The door was promptly opened by a young footman.

"Good morning," Anne said briskly. "Be so good as to inform his lordship that Lady Anne Deveril is here to see him."

The footman didn't question her identity. Indeed, he appeared to recognize her. And why not? She was herself an earl's daughter, and one of some notoriety thanks to the conduct of her famously eccentric mother. A widowed countess couldn't garb herself entirely in black for years on end, traipsing about the city to consort with crystal gazers and mediums, without drawing some degree of attention to herself. Anne had long accepted that she must bear some guilt by association.

"Yes, my lady." The footman stepped back for her to enter. "If you would care to wait in the library, I shall see if his lordship is at home."

Of course he was at home; in his greenhouse, no doubt. Anne had little intention of actually seeing the man. She nevertheless permitted the footman to show her into the earl's spacious library while he trotted off to find his elderly master.

The twin fragrances of pipe smoke and parchment tickled her nose. Lemon polish, too, though there was no sign that the maids had done any recent tidying up. The library was a place of spectacular clutter.

Bookcases lined three of the walls; leatherbound volumes on botany, agriculture, and natural history pulled out at all angles as if an absentminded researcher had wandered from shelf to shelf withdrawing tomes at random only to change his mind midway through extracting them.

The fourth wall was entirely covered in framed sketches of flowers and greenery. Some images were produced in pencil and some in delicately rendered watercolor. They were—along with the teetering stacks of botanical journals and drooping maps that spilled over the sides of the earl's carved mahogany desk—evidence of his prevailing passion.

Lord March's love of exotic plants was legendary. He'd spent much of his life traveling the globe, from the wilds of America to the highest peaks of the Himalayas, bringing back rare seeds to nurture into bloom.

A distracted fellow at the best of times, but a kind one, too, as far as Anne recalled. It had been a long time since she'd darkened his doorstep. A lifetime, it felt like.

She tugged restlessly at her black kid leather gloves as she paced the worn carpet in front of the library's cavernous marble fireplace. She'd never excelled at waiting for unpleasantness to arrive.

Fortunately, she didn't have to wait long.

"Hello, old thing." A familiar deep voice sounded from the library door.

Anne spun around, her traitorous heart giving an involuntary leap in her breast.

Mr. Felix Hartford stood in the entryway; one shoulder propped against the doorframe. Lord only knew how long he'd been observing her.

She stiffened. After all these years, he still had the power to discompose her. Drat him. But she wouldn't permit her emotions to be thrown into chaos by his attractive face and figure. What cared she for his commanding height? His square-chiseled jaw? For the devilish glint in his sky-colored eyes?

And devil he was. The very one she'd come here to see.

"Hartford," she said. Her chin ticked up a notch in challenge. It was a reflex. There was no occasion on which they'd met during the course of the past several years that they hadn't engaged in verbal battle.

This time, however, he made no attempt to engage her.

He was wearing plaid trousers and a loose-fitting black sack coat worn open to reveal the dark waistcoat beneath. A casual ensemble, made more so by the state of him. His clothes were vaguely rumpled and so was his seal-brown hair. It fell over his brow, desperately in need of an application of pomade.

There was an air of arrested preoccupation about him; as if he'd just returned from somewhere or was on his way to somewhere. As if he hadn't realized she was in the library and had come upon her quite by chance.

An unnatural silence stretched between them, void of their typical barb-filled banter.

Greetings dispensed with, Anne found herself at an unaccountable loss. More surprising still, so did Hartford.

He remained, frozen on the threshold, his usually humorous expression turned to stone on his handsome face.

At length, he managed a smile. "I knew one day you'd walk through my door again. It only took you"—withdrawing his pocket watch from his waistcoat pocket, he cast it a brief glance, brows lifting as if in astonishment at the time—"seven years to do it."

She huffed. "It hasn't been seven years."

"Six and half, then."

Six years and five months, more like.

It had been early December of 1855, during the Earl of March's holiday party. She'd been just shy of seventeen; young and naive and not formally out yet. Hartford had kissed her under a sprig of mistletoe in the gaslit servants' hallway outside the kitchens.

And he'd proposed to her.

But Anne refused to think of the past. Never mind that, living in London, reminders of it were daily shoved under her nose. "You're not going to be difficult, are you?" she asked.

"That depends." He strolled into the room. "To what do I owe your visit?"

"Presumptuous, as always," she said. "For all you know, I'm here to see your grandfather."

"My grandfather is in his greenhouse, elbow deep in chicken manure. If it's him you've come to speak with, you're in for a long wait."

She suppressed a grimace. There was no need for him to be crass. "Really, Hartford."

"Really, my lady." He advanced into the room slowly, his genial expression doing little to mask the fact that he was a great towering male bearing down on her. "Why have you come?"

Anne held her ground. She wasn't afraid of him. "I've come to ask a favor of you."

His mouth curled up at one corner. "Better and better." He gestured to a stuffed settee upholstered in Gobelins tapestry. "Pray sit down."

She nimbly sidestepped him to sink down on the cushioned seat. The skirts of her black carriage gown brushed his leg as she passed, silk bombazine sliding against fine wool in an audible caress of expensive fabric.

Her pulse thrummed in her throat.

She daren't look at him, instead focusing on the business at hand with renewed vigor. Withdrawing her copy of the *Spiritualist Herald* from beneath her arm, she smoothed the wrinkled pages out onto her lap.

He remained standing by the fireplace. "What do you have there?"

"First things first." She forced her gaze to meet his. "You've doubtless heard of Captain Blunt's abduction of Miss Wychwood?"

His brow creased. "Abduction? That's quite a charge."

"Do you dispute it?"

"I haven't enough of the facts to do so. Still—"

"Allow me to enlighten you." She sat rigidly on the settee, the dire facts of her friend's unfortunate situation putting starch in her spine. "Captain Blunt, an ex-soldier of dubious fame, has spirited away a vulnerable heiress and married her against the advice of her friends and her family, possibly against her own will. If that's not a crime—"

"He's a war hero," Hartford said, as if that excused everything.

"He's a villain," Anne countered. "He stole her from her sickbed. Did you know that? Quite literally carried her away from her parents' house in Belgrave Square and conveyed her to his haunted estate in the wilds of Yorkshire, just like some rogue in a penny novel."

"Miss Wychwood's circumstances were far from ideal. And she had no objection to Blunt, not on the few occasions I saw them together. Given that, your conclusions are hasty at best."

"I don't require you to validate them. Miss Wychwood is *my* friend, not yours. It's my duty to see that she's all right. I won't rest until I can assure myself of the fact."

A shadow of irritation ghosted over his usually humorous countenance.

Anne had observed the expression before. "You don't approve of my friends."

"As ever, you presume to read my mind."

"I'm not reading your mind. I'm reading your face. And anyway, it doesn't matter. I don't care what you think of my friends."

Hartford's jaw tightened imperceptibly. "Shall I tell you what I think?" He didn't wait for her to answer. "You use your friends as a shield."

She scoffed. "I most certainly don't."

"You travel with them in a pack—a pack that grows with every passing season."

She opened her mouth to object, but Hartford ploughed on, unconcerned with her protestations.

"First there was only Miss Wychwood," he said. "Then there was Miss Hobhouse. And now Miss Maltravers." His smile turned wry. "The Four Horsewomen."

"Yes, yes, it's quite diverting, I'm sure." To someone with a pea brain, she added silently.

Four Horsewomen indeed.

Though Anne supposed it was preferable to the tired epithet he'd previously used. Until Miss Maltravers had arrived in London, Hartford had been calling Anne and her friends the three Furies.

"Not diverting," he said. "Merely interesting. I wonder why you need their protection."

Her chin ticked up another notch. "I'm here, aren't I? Unescorted. Unprotected."

She hadn't had much choice in the matter.

Julia was somewhere in Yorkshire, a prisoner of the evil Captain Blunt. Evelyn Maltravers was in Sussex awaiting the arrival of her beau, Mr. Malik. And Stella Hobhouse—dear Stella!—was presently cloistered with her dour clergyman brother in George's Street. Newly returned from accompanying him to an ecumenical conference in Exeter, she'd been tasked with transcribing his mountain of notes.

Not that Stella would have understood Anne's reasons for calling at the Earl of March's residence. When it came to Felix Hartford, Anne preferred to hold her secrets close. Nothing good could come of sharing them, not even with her dearest friends.

"Unwise of you," Hartford said. "You should have at least brought a maid."

"To visit an aged family friend? Your grandfather is no threat to my reputation. That's why I asked for him."

"In hopes that I'd show up eventually?"

"You always do where I'm concerned." The words were tantamount to an accusation. Anne's stomach trembled a little to say them aloud.

His smile faded. "What do you want of me, my lady?"

"What I want," she said, "is for you to write something very particular in the next column you publish in the *Spiritualist Herald*."

He stilled. A look of uncommon alertness flickered at the back of his eyes. "I don't have a column in the *Spiritualist Herald*."

"Nonsense," she said. "Of course, you do. You have columns in several publications. The *Spiritualist Herald*, the *Weekly Heliosphere*, *Glendale's Botanical Bi-Monthly*. I could go on."

"You're mistaken."

"I'm not. You're Mr. Drinkwater, aren't you? And Mr. Bilgewater, and Mr. Tidewater. You know, you really should diversify your pseudonyms—*and* your turn of phrase. It's recognizable to anyone who knows you."

His gaze sharpened, holding hers with an air of unmistakable challenge. "And you know me, do you?"

"Regrettably," she said, "I do."

It took a great deal to shake Felix Hartford's good-humored equanimity. He prided himself on his ability to see the absurd in every situation. No matter if it hurt him. No matter if it broke his heart.

But today was no ordinary day.

He'd been up since before dawn broke, attending to yet another remnant of his late father's distasteful legacy. An unknown legacy as far as society was aware. Hartford wished he might have been spared the knowledge of it as well.

There had been no chance of that.

His own mother had unloaded the burden onto his shoulders, confessing every sordid detail from her deathbed nine years ago. Hartford had been only twenty at the time, little equipped to face the reality his mother's dying words had wrought.

Lack of readiness hadn't alleviated his responsibilities.

He'd begun to view his father's secret life as the many-headed Hydra of mythology. Nothing was ever fully resolved. Just when he'd lopped off one of the sea serpent's poisonous heads, two more grew in its place. He was tired of it and, after this morning's events, quite tempted to wash his hands of the business once and for all.

And now this.

Her.

Lady Anne Deveril was the last person he wanted to see at the moment. And, rather paradoxically, the person his heart most yearned to speak with.

But not about his family's past.

And not about *her* family's either. It was a past her mother seemed to cling to with increasing determination. Anne clung to it, too, in her way; a willing victim to Lady Arundell's obsession with the dead.

Per usual, she was clad in lusterless black bombazine. An aggravating sight, though her mourning gown was one of impeccable cut. It molded to her delicate frame; the tightly fitted bodice, with its long row of dainty jet buttons, emphasizing her narrow waist and the lush curve of her magnificent bosom. Full skirts swelled over her hips in a voluminous sweep of fabric that made the most sensuous sound, rustling over her layers of petticoats and crinoline, when she moved.

He felt it as much as heard it, tickling his senses and thrumming in his blood.

Thank heaven she'd agreed to sit.

A seated Lady Anne was far easier to deal with than an Anne in motion. And she was almost always in motion, whether striding about in her mother's wake or galloping down Rotten Row in company with her bluestocking friends. Mounted Amazons, all—and just as formidable.

He chose his next words with care. "Whatever it is you think you know—"

"What I know," she said in the lemon-tart tones of a British schoolmarm, "is that you never met a frivolity you didn't like. These columns you write are another of your childish diversions, clearly. I'm not here to judge."

"No?"

"I'm here to make use of you." She tapped one kid-gloved finger on the cover of the printed journal on her lap. "All you need do is say something of a spiritualist nature about this house of Blunt's in Yorkshire."

"Is that all?"

"Yes."

"And what am I to say?" He paused, adding, "If I *am* this Drinkwater fellow you claim."

She was, unsurprisingly, prepared with an answer. "There's no need to reinvent the wheel," she said. "Blunt's estate is already rumored to be haunted. You need merely expound on the fact with an emphasis on immediacy. You might say 'the veil between worlds is closing soon' and that 'all practitioners of a serious bent should journey North to take advantage of it.' I'll do the rest."

His mouth quirked briefly. She was so confident in her plan. So all-fire determined. It was one of the things he'd used to admire most about her, this unwavering confidence she had in herself. "Have it all planned out, do you?"

"Naturally." She moved to rise. "All that's required is for you to do your part. I'll do the rest."

"Manage your mother?" His amusement at the situation flickered out as quickly as it had arisen, extinguished by half a decade of bitterness. "Forgive me if I take leave to doubt your capabilities on that score."

She fixed him with a withering look as she stood, brown eyes sparkling with flecks of gold, like strong spirits ignited by fire.

It brought to mind the game of snapdragon they'd played six and a half years ago, here in this very house, at a Christmas party hosted by his grandfather before he'd left on his 1856 expedition to India. Brandy-soaked raisins and nuts had been set aflame on a silver plate. The young people in attendance had taken turns snatching the sweet treats from the fire.

Anne had been fearless, of course. Heedless of being burned.

And she *had* been burned.

Hartford had caught hold of her scorched fingers a split second after the flames had licked them. He'd drawn her away from the game, taking her down to the kitchens so that Cook could soothe Anne's burns with cold butter from the larder.

It was as they were leaving the kitchens that it had happened.

The two of them, alone in the servants' hallway, the light from a gas wall sconce shimmering in the threads of Anne's hair. Like spun gold it had been, swept back in a glittering net. He'd felt the silken strands with his fingers as he'd tipped her face to kiss her under the mistletoe. Her voluptuous mouth had trembled beneath his. He'd trembled, too.

"I've been wanting to do that all night," he'd said, rather unsteadily.

There was no use pretending. They both remembered it. And not only that kiss, but everything that had come after it.

Would that he could forget!

"You may say what you like," she said, "so long as you do what I ask of you."

He leaned back against the mantelpiece, folding his arms. "Why should I exert myself?"

"*Why?*" she echoed, her temper visibly rising. "For novelty, if for no other reason. Lord knows you've done nothing honorable or responsible in your life."

His temper briefly flared to match hers, the harsh scrape of suppressed resentment deepening his voice. "You know nothing of my responsibilities."

"I know that you live only to find amusement for yourself. Is it too much to hope that you might, for once, do something useful? Something that might help another person besides yourself?"

"Help you, you mean."

"It's not helping me. It's helping Miss Wychwood. Whatever you may think of me, she's done nothing to earn your hatred. She's a sweet and gentle soul who even now might be in the utmost peril. If you—"

"I don't hate you," he said gruffly.

She broke off. "I beg your pardon?"

"I said that I don't hate you. I've never hated you."

"Well . . ." A rare expression of vulnerability stole over her face. She masked it instantly, bending her head as she smoothed her gloves. "In that case, you won't mind doing what I ask."

"Would that it were so easy."

"It's not difficult, surely. I can write the column myself if needs be. All you need do is see that it's published as soon as possible."

"Writing it isn't the difficult part."

She gave him a suspicious look. "Then what?"

"I told you. I'm reluctant to exert myself."

"Hartford—"

"I see little incentive to do so." He managed a thin smile. "As you so rightly pointed out, I'm a selfish ne'er-do-well who thinks only of my own amusement."

"I didn't—"

"Now," he said, "if there was something in it for me . . ."

The last vestige of Anne's self-restraint crumbled in spectacular fashion. Her countenance hardened to marble and her hands dropped to clench at her sides, crumpling the pages of the *Spiritualist Herald* in her fist. She bore down on him like one of the mythical Furies he'd so often accused her of being. "Why you arrogant blackmailing rogue!"

His heartbeat quickened as she approached. Anne in a rage was thrilling sight to behold. "It's not blackmail. It's an exchange. Something you want for something I want."

"And just what *do* you want?"

The idea struck him all at once—a lightning flash of genius. Or possibly madness. Tomorrow he'd likely regret the raw honesty of his words, but in this moment they seemed right. They *felt* right. "I want you," he said.

She stopped mid-stride. Her mouth fell open. "*Me?*"

"You," he said. "And not like this. Not here in London, dressed in black, like some wraith at a funeral feast. I want you in Hampshire. And I want you in color. Red, preferably."

She looked appalled by the suggestion. "I am *not* wearing red. Besides, what on earth is in Hampshire?" Understanding darkened her gaze. "You can't mean Sutton Park?"

Sutton Park was the seat of the earldom of March. Hartford descendants had been living there for centuries. Grandfather hadn't been the best custodian of the place during his tenure as earl. He preferred traveling the globe to languishing in the English countryside looking after his estates. Still, the great house occasionally served a purpose.

"He's hosting a house party for the holidays. Gentlemen naturalists, mostly. A few tradesmen, too, I believe. Perfumers and the like. My grandfather plans to give them some of his newest strain of hybrid roses."

Her eyes locked with his. "You're talking about a Christmas party."

Another Christmas party, she might have said.

"So what if I am?" he asked. "Is Miss Wychwood not worth the sacrifice?"

"My friends are worth anything," she retorted.

"Then you know what you must do."

Anne glowered. Folding her arms, she paced the length of the room, skirts twitching as she walked. She looked rather magnificent.

"There'll be other ladies there," he offered helpfully. "I expect my aunt will have a whole contingent of eligible young misses to throw at my head. Perhaps you can help me choose one?"

She shot him a sour look.

"It's high time I married. A fellow wouldn't want to end his days gathering dust on the shelf."

He was pushing his luck and he knew it. Nettling her past all bearing. It had become a habit in his dealings with Anne. Anything to get a reaction from her. To rouse her from this infuriating role she'd chosen for herself as a mute, obedient, unquestioning shadow to her overbearing mother.

An angry Anne was preferable to one that was fading to nothing before his eyes. Slipping further away with every passing season.

Though why he should care anymore, he didn't know.

"You could bring your horse," he offered. "Spend the whole two weeks riding if you like."

Her brows lowered in a scowl. "So long as I don't wear black?"

He shrugged. "A small price to pay."

Her skirts swished about her legs as she paced back to the fireplace. "December is a long way away. A great deal could happen between now and then."

"It could," he conceded. "Regardless, if I do as you ask—if I write this drivel to convince your mother to travel to Yorkshire—I'd expect you to hold up your side of the agreement, no matter what the intervening months might hold."

Anne came to a halt in front of him. Her elegant features set with a sudden resolve. It was the look of a determined lady willing to endure the bitterest of medicines in order to vouchsafe a cure. "Very well," she said at last. "You have yourself a bargain."

USA Today bestselling author **Mimi Matthews** writes both historical nonfiction and award-winning proper Victorian romances. Her novels have received starred reviews in *Library Journal, Publishers Weekly, Booklist,* and *Kirkus Reviews,* and her articles have been featured on the *Victorian Web,* the *Journal of Victorian Culture,* and in syndication at *BUST* magazine. In her other life, Mimi is an attorney. She resides in California with her family, which includes a retired Andalusian dressage horse, a sheltie, and two Siamese cats.

CONNECT ONLINE

MimiMatthews.com
❐ MimiMatthewsAuthor
🐦 MimiMatthewsEsq
📷 MimiMatthewsEsq